The Holy Man's War

THE MYSTIC ISLE LEGENDS
Book One

The Holy Man's War

Theodore J. Nottingham

Nottingham Publishing
Indianapolis

Dedication

To Rebecca, the love of my life, without whom the journey would not have been possible, and to our daughter Ashley who finds such kinship with the land and peoples filling these pages.

THE HOLY MAN'S WAR
By Theodore J. Nottingham

Cover design by Barbara Rogers
Front & back cover illustrations by Dale O' Dell
Typesetting by Robert Coalson

ISBN 0-9664960-2-7

Library of Congress catalog number 98-68401

Published by Nottingham Publishing

http://tedn.hypermart.net
tnottingham@usa.net

Printed in the United States of America

Part One

The Druid's Isle

chapter one

FROM THE gaping mouth of a giant fireplace came a chilling whisper as the last surviving log suddenly crumbled into a cloud of ashes.

Glowing deep within shadowed crevices, the living black pearls of the wizard witnessed this transmutation among the flames. And it caused the old sage to drift away on wings of celestial reveries.

Soon, all matter vanishes. This spinning rock of interstellar dust must crumble as well, leaving its sunsets, its blue heavens, its myriad creatures to stir in the memory of some melancholic angel.

Beneath the heavy folds of his black tunic, a crooked finger crept into the humid night air. It rose to the cascade of his unkempt beard and gently caressed its steep slopes. Ashes! All!

This huge fireplace which so inspired him now, as it did most every evening when human existence became suspended and spirits murmured louder for him alone to hear, this gloomy fortress too shall be no more. The glacial cobblestones under his feet, shaped in obscure ages before the onslaught of barbarian invasions, were as fleeting as his withering body.

The sage slowly lifted himself from his colossal chair whose wood twisted in grimaces of grotesque demons, and glided in his flowing robe to the edge of the flames.

They reached for him as savage tongues thirsting for more victims.

The trembling shadows spoke to him of his lover—Death. Four decades had he courted the Grim Reaper. His thoughts, visions, experiments, his very life-force had been impregnated by the awesome presence of that silent Master. The promise of peace, freedom—Eternity—carried him far above the terrors of the Invisible.

Now, upon this wintry eve, while the planet slept beneath sheets of frost, and its inhabitants dissipated in vaporous dreams, this dreaded wizard of the haunted moors, a son of holymen from distant lands, mighty sorcerer and voyager to the realm of spirits, Ubarra the Magician shivered in the shadows of the night. An icy breath had touched his cheek! His soul stood before the whispering abyss of the Unseen. He had felt the first pull of his spirit's struggle to escape, to soar homeward.

The flames laughed at the pale old man. They knew consummation to be his fate, dust his only future.

What secret horror rose thus in this disciple of Death, this loyal scholar of the Unknown? Forty years had he prepared for this moment of union. He was leaving nothing behind but a dried sack of fragile bones, a musty robe, and some dust-covered parchments containing wise imaginings of the cosmic mystery he was suddenly being called to partake in on this silent, moonless night. Not a creature in the human world to regret, not a fond moment to bless with one last bitter tear. Solitary bleakness had filled the days of his life.

A vague terror rattled his ancient skeleton, shaking off the rotted fruit of dignity which he had carried about in every gesture, every glance, every word. From bleakness to fathomless bleakness, thus he sensed his fate! A sunless, formless isolation more hushed than the darkest dungeon of his secluded lair. Infinite nothingness!

The aged sorcerer fell to his knees. A darting flame

licked his beard, blackening several strands. His wide-open eyes were blinded to the outside for their gaze had turned fully inward. In these precious, vanishing moments, he could clearly see his tragic error. He had endeavored to prove beyond doubt that the soul would exist without its vessel of flesh, but had never considered how to nurture it so that it might enter higher realms of the spiritual universe. He had ordained his own hell— to consciously know himself as a soul without the anchor of a body, caught between the tomb and blissful Eternity. For the keys to those gates lay in a province he had never visited while on this planet: his heart. He knew himself, in the flash of certain vision, to be a captive in the desert of dimensionless void, a wanderer in the regions of Naught.

"Waaiit!"

The soundless cry roared within his breast.

An answer came from the chilled darkness beyond the walls. Thunder growled over the mountain chain, warning all to beware.

The wizard raised his wild gaze toward the humid beams sighing beneath the weight of the mammoth dome. He seemed to be looking into the face of merciless Infinity.

"A moment more . . . "

The desperate whisper escaped his lips and vanished with a hoarse echo.

A dim flicker beckoned from the fireplace as the magical warmth died away amidst an island of glowing ashes. Silence fell like a heavy cloak over the vast, barren chamber of stone. The dying moment seemed to reflect the sorcerer's evaporating inner world. His aloneness weighed upon him more than it ever had in his long hermit's life. The surrounding darkness announced his apocalypse.

He rose weakly and breathed in the damp air. A strange glow returned to his eyes. In a final supreme effort, he conjured forth all the powers he had fathered on mystical eves under the moon's stern glare in holy places unknown to men. All his learning, all his endless ponderings which had carved such furrows in his features, all his visions, perceptions, elevations, the inner gold he had transmuted through a life of struggle and perseverance, boiled upward from the depths of his being. His shriveled face burned with scarlet shades as the intensity of his concentration heated beyond human capacity. Seething energy erupted from the whirlpool of his spirit in a mad endeavor to halt Time-the-Destroyer in his conquering charge, to breathe a moment more and strive to comprehend Divine mysteries.

The skeleton fell upon the stones, contorting in an unearthly battle. Death, who had been hovering impatiently since sunset, fought his valiant prey, enraged. The old man was defying natural laws, Death's loyal servants. The chamber quivered in the tension emanating from the wriggling corpse refusing to be abandoned.

A solitary bat descended from the heights of the dome, disturbed by the twisting shadows dancing a demonic duel in its haunt. Its frantic flight carried it down through silent spaces to the ghastly scene of the wizard's desperate fight. The stubborn cadaver's gasps to remain in its element were swelling to a macabre crescendo. The night creature fluttered nearby, curious and dismayed.

Suddenly, the struggle halted. The disheveled body lay utterly still, white spheres staring from sunken orbs. A frightened hush returned to the ravaged chamber. Stillness settled over the gruesome scene. A faint whistle announced the final passing of the once roaring fire.

The bat hurried round the walls, risking several approaches to the rigid form. The mouth hung open in a grimace of desperate resistance. A breeze, hurled onward by the growing storm, raced across the floor and caught itself in the long white hair. The chamber felt itself a crypt, respectfully restraining its creeks and moans. Tranquility, majestic emperor of the galaxies, entered this small alcove lost in a corner of its measureless kingdom.

The rugged countryside held its myriad breaths. Not a leaf seemed exposed to rustle in the trail of some passing wind or spirit. Not a howl echoed from a sad, lonely creature. Time had ceased . . . There was no movement to betray its illusion. Everlastingness revealed itself to the secretive stars.

But its disrobing was brief. A vicious clamor sounded across the jagged summits on the horizon. Lightning had gathered to rip through the sacred vision of Eternity, Nature's nemesis.

The little bat dove back into its well of darkness, terrified. The cadaver's eyes had rolled back into its empty sockets. And something was staring through them!

A GRIM dawn wearily opened its pale eye and gazed across the bleak horizon of still waters.

The North Sea had raged throughout the night, under sister twilight's clandestine mantle. With the rebirth of Light, she now retreated behind her mask of inconspicuous serenity, soft and charming as her master the Sun wished her.

Only a trace remained of her evil temper. Carried by graceful, soothing waves, the body of a man was gently laid upon the stark shores of the Nordic isle of Mallor, a sinister claw rising from the turbulent depths of the ocean floor. Shattered fragments of a handsome ship were placed by his side, gifts from mocking doom: golden chests, polished barrels, the head of a proud mast, all covered with a mourning veil of algae. The sea was satisfied with her feast of victims, thirty Roman sailors, and disdainfully regurgitated the tall, emaciated frame of Hadrian Aldius.

He lay unconscious in the warm sand, a battered puppet of Destiny, helpless and alone as once in his mother's womb. Past, friends and glories had vanished forever, like the great vessel scattered over the waves. Vanished were the illustrious days in Egypt, at the head of noble legions; gone were the profound years alongside a spirit almost too divine to be held in human flesh, his stoic teacher; gone too was his courageous struggle as tribune for the poor of the Empire which finally forced him into exile so as to escape the knives of hired assassins. All was gone . . . His very name would ring hollow now, its distinguished sound unbefitting the trembling, abandoned creature in the sand.

The silhouette of an aged fisherman appeared over the edge of the desolate cliffs, summoned by Fate to discover her favored child. It was not yet Her pleasure to devour him.

A gentle spray fell from the drooping belly of grey clouds. The fisherman hurried his step, seeing that the waves had already forgotten their mercy and were drawing the limp form back into the insatiable abyss. He splashed into the shallow foam, caught a drifting arm, and pulled the body from the clutches of the treacherous sea.

He turned the hideous catch upon its back and stared into the vacant face. For an instant, he was filled with wonder at the calm features of eternal rest. They seemed to reflect what the waves murmured, what the rain moaned, what the breeze foretold. Such tranquility . . . A thought shook him out of his trance. Ought he awaken this man from the pure, dreamless realm he had entered? Ought he drag him back to the pain and madness in which his fellow humans wallowed?

The old man found himself kneeling upon the man's chest, beating the silent heart. The feeling that he had suddenly been ordered into this action despite his wish was too fleeting and bizarre for him to consider.

The body twitched, and a violent cough announced the soul's reentry into the veil of matter. Cool drops from the sky kissed his cheeks, eyelids, and lips, begging him to return to this lost world falling through one of the darkest nooks of the Universe.

The fisherman stood and backed away. The corpse was inhabited again. It terrified him to see the haggard skeleton shiver, twist, and move. He knew he was witnessing a fragment of the sacred mystery of Creation. Something was being born in the sand within the narrow confines of fleshy walls. The dawn of Humanity seemed enacted again: alien spirits entering this planet's sphere through the passageway of flesh and blood.

The eyes opened and sadness glimmered through their clouded gaze. An awesome sensation drifted through these two men caught in this eerie scene upon the desolate beach. The merging of the invisible with the visible halted all sense of reality. The illusion of form became transparent, revealing a glimpse of the cosmos within and beyond it.

The sky tore open over the sharp teeth of the cliffs and released a crackle of thunder. Rain whipped across the sands. The sea began to shiver in anger. Nature ferociously reclaimed her dominion over her insubstantial kingdom of matter, enraged that her mask had been lifted once again.

The old fisherman, his huge beard fluttering about him like an unconquerable flag round a sturdy mast, pulled off his cloak and covered the trembling survivor. He was no longer afraid. A man was cold and that was all he had to know.

chapter two

THE TOWN of Elkar lay nestled between two barren peaks known as the "Devil's Horns," so named for their sharp, curved summits.

A violent river rushed by the old mossy walls surrounding the budding civilization. It bled into the warring waves of the North Sea, that raging monster whose foam had born the human beasts from the land of ice. Elkar had grown from the remnants of their camp as fishermen, peasants, and wandering thieves had slowly, like starving rats, infested the disturbed ground, drawn by strange relics of broken pots and fences.

The mountain's wilderness offered no refuge to these desperate creatures. Its children still bore shapes of the planet's earliest dwellers. Giant birds ruled the remote heights; savage wolves, bears, mutants from the saber-toothed scavengers, roamed the black forests which crawled up the forbidding slopes. Dawn often revealed horrid scenes of death and destruction, while day shivered with fear across the mighty wasteland.

The Vikings' fruitless raid upon these silent shores had served to clear the woodland and little else. Their short visit had left a seed which desperate need soon fertilized. In this grisly wound of raped wilderness, humans had managed to build a sense of safety and well-being which satisfied their simplest desires. New generations brought embellishments to their survival as the community naturally divided into groups of various interests and skills. Through cycles of births and deaths, the little society turned in upon itself, inbreeding its energies, fearfully grasping onto the apparent security of squalid streets and stifling proximity. Within the breadth of one century, the magnificence of the mountains, forests and lakes had vanished beneath the putrid interests of conniving merchants, noisy markets, feudal disputes, and base ambitions. The oneness of the cosmic heartbeat within all things, so revered by the ancient religions, had been forgotten and left to the secret world of the druids.

At the tip of the wilderness' tentacles, which slivered to the very edge of the town walls, cottages of lone beings stood courageously in the dangerous shadows, disdaining the smell of terror and dependence rising from the sordid labyrinths of back alleys. One of the furthest removed from the human whirlpool was the old fisherman's hut. It had stood for thirty years in the shaded light of a small, quiet clearing. Children had once graced its little doorway. The aroma of boiling soup had blended with Nature's sacred incense, carried on the billows of a kindly fireplace. Birds had nested over the warmth of the family, whistling gay melodies inspired by the tender peace.

But the fisherman lived alone now. The birds sang to themselves high in the dark foliage, and the chimney seldom breathed. For all that sweet life had disappeared, leaving the clearing abandoned and forlorn. The old man had stayed on the sight of his former happiness out of some odd sense of duty. Perhaps he thought the spirits of his wife and three daughters lingered about, awaiting him.

It was here that he brought the barely living body with which his mother the sea had charged him.

Only the slow movements of the patriarch had inhabited the little room made of mud, rocks, and rotting beams since that evil night two decades past when strangers from the mountain gorges had descended upon this humble paradise and slaughtered the meek children of the Uncreated.

The shadowed objects seemed to turn a suspicious glare upon the unexpected guest. The bed creaked loudly beneath the foreign weight, as though resisting the intruder. The fire took long to tease into warmth, inhospitable and aloof in its domineering corner.

The first quivers of light beneath the crackling wood almost pulled back into non-being, frightened to find themselves mirrored in the vacant eyes of the old man. A soft mist from the crevices of his grieving soul somehow escaped the bolted ceiling of his weather-worn face. It faded quickly as the strong winds of will chased the pain far back into its abyss of sorrow. Somehow, the presence of another creature, miserable as he was, as beaten and alone, yet still stubbornly alive, caused him to remember the weight of his existence. For countless days, months, years, the sea had lulled his torment into a restless sleep, and the cry of lone birds and the silent death of the sun had hypnotized him into a trance mistaken for acceptance.

The flames rose before him, sensually tickling the branches and logs they would soon devour. The heat reddened his rugged cheeks and dried the pearls of rain caught in his beard. Outside, leaves beaten by the angry downpour rustled in a gentle chorus of resignation. The flames smiled and wiggled, ecstatic within their rising warmth. For an instant, the old man thought he felt a timid contentment caress his decaying heart. He quickly dismissed it from his presence, but was nevertheless concerned that its ray had slipped through the bleak mourning veil he never lifted. What was it in this moment that had almost made him live again?

The bed creaked. Suddenly, the old fisherman was overwhelmed by the certainty that the man laying in the shadows behind him was always meant to have been there! He sensed that the chaos, struggles, and despair which had carried him over so many solitary seasons to this instant before this strangely glowing fire, had carried in their torrent, as purpose and cause, the destiny of that foreigner whose ordained path now merged with his. That perception of Fate's guidance flashed before him, clear and unquestionable. He felt himself no longer staring into a blazing fire, but into a crack, a passageway to Eternity. He saw himself from outside his body, sitting there as he had always sat there, as he would always sit here in this point of Now. Suddenly, infinite dimensions seemed to gush open on all sides as though he had fallen into a fathomless void which extended all around him. Space, infinity, timelessness dissolved him. Nothingness engulfed him, imploded from within his endlessly widening inner world.

But the old fisherman held on as he had so many times in the midst of a wild North Sea storm where he had first encountered the fierce presence of infinite, merciless Power.

The rain whispered a monotonous, soothing chant over the roof. The wood sighed and floated off into smoke. The old man felt his hands knotted together in a fearful grasp. Drops of blood appeared where his nails, long and sharp, dug into his flesh. He breathed deeply, as deeply as he would upon a cliff swept by the pure winds of the boundless ocean. He felt himself "solid" again, securely fastened to his strong frame, anchored to what seemed like reality. That vacancy with which he masked his gaze spread her dullness over his features once again. All was as it should be . . . except for a sharp creak suddenly rising from the bed.

The fisherman turned and was hit by the sight of the pale, trembling corpse sitting up, staring an intense, probing look into him. The unearthly gaze of the bloodshot eyes was tempered by the weakness of shivering shoulders, and the fisherman escaped the fear of the cavernous stare by reaching for a pot of cold victuals which he hung over the flames.

"Hungry?"

THE GIANT fingers of a monstrous fog slowly crept over a rampart of hills hiding the sea's volatile moods from the sons of earth. Its white claws seeped into the pine forests, swallowing them, blending their proud shapes into the formless clouds. Soon, the valley would no longer exist, its meadows, rivers, dwellers vanished in the invading mist.

Through the rolling fog appeared a tall silhouette stumbling along a forest path. The figure seemed to be hurrying at the edge of the claws of fog, struggling to flee from their blinding grip. Long waves of hair flew about the person's head, frightened by their master's wild race. The ocean of cloud tumbled over its prey and a cold wind whirled about the flowing robes like a vicious conqueror tormenting its captive.

The woman stopped, breathing heavily. She leaned against an ancient oak and watched the insubstantial marauder gallop onward into the woods, obliterating all familiar shapes. Her strong features were almost manly though illuminated by a savage, feline glow all the more intensified by the fact that she was lost in the heart of the forest. It would be a long time before the mist lifted and the path to her dwelling rediscovered. Long, sinewy fingers rose to pull black strands from her moist forehead, revealing hard nails gleaming like spikes. Her large, piercing eyes shot arrows into the nearby fading trees. Not a hint of weakness appeared on her rugged yet graceful face. She was a woman accustomed to dangerous circumstances. The heavy flap of a silent bird whispered above her and vanished into the grey void. Without hesitation, the woman followed the eerie sound.

Grundler the fisherman placed another log in the blaze and rubbed his numb fingers.

His guest leaned against the warm stone and pulled the heap of furs tighter around him. He sipped from a steaming bowl trembling in his hands.

"What is this island called?"

Grundler sat on a trunk facing the fire.

"Mallor. After the god . . . "

"What god?"

"The god of the wizards."

"Is there a ruler here? A chieftain?"

"I've heard that we have a king. King Gallarix, a Visigoth leader who claimed these regions some time ago. I've never seen him or his men. But they are not the true masters of this isle."

"Who is then?"

Grundler turned to his visitor and waved his hand in the air.

"They are."

The Roman looked up, then back at the man who had saved him from death, not understanding. But the heavy, sunburnt wrinkles were as impassive as the island's cliffs. He would say no more.

Hadrian finished his soup and placed his numb hands over the fire. The two men sat in silence. Outside, the fog curled around the cottage and swallowed it up.

"I owe you my life," Hadrian Aldius stated simply.

The old fisherman said nothing. He wasn't sure he had done the man a favor.

"I've heard that Roman citizens are not much cared for in these northern regions."

Grundler shrugged.

"I haven't seen a vessel of the Empire near our shores for longer than I can remember."

"We've been busy protecting our Eastern borders."

Grundler turned to his guest for the first time.

"Protecting what? There's nothing left to protect."

A heavy shadow fell over the Roman's features. Even now, at the ends of the earth, he could not accept the unacceptable.

"We . . . we still have an Emperor . . . "

Grundler raised his large fisherman's hand and cut him short.

"Your empire has been rotting for years. Even a poor fisherman on the edge of your territories knows this. Everyone on this isle has known about the end of your civilization long before Alaric plundered Rome."

"They have?"

Hadrian was intrigued. He had assumed that only the most primitive peoples lived in these parts.

"The druids foretold it to our ancestors."

"What omens would have revealed such knowledge?"

Grundler looked out the window at the grey world which had invaded his clearing. The devouring fog suddenly seemed full of eyes, watching them and listening to their conversation. The fisherman turned pale. His guest noticed the strange state which had overtaken him.

"What powers could have prophesied this calamity?" he asked again.

This time Grundler rose to his feet and hurried away as though the demons of fear had just flown down upon him like wild furies and gripped onto him with their claws.

"What is it?" the Roman inquired, feeling his warrior's

blood course faster through the banks of his flesh, in tempo with the old man's sudden fear.

"No more questions!" Grundler bellowed. He looked back at the man whose life he had saved and tried to conceal his inner turmoil.

"I told you already. . . This is the Isle of Mallor. There is more than rock and vegetation here!"

"More?" Hadrian asked with burning interest.

Grundler glanced out the window, as though expecting to find a face reproachfully staring at him for revealing as much as he had. He suddenly let out a shout. In the window frame, partially dissolved by the shroud of mist, were the piercing features of the woman who had lost her way in the forest.

Hadrian jumped to his feet, alarmed by the man's terror. But the face was gone by the time he turned to the window.

"You are going to make a corpse of me again, friend!" he exclaimed, sitting back down on the bed, still weakened by his encounter with death. "What has come over you?"

Grundler stood frozen like a statue in the corner of his cottage. He was breathing heavily, struggling to free himself from the hurricane released in his breast. The Roman wrapped a blanket around his muscular frame and leaned toward the fire.

An ominous atmosphere crept into the small room, seeping through the walls along with the rolling fog. Hadrian felt a strange nostalgia for the peace he had briefly tasted in the salty waters of the North Sea. It seemed so remote now. What kind of a world had he been brought back to?

A loud rapping at the door suddenly broke the spectral silence. The fisherman did not move. Hadrian looked over at him, surprised. The simple man of the sea was more of an enigma than he had imagined.

The pounding started again, like a hammer forcing nails into hard word. Grundler seemed to come to his senses with a jolt and suddenly rushed over to his guest. He threw another blanket which hung near the fire over his Roman cloak.

"Don't say a word! She'll recognize your accent," Grundler ordered as he moved to the door.

Hadrian instinctively searched for his cutlass. He noticed that his host had slipped it beneath an old fishnet sprawled out in a corner of the room. Grundler opened the door. A cloud of fog burst into the cottage, carrying the dark woman in its twirling mist.

"Why did you make me wait so long?" she asked angrily. Her voice was shrill and harsh like the sound of an ax cutting into a mighty tree.

"I was not expecting company . . . " he answered hesitatingly. "What are you doing in this part of the forest, Hyndla?"

"I lost my way in the fog," she responded irritably, throwing back the sleeves of her cloak to warm her hands by the fire. Her eyes fell upon the tall man seated by the hearth.

"Who is this?" she asked sternly.

A cold wind rattled the door which Grundler had not shut fully, as though providing an ominous answer to her question. Grundler slammed the door and bolted it against the whistling intruder. Hadrian attempted a smile as the sorceress studied him. Her icy stare caused him to tighten the blanket around his shoulders. She examined him fiercely, taking in everything, from the heritage of his bone structure to the spark of intelligence and learning in his eyes.

"You pulled this man from the sea!" she cried out.

"Yes, I did," Grundler responded defiantly.

"How could you?" Hyndla shrieked. "Did you forget the curse?"

"No," the fisherman said quietly, "I did not forget."

The woman leaned her face toward his until it was within inches of his whiskers and pierced him with her wrathful glare.

"Do you want to destroy us all, you old fool?"

"I don't want to destroy anyone. I'm tired of destruction. That's why I pulled him from the waves."

"But we've been warned . . . !"

She abruptly interrupted herself and turned toward the Roman who was listening intently.

"What importance is it to you if I live or die?" he asked.

"He's a Roman no less!" she exclaimed. "What madness has taken hold of you, Grundler?"

Hadrian stood, angered by the woman's blatant wish for his death.

"The man saved my life! That is a noble deed in all parts of the civilized world!"

Hyndla swung around and faced him. Her black locks fell across her face liked giant spider legs seeking to hide the wild fires smoldering in her eyes.

"This is not the civilized world, Roman! This is the Isle of Mallor!"

"I've traveled to a hundred islands across five oceans! What makes this island different than any other?"

The woman hurried to the door.

"At least you've kept your mouth shut, Grundler! But that won't save you now. What is done is done!"

"Damn them! Damn them all!" the old fisherman cried out from the depths of his tormented soul.

"Don't waste your curses. You know they already are. And I'll tell you this, in the name of the kindnesses you've shown me all these years. He has come back. This very night, he came back from among them, just as he foretold it!"

A look of horror spread over the fisherman's features.

"And that is who he has returned for!" she added,

pointing to the Roman standing by the hearth. "The gods be with you, old man. May they have mercy on us all!"

With that, she disappeared into the fog, leaving a trail of fear and impending doom behind her.

chapter three

ULBREK WAS a giant of a man. Legend had it that he had been fathered by a savage Viking chief on the night of the harvest moon while the druids performed their most sacred rituals. Whispered tales suggested that he was part beast, the product of some unspeakable act. Whatever the truth of his begetting might have been, Ulbrek was a man forever smoldering with wild, untamable rage.

Only strangers from the fog-shrouded marshlands had dared to face him in combat. And not one of them had survived. Nor was much left of their corpses when the butchery was complete. The townspeople had come to fear Ulbrek more than any of the witches and demons said to infest the forests. For the deeds of those unearthly beings were only hearsay, whereas the giant's temper was a daily occurrence, as familiar as the sound of thunder. Indeed, when Ulbrek roared at some unfortunate creature, it was heard throughout the town and turned the blood cold.

There was only one human being who controlled this tempestuous, brutal man. Her name was Ethrain and she was his very opposite. Strong and graceful, with the mind of a sorceress, she was the only beautiful being in the valley. All the men loved her from afar, and stories of her rare beauty were carried across the seas to other isles. But no one dared approach to ask for her hand. For behind those piercing blue eyes and radiant sunshine curls, there lurked a dark secret that none could unlock.

Those who had survived to an advanced age claimed to know a part of her mystery. In the circles of widows it was agreed that Ethrain had often been seen scurrying up the mountain path which led to the haunt of Ubarra the fearsome warlock.

It was known that she had no family. A lonely old woman well acquainted with the dark arts had found her near her home in the depths of the woodland. She kept the abandoned infant and raised her as her own. It was only in her seventeenth year that Ethrain appeared on the outskirts of the town, gathering rare herbs.

Since then, she was often seen at the market in the town square in the company of a huge grey wolf who followed her with extraordinary loyalty and affection.

Like all the other men, Ulbrek longed for the moment when she would appear out of the forest mist and gracefully step through the beaten mud of Elkar. All the joy of his miserable existence was contained in that instant, that enchanted vision. His love for this angel of the wilds was such that, on the occasion of her last appearance, he had slashed a man's throat for daring to whisper her name with lust in his eyes.

As the shimmering sun reached its zenith, the harmonies of the marketplace echoed across the town. Peasants from the three valleys cut out of the mountainside had arrived in carts, on the back of oxen, and by foot to sell their meager wares. Market day was always a festive occasion for the people of Elkar. It rivaled the religious ceremonies practiced in reverent rhythm with the movements of celestial bodies. The community grew to four times its size and there was always a fascinating new face in the crowds. Alongside the relentless bantering were heard stories from distant lands. Tales of the rampaging eastern hordes were among the crowds' favorites, along with the conquests of the Goths and the mysteries of the desert nomads.

But the most eagerly awaited accounts concerned the fate of the great Roman Empire. Roman legions had not been seen for decades and the sagas of the latest heroes were no longer sung of noble centurions but of bloodthirsty Vandal chieftains. The last gasps of the decaying Empire were felt by the most ignorant woodsman in the farthest reaches of the known world. A profound and inescapable melancholy had seeped into the psyche of the peoples of the West. It was as though one of the immortal gods had died after all and the cosmos could never be the same. Or perhaps the security of a great Mother figure had vanished, leaving her children lost and terrified.

The stories told in the marketplace clearly expressed the utter chaos which now roamed the earth. If divine Rome could fall into ruins, then all power was uncertain and suspect. There were no kings or emperors with right of rule any longer. There were no laws, no teachers, no generals. There was only ambush and bloodshed and darkness. No storyteller ended his tale with hope and joy. Such outcomes were not a part of people's experiences.

Ulbrek stepped into the heat of the day, dazed by the acrid mugs of wine he had consumed moments before. He always drank avidly on such days, seeking to drown the agony which would undoubtedly eat at his insides the instant Ethrain appeared before him. In such a state, the giant was a greater terror than ever. His colossal anger could erupt over anything, upon anyone. And the jagged edge of the cutlass he always wore in his belt bore witness to the results of his outbursts.

His mood was especially volatile on this day, for he had heard a rumor from the corner of the tavern which was his alone. Someone had seen Grundler the fisherman pull a cadaver from the ocean waves and carry it off in the direction of his dwelling. The solitary Grundler was hated by all the men in the town, for he had rejected their company and cursed their way of life. No one ever came near him and he asked help of no one. In a land of desperate survival, this was anathema to the most basic human instinct. Every person whose fate it was to be born upon this isle was under sacred obligation to assist the needs of the community. Even Ulbrek had been known to lend a hand in times of crisis.

But the grim fisherman refused to take part in the common good. Since the tragic butchery of his family, he had turned away from humanity. Resentment had festered in the town every since. The men were on the lookout for years, awaiting the moment when they could vent their revenge on the one who despised their fears and their needs. The rumor sparked the smell of blood among them. Especially when it was reported that Roman artifacts had been washed ashore.

Among all the hatreds which poisoned their souls, none was as heinous as the loathing of soldiers of the Empire. The shadow of Caesar still lived among them though centuries had flowed by since the fateful day the great general crossed the Rubicon. The imperial armies had pillaged every village in every valley upon every isle. Not a family could be found which had not received a tale of Roman atrocity from the previous generation. Only a few wizards and druids had escaped the humiliation of captivity. Rome was the great common enemy for peoples who had few bonds among them. The rumor of a Roman in their midst was enough to boil the blood to a murderous frenzy.

The giant rubbed his bloodshot eyes and peered through the haze of the noonday sun. He glared at the people milling about like ants crawling over the remnants of an encampment. Market day always intensified his terrible curse of lifelong loneliness. On ordinary days, when the men were off working and the sleepy town streets were visited by an old widow or two, he could bear his burden more comfortably. The silence of the day united him with other lonely creatures washed upon the alien shores of Mallor. But when the noise of human community, the laughter of children, the rumble of conversations filled the air, Ulbrek was virtually asphyxiated by the sense of being buried alive within his prison of flesh. He was not accepted as part of the human family and the fear he instilled in others was no consolation. Beautiful Ethrain was the only person who had ever smiled at him.

She appeared in the shimmering glow like a radiant angel descended from the heavens. Ulbrek spotted her immediately and his heart nearly burst with excitement. She stepped into the square as lightly as though she were still dancing in the wild meadows of the valley. Her wolf followed by her side, creating a wide path for her as strangers hurried away from one of the forest's most savage predators.

She wandered by the stalls, examining the wares with the wonder and curiosity of a child. Men and women turned to look at this rare, untamed beauty, but no one dared to talk to her. Like the giant, she too was isolated from the hordes of humanity, for the very opposite reason. There was something too unearthly about the young woman for people to accept her as one of them. The group needed conformity, similarity, and a common mediocrity to feel at ease with itself. Anything else was foreign and suspect.

Large beads of sweat gathered on Ulbrek's forehead as he followed Ethrain from afar. His very soul seemed to leak from his pores in tears of desperate longing. It was not her body he wanted, for he worshiped her like a goddess. Ulbrek lived for her smile, for the friendly twinkle in her sky-blue eyes, for an instant of affection and approval.

He would never forget their first meeting. It was on the moors, at the foot of the Devil's Horns where walls of thorns and caves infested with bats and man-eating creatures assured the privacy of the wasteland. He was returning from the marshes where he had been fishing. A terrible incident had just taken place. While sitting peacefully on the edge of the waters, three marauders from the far side of the isle, where men still lived as beasts, attacked him. They wanted nothing from him, only to kill him because of his size and looks. Like a hounded bear, Ulbrek attracted hatred by his sheer appearance.

They covered his body with gashes, striking him with their crude spears before he could fight back. In a bloody whirlwind of rage and terror, he grabbed each of his assailants and broke their necks. When the struggle was over, he was left badly wounded and weeping like a baby at his wretched plight.

Ulbrek stumbled back onto the moors and collapsed in the cool grasses of the plains. Colossal clouds gathered overhead as though covering the world with a death shroud. The giant closed his eyes and wished himself into the realm of the dead where peace would come to him at last.

Raindrops fell on his distorted features and soothed his pain. He felt his sorrowful spirit rising out of the dungeon of his cursed body and he smiled perhaps for the first time in his life. But suddenly he felt a new sensation, one that brought back an ancient, forgotten memory: the soft caress of human flesh upon his brow. He thought it was the fleeting vision of his sweet mother who had left him alone and unloved in his third year.

A profound peace entered his heart and he felt sure that he was being freed from the shackles of life.

Then he felt it again. It was as real as the heavy raindrops which were mixing with his tears and gliding down the sides of his face. But he hesitated to open his eyes for fear that he would be pulled from this place of quiet and rest to be thrown back into the furnace of life. Yet the gentle caresses called to him like a mermaid's song in the midst of a deadly storm. Human love reached into his soul and raised it from its deathbed.

He opened his eyes. Kneeling over him was the most beautiful face he had ever seen. It was Ethrain. Her eyes sparkled with tears as she softly caressed his forehead. For a long time, he stared at her in wonder as she brought him back to life. His violence and anger were utterly drained. He felt like an infant in his crib looking up at the life-giving love of his mother.

"Drink," she finally whispered as she placed a water sack to his lips.

For hours he lay on the wet moors as she nursed his wounds with a mixture of mud and herbs. Not a word was spoken between them. He watched her, almost afraid to breathe for fear that the dream would dissipate and he would find himself the victim of a cruel trick of the gods.

When she had finished, she gave him to drink once more and then hurried away. He lay there until nightfall, weeping with joy. The next day he returned to the town and took up his gruesome existence with less despair, living each moment to remember the enchanted dream on the moors when another human being had cared for him. Weeks passed by before he saw her again, but he was too timid to approach and speak to her.

On this day, however, with the heat of ale in his veins, he decided to do more than watch Ethrain from afar. He came up behind her, mesmerized by the golden hair which shone like the sun and seemed to reveal the kind spirit that had nursed him back to life. He stood there, speechless, and suddenly aware of all his physical defects. The wolf turned around and growled at him. Ulbrek hardly took notice, for his heart and soul were entirely focused on Ethrain.

Suddenly, a loud commotion exploded nearby. Screams and curses and falling stands broke through the harmonies of the market songs. Men streamed from everywhere toward the source of the turmoil. A great circle was forming around a struggling figure who was evading the blows and objects being hurled at him by the angry crowd. Ulbrek recognized him as Grundler the fisherman.

A shriveled old widow was leading the crowd in its wrath.

"You brought him onto our shores! You've cursed us all!" she screamed.

"Stone him!" voices shouted in chorus.

Grundler raised his arms to protect himself from the rocks and sticks which rained down upon him. Ethrain watched in horror, then suddenly turned to find Ulbrek standing behind her. He smiled a toothless grin at her.

"Help him," she said softly.

Ulbrek did not hesitate. Without a second thought, like a man under a spell, he obeyed her wish.

The ranks of the angry crowd were swelling like a Hydra from the depths of the sea. The news of Grundler's catch was going through the town like a fire storm. And everyone knew what it meant: the reclusive old man who had turned his back on them was now the cause of their apocalypse. The thirst for his blood was enhanced by the fact that he had come to market to purchase items for the Roman.

A man in hunter's gear, with muscles the size of barrels, broke through the press of bodies and grabbed Grundler's arms, pinning them behind him.

"You're a dead man, Grundler! I've waited for this moment for many years!"

Agnar was the wealthiest man in the town. He had taken over the leadership of the community by sheer force and created a standing army of men at arms who followed his every order. From a common thief and murderer, he had become the warlord of the isle and had been chosen by King Gallarix as his representative and tax collector.

Two of Agnar's men hurried to their chief and struck the old fisherman.

The crowd roared with a frenzied call for Grundler's death. Seeing gore would provide special entertainment for the market day.

"Strip him!" Agnar shouted as he held the old man in an iron grip.

The fisherman struggled as best he could, but his age was against him. He was forced to watch his own humiliation and destruction. Suddenly, bodies flew aside and the crowd was split in half by the onslaught of the giant. Ulbrek burst into the center of the vicious circle and grabbed Agnar's men by the hair. He crashed their skulls together with incredible force and threw the limp bodies aside. Agnar stepped back, holding onto the fisherman.

"What are doing, Ulbrek? You have no cause to defend this man!"

Without a word, Ulbrek moved toward them.

"Stay back! Stay back or I'll . . . "

The giant yanked Grundler from Agnar's grip and brought his fist thundering down on the strong man's head. Agnar's knees gave way. He tried to pull out his cutlass but another blow threw him into the stunned crowd.

The townspeople, now utterly silent, made way for the giant as he impassively walked off holding Grundler by one arm like a discarded puppet. Agnar sat up in the dirt, his head pounding with a fierce ache.

"I'll kill you for this, Ulbrek! You and your fisherman!"

Ethrain hurried off toward the town gates, followed by the plodding giant and the old fisherman. Her wolf looked back and growled. The beast could sense the smell of danger rising from the crowd.

The strange trio disappeared behind the walls which kept the wilderness from creeping into the town. But another wilderness had already penetrated the hearts of the people of Elkar. Everyone knew that Ragnarok, the Day of Destruction prophesied since the dawn of time, was finally at hand.

chapter four

HADRIAN ALDIUS walked through the clearing where the cottage stood. The leaves rustled in a soothing breeze and glimmered with golden drops of sunlight. The air carried a faint scent of sea breeze, reminding him that he stood on an island surrounded by ferocious waters. A subtle joy filled his heart as he slowly moved through the sanctuary of natural wonders. Great varieties of plants and flowers and trees, many reaching so high into the sky as to obscure the blue spaces above, surrounded him with the powers of life. A tiny family of mushrooms in the green shadows spoke to him of peace.

He had seen so much in his thirty-five years on earth. As a child of an old Roman family, he had inherited a warrior's destiny and, in another century, would have headed numerous victory parades beneath the blessing of the Emperor. Perhaps as an old man he would have become a senator and shared in the glory of law and philosophy so nobly upheld by men like the immortal Cicero. But none of that was to be his now. He was born in the twilight of the Empire when barbarians shared the seat of power with the weakling descendants of the mighty emperors. The whole world had crumbled along with the great monuments of Rome. Misery, famine, constant pillaging had replaced the deeds of Marc Antony and Octavian. The royal eagle of the Roman banner which had once stretched across the world was thrown asunder beneath the thundering hooves of Attila's Huns.

Across his beloved Italy, thousands of acres of fertile land went untilled, countless farms were in ruin. The great cities of his youth, Bologna, Piacenza, Rome itself were devastated and depopulated. The Empire was run by greedy merchants, bribed generals, and men of perverse ambition whose primary effort was to avoid assassination during their short reign.

From the age of fifteen, Hadrian had been on the battlefields, fighting under the man they called "the last Roman," the great general Aetius. He had fought in Spain and Africa, alongside Visigoths and Vandals, centurion to the most ragged, motley legions ever to disgrace Rome. He had met the great men of his day, King Theodoric, the mighty Gaiseric, and had seen with his own eyes the Scourge of God, Attila, Master of the Huns.

Less than a year had gone by since that battle on the Catalaunian Fields, outside of Troyes near the banks of the Rhine. There General Aetius had joined with the warriors of Gaul to stop the invasion of half a million Huns. There had never been a battle such as this before. Some one hundred and sixty thousand men were killed in the carnage. Attila retreated for the first time, but the victors were left decimated. Within six months, Attila had invaded Italy.

The battle of Troyes had crushed all of Hadrian's ideals of glory. Until then, he had imagined that, through Roman discipline and honor, the devastation of the Empire could be halted. Like other children of Rome who attempted to maintain the legacy of moral and ethical standards established by their noble ancestors, he refused to accept that a magnificent civilization which had once tamed the world could die and disintegrate like the corpse of a common farm animal. With the vanishing of

Roman law and order could only come centuries of darkness where humanity would revert to its bestial origins. How could a thousand years of glorious learning and art turn into smoldering ruins trampled over by nomadic barbarians from distant lands?

But he had now seen too much death and destruction to indulge his fantasies any longer. Upon returning from the blood-soaked fields where he had left the mangled cadavers of every friend of his youth, Hadrian turned away from his military career for the politics of Rome. Perhaps as a tribune he could influence the sordid minds that were turning the great city into the cesspool of the world. Every street corner was a brothel and every other child a beggar. Human misery was so intense that the annihilation of the city seemed almost a blessing.

Hadrian found himself more repulsed by the Roman Emperor Valentinian than he had been by Attila. He knew that only evil would come from such a weak and manipulative individual wielding so much power. Traitors and liars had replaced senators and consuls. The dagger and the cup of poison were the only diplomacy of the day. Hadrian understood then that the spirit of Rome was dead.

He had been bred as a soldier since earliest childhood. His father was one of the most honored generals in the Empire. When Hadrian was only two years of age, his father proudly held him in his right arm as he trotted at the head of a mighty victory parade. Little Hadrian had watched in wonder as the crowds cheered his Daddy and the chained prisoners of war were marched past him.

General Aldius had slowly walked up the great marble stairs leading to the colossal seat where a frail old man, the Emperor, awaited him with a benign smile brightening his deep wrinkles.

When he was only nine, Hadrian was taken to his first battlefield and exposed to the horrors of human violence.

Standing at the side of his imperious father, among grim centurions whose tunics and weapons were still wet from the carnage, the young boy understood that he had to repress his gut-wrenching repulsion. But more gruesome than rigid corpses strewn across the land was the fact that he knew he had suddenly killed something within him: his heart. From that day forth, Hadrian had lost contact with his emotions. The little boy standing in the bloody field saw the innocence of his childhood crumble, never to rise again.

Any gentility in his soul was further crushed beneath a harsh, relentless military training launched by his father who wanted a son who would grow up to be a valiant warrior and carry on his glory. No Roman child was submitted to a more suffocating regime. By the age of sixteen, Hadrian was an expert swordsman, a fine athlete, and an initiate in the legendary Roman strategies of war.

But his experience of life was reduced to the surface realm of the physical, the limited world of the senses. When he began to exert his skills in war, the last shovel of dirt was thrown on the coffin of his soul. There was no place in hand-to-hand combat for any awareness of life's higher purposes.

It wasn't until his father fell from his stallion in the midst of a fierce battle with the Teutonic tribes that Hadrian came face to face again with his lost self. The barbarians had broken through the Roman front and surrounded them on all sides. General Aldius reared his horse, raised his sword and called on his men to charge through the raging hordes. Stunned by their leader's boldness, the ragged soldiers rose up with new courage and hurled themselves upon their enemies.

The battle raged on until the sun began to fade. The legions broke through the ranks of the blond-haired giants and turned back upon them with the savagery of warriors sensing oncoming victory. Hadrian saw the ax enter his father's side. The General fell from his horse but his foot remained caught in the stirrup. Hadrian made his way past the struggling soldiers with great sweeping blows of his sword. He dashed toward his father and arrived just in time to see a Goth shove his blade into the General's chest as he was dragged about by his horse. With a terrible cry, Hadrian struck the barbarian, killing him instantly.

He knelt by his father and saw his life-force escaping him, as though seeking to return to its origin, leaving behind the broken corpse which had tempted death one time too many. His son held him in his arms and was soaked by his blood. For the first time, his mighty inner wall cracked. The pain was greater than an enemy's spear piercing him through and through. Huge salty tears burst from his repressed soul and, for an instant, the face of a lost, frightened boy appeared from behind the centurion's mask.

The General' eyes had nearly lost their sight, but his powerful hand managed to tighten around his son's arm. Hadrian felt the warmth of love come through the gripping fingers, a love never before expressed.

"Father . . . "

Some echo rising out of his subconscious involuntarily escaped from his imprisoned depths. The weakening grip was the first and only hug he would ever receive from the man he so loved and revered. Hadrian lifted him up and embraced his dying father. The sound of battle had disappeared and a great silence enveloped them, as though some cosmic force was making room for this fleeting encounter between father and son.

In this hurricane's eye, Hadrian's soul blended with his father's departing spirit. His armor of manly strength fell from him like dried snake skin and revealed a new man, a true man. The soldier's brutal teaching which his father had instilled within him leaked out and joined with the streams of gushing blood.

The great man's intimidating power was now gone from his haggard face. The faded eyes had lost their eagle's glare, and the square jaw was slacken and no longer under his control. Looking into the vulnerability of mortal man, Hadrian was struck with the undeniable fact that all pride, all power was doomed to sink helplessly into the abyss of nothingness. And no victory parade, no emperor's crown, no adoring throngs could hold back the final stripping away of these illusions.

The hand slipped from his forearm and splashed in the red pond. Hadrian kissed his father's forehead and gently laid the old soldier down in the trampled grass. He hardly noticed the beautiful peace spreading through the aquiline features he had so loved. The silence began to break up with the guttural sounds of battle, but the grieving son remained unaware of his surroundings. He could still feel this father's grip on his arm, his final goodbye, his blessing, his message of love.

Out of his pain came a sudden storm of anger. He wanted to curse the cadaver stretched out before him. Why had he not shown him such affection when he was alive? Why had he kept it in and treated him like one of his lieutenants, rejecting all claims of filial attachment? Why had he made him into a heartless warrior, a death-dealing beast dressed in a glimmering cuirass and golden straps so as to honor the savagery of his evil work?

Hadrian looked up in time to see a Teutonic tribesman leap upon him. He fell back and wrestled with his adversary. The man was nearly twice his size, but Hadrian's rage was indomitable. In a flash, he turned him over and straddled him, grabbing the huge ax-wielding hand. With a great yell, he brought the barbarian's weapon down on his head and let the whole weight of his body drop on the iron blade. The body shook and was soon still as a log. Hadrian rolled off of him and remained on his back to catch his breath. Up above the carnage, ephemeral clouds floated by on an airy ocean of deep blue. A gentle breeze carried the white billows across the warm and brilliant space.

"That's what I want!" Hadrian thought to himself in a semi- delirium. That peace, that rhythm, that glorious living poetry was his birthright as a child of the earth and of the sun. He had known that as a boy but the knowledge gained through wonder had been stolen from him before he could recognize it as one of Life's great treasures.

Now, covered with blood, seared to the core of his being by the loss of his father, Hadrian was forced to see what had been before him all along. He no longer cared if he ever rose again. Had a barbarian stood over him in that moment, he would have hardly blinked as the weapon came down upon him. What senselessness, what wasted time he had been lured into! How bewitched he had been by the drums and trumpets, the marching feet and flying standards, the glitter of helmets and clanging of sharp metal. No more! He was not born for this. The child in him had been resurrected and had taken hold of his consciousness. If he lived through the day, he would find another path to follow.

Hadrian suddenly felt himself lifted to his feet. He turned with utter disinterest toward his assailants and recognized his soldiers. The battle had been won.

He set sail for the furthest regions of the Empire both to escape his enemies at court and to find some refuge from the horrors all around him. If anything still drove him on it was the desire to find some peace before he turned to dust. A vague intuition within, stirred to life by the remembrance of his wise tutor, insisted that, even if the world sunk into depravity, the individual could still journey toward the summits of enlightenment. In spite of his stubborn belief in Providence, he felt he had been born in the wrong time, that he was an aberration, a man out of time dropped into the dark waters of the last days to witness the full spectacle unrelieved by the merciful blindness of ignorance.

Now he stood in this strangely quiet clearing, a chance survivor of Fate's latest blow. He had nothing left, not even the treasured writings of the philosophers which he had carried across the battlefields of the Empire. He was alone in an alien land.

In the silence of Nature, a thought suddenly entered his mind that made his strong frame shiver. Though he had come to the end of his life as he knew it, and that Hadrian Aldius, son of generals and patricians was no more, a new life was about to be born, a new man made ready to fulfill his ultimate destiny.

Branches crackled nearby and stirred him from his thoughts. Grundler appeared from the woods, followed by Ethrain and Ulbrek. Hadrian was astonished at the sight of the newcomers. They looked as though they had been summoned out of some Nordic myth, come in the flesh to fulfill ancient prophecies.

Ethrain was immediately bewitched by the noble allure of the Roman aristocrat. She had never seen a cultured man before whose physical power was matched by the depth of his thoughtfulness. All she had ever seen of men was brutality, drunkenness, and sexual depravity. She had been told in her childhood of virtuous princes in far-off lands whose handsome looks were matched by a shining spirit. But such men were more of a fantasy than the flying dragons of old. She had once met a druid with gentle eyes but the secretive priests were not subject to a young girl's romantic fancy.

Hadrian felt a thrill ring through his entire being at the sight of the youthful Nordic beauty. Though her cloak was ragged and her furs muddied by a life in the woods, she sparkled with purity. Her bright, crystal-like eyes mesmerized him and for a moment lifted him above his deep melancholy. She was a young Venus incarnate, full of life and love and mystery.

Ulbrek saw the electricity flash between them and his rage exploded like a great mountain waterfall. He suddenly rushed toward the Roman, pulling the cutlass from his belt.

"No!" Ethrain cried out as Hadrian leaped aside to evade a deadly blow.

The giant was dazed with anger and pain for he knew without a doubt that this man would take his Ethrain away from him. He swung at him wildly, deaf to the pleas of his sweet angel.

At his master's command, the wolf sunk his teeth into Ulbrek's leg and forced him to the ground. Hadrian grabbed the great arm which held the blade and twisted it until the weapon dropped. He instinctively took up the weapon and would have pierced the giant's throat had a soft hand not fallen on his arm like a feather from heaven.

Hadrian lowered the knife, embarrassed by his own violent reaction. Ulbrek grimaced in pain as the wolf held on to his leg.

"Let go, Fenrir!" Ethrain called out.

The animal released the bloody limb and hurried back to its master. Ethrain examined the wound.

"I'll stop the bleeding, but you must promise me never to do that again!"

Ulbrek opened his eyes and looked with deep sadness upon the young woman.

"Will you do as I say?" she asked in an insistent tone.

Ulbrek nodded sheepishly, ashamed to have made her angry at him. Despite the madness in his breast he would never again do anything which would darken the light in her eyes.

Grundler took from his belt the coin purse with which Hadrian had entrusted him.

"I was not able to purchase the garments you wanted," he said gruffly. "But it won't matter now. You will have to leave very soon. They know you are here and they will be coming for you."

"Where can I go?" Hadrian asked nervously.

"I don't know," the old fisherman answered. He marched off toward the cottage, his shoulders collapsing forward under the weight of fatigue. He knew he would soon be seeing his loved ones again.

"What do you mean they will be coming for me?" Hadrian called out. "What am I guilty of besides surviving a shipwreck?"

Grundler entered the cottage without answering. Hadrian turned to the young woman who was watching him with expectant eyes. A wisp of golden hair shivered in the breeze as though beckoning the Roman toward his inescapable destiny.

Ulbrek sat against a massive oak tree, holding the leaves Ethrain had placed over his wound. Gloom drifted over him like a storm cloud. He had never had to control his fierce temper before and back down from an adversary. But he was now helpless as a child under the spell of the young woman who had showed him kindness.

Hadrian approached Ethrain. Fenrir did not growl, for even the wolf could sense that his mistress was greatly attracted to the noble foreigner.

"My name is Hadrian Aldius. I come from Rome . . . "

Looking into the untamed beauty of this woman of the wilds, the centurion saw new purpose for living.

"I know," she whispered timidly.

"You know?" Hadrian responded in bewilderment. It seemed that everyone on the isle knew of his coming except him. His vessel's course had been set for the isles of Britain, not for this forbidding protrusion of misty stone and savage vegetation.

"What do you know?" he asked, lost in the radiance of her youthful features.

"The druids foretold your appearance among us."

"I thought Caesar had destroyed them centuries ago!"

Ethrain smiled a mysterious smile.

"Seers have been among us since the dawn of Time. Not even mighty Rome can put an end to them. The druids come from realms which cannot be reached on horseback or by ship."

"Are there still practicing druids on this isle?"

Ethrain moved away, unwilling to reveal anymore.

"There is much more than nocturnal ceremonies here. You do not know this?"

"No!" Hadrian exclaimed in exasperation. "I have never heard of the Isle of Mallor before it shattered my ship and killed my companions!"

Ethrain turned and faced him. A strange glow came from her eyes.

"Then for all your learning and power, you know nothing!"

Hadrian was struck by her ominous tone. His pride reacted defiantly but was halted by the remembrance of the wisdom of Socrates: those who think they know, do not.

"You may well be right," he stated humbly, feeling a vulnerability he had never experienced before, as though he were standing in the midst of invisible forces swirling about him.

"Perhaps you can teach me," he added softly.

"Perhaps . . . "

She walked away with a coquettish air. Suddenly, she paused and a grimace of fear distorted her features. A cold wind had caressed her with a menacing touch. Her playfulness disappeared as she remembered the great dangers involved for those who would deal with the newcomer.

"What is it?" Hadrian asked, noticing her sudden change.

Fenrir's ears perked and Ulbrek jumped up. Something evil had entered the clearing and wrapped itself around Ethrain.

"Begone!" she cried out. In frenzied fear, she drew circular signs in the air with her hands and emitted a spell in a strange tongue. The wolf howled in a high-pitched, eerie sound which sent shivers up Hadrian's spine.

Ethrain dashed off into the woods, followed by her companions. Ulbrek turned back and pointed a huge finger at the Roman.

"Stay away from her!" he growled in a deep, thunderous voice.

Hadrian called after her, but within moments the thick underbrush had swallowed them up. He stood in the clearing, filled with apprehension. He too could sense that some wicked presence had swept through the sweet-scented air of the woodland. Never before had he experienced such a certainty over the presence of something unseen. Never before had he faced such an adversary. Yet there was something vaguely familiar about the presence, like the premonition of rain or the quality of silence before an oncoming storm.

Hadrian studied the foliage around him, searching for an alien movement. But all was calm. Even the gentle breeze had died down. Leaves no longer rustled, tuffs of grass no longer danced to the rhythm of the ocean's breath. The birds no longer sang in the trees. Something, or someone, had rendered nature utterly motionless. Terror held the landscape in a tight, unearthly grip.

chapter five

THE MASSIVE stone stood at the top of a secluded hill in the shadows of a gargantuan oak tree whose branches fanned out across the sky like an exotic bird of the East. The dolmen had been placed there in unrecorded ages when the druids ruled the land. It had been the sight of unspeakable mysteries when distant stars aligned with the obelisk and set in motion powers within the stone.

The megalith was a silent witness to a time when initiates knew of forces beneath the earth containing the key to the secrets of the universe. Hidden schools from the four corners of the world had received and passed on such knowledge. Mayan priests, the Chaldeans of Assyria, the Magi of Persia, the High Priests of Egypt, the students of Pythagoras had all partaken in the life-giving learning which had come down from a source beyond the sun. The druids were the last to know these secrets and had kept them alive through an oral teaching which had left no trace in the outer world. The depths of their spiritual treasures were hinted at by the remnants of temples such as the one found on the plains of Salisbury by the river Avon, known to history as Stonehenge.

With the coming of each season, the druids would gather in their long white ceremonial robes and enact ancient rites in the ghostly light of moonglow. From across the cosmic spaces, beyond the outer edges of the solar system, aligned with stars never seen by human eyes, a forcefield, attracted as by a magnet, would reach down into the mists of the blue planet and ring within the crystals of the stone. Men of great wisdom would lift their spirits in ecstasy and combine their radiant energy with the power entering the stone from above and from below.

The great menhir rose over two underground streams which crossed immediately below its base. This was one of the most active rocks in the region. At every moon phase it would vibrate ever so slightly, its inner quartz filled with such surges of energy that anyone who touched it, or focused its power through ritual, would be harnessing forces greater than lightning. Upon closer inspection, one could notice that the lower sides of the rock had become vitrified, molten by an unearthly heat. No bonfire could have created such intensity.

Now the dolmen stood forgotten on the cliff. It rose in splendid isolation, a witness to another age when men were not ruled by warrior instincts. Squirrels scampered around the rock, avoiding its touch for they had learned long ago that a strange sensation emanated from its core. Nor did birds ever rest upon its oval summit. The mysterious stone was abandoned by all.

Without the guiding power of the priests, the cosmic beacon was but a useless monument. Its link with other such sights, Silbury Hill, the Glastonbury Tor, Stonehenge, so meticulously designed by sages of yore, meant nothing to the pillaging tribes of the Picts, Alamans and Saxons whose only concern for the heavens was that they not fall on their heads.

Two visitors still came to the megalith when the moon was full. This very eve, as the earth's axis shifted with the arrival of the spring equinox, they would come before the dolmen and fill themselves with its strange power.

A giant owl let out a piercing cry as the forest fell prey to the darkness of night. Shadowy creatures furtively wandered among the great oak trees, in search of food. The tiny clearing where the living stone looked up at the heavens was flooded with the dim bluish light of the moon. It seemed to be patiently waiting for its masters, oblivious to the ravages of passing time and the annihilation of those who had placed it there and knew its secrets.

But this eve was different. Someone was coming, someone who knew the spiraling currents within the dolmen and could direct them for his purposes. Rustling leaves broke the silence and announced his arrival. A tall figure stepped into the clearing and came to stand before the sacred stone. The ghostly light seemed to welcome the visitor as though he were part of its eerie atmosphere. The silhouette, the dolmen, and the moon seemed linked by the invisible forces which soared between them. It was as though they were not separate entities but blended together beyond the fragile walls of matter giving the illusion of distance and separation.

Slowly, the black-robed man approached the dolmen, raising his arms like giant wings spreading for flight. He placed his old, withered hands upon the stone. The crickets suddenly stopped chirping. A hum filled the clearing as the stone began to shake and the man's body shiver. From the depths of the earth came a power current so strong that the silhouette was thrown back. It was immediately followed by the loud, frantic flapping of owls' wings as the night creatures hurried from their trees to escape the unnatural sound.

The tall figure raised his arms toward the black skies. A glow radiated from the eagle eyes of the wizard Ubarra. He looked toward the giant, cold eye of the moon and whispered hoarsely: "The Time has come!"

Suddenly, the clearing was filled with sounds. Voices,

moans, laughter, shouts and shrill cries. Mingling with the moonglow, ethereal shapes swirled in the air, appearing and disappearing as though caught between the realms of spirit and matter.

Ubarra kept his arms held high and watched the bizarre movements with wild amazement.

"Come to me!" he shouted. "I've been waiting so long! Come to me!"

A wisp of light formed a few feet from him like smoke blown by a whirlwind. It writhed before him, struggling to take shape. Ubarra mumbled out an incantation in a strange tongue, turning scarlet with strain.

"I am here!" a low, gravelly voice said with a snicker. The unearthly voice sounded like the rumble of distant thunder.

Ubarra whirled around and found standing before him a little, heavy-set man wearing a broad-rimmed hat and blue cloak. He had only one eye and from it came a beam of light sparkling with arrogance.

The old warlock studied him carefully. He was surprised by the almost humorous appearance of the odd little man.

"Don't be fooled. It is I!" he said in his unnatural voice.

"Odin!" Ubarra whispered in awe.

"My appearance is different in the upper world, but there too I am not what I seem to be. You of all humans should not be fooled by the visible!"

"You look just as the myths have described you . . . " Ubarra said breathlessly.

"This is not my first visit to the middle world," he growled. "But it may be my last if we do not accomplish what has been ordained!"

"I am ready," the old wizard stated with determination.

"Certainly you are. We have not risked your travel to our world for nothing. We are depending on you now."

"What do you command?"

Ghostly figures continued to dance about the clearing as the old wizard and the strange little man spoke. The outcome of their meeting would determine who would be the rulers of earth.

ETHRAIN WATCHED from the window of her little cottage nestled deep in the woods. Outside, Ulbrek sat on a tree trunk carving a massive walking stick with his cutlass. She had chosen to keep him as her guardian now that she had experienced her first encounter with the unseen forces whose presence heralded the dawn of the great confrontation. She knew that fear and violence would soon sweep across the isle and that death would reign over them as it never had before.

The young woman watched the movements in the maze of trees. Since sunrise, she had anticipated the arrival of the Roman. She knew Grundler would bring him to her, just as she knew that the peace of her youth was shattered forever. From earliest childhood, Ethrain had known that she would play a vital role in the drama that was to be staged on this unholy isle. Her years of dancing in the meadows and laying by waterfalls were always unsettled with an undercurrent of tension which told her that colossal events were being prepared and that she was merely waiting for the fateful moment when they would be set in motion.

That moment had come. And she was ready to fulfill her destiny. The witch Hyndla had taught her well how to read omens and deal with visitors from the realm of the Aesir, the warrior gods gathered in the halls of Valhalla. Ethrain had learned of the different worlds which contended for the dominion of earth. She understood that the world of sight and touch and scent, Midgard the middle world, was but one of three levels of existence which intersected each other here on the Isle of Mallor, the gateway to the realm of the gods. Then there was Niflheim, the world of the dead where the roots of the Guardian Tree, Yggdrasil, which rose through all three worlds, were forever gnawed upon by dragons and serpents seeking to return all life into the black abyss from which it came. Sages spoke of the worlds of Svartafheim, the land of the dark elves and Alfheim, a land of light. In all there were nine worlds along the three levels of the cosmic spiral. The number was more of a symbol than a map of actual places. To those who could read the signs, it spoke of death and rebirth, the ever-recurring cycles which affected all things, including human beings and their civilizations. This was a period in which the end had come and a beginning was soon to be born.

Ethrain had not only learned these ancient tales like all other children of the northern lands, but she had been initiated into the awful truth that these myths were incarnated in the realm of matter and were the driving force behind the events of human history. Hyndla had taught her the dark secrets of recognizing the presence of spirits who had taken possession of men and women to accomplish their purposes. She had shown her how to escape their clutches for their powers were limited when they entered Midgard. And she had learned which to trust and which not to trust. Few of the gods wanted the welfare of humanity. Their battle was with the forces of Jotunheim, the outer world of the giants, the powers of chaos. They struggled for dominion over the world of men where they could manifest their essences in physical form.

Ethrain knew that the fate of the middle world, the world of her beloved meadows and pine trees, birds and sea creatures, was soon to be decided. The giants had vied for the minds of men and won. The cruelty of the age was but a reflection of the darkness in men's souls and the gods' patience had come to an end. Either they regained control over Midgard and it once again became a place of peace and transformation, a stepping stone to higher realms, or it would have to be conquered and annihilated before it dragged all creatures into the void of non-being. For earth was the cocoon in which spirit and matter commingled to create the miraculous metamorphosis which elevated beasts to the spirit realm. The cosmic experiment was coming to an end and Ragnarok, the battle of the End Cycle, would determine its results. The middle world of men would have either elevated Creation or ruined it.

The Isle of Mallor was the crossroad for these turbulent worlds, the outpost of Midgard and the entryway to Avalon, the dimension of spirit. Gods and men had commingled here for generations, both blessing their descendants with extraordinary powers and burdening them with the curse of seeing into the fearsome abyss where their fate was being decided.

At the tender age of seven, Ethrain had been informed that she would be the guide and finder for the man who was to be the turning point at the dawn of the era of Ragnarok. She had lived in fear of this terrible responsibility but now that she had looked into his eyes, she was freed from her apprehension. She knew that in his effort to save their world, he would be saving her from the lonely life she had known till then.

Ulbrek jumped to his feet as Hadrian and Grundler appeared from the woods. He raised his staff but did not move, waiting for his mistress to give him orders. Ethrain hurried from the cottage.

"He insisted on seeing you," Grunlder stated with embarrassment. "I am too tired to argue with him."

"You did well, Grundler," Ethrain replied, her eyes riveted on the Roman.

"He cannot stay at my home any longer. Agnar will

be coming for him today."

"I know where he can stay," she declared. "But what about you? How will you avoid Agnar's wrath?"

The old fisherman almost let a smile escape from his frowning features.

"He will not find me. I will be at sea where I belong."

Hadrian turned to the man who had saved his life and addressed him with affectionate concern.

"You cannot stay out there forever. You'll have to return before the storms toss you on the island's breakers."

"No, I do not intend to return."

"Where will you go?"

"To my family. They have waited long enough."

Hadrian did not understand what the man was saying. He assumed that his family was on another island.

"How can I thank you for saving my life?"

"Don't thank me. It is still to be decided whether I did you a favor."

"You have done us all a great favor, Grundler," Ethrain stated as she came up to him and surprised him with a kiss. The old man hadn't felt the soft touch of a woman's sweet caress in so long that it almost melted his heart. His eyes filled with tears at the memory of his beloved.

"The people of the isle think I have cursed them with what I have done. I hope I have! I hope the anger of the gods falls upon them all. Perhaps they will understand what I have tasted all these years."

Ethrain placed her hand on his cheek.

"Don't be bitter any longer, Grundler. You are about to be freed from your solitude. And you will be forgiven everything for bringing this man among us. Your goodness may have saved us all."

"Now that would be an irony worthy of the gods! That I should be the one to do such a thing when I have hated human beings for so long!"

"Then why did you not let him die?"

Grundler hesitated. He looked over at the stranger who smiled at him with gratitude.

"He looked so cold and . . . alone . . . "

Hadrian took him in his muscular arms.

"Why don't you stay with me. I will take care of you now."

"No," Grundler responded sadly. "You will need every ounce of your strength and courage to face what lies ahead. And I do not want to be there to pick up your body again."

"I intend to stay alive for a long time, old man!"

"You have no idea what awaits you. I dreamt last night that this isle was consumed by fire. I fear for you. I fear for the two of you. I hope you do not come to curse me for what I have done."

"You have fulfilled our lives, Grundler," Ethrain stated gently as she offered him a grateful smile. "Your act of kindness toward a stranger will affect countless peoples. It will reverberate through mighty events for generations."

Hadrian took him by the forearm in the Roman show of brotherliness.

"My friend, I will honor you in all that I do from this day forth. You are the father of my new life."

"They say that the gods will damn me forever for bringing you ashore . . . " the old man responded with melancholy.

"I have heard of a God greater than the rest, the God of the Christians, who damns no one."

"It was not my intention to set Ragnarok in motion. I always believed that it was a storyteller's fantasy. But now, I am not so sure."

"What is Ragnarok?" Hadrian asked, confused again.

"Ethrain will explain everything to you," Grundler said,

relieved that someone else would have to reveal what lay ahead.

The young woman looked up at him with the blush of shyness on her cheeks. Hadrian smiled at her and her eyes sparkled with glee. Grundler knew that they would care for each other for the rest of their lives. His work was done and he was free to go. He understood that it was for this that he had been held back all these years from joining his loved ones.

The old fisherman turned his back on them and headed in the direction of the ocean where his faithful boat awaited him. It would take him to the Spring of Hvergelmir where the waters of the earth are born and where men of the sea are welcomed and offered the peace which has eluded their tired souls for so long.

chapter six

"I MUST take you to Hyndla."

Hadrian walked alongside Ethrain as they wandered through the forest. Ulbrek walked behind them at a distance, accompanied by the wolf who had taken a liking to the giant.

"Who is Hyndla?"

"She is the mightiest witch on the isle."

"Why must I see a witch?"

"Because she will tell you what you must do."

"Don't you know what I must do?"

Ethrain stopped walking. Hadrian looked deeply into her eyes.

"You know something, don't you? You know why it is that I am here."

He suddenly fell silent as he saw movement from the corner of his eye. He turned abruptly. Ethrain followed his gaze and looked up to see a giant oak tree reaching high over its neighbors. It was one of the oldest trees of the forest with a trunk several times the size of its neighbors.

"I've seen that tree before!" Hadrian cried out in amazement.

"No, you haven't," Ethrain stated bluntly. "There are none like it on any isle from the land of the Celts to the haunts of the Vikings."

"I have seen this tree before, I tell you!" Hadrian insisted.

"Well, if you have traveled the world as you say you have, you shouldn't be so surprised."

"No, this is different. I remember it from some strange place . . . Perhaps in a dream . . . "

"What sort of a dream?" Ethrain asked, suddenly intrigued.

"I dreamt that I was lost in the land of the dead . . . "

Hadrian stopped short. He was struck by the realization that he had indeed been dead several days before. It must have been only moments before Grundler brought him back to life, but the sight of the tree was stirring memories revealing a vaster time period than the seconds of darkness in the murky waters.

Ethrain studied him closely. She was familiar with such journeys.

"Tell me what you saw."

"This great tree . . . surrounded by thick fog . . . I couldn't see the top branches."

His face suddenly turned pale as the bizarre images appeared before his inner sight and gave him the discomforting feeling that he was caught between two realms of reality. A strange inner vertigo took hold of him.

"That must have been Yggdrasill, the Tree of Life at the center of the worlds."

"I've never heard of such a tree . . . "

"You haven't? Then you Romans should have learned from the peoples you tried to conquer. You might have avoided being overrun by the eastern invaders. Yggdrasill rises through the three levels of the nine worlds where we, the giants and the gods live. Did you see the Norns?"

"The what?"

"The three Norns who guard the Well of Urd beneath the first root."

"I did see a well!" Hadrian exclaimed excitedly. "And

there was a woman seated by it. She was . . . she was calling to me. And two other beautiful maidens came out of the mist. They too called my name."

Ethrain brought her hands to her face in amazement.

"Those were the Norns, the goddesses of destiny. Did you see anything by the second root? It descends into the Spring of Mimir."

"I heard its running waters . . . "

"It is the source of wisdom. The ancients say that Odin sacrificed an eye to drink from its waters. And Heimdall, the watchman of the gods, left his great horn on its banks."

"I saw it! I saw the horn shining even though there was no sun to reflect upon it!"

"That is the horn he will use at Ragnarok."

Hadrian suddenly winced as the strange images became clearer.

"There was someone else by the tree . . . "

"Someone else?" Ethrain asked with great surprise.

"A dark shape . . . An evil figure . . . He was watching me from behind the tree."

"Can you see his face?"

"Yes! Yes, I can."

"Describe it to me."

Hadrian closed his eyes and tightened every muscle in his face, focusing on the returning memories.

"He had a very long beard. His face was bony and thin . . . and very old . . . His eyes were terrifying . . . like torches on a pirate ship."

"What did he do?"

"He shouted at me. I think it was a curse. Then a great cloud of mist rolled in and I lost sight of him."

Hadrian opened his eyes on the tangible reality before him. It seemed no more real than the hazy images which had just floated up from some secret recess of his soul. He turned to Ethrain and noticed that she had grown pale. She brushed a lock of golden hair from her eyes and he saw that her hand was trembling.

"What is it, Ethrain?" he asked, feeling the cold wind of her fear enter his breast.

"I know the man you saw."

"How is that possible?"

Ethrain raised her bright blue eyes and peered at him sadly.

"Haven't you understood yet that all things are possible on this isle? You have described the man I have hated from the day I learned to walk."

"I never imagined that you would hate anyone," Hadrian said softly.

"That is because you do not know Ubarra!"

She hurried away toward the great oak tree.

"Who did you say?"

"Ubarra the wizard. If you met him in the land of the dead, then you will surely come upon him here in the middle world."

Hadrian approached her. He wanted to comfort her but knew that it was too soon to take her in his arms, even though the desire to do so gnawed at every fiber of his being.

"What is so fearsome about this man?"

"He is a mighty wizard, the last of the druids. He has helped the giants spread terror across the world in revenge for the murder of his priesthood. Everyone on the isle fears him greatly."

"Do you fear him?"

"Yes, and you should also. His powers are unlike any you will ever come upon."

"I have faced powerful adversaries on the battlefield. I've fought Huns with my bare hands."

"That is child's play compared to the dangers of confronting Ubarra."

"Surely he is only a mortal man."

"Yes, but there are men . . . and women . . . who have encountered the gods on this plane and have mingled with their powers."

"Do you mean that your gods walk the earth?" Hadrian asked suspiciously. He knew well all the myths of Zeus and his wanderings among mortals, but had never thought there could be any truth to them. Reason had long replaced the mythopoetic spirit of his people. The powers of logic and analysis had recreated their world and structured it according to that which man's mind could understand.

"You think I'm just an ignorant barbarian, don't you?" Ethrain stated angrily. "You Romans will never lose your arrogance, even as your empire sinks into oblivion before your very eyes!"

Ulbrek watched them closely, alerted by the tone of her voice. He relished the thought of killing Hadrian at the first opportunity.

"I don't think you're a barbarian! But I was educated in the best schools in the world, and I left behind my childhood superstition long ago."

"Childhood superstition you call it! Why am I risking my life for you?"

"Are you risking your life for me?"

Ethrain walked up to him and placed her hands defiantly on her hips.

"You cannot be that stupid, Roman! Many people are going to die because of you, beginning with poor Grundler! And I may be the one to follow him!"

"I am not responsible for any of this!" Hadrian shouted in rage. "I want nothing to do with your cursed isle! I was seeking peace and quiet at the far edge of the world, not this madness! Maybe it would have been better if the waters had swallowed me up!"

He leaned against the giant oak tree and closed his eyes. He was tired of struggle and violence and talk of wizards with supernatural powers. Why could he not be left alone to end his days planting lettuce on some remote landscape?

Ethrain felt his melancholy and realized that he was an unwilling victim of Fate, an innocent child caught in the web of destiny, forced to face the most terrible adversaries imaginable. She knew already that he would never find the peace he so dearly sought. There was a great work to be done, a vital role for him to play for the future of the race.

She moved toward him with the grace of a butterfly, as though tiptoeing through the grass to avoid any sound which might disturb his sorely needed rest. He opened his eyes to find her standing before him, a vision of beauty in this savage wilderness, an angel come down to carry him through the battlefields he could not escape from.

For the briefest moment, he thought she actually was an ethereal being hidden behind the mortal mask of humankind. His heart leaped in a wild hope that, beneath the dead weight of his reasoning mind, there might still be the child's wonder for a world teeming with miracles. But then Ulbrek appeared in his sight, deformed and ugly with venomous energy, and he knew that he was still in the land of pain and destruction.

"No, Ulbrek!"

Ethrain grabbed the giant's massive forearm and kept it from crashing down on Hadrian's skull. The wolf growled at his new companion, warning him that he would be leaping at his throat momentarily.

"I don't want you to hurt him!" Ethrain cried out. "Not ever!"

The huge man stepped back, overwhelmed by the feel of her touch. He looked down at her thin hands around his rugged flesh, mouth dropping in astonishment.

"You are to protect him, Ulbrek. Protect him for me! Understand?"

She stared at him with her striking blue eyes, looking for some sign of comprehension. His eyes met hers and immediately turned away, unable to bear the intensity of her beauty and spirit. He nodded in meekness and moved away to nurse the pain of having disappointed her again.

"Who is this creature?" Hadrian whispered as he studied the giant suspiciously.

"He is with me," Ethrain responded simply.

"I can see that, but why is he with you?" the Roman insisted.

"Because he has no one else."

She walked away from him and went to pick some herbs rising at the side of the great twisted roots stretching out like some prehistoric monster's gnarled fingers. Hadrian watched her with admiration and wonder. He had never met such a woman before. In Rome, no self-respecting young lady would allow such a grotesque creature anywhere near her; even less would she have compassion on his condition. Except for the few who took seriously the Empire's new religion which Constantine had enforced upon the world after a miraculous victory.

All his life, Hadrian had hated the strange new faith brought from the dusty lands of Judea. His family had bred him on the old gods who were as precious to them as the glorious days of Rome. The shrinking world of patricians and privileged members of the Emperor's court believed vehemently that the destruction of the Empire, and therefore of all civilization, was the direct result of unfaithfulness to the beloved myths of their ancestors. For generations, mystery religions from every culture had found their way to the heart of the Roman world, but none had ever threatened to destroy the pantheon of deities. They had been accepted along with the strange clothing and bizarre hairstyles which filled the teeming streets of the city.

But those who called upon the name of the crucified one were of a different sort. Three hundred years of martyrdom had not weakened their faith. In fact, it had done the opposite. After a time, some spectators in the arenas could not help but wonder what sort of religion it was which gave such courage to its adherents before the hungry beasts of the Circus Maximus. Moreover, their astonishing habits of assisting the poorest of the poor, of making themselves humble servants of those in need, had finally torn Jupiter, Venus, and Mars from their marble pedestals.

Hadrian had rejected all his father's beliefs but that one. The Christians were more dangerous than the Huns for they had broken through the dreams of a people and thrown their idea of the order of the universe literally upside down. After leaving the legions, Hadrian had gone to find wisdom in Greece, among the stoic philosophers who carried on the legacy of great minds like the incomparable Epictetus. There he came upon the genius of Plato, the mysticism of Pythagoras and the serenity of the human mind turned in upon its transcendent center and detached from the follies of humanity. After years of violence and worship of physical prowess, Hadrian was satisfied that he had found the truth.

But every time he encountered a real Christian, not the kind that sought tax breaks by claiming to be a member of the Emperor's favorite religion, but the kind that daily performed acts of selflessness, Hadrian had the uncomfortable feeling that something was incomplete in his well established system of thought. He buried the feeling immediately yet it never failed to reappear as it just had upon hearing Ethrain's words of compassion.

He walked over to her in an effort to shake himself free from the unsettling sensation.

"Can you interpret dreams?" he asked.

Ethrain continued her careful picking of herbs.

"Maybe . . . "

Hadrian smiled, thinking she was teasing him.

"Maybe?"

"Sometimes a dream is not a dream."

He tried to wrap his mind around that thought, to no avail.

"What did you say?"

Ethrain stood up, stretched her back and placed the plants she had picked in her satchel.

"You didn't dream that tree. You were there."

"That's . . . That's not possible."

"For your mind, perhaps, but not for your soul."

She returned to her picking.

"These are wonderful herbs. I haven't seen so many since . . . "

"Do you actually believe that I was in some other world?"

"I know you were," she stated without looking up.

"How can you be so sure?"

Ethrain stood up, irritated.

"You ask too many questions, Roman! So I will make it very clear to you."

She took a deep breath and looked around, searching the underbrush for listening ears.

"You are here for a purpose, whether you like it or not. And I am here to help you in this purpose, whether I like it or not."

"What purpose?" Hadrian asked at the limits of his frustration.

"You are here to keep the world from falling into darkness and to initiate the new cycle which must take place."

Hadrian stared at her for a long moment. She turned back to her plants. Up above, the branches of the tree let out a loud shiver as a huge black crow suddenly rose into the sky. Ethrain looked up and quickly veiled the fear that clouded her eyes. Hadrian heard nothing, struck dumb by her statement. His mind was refusing entry to the words she had spoken because their impact would have crushed him like a falling temple column.

"What barbarian nonsense is this?" he heard himself cry out.

She looked at him and sadly shook her head.

"Do you also believe that the sky is going to fall on your head as the Franks do? Maybe I'm to hold it up for you!" he said with a snicker.

"You will have to accept this quickly, Roman. There isn't much time."

"Not much time?" he shouted, his anger increasing. "I thought we were dealing with gods who had all the time in the world!"

"We are . . . "

"We are?" Hadrian cried out, stupefied. "What do they have to do with all this nonsense?"

"The gods are seeking to take control of Earth back from the giants."

"So the world is controlled by giants? What kind of giants? I hope they're not like him!" he stated sarcastically, pointing to Ulbrek who leaned against a tree, glaring at him hatefully.

"No, they are not like him," Ethrain replied calmly. "They are from the lower world."

"You mean to say that they are invisible, from the realm of spirit?"

"Yes, except when they act through humans."

Hadrian threw up his arms in exasperation.

"So they crawl beneath our skin and control our behavior?"

"If we let them . . . "

"How can you believe such primitive foolishness? You've got a bright, healthy mind."

Ethrain had enough of his insults. She approached him defiantly.

"Can't you see what is happening in our world?"

"Of course I can! I've travelled it several times. The Huns are at our eastern borders. The Angles and the Saxons are invading the Celtic lands. The Picts and the Scots are descending from the North . . . "

"And your empire is vanishing before your very eyes!"

"No!"

"Yes! Yes, it is dying and will never rise again!"

"What do you know of these things? You live on one of the remotest isles in the known world! How can you judge the affairs of the Empire?"

Ethrain's eyes gleamed with outrage. She did her best to control herself.

"There are things foretold and things prophesied and things determined which are beyond the grasp of your understanding!"

"Are these tales of the druids that you speak of?"

She nodded reluctantly. She knew his people had great disdain for the luminous wisemen of her homeland.

"Those crazed old men with scraggly beards and mistletoe on their heads! They worship rocks! How can they read the course of Fate?"

"They can no longer because your legions massacred them!" she cried out bitterly. "But your people failed in their murderous task. They left Ubarra alive!"

"Him again! So he is a druid and a wizard?" Hadrian questioned mockingly.

"Beware of mocking that which you do not understand, Roman!"

With that, she turned away and headed into the woods. Ulbrek hurried after her, along with the faithful wolf who growled at Hadrian as he passed him by. The Roman watched them disappear into the thick foliage. He felt ashamed at having argued with the young woman who had come to his aid. But at the same time, he felt a sudden sensation of freedom. Perhaps if he hurried for the shore, he might find a boatman to take him away from this forsaken isle so filled with strange tales and stranger inhabitants.

He headed in the opposite direction, a new thrill lifting his spirits. Could it be that he might walk away from this living nightmare and search again for the peace he had come so far to find?

chapter 7

THE SUN had fallen behind a black mountainous cloud which hung over the horizon like a death cloak. An icy wind whistled down from the peaks of the Devil's Horns, heralding the approach of a Nordic storm.

Hadrian tightened the well-worn cape given to him by the good fisherman and hurried his step toward the restless shores. The waves had risen to ferocious heights, hurled on by the oncoming storm. They crashed upon the rocks of Mallor like angry beasts seeking to destroy their prey. Hadrian came out of the woods and found himself on the edge of a cliff some hundred yards over the turbulent waters.

The Roman realized that his escape would be as dangerous as his stay. He looked back at the scrawny trees permanently bent by the merciless winds that howled across the North Sea. The twisted, petrified forest seemed the very expression of the spirit of this rugged isle. The tortured trees were the incarnation of the macabre spirit realm which thickened the atmosphere with dread and fear.

Hadrian headed down the cliff, slipping on loose rocks that hurried ahead of him, slapping into the wet sand below. As he scampered to the tiny mound of beach, he noticed a small boat partly hidden amid the boulders.

Had his luck returned to him at last? As his feet sunk into the sand, he slowed his pace, aware that going out into the angry waves in a rowboat was virtually a death wish. He remembered the terrible feeling of drowning which he had experienced only a few days before. A powerful shiver shook his body at the thought of those final moments when every face he had ever known flashed before him in a final farewell, a condensed summation of his earthly life. Such an experience could not be lived through without the overwhelming realization that time and space which had always been the concrete blocks of his existence were as flimsy as the algae floating on the surface of the open sea's mighty abyss.

But he pressed on, remembering the bizarre tales he had been told about gods and Fate and human destiny. He came around the great rock scarred by centuries of beatings from the ocean froth and stumbled over the debris of a shipwreck. As the body of the skiff came into view, it looked strong and well built by knowledgeable hands. But then he saw it. The blood stained the bottom of the boat and spread out into the sands from a source on the other side of the craft.

Every muscle tensed in the Roman's powerful body. His breath caught in his throat and his heart suddenly pumped at a frantic pace. He followed the red stream and came upon the grotesquely mutilated corpse of his friend Grundler the fisherman.

A shout rose out of his soul, echoing across the coastline, above the crashing waves. A desolate seagull's cry followed the agonized yell, as though answering the man's pain with empathy. Hadrian knelt by the body and placed his hand over the open eyes of the old man. He had seen many corpses in his day, in various stages of destruction. But there was something especially evil about the wounds inflicted on the fisherman. The killers had clearly wanted to see him suffer. Hadrian could feel his face turn scarlet with rage. He hadn't known such outrage since his father's death. The thirst for vengeance rushed, uncontrollable, through his being.

Grundler's beard fluttered in the ocean breeze that had caressed his cheeks for more than half a century. The white hairs seemed to cry out in indignation at the odious mistreatment of a man who so deserved the peace of his last days.

Hadrian turned away, unable to look at the man's features any longer. Suddenly, he spotted a small silhouette peering at him from the rocks at the foot of the cliff. He jumped to his feet and dashed toward the boulders that stood like broken teeth in the open mouth of a dead giant. A terrified little boy scampered through the slippery stones. Hadrian grabbed him with both hands and lifted him into the air. The boy kicked and screamed like a fish out of water.

"Don't kill me! Don't kill me!"

The Roman turned the boy around and shook him until the child stopped kicking.

"I won't kill you if you answer me truthfully. Did you see what happened?"

The boy stared at him as though not understanding, every bone in his body shaking like an autumn leaf. Hadrian turned the child's head toward the inert body laying near the boat.

"Did you see who killed that old man?"

The boy shook his head affirmatively.

"What did they look like?"

"A big man . . . All in brown . . . And two others . . . "

"Do you know that big man's name?"

"No . . . But I've seen him in town . . . "

Hadrian took a deep breath to restrain his violent rage.

"I'm going to take you there, boy, and you're going to show him to me."

A grimace of terror distorted the child's features.

"He'll kill me!"

"No, he will not."

"Yes, he will!" the boy cried out, obviously still in shock from the horror of what he had witnessed.

"He will not hurt you, I give you my word as a Roman centurion! He won't be hurting anyone ever again!"

"But . . . He's very strong and mean!"

"I'll be meaner!" Hadrian shouted wrathfully. "Take me to the town!"

The boy could not control his shivering and was so traumatized that he seemed about to lose consciousness. Hadrian released his grasp and patted the boy's head.

"I'll get you a nice hot meal."

The boy smiled meekly. Hadrian picked him up in his arms and headed off toward the cliff. The hope of leaving the isle had vanished in the heat of his outrage. Poor Grundler's tragic end would not go unpunished.

HADRIAN ENTERED the forest and retraced his steps. He released the boy who knew the path well and led him through the shadows of the dense foliage. The storm clouds had made their way across the waters and were now gathering over the isle, turning day into night and threatening the onslaught of a violent downpour.

Even in the midst of his raging anger, Hadrian could feel the tug of his stoic master's teachings, calling him to return to detachment and inner peace. But the old man's face kept haunting his mind, that face which had offered such generosity to a desperate stranger.

They hurried through the woods, hoping to find their way to the town before the heavens opened their entrails over the earth. They soon came upon the clearing where the mammoth oak tree reigned. The great tree rose before them with the presence of a mythic colossus, stretching his arms toward the darkness above. A cold sweat glistened on the Roman's forehead. It came from some mysterious intuition rising out of an unexplored part of himself. There was something ominous in the clearing. He took hold of the boy's arm to keep him from going any further. The child looked up at him, his wide brown eyes filling with fear at the sight of Hadrian's expression. He turned toward the great tree and searched the shadows for signs of danger.

Hadrian's right hand instinctively wrapped itself around the hilt of his weapon. But he knew that his little sword would be of no use. Whatever was out there, it was beyond the reach of iron blades. Hadrian took a step toward the tree, intending to circle the immense trunk with the expectation of finding whatever it was that filled the clearing with such dread.

His mind began to swim and he became faint as he felt himself stepping back into the dream he had revealed to Ethrain. There was no fog and the smell of rain had not permeated the air as it did now, but the act of coming around the trunk seemed to be the very experience he had dreamt. He was losing track of reality, as though the anchor that held him in the physical realm had broken loose.

A silhouette stepped out from behind the tree, tall and imposing, dressed in flowing gowns. A bolt of lightning cracked across the sky and lit the clearing with a white, ghostly light that suddenly unveiled the features of Ubarra the wizard, last of the mystic druids.

His eyes were fireballs of power and hate. They were glazed with an unnatural glow that only added to the thunderous glare aimed at Hadrian. He stood there, holding a large staff, his other hand pointing at his nemesis. The Roman immediately recognized him as the man in his dreams. He felt his body freeze up like never before. No adversary had ever overwhelmed him to the point of losing control. But this fierce old man radiated more menacing power than any ax-wielding Goth or scarred Hun warrior lusting for blood.

The figure before him suddenly vanished as the stormy darkness returned. His visual disappearance freed Hadrian from the terror that had turned him to stone. His military training took over and he threw himself to the ground. Just then, a ray of reddish light shot through the air, emanating from the wizard's finger, and exploded in the space where Hadrian had stood.

The Roman rolled quickly to the other side of the trunk and felt a searing beam of heat shoot right above his head. He leaped to his feet and dove over the massive roots covering the earth like piles of petrified snakes. Then he heard a scream. He turned around in time to see the young boy fall to the ground, smoke rising from his clothing.

Hadrain drew his sword in a blind rage. Lightning crashed over the forest and once again lit the clearing. The mighty druid stood over the child, looking down at the little corpse. He seemed unmoved, merely examining the results of his strange powers. He turned in time to see the Roman sword flying at him. It struck him in the shoulder and he fell without a sound.

Yelling like a wild man, Hadrian rushed toward him. At the same moment, a thunderous downpour crashed to earth. Hadrian slipped and fell over the roots. He jumped back up and raced toward his gleaming sword. He grabbed it and heaved it up in order to bring it back down upon the wizard. But the blade sunk into a mud puddle. Ubarra had vanished!

Hadrian frantically searched the ground with his blade, then fell to his knees and tapped about for the body he had seen fall. Lightning exploded again, this time striking a tree on the edge of the clearing, sending sparks showering everywhere. In the light, Hadrian saw his sword. There was no blood on its tip, yet he had seen it strike the sorcerer.

Hadrian sprawled in the mud and wept. The emotions of the day and the astonishing events he was faced with had overwhelmed his reason. He lay in the mud, near the little boy's body, and let the heavy rain slap his face and blend with his tears.

Once again, he was helpless and frightened, as vulnerable as the poor child whose life had just been torn away from him by malefic powers that the centurion had never encountered before. He wanted to die, to escape forever from this world which was not only cruel and merciless, but unknown and terrifying.

The rain fell hard upon the earth and the skies rumbled with torment. The mighty tree stood defiantly before the assault of the unleashed storm. Its higher branches shuddered in the cold winds and leaves were torn away and swept into the black heavens.

The beating rain soothed the agony broiling in Hadrian's chest. Soon a deep calm spread through his soul, even though his body was whipped by the violent weather. The mud splattered his face and clothing but he felt nothing. An unexpected quiet within took him far from the horror and darkness of the outer world. His strength began to return to him and he breathed deeply and slowly, swallowing the icy waters which washed his helplessness away.

The storm seemed to rage forever. By the time it had moved on, Hadrian was shivering from head to foot. He opened his eyes. A grim light cut through the clouds, reflected in the glistening raindrops covering the landscape. The howl of night creatures filled the air again.

Hadrian sat up. He looked at his drenched, mud-covered clothing as though it belonged to someone else. His sword lay at his side like a loyal friend. He rose and returned it to its sheath.

His eyes fell on the dead boy. He picked him up in his arms and noticed a large charred spot on his chest. He could not but wonder at the fearsome power of the strange figure who had tried to kill him. The weight of the limp body was a testimonial to the reality of the mysterious forces of which Ethrain had told him. His highly trained logical mind was faltering and he knew it would crumble in the face of supernatural experiences that awaited him on this isle. He would never again mock the beliefs of the natives of Mallor. Clearly, there were things here on the edge of the world which no Roman philosopher had ever imagined.

Hadrian buried the child, digging a grave in the soft black earth with his weapon. He was cleaning the sword when he heard a crackle in the underbrush. He wasn't sure if he had the strength or the desire to fight for his life again. But when he saw the golden locks of young Ethrain, he suddenly awoke to the fact that he still craved being alive.

She came up to him, expressionless. Her companions obediently remained at the edge of the clearing. She looked him over and glanced at the fresh grave. Hadrain peered at her in amazement as though seeing her for the first time. Her youthful vitality underscored by eyes gleaming with serenity and sharp intelligence made her more beautiful then any statue of Venus. She radiated mystery and compassion, strength and vulnerability. Hadrian felt a tremendous avalanche within, as though his inner armor was melting in the heat of a roaring furnace fired by flames of a feeling he had never known before. Standing in the wet and muddy clearing, beneath the towering tree full of some mystic emanation, Hadrian recognized and accepted the fact that he had met the only woman who would ever give him happiness and fulfillment.

Without a word, he took her in his arms. She did not

resist. He hugged her and experienced the merging of his soul with hers, the consummation of unspoken affection, the fateful joining together with the soulmate he had travelled the world to find.

chapter eight

"HYNDLA AWAITS us."

Ulbrek stopped chewing on the rabbit leg.

"The witch?"

A look of fear rippled across the giant's features. Hadrian looked up from his meal and gave Ethrain a questioning glance.

"She is the only one who can tell you how to fight Ubarra."

Hadrian choked on his food.

"I don't want to fight that creature!"

Ethrain looked at him sadly.

"You have no choice. He will seek to destroy you until he succeeds or until you destroy him."

"But I'm just a man. Who knows what he is!"

"He was just a man . . . once."

"No man could ever do what I saw him do!"

Ethrain turned her gaze on the fire, a strange melancholy darkening her magnificent blue eyes.

"Something has happened to him. His powers were for good . . . "

"There was nothing good in what took place in that clearing! When I saw him look at that poor boy as though he were some dead animal, I knew I was faced with pure evil!"

He noticed tears sparkle in Ethrain's eyes.

"Why do you weep?" he asked softly.

Ethrain shook her head and wiped her eyes, not wanting to respond. Hadrian studied her curiously for a moment. A strange feeling made its way to his mind as he pondered her unexpected emotion.

"What does this wizard mean to you?" he asked.

Again, she wouldn't answer. He moved closer to her. Ulbrek and the wolf both looked up, ready to protect her from the Roman intruder.

"You mustn't hide anything from me, Ethrain. I am ready to give my life to rid this isle of its evil."

Ethrain turned to him, letting the tears roll down her cheeks.

"You don't know what you're saying. Mallor is a gateway to other worlds, worlds which control us. Your role will be to do their bidding. All you can do is choose which world you will serve."

"Which world will I serve if I were to kill Ubarra?"

"I . . . I'm not sure . . . He was once a great druid, a healer and a teacher. It was Rome that darkened his soul."

"Rome?"

"I told you . . . The massacre of his brotherhood killed his heart. I don't know him anymore . . . "

She had said too much and bit her lip regretfully.

"What do you mean? How do you know this man?"

Ethrain stood and hurried away. Hadrian jumped to his feet and would have pursued her but Ulbrek stood in his way.

"Let her be!" the giant cried out.

Hadrian was not about to struggle with him. Besides, he realized that there was no point in pressing Ethrain. He would have to find his answer some other way.

They spent the night in a cave in the foothills of the Devil's Horns. Ulbrek and the wolf slept restlessly near the entrance, protecting the two lovers in the depths of the mountain.

At sunrise, they were already on their way to the far side of the isle, toward the swamplands and moors where few dared to wander.

A strong wind howled across the desolate plains, carrying the scent of the open sea. Ethrain had given Hadrian a heavy fur cloak which once covered the entire frame of a great white bear who had found his way to Mallor on floating icebergs descended from the far north, the last remnants of the ice age. It had been in her possession since earliest childhood. She was found wrapped in it by the old woman who saved her from the wilds where she had been abandoned.

On the way to the moors, they stopped at Ethrain's home, a little cottage situated in the forests that cut through the isle like the ragged mane of some monstrous beast. Hadrian was struck with the isolation and crudeness of Ethrian's cottage and admired the strength of character evident in this child of the wilderness. She lived alone with her wolf, as though awaiting the man who would free her from this solitary life. The widow who had found her in these same woods had died several years before, leaving Ethrain with the hut, a few tools, and a great spear that had been fashioned by the woodsman who first brought the old woman to these forests.

Hadrian now held the spear in his hand, finding new confidence in the mysterious mission with which he was entrusted. The blade was made of a heavy chiseled stone with a polished, sharp tip as deadly as any iron weapon. The staff, made of the finest oak, was over six feet in length.

Compared to his centurion's little sword, this weapon was like having an arsenal at his command. He no longer feared the beasts of Mallor, either man or animal. As for the invisible powers he would have to confront,

Hadrian chose to let Fate have its way, as it would in any case.

They journeyed across the flat landscape, struggling against powerful winds. Hadrian felt invigorated by the fresh currents swirling around him. His massive cloak and heavy spear made him feel twice as strong and far removed from those awful feelings of helplessness he had tasted too many times these last few days. But the greatest source of his new vitality was born from the love he shared with Ethrain in the depths of the cave. He had never known such an overwhelming sensation of transcendence. He had been the giver and the receiver, the lover and the beloved, himself and not himself. Together, they had found a merging, a oneness which broke through every illusion of physical separateness. They had loved each other in spirit as well as in the flesh. Their caresses became sacred rituals leading into a holy of holies in the depth of their being where they discovered a vaster Self that was a part of an unspeakable wholeness which defied all understanding.

He put his arm around Ethrain and smiled at her. She nestled at his side, radiant with joy. Her harsh, lonely life was over. She blossomed overnight into womanhood and discovered the wondrous new horizons of her feminine nature. Her cherished independence was only enhanced by the power of her love. She had never known such potent magic.

THE COMPANIONS were halfway across the plain when they came upon a bizarre monument standing alone in the very heart of the wilderness. A large rock rose over a mound of tightly packed dirt. A niche was carved out of the stone and, within it, was lodged a human skull.

"What sort of a sign is this?" Hadrian asked.

"It's a burial ground for the ancient druids."

"Is it one man's grave?"

"No. There is a shaft cut some fifteen feet into the earth where the bodies have been placed. The skull is the severed head of a victim sacrificed to the gods."

"They sacrificed human beings?"

"In the old times . . . "

"So Caesar was right when he reported that the druids were savages!"

"No! These were their forerunners. The druids were wisemen. They held to the teachings of a Greek master."

Hadrian turned to her, astonished.

"What? How did the Greeks reach all the way to this forsaken place?"

"Through Gaul . . . Our druids met each year in that land. I've heard that they left from these very shores."

She pointed to the distant beaches on the far side of the moors.

"Do you know which Greek master it was?"

"I've heard the name. But I don't remember it."

Hadrian marveled at the fact that this child of the wilds even knew there was a people known as Greeks. Again, he realized that Mallor was not like the other primitive rocks in this violent sea. There was more enlightenment here than among the Angles, and the Franks. This was indeed an extraordinary spot upon the earth.

A strange thought suddenly took hold of him. "Why not?" he wondered to himself, remembering all the other unexpected events that he had witnessed on this isle.

"The name wouldn't be Pythagoras, would it?"

"That's it!" Ethrain exclaimed. "Do you know the master's teachings?"

"I've been privileged to hear some of them."

"Then you know about life beyond death!" she said, her excitement growing to new heights.

Hadrian marvelled at the young woman.

"How does a daughter of Mallor know of this great man's philosophy?"

"You still see us as barbarians, Roman!" she said with a smile. "I was taught by druids. This wisdom comes from the most high and ancient sources. I know of things that have never been whispered in the great halls of Roman learning."

Hadrian felt a surge of energy flood his being, rising out of the secret core of his soul. He had long sought that life-giving knowledge passed on by sages from time immemorial.

"Are the teachings of the druids written down?"

"No. Every precious thought has been transmitted through the memories of those who know. Nothing has been left for the eyes of the vulgar."

"But if most of the druids have disappeared, so will their knowledge!"

"There are enough of us to carry it on for the next generation," Ethrain stated with a mysterious expression.

"Have you been given their treasures? Are you an initiate?" Hadrian asked, astonished.

"I will only say that I am here to join with you on the mission which was foretold in the days when druids from all the lands would come to our shores at the spring equinox."

Hadrian knew he was not to pry any further. But he realized that Fate had hurled him into something of great importance, something which went beyond anything he had ever experienced. He understood intuitively that his love for Ethrain was an integral part of some cosmic plan that might indeed impact the history of humanity.

He took her hand and they moved on. They walked until late afternoon before reaching the boggs on the southern tip of the isle.

HYNDLA'S HOME was a large building powerfully constructed with entire oak trees. It had stood for many years and had first belonged to some prominent leader of the secretive druids. The structure stood on a hill surrounded by deep marshes and treacherous quicksands. Even more menacing were monuments of ancient gods standing behind every tree and rock in the area. The moss-covered carvings were simple but bore striking expressions that were both frightful and fascinating.

A bright light flickered from within the building, rendering it all the more out of place in this wretched, alien landscape. Hyndla seemed to be expecting them for she came out as they climbed the hill and impassively watched them approach. Though she looked at Hadrian suspiciously, she no longer appeared enraged at his presence among them.

Ethrain embraced her warmly, and Hyndla caressed the wolf who knew her well and licked her hands affectionately. Ethrain took Hadrian by the arm and brought him face to face with the powerful woman.

"This is Hadrian the Roman."

Hyndla looked him over sternly.

"We've met," the Roman said awkwardly, attempting to offer her a smile of reconciliation.

Hyndla's features darkened as she immediately perceived the bonds that had developed between Ethrain and Hadrian. Disdain curled her lip downward into an unfriendly grimace. Hadrian shrugged at the witch's grim temperament, and he gave up trying to establish a warmer relationship. His Roman pride had never been interested in trying to make people like him.

They entered the building. Countless plants filled the large room. Great roots hung from the rafters. A giant hearth was occupied by several huge cauldrons. The light-colored logs softened the impression of the room even though it was filled with strange and disturbing objects. A giant fur blanket separated Hyndla's living quarters from the space which served as some sort of kitchen-laboratory. This was a place where potions of all sorts were created; whether for good or evil it was hard to tell.

Amulets and talismans hung along the walls like supernatural ornaments. Hadrian recognized several of them, surprised to find figurines from distant eastern lands, beyond the kingdom of the Huns and Mongols. How they had made their way to the other side of the world was a dark mystery. Hadrian wondered if there might be some secret civilization that linked and perhaps controlled the established ones. Clearly, there was travel and interaction occurring outside the main currents of trade and diplomacy, a stream of activity uncontrolled by the military powers of the earth.

Hadrian noticed a preponderance of Nordic carvings. He recognized the gods and demons of Iceland, the hexes of the Viking peoples, and the war symbols of the Danes. There was even a crucifix carved in the Celtic manner, possibly by the lone missionary to the wilds of Ireland, Patrick the Briton.

The Roman had never seen such a gathering of differing religious images. In fact, he had only seen them in separate lands among separate peoples. Only in crossing frontiers on his way to war had he come across these strange symbols.

A dwarf appeared from behind the curtain, a plump little woman in black clothing whom Hyndla had taken in as a servant.

"Offer our guests to drink," Hyndla ordered.

She pointed to tree trunks and mounds of fur near the hearth. The group dropped on the makeshift chairs, exhausted by the journey. Before seating himself, Hadrian came up to Hyndla.

"Grundler's been murdered," he said sadly.

The fiery woman stared into his eyes and seemed unmoved except for a slight facial twitch that betrayed some deep emotion.

"He knew it would come to that," she stated coldly.

"I will find the killers and avenge him!" Hadrian whispered hoarsely, his rage erupting from its lair.

"The killers were puppets in the hands of the spirits. It was foretold that the one who helped the Roman would suffer a terrible death."

Hadrian glanced at Ethrain.

"Yes, that same fate awaits her because she has joined with you," Hyndla said, knowing what he was thinking.

"No one will hurt her! I swear it on all that is sacred!"

Hyndla looked at him with a mocking sneer.

"You have no power, Roman. If the spirits choose to act, the best you can do is to accept what they ordain."

"I tell you that no harm will come to Ethrain as long as . . . "

"As long as you are alive," she stated sarcastically.

"I will break through the gates of Hades itself to protect her!"

"You may have to do that."

"Then I will!"

They stared at each other in silence. Hyndla's harsh features relaxed and a sparkle of warmth appeared in her dark eyes as she witnessed the Roman's mighty determination fired by great courage and greater love.

"I will pray for your safety, Roman," she whispered.

Hadrain was surprised by her sudden change of attitude. She turned away from him before he could find out the source of her feelings. What was her relationship to Ethrain?

The dwarf served a delicious hot brew to the group in large mugs crafted in some other age. Ethrain explained what had happened in the forest clearing and why they had come to her.

Hadrian learned that the witch was a sworn enemy of the wizard, nurturing a terrible hatred born from some secret deed which had taken place between them years ago. Once again, he heard of legends that were now becoming reality.

"The dark forces of the underworld have taken control of men's souls," Hyndla said. "And the gods now want to reclaim their rightful dominion over this world."

She explained that humans had been left free by the powers of the upper world to choose which influence they would place themselves under. They had chosen the dark forces.

"How will the gods do this?" Hadrian asked with hesitance, already cringing at the answer.

"They will war with the giants of Jotunheim."

"What will happen to humanity?"

"Our middle world may be destroyed."

"Why?" Hadrian asked, horrified.

"Because we have disappointed the higher powers and have reduced the earth to a battlefield feeding the hunger of the underworld for death and destruction."

"Do you mean that the gods have given up on us?"

A melancholic expression fell over Hyndla's aquiline features. She did not answer. Ethrain took Hadrian's hand.

"They have given up on this cycle of history. The time has come to begin anew. The old world must either give birth to the new or die in labor."

"But the gods of Valhalla do not want to start again," Hyndla stated in solemn tones. "You have called upon us the wrath of both the gods and the giants."

"How have I done that?" Hadrian cried out.

"It is you who will lead us into a new cycle of civilization," Ethrain said softly.

"The gods will seek to destroy you because they have lost faith in humanity. And the giants will attack you because they wish to maintain their stronghold over this world," Hyndla exclaimed grimly.

"How in the name of all that is holy can I accomplish anything under such conditions?"

"You will have to trick the gods and confront the giants," the witch said.

"No man can do such a thing!"

A deadly silence fell over the room. Ulbrek drank from his mug loudly and a crow let out a plaintive cry from its cage in the back of the building. The wolf yawned and stretched, unconcerned with the troubles of his human companions.

Hyndla tossed another log on the fire and turned her back on the grim Roman.

"You will have to attempt it now that you are here," she said coldly. "You have no choice in the matter."

"Why is Ubarra trying to kill him?" Ethrain asked.

"Ubarra is dead. His soul has been enslaved by the gods."

"What sort of gods could be so cruel?" Hadrian questioned.

"They are the warrior spirits of Valhalla. The demiurges who reign over this part of the universe."

"Do you mean that they are not the highest gods?"

"Certainly not. The sacred Absolute has no form or name."

"Will this Absolute let our world be destroyed?"

"The decision is ours alone. Your people chose the ways of brutality as have most of the other races. And that choice has determined the future."

"Are the gods evil?" Ethrain asked.

"Not evil, but neither are they willing to let humans offer earth to the dominion of the underworld."

"How do you know these things?" Hadrian asked suspiciously.

"I know . . . "

Hadrian would have protested her vague response had he not caught sight of her fearsome expression. The woman seemed terrified at her own knowledge of things to come. He could tell that she had encountered something supernatural which had left its mark on her.

"How do we trick the gods?" he asked her.

"Change the course of events!"

She looked at him with a terrible glare as if daring him to his ultimate challenge.

"Find the envoys of the dark forces," she continued, "and keep them from conquering the earth."

Suddenly, Hadrian understood. In a flash of insight, he recognized what Grundler, Ethrain and Hyndla had been trying to tell him all along. The illusion of men acting from their own will crumbled like an old wall struck by a battering ram. And out of the smoke of human arrogance, he saw clearly that they were puppets on a stage where the forces of light and darkness warred in a fatal struggle. His military knowledge revealed to him the death grip in which civilization found itself.

"Attila!" he cried out.

Hyndla shook her head knowingly.

"I am to destroy Attila before his armies spread across the entire world!"

"If that happens, the druids have said that darkness will fall over humankind for uncounted generations. The giants will be the victorious rulers of earth."

Hadrian took his head in his hands. He knew only too well what an impossible feat this would be.

"What of Ubarra?" Ethrain wondered.

"You must meet with him and make him understand that he is only going to plunge us all into the fires of Ragnarok unless he realizes that the Roman is our only hope!" the witch of Mallor declared in solemn tones.

chapter 9

THE COMPANIONS spent the night in Hyndla's home. Hadrian was assaulted until dawn by a dream unlike any other he had ever experienced. Hundreds of strange faces appeared to him in a dizzying dance of shadows and light. Some whispered, some shouted. But all had the same message to give him: "Save us! Save us from destruction!"

The faces gave way to landscapes, some of which were familiar to him. The great Alpine forests appeared to him. He felt himself lifted above the highest branches of the majestic fir trees. Then he found himself flying over the white peaks of the mammoth mountain chain. The awesome sight then transformed into another landscape, one Hadrian had never seen before. An ocean of endless rolling hills, barren and desolate appeared beneath him. Hadrian's soul was breathless with ecstasy under the spell of this sensation of flight. He felt freed from the bonds of flesh, escaping the anxieties of life. He no longer experienced himself as a man imprisoned in a cage of bones and sinews, but as a spirit as free as the wind that howled across the seas.

The odd terrain gave way to another vision. It was night now and a thousand sparkling campfires spread out before him, designing the outline of a city as vast as

Rome itself. Somehow, he knew what city it was. A powerful feeling of dread shot through him and seemed to break his flight. He felt himself falling toward the massive gathering of tents and oddly shaped buildings. A paralyzing fear took hold of him. He thought he would witness his body splatter on the rapidly approaching ground.

But he landed as light as a feather in a large hall. The dark room was empty at first sight, though the air seemed packed with the tension of impending doom. Confused by the abrupt change of scenery, Hadrian took a hesitant step forward. He listened to the loud echo of his footsteps, worried that someone might detect his presence. The eerie sound bounced across the stone floor and humid walls and suddenly mixed with another echo which grew into the sound of laughter, a horrid, terrible laughter.

Hadrian looked over at the head of the great table in the far corner of the hall. A large silhouette sat in the center chair. A dim glow emanated from slanted eyes. The laughter became demonic and the Roman felt a cold sweat moisten his forehead. He knew he was in the presence of unspeakable evil.

The figure stood. It had the bulk of a mighty bull and the presence of an all-powerful king. Hadrian recognized Attila, whom the world called the Scourge of God.

He abruptly awoke and sat up. The room was utterly silent, lit only by a ray of moonlight streaming through an open window. It took him several moments to identify where he was. The place was as bizarre as the images in his nightmare. He looked about frantically, expecting to find the savage Kagan of the Huns standing behind him. The horrid laugh still rang through his mind, haunting him with an overwhelming sense of danger. He breathed deeply and wiped the hot sweat streaming down his cheeks. He heard Ulbrek's loud snoring nearby and felt a wave of relief rush through him. Never had he imagined that the giant's presence would be comforting to him.

Suddenly, he saw a shadow move across the dim blue light penetrating the room. He peered into the darkness and made out a silhouette standing by the window. The form was familiar to him, terribly familiar. It instantly sent his adrenalines burning into his bloodstream like wildfire. Ubarra stood by the window!

Hadrain was about to jump to his feet when he saw the wizard lean into the light and look down upon Ethrain's sleeping form. There was a sad gentleness in his movement and for a moment all dread left his presence. The Roman sensed that the druid was not here to kill him so he remained frozen in the darkness. He watched silently as Ubarra lowered his bony hand over Ethrain's head. Somehow, Hadrian knew that the old warlock would not harm his beloved. He could see Ubarra's features now and what he witnessed astonished him. There were tears sparkling in his eyes. They fell onto his cheeks in big drops and wet his great white beard as though he were caught in a sudden spring rain.

The wizard's hand hovered over the young woman. His crooked fingers became graceful as they spread apart and radiated an affectionate energy, a blessing upon Ethrain.

Hadrian held his breath. A great melancholy unexpectedly filled his heart as he saw his dreaded enemy weep with stoic nobility. This was not the beast who had coldly destroyed the young boy in the forest. This was an old man broken by great pain and reaching out with a love that would not be reciprocated.

Suddenly, Ubarra turned toward Hadrian. He had sensed that he was being watched with that awareness of a lion detecting the presence of its hunters. Though Hadrian sat in darkness, he knew that the wizard could see him. His heart pounded out of control as he watched the sad eyes turn fierce and the tears dry instantly in the heat of rage.

Slowly, the wizard's hand rose through the air and turned toward Hadrian. One finger pointed directly at his head. The Roman raised his chin in proud defiance. If his time to die had come, it would be with dignity, not with fear.

The crow's raucous cry broke the deadly silence. Ubarra looked down at Ethrain and saw her move. He stepped into the shadows as she sat up. Hadrian blinked and rubbed his eyes. The astonished Roman realized that the wizard had vanished from the room.

POOLS OF red light reflected the bloody sunrise in the myriad tiny lakes cut into the rocky flatlands. The pools looked like giant drops of blood fallen from some wounded colossus stumbling across the desolate land.

The scarlet sky expressed Hadrian's mood. He had not slept after the strange incident and his mind was turbulent with chaotic thoughts. He knew his dream was a message, a warning from the future. And he vaguely sensed that the crow's timely cry had kept him alive for some more gruesome fate.

Ethrain walked alongside him in an opposite state of mind. She was full of joy and mirth. When he had asked her what the cause of her happiness was, she could only say that she had awakened with a marvelous sensation of peace that tingled through her from head to toe.

"Do you realize what lies ahead?" he asked cynically.

"We have no choice in the matter. So why worry?"

"Why worry?" Hadrian exclaimed. "We are asked to destroy the greatest military leader in the world or face the wrath of gods and demons alike!"

"I would have thought that you had a liking for adventure."

"I've had all the adventure a man could ever hope for."

"Would you rather work the land and sit by the hearth in the evenings?"

"Perhaps . . . "

"You were born to be a man of action, Hadrian Aldius, just as I was born to be a daughter of Mallor."

"Does that mean we are forced to live as such to the end of our days?"

"Of course. Does a wolf cease to be a wolf halfway through its existence?"

Hadrian couldn't argue with that statement. But he wanted to argue with something. There had to be a way to bemoan what had been thrown upon him since his shipwreck.

"Why didn't you leave the island when I gave you the chance?"

He turned to her, stunned.

"What do you mean?"

"You know. . . When I left you in the clearing. You were near the shore. Why didn't you escape all this?"

"Did I really have a choice?"

"Yes! We humans are not wooden puppets. We're living puppets! There are choices we can make. Neither the gods nor the demons have full control. That's what makes us valuable to them. It is our willpower which they struggle for. If we were mere sheep, we would be of no use to them."

"But what of possession by the spirits? Do they not have command over us as a captain does over his ship?"

"Certainly. But the captain only controls the rudder and the raising of the sail. He has no say over the wind and the waves."

They walked in silence for a moment.

"What are the wind and the waves to us?" he asked, almost embarrassed to acknowledge that the young woman who had probably never seen a book in her life had more wisdom than a highly educated Roman patrician.

"Our true nature. We are spirit as well as flesh. And though we seem so much weaker than the powers of Valhalla and Jotunheim, we actually arise from a much greater source than they."

"What source?" he inquired breathless with curiously.

She looked up at him in surprise.

"Don't you know?"

"No," he said irritably. There were limits to how much humbling of himself he was willing to go through. "But I'm sure you do."

"Of course!" she said with glee. "Religion would have no purpose if it didn't reveal them to us. Why else do you have temples and priests?"

Hadrian was dumbfounded by her insightfulness.

"So tell me, what is the source from which we arise?"

"Such knowledge cannot simply be given over to the ignorant. One must be made worthy of it."

Hadrian's ears turned as red as the sky.

"How dare you call me ignorant!"

"Well, aren't you?" she responded with a twinkle in her eyes.

"No! I've studied the teachings of Pythagoras, Plato, Epectitus . . . "

"And you still don't know the answer to your question!" she interrupted. "What good is that kind of knowledge?"

"And what makes you so sure your knowledge is correct?"

"Experience," she answered simply.

Once again, Hadrian could not think of a response. He looked back at their companions who moved slowly over the rocks at a respectful distance. They were headed for the Place of Power where Hyndla performed her rituals. She had assured Hadrian that there were spells which could protect him from Ubarra's unworldly powers.

Hyndla led the way, walking silently ahead in an intense state of concentration. Ulbrek and the wolf followed behind, unconcerned with anything but the next meal. Hadrian decided to take his chances.

"Why does Ubarra care for you?"

As he had expected, his question struck Ethrain like a bolt of lightning.

"You are talking foolishly, Roman," she responded after regaining her composure.

"You told me that experience does not lie."

"I don't understand you."

"He was with us last night."

"Who?"

"Ubarra!"

Ethrain turned pale and Hadrian thought he detected a tremble on her lips.

"How is that possible?"

"He stood over you."

"You must have been dreaming!"

"I had a dream last evening, but that was not it. I'm telling you that I saw him as clearly as I see you."

"What did he do?" she asked in a whisper.

"He wept."

The words pierced her heart. She let out an involuntary moan. He took her by the shoulders.

"What is he to you, Ethrain? You must tell me!"

She pulled away and ran toward Hyndla. They spoke in hushed tones and the witch put her arm around Ethrain, hugging her as only a mother can embrace her child.

Hadrian studied them closely as they walked ahead of him, arm in arm, apparently consoling each other. A wave of emotion suddenly crashed upon the shores of his heart. He felt the same deep melancholy that had invaded him the night before. He no longer needed an answer.

He knew. His heart knew. Hyndla was Ethrain's mother and Ubarra was her father!

They reached the plateau overlooking the waters of the North Sea. A great circle was drawn in the rock surrounding a gigantic dolmen which rose like some monstrous skull staring out at the horizon.

"What is this place?" Hadrian asked.

"This is the most sacred point on the isle," Ethrain whispered. "It's a great privilege for you to be here."

"I'm honored," Hadrian said sarcastically.

Ethrain threw him a dark glare. She was becoming wearied with the Roman's lack of reverence for the mysteries of her people.

"I'm more interested in why you've kept from me the fact that the man who wants to kill me is your father."

"Silence!" Hyndla ordered as she approached the jagged obelisk in the center of the circle. She pointed at Ulbrek and motioned for him to sit at the far side of the clearing. She then turned to Hadrian and ordered him to approach.

The Roman looked at Ethrain, somewhat intimidated. He sensed that something unusual was about to happen. The young woman gently pushed him forward.

"It must be this way," she murmured.

Her soft tone eased his concern and he stepped into the circle. Hyndla came up to him and stood inches from his face. Her eyes were glazed with striking inward intensity.

"Roman, you are about to be initiated into one of the great secrets of the druids. Only through this knowledge will you be able to fulfill your mission."

A strange thought entered Hadrian's mind. He had the distinct impression that Hyndla still loved the wizard despite her insistence on his demise. Was it truly for the good of humanity that she wanted him dead? Or was it unrequited love and past mistakes controlling the events of which he was now a part?

"Clear all thoughts from your mind," she whispered sternly.

Hadrian detected resentment in her voice as though she had read his mind. Suddenly, she slapped him across the face. He barely managed to control his warrior's reaction as every muscle in his body tensed with anger.

"Give me all your attention!" she commanded.

The stinging pain reddening his cheek had accomplished its purpose. Hadrian was fully focused on her.

"All obstructions must be removed from your body," Hyndla said as she yanked on his ring. Ethrain came up behind him and unbuckled his belt. He felt his sword being taken away. Ethrain then unbuckled his boots and slipped them off his feet as Hyndla forced him to maintain eye contact with her. She then untied the cords of his cloak and tossed the heavy clothing aside.

A cold sea breeze enveloped him, shivering through his light tunic. Hadrian experienced a rare vulnerability invading his being. He felt naked in the harsh elements surrounding him. Never had he been so humiliated, and yet he knew that he had to comply.

"Follow me," Hyndla whispered as she turned away and approached the dolmen.

Hadrian walked awkwardly behind her. She took his hands and placed them on the icy rock.

"Step back," she said as she pushed his legs away, forcing him off balance.

Hadrain clenched his jaws and leaned his weight against the stone. He closed his eyes and wished himself elsewhere. A moment that seemed like eternity went by. Hadrian focused his attention on the rhythmic sounds of the ocean tide far below. He concentrated as best he could to keep his thoughts away and his mind empty. The awkwardness of his condition assisted him in maintaining a silence within as he separated himself from his body.

The cold wind caused his body to shiver. He breathed deeply and found that it was no longer a strain to keep his mind free from disturbances. The very desire to be out of his body, removed from this humiliation, lifted him into a strange detachment. Again he focused his attention on the slow splashing of the calm sea.

His entire body shivered with cold. As his consciousness left the song of the ocean waves and returned to his shaking body, he realized that it was more than the weather that was causing him to shiver. He became aware of his hands against the rock. They were hot as coals and pulsating as though an energy was penetrating them from the giant rock and filling his body with a new power. The shaking grew more intense as the force field invaded him.

The energy from the rock reached its peak and vibrated through him from head to toe. Hot perspiration covered his whole body all at once as he lost all control of his muscles and entered a convulsion which shook him back and forth. Completely released from his willpower, his soul seemed cut loose from his body and sent adrift into some other realm. Though his heartbeat rose to a frenzied pace, he could no longer feel it pumping within. In an explosion of energy, he seemed to break through the barriers of the physical and plunge into a land of ecstatic intensity. He had broken away from himself as a ship torn loose from its anchor and was gliding in unknown waters, free and transformed.

Suddenly, he felt an immense presence surrounding him. Though he could not tell whether his eyes were closed or not, he could see with another sight a universe of brilliant light. The sense of the presence expanded with the light and suddenly burst into a myriad colors. Countless beings stared at him through the shimmering hues. They extended further than the ocean's horizon and higher than the most distant star. Overwhelmed by the vision, Hadrian felt himself melt in the searing heat of these innumerable spirits. Dark colors mixed with golden light, melodious sounds blended with deep, relentless hums. Angelic figures of light seemed to coexist in multiple layers of living forms extending into a dizzying abyss of infinity.

He felt like a seagull floating out to sea carried along powerful currents.

Then the shapes and sounds hurled toward him as if they were about to crush him into nonexistence. He heard himself scream in sheer terror and suddenly found himself staring at his hands spread out against the dolmen. They were scarlet and shaking like storm-tossed leaves. Someone grabbed his arms from behind and he felt himself torn away from the sacred stone. He fell on his back, at the feet of Hyndla and Ethrain. For a time, he continued to shiver uncontrollably. The soothing song of the waves caressing the shoreline slowly calmed him down. His sight focused on Ethrain's gentle features. She was watching him with great concern and love. Her face eased the dread knotting up his chest and the thundering heartbeat became more regular.

Ethrain kneeled down beside him and poured cool water over his lips. She wet her fingers in the water sack and gently stroked his forehead and cheeks.

"You're with us again," she whispered. "You're safe."

Hadrian continued to stare at them with wide, unblinking eyes. The alien force within still held him in its grip and kept him from regaining control over his body.

"You have seen the world as it truly is," Hyndla stated in a friendlier tone than she had ever used before. "Once you are familiar with it, you'll find that it need not be feared. But neither must it be forgotten!"

"Take a deep breath if you can," Ethrain whispered.

Hadrian breathed in the salty air. The scent of the sea

made him feel better, as though proving that he was back in familiar territory.

"You must lay still until the shivers are gone," Hyndla advised him as she and Ethrain massaged his convulsing muscles.

Hadrian continued to breathe deeply. He had never felt so helpless before. But that weakness didn't bother his warrior's pride any longer. He had seen something he could never have imagined in his wildest dreams. The philosophers he studied had made references to these spiralling worlds of spirit but that knowledge had only been interesting theory or religious belief, not genuine experience. His whole view of life had been completely shattered in those few moments. The visible world would never be the same again. Matter was no longer the all of things but windows onto an infinity inhabited by unutterable beauty and power. Time itself had been revealed as an illusion masking dimensions which converged in the simplicity of the passing moment.

Hadrian drank deeply from Ethrain's water sack. He poured the cold liquid on his head and let it run down his neck and shoulders. Ethrain laughed.

"Now what do you think of our barbarian ways, Roman?"

Hadrian turned to her and found that no words came to his mind. He looked out over the great ocean. It too had changed. Where he had once seen water and danger, he now saw mystery and wonder. He perceived eternity written in the foam that fell upon the sands in an endless cycle of departure and return. He heard a great longing in the bleak cry of seagulls, the longing of souls exiled from their true homeland. The breeze whispered secrets to his ear and the sky, the awesome blue zenith, became a world filled with life rather than a void where clouds traced their melancholic passage.

Finally, the vast space within his mind narrowed to his intellectual faculties and he was able to speak.

"Have you seen what I have seen?" he asked Ethrain in a hesitant voice.

"I have . . . "

"How is it that . . . ?"

"No questions!" Hyndla interrupted. "Do not let your mind reduce what you have experienced to the smallness of your thought."

Hadrian noticed that he was no longer offended by the woman's stern and haughty behavior. A new feeling had entered his soul, a feeling which untangled him from the darkness and ignorance of his petty but well groomed pride. It was the feeling which all his spiritual teachers and their teachers before them had manifested. Humility was its name.

"We will teach you how to make use of what you have witnessed," Ethrain told him gently.

"Or rather how to make yourself an instrument to be used by higher powers," Hyndla corrected. "You will have to distinguish between forces of light and forces of darkness, both of which will seek to manifest through you."

"Are these the gods and giants you have told me about?" he wondered.

"What did I tell you about questions, Roman?" Hyndla replied angrily. "Is your mind so wooden that it must rule over every mystery you come upon?"

"Both gods and demons are but a small form of these powers," Ethrain stated, overlooking the witch's disapproving look. "Just as we are even a smaller expression of that world."

They helped Hadrian to his feet and assisted him in taking small steps until he regained his equilibrium.

"What you have seen will not give you the powers which Ubarra possesses. But you will learn to call upon them for assistance," Hyndla said as she handed him his sword. "They will protect you much better than this piece of steel."

"May I ask what happens now?"

"You will go to Elkar and purchase the necessary materials to defeat Ubarra."

"Can anything made of matter defeat him?"

"No, but going to Elkar will."

Hadrian looked at her with surprise. But he knew that he was not to ask anymore questions.

chapter 10

HYNDLA INSISTED that Ulbrek and the wolf remain at her home while Ethrain and Hadrian returned to the town. She gave the Roman an amulet which was carved from the most ancient dolmen on the isle.

"It holds the powers which you discovered yesterday, though in much weaker form. To receive them, you must learn to quiet your mind and soul and focus your attention. Hold the amulet in your right hand and you will feel its powers come through you."

Hyndla gave them two horses for the trip to Elkar. The Roman recognized them as the rugged ponies which the Huns had introduced into the West. He didn't even try to find out how the beasts had found their way to Mallor. Apparently, everything human and otherwise seemed to pass through this strange and terrible island.

Within a day's ride, they had crossed the flatlands and found their way back into the forests on the far side of the Devil's Horns. As the sun was setting over the mountains, they decided to stop at Ethrain's hut and enter the town at dawn the following day.

Hadrian went out to find kindling for the fireplace as Ethrain prepared a meal for them. He had barely entered the forest when three men appeared before him. In the shadows of twilight, Hadrian recognized Agnar.

"You must be the Roman!" the evil man cried out. "We've been looking for you everywhere. I should have known you had joined company with the witch's daughter."

Hadrian drew his sword as his anger gushed to the surface.

"You're the vile creature who killed Grundler!"

"So you found his body, did you? You'll be happy to know the old fool didn't betray you. But, as you can see, all his suffering proved useless!"

The men laughed. With a terrible yell, Hadrian swung his sword and attacked them. One of the men stepped in front of Agnar and took the blow across the side of his head, saving his leader's life. Before Hadrian could swing again, the other man struck him in the chest with his spear. The sharp point was stopped by the amulet but the power of the blow knocked Hadrian off his feet. As he jumped up, Agnar brought his great ax down upon him and sunk it into his shoulder.

Hadrian cried out in agony and tried to strike him with his sword but the other man blocked the blow and hit his wrist with the shaft of his spear so hard that Hadrian dropped the weapon.

The spear whistled through the air and planted itself in the Roman's thigh. Hadrian collapsed, his blood raining down upon the forest floor. Agnar pulled his ax from Hadrian's shoulder and watched him squirm. The other man drew a long knife from his belt and was about to strike a fatal blow when Agnar stopped him.

"Wait! I want him to die slowly. Tie him to the tree."

He unwrapped a cord from his waist and gave it to his companion. The man tied Hadrian's hands together as the Roman moaned in pain. He then wrapped the cord around the tree and swiftly fashioned a sailor's knot. Agnar grabbed Hadrian by the hair and lifted his head up.

"The smell of blood will draw the wolves down upon you before the moon rises. We'll be back to see what's left of you after we take care of Ethrain."

He threw the Roman's head down and snickered. Hadrian nearly fainted from the pain. He watched desperately as they hurried off to the hut.

Agnar burst into the room as Ethrain was filling a pot with vegetables. She jumped away and called out for Hadrian. Her cry carried all the way to the tree where the wounded man groaned in horror. He tried to raise himself but the deep cut in his shoulder paralyzed him with pain.

Agnar grabbed Ethrain and pinned her arms behind her back.

Hadrian felt his life force drain out of him as quickly as his blood which flowed out among the leaves. He knew the cut in his shoulder was a bad one, though the spear had only caused a flesh wound. He couldn't accept that he had been granted that extraordinary vision for nothing. It would vanish with his last breath. This caused him more agony than the fear of beasts soon to be attracted by his blood. Was all that talk of Fate meaningless, a great illusion which the likes of Agnar could mock as they raped his beloved?

At the thought of Ethrain, he felt a burning sensation on his chest. It was the amulet! He had forgotten it even though it had already saved him once from the spear's sharp blade. In a supreme effort, he shook on the rope. He could hardly move his hands but there was enough cord to bring them toward his chest. Writhing in terrible pain, he lowered his hands as blood surged out of his open shoulder. He grasped the stone with both hands and nearly lost consciousness again.

"The right one . . . " The words came to him as though Hyndla were speaking to him in his mind. He clasped his right hand around the amulet and held it tight.

"Save me, mighty gods! Save me so that I may protect Ethrain!" he begged in a silent scream.

Then he remembered that he was not to have thoughts in his mind. But the stone burned his hand like a hot coal. He dimly realized that his prayer, rising from the depths of his soul, had acted more powerfully than the vacant concentration which he had been told to perform.

A new strength entered his arm and raced down the side of his body.

"Not for me, but for your child!" he cried out. The sizzling energy flooded him completely and he suddenly found himself clear headed, and relieved from the wrenching agony. He sat up against the tree and felt a sharp object cut into his thigh. It was his sword! They had forgotten to remove his sword, assuming that he was too weak to make use of it.

For an instant, he hesitated. What would happen if he let go of the sacred stone? A scream rang out from the hut and Hadrian lunged for the sword. He hacked at the rope with new vigor and was soon freed from the tree. He then placed the weapon between his feet and inserted the blade through the rope binding his hands. Gritting his teeth with pain, he rubbed them back and forth with all his might. He could feel the flesh tearing in his shoulder, but he was now beyond physical torment, as though a part of him had stepped out into that dimension he had experienced on the plateau. But this time, it wasn't curiosity that motivated him. It was love. And the force of the stone erupted within him.

His hands were quickly freed. Though he felt disconnected from his torn body, he had the presence of mind to rip his tunic and wrap it around the wound, slowing the flow of blood. He leaned against the tree and with a shout rose to his feet. His head was spinning and he thought he would lose consciousness but he grasped the amulet and the dizziness left him.

He hurried to the hut as though the fever of every battle he had ever fought were bursting through him at once. He stumbled into the doorway. Agnar turned around and his mouth fell open in astonishment.

"What in the name of . . . !"

Hadrian charged like a mad bull. As Agnar leaped at him, the Roman smashed the hilt of his weapon into his forehead. The man fell to the floor, unconsciousness. The other man released Ethrain, a look of sheer terror in his eyes. Hadrian threw himself on him and wrestled him to the ground. The man grabbed his knife but Hadrian took hold of his wrist and twisted his arm, pointing the knife directly at his chest. He dropped his whole body weight on the weapon. Within moments, his adversary was motionless.

Hadrian rose with difficulty and cut the ropes holding Ethrain down. She threw herself in his arms, weeping uncontrollably. Hadrain soothed her as he felt his strength seep out of him. His legs gave way and he crumbled to the ground, taking Ethrain with him.

A terrible roar burst across the room. They looked up in time to see Agnar rising to his feet. His face distorted by a demonic grimace, he stepped toward them, aiming the sword at Hadrian's head. Ethrain placed herself in front of him to protect him from the blow. Agnar advanced and raised the sword with both hands. Hadrian was too weak to move Ethrain out of the way.

As the blade was about to come down upon them, they saw Agnar's body suddenly smash against the wall with such force that his neck broke and he slumped to the floor, lifeless. In the doorway stood the gaunt figure of Ubarra, his hand aimed at the evil man.

The wizard's eagle eyes were boiling with rage. He looked down at them. Hadrian held Ethrain against his heart, no longer able to do anything but face death with a soldier's courage.

Ubarra approached them. His harsh features gleamed with unearthly power. He raised his hand. It took the same shape it had manifested the night Hadrian had seen him standing over Ethrain.

"You have saved my daughter, Roman."

The voice was deep and resonant with an unnatural quality, as though it echoed from some far away place. An intense silence fell over them. Only the drops of Hadrian's blood falling to the floor disturbed the awful silence.

Ubarra came closer and leaned over them. He placed his hand on the blood-soaked tunic wrapped around Hadrian's wound. The Roman held his breath. He had never seen Ubarra's features up close. The skeletal face was lined with deep crevices of sorrow and the eyes had a transparence that revealed a strange light as from a distant star.

Within moments, the blood had stopped flowing. An incredible heat emanated from the druid's thin hand as it absorbed the pain it was touching. Ubarra pulled it away and straightened his back with difficulty.

"I will not seek to kill you, Roman. Even if the gods destroy me forever. I will not kill the man who rose from the dead to save my Ethrain."

Bursting into tears, Ethrain stood and embraced the old wizard. A deep sigh escaped him and his tired eyes sparkled with a rare joy. Hesitantly, he put his arm around her.

"Father!" she cried out. "Why have you waited so long to give me your love?"

"It is too late to change anything now. My mistakes will haunt me even in the other world."

He looked down at Hadrian who watched on in amazement.

"My son, your people massacred everything I cared for.

But you have washed their evil away in this one act. And you have allowed me to be with Ethrain one last time."

"No, father. Stay with us. Let us make up for lost time."

"I am no longer in time, my daughter. I am here only by the wishes of Odin who would have me be his butcher. But I am done with bloodshed."

"Don't leave me!" she cried out in despair.

"You have another man to care for you as I never could. I will be of more use to you out of this old carcass. There is much to be done if you wish to live in peace together."

"I beg of you . . . "

"No, child. I have failed you in this life as I failed your mother . . . and as I failed myself."

He took her face in his trembling hands.

"But I promise you this. The powers I have gained at this terrible price will be used for your happiness. Before the gods take their revenge upon my betrayal, I will grant you your deepest desire."

He kissed her forehead as tears streamed down his wrinkled cheeks.

"I love you, father. No matter what you have done."

"That is my only happiness, Ethrain. And I will bless the two of you with my legacy. Rise, Roman."

Hadrian obeyed him and found with astonishment that his body was able to comply. The old druid placed one hand on Hadrian's head and the other on Ethrain.

"The road ahead will be full of great danger, but the might of the druids will be with you. The spirit of my brotherhood will accompany you and assist you. Your success will be our final victory and we will not have died in vain."

He pulled them together and stepped away.

"Do not commit my errors. Let your love guide you in all that you do. It is the only path to true life."

Hadrian and Ethrain embraced each other. Both were

weeping. They kissed through their tears. Then they turned to Ubarra, but there was no one there. He had vanished, yet they knew he would be with them always.

chapter eleven

THE LARGE crystal triangle was placed in the center of a round table. A yellowish light emanated from it, spreading across the darkness in ghostly shapes.

Hyndla stared intently at its center where a beaming white light sparkled. Ethrain and Hadrain sat on either side, waiting for something to happen.

The witch had been looking at the strange object, silent and motionless, since sunset. Her stern, hawklike features were more somber than usual. News of Ubarra's incredible words had cut through her heart as deeply as they had through the two lovers. She seemed to have aged ten years in one afternoon.

The mighty druid had abandoned her for his mystic work as he had Ethrain. Hyndla had known him her entire life and it was as a fresh young fisherman's daughter that she had fallen in love with the mysterious man. He had kept her under his wing for a few years, teaching her as an apprentice rather than as a wife. When the Romans descended upon them, he disappeared into the mountains and left her brokenhearted and with child. The townspeople rejected her as well and a desperate Hyndla had to give up her infant to someone who had the means to care for her. Like her only love, she became a grim recluse, developing powers and knowledge beyond the sphere of human wisdom.

Now that Ubarra had left her forever, she felt forsaken once again. Somehow, his presence had kept a spark of love and hope alive in her all these years. He had been her master, her lover, her teacher, her object of wrath. There was nothing left to love or hate now, and she knew that her life had ended with his.

Sitting before the crystal, Hyndla focused all the powers she had bred through a lifetime of toil and misery. This would be her final act and it gave her some measure of satisfaction that it would be for her daughter. Her terrible isolation and suffering had been numbed by the druids with the gift of one of their most sacred objects. She was the keeper of the crystal for these last thirty years, hiding it beneath her wooden floor, waiting for the time when it was to be used again. And that time had come.

The crystal suddenly exploded with multicolored lights. They shot across the room like beams from another world. The wolf let out a howl and Ulbrek took hold of his animal friend to comfort him. They sat in the corner and, as they had so often before, watched the inexplicable take place before them.

Hadrian's eyes widened in astonishment. He would never get used to the magic present in this primitive wilderness. Ethrain held her breath, thrilled with the brilliant display. The colors soon merged into a blood-red beam which spread in all directions, bouncing off the walls and onto the ceiling. Soon the entire room was the color of the light glowing from the mysterious object.

Hyndla peered more intensely than ever into the center of the crystal. Hadrian followed her gaze and noticed that an image was taking shape deep within the multi-layered triangle. He let out a gasp as a human face took shape within the prism of stone. It was the same face he had seen in his dream and on the battlefield. The image expanded until it filled the entire transparent rock. It was the face of Attila, Kagan of the Huns.

Hyndla raised her hand, expecting Hadrian to ask a question.

"Watch!" she said solemnly.

The disembodied face soon gave way to another face. It was a beautiful woman, bearing the strong features and thick brown hair of the Gauls. The ornaments on her ears and neck revealed her to be a princess of high order among the Burgundian tribes who lived by the great Rhine river.

The image merged with the dreadful features of Attila. His Hun's scars running down his cheeks, his wide cheekbones and small, piercing eyes were strangely imposed over the refined face of the princess.

"That woman must be his queen," Hyndla whispered.

Studying Attila's features at this proximity, Hadrian had the unexpected intuition that the powerful, cruel man was indeed an instrument of darkness. Despite his personal charisma and strength, Hadrian saw him as a puppet of the underworld. He also realized that he was merely a human being who, however fierce and mighty, was nevertheless a man. A man who could be defeated.

"She holds the key to what you must do."

The image faded and another picture appeared. It was a fortress, or rather a town encompassed by tall, wooden walls.

"This is where you must go."

"Where is it?" Hadrian asked.

"Wait and you will see."

The picture changed again. Great Alpine mountains appeared, much like the images in Hadrian's dream. Visions of northern pastures followed one another until finally a great river came into focus. Hadrian peered at it intently.

"That's the Rhine!"

"You know this place?" Hyndla asked.

"Yes, of course. I've crossed it many times. I've fought there . . . and I saw my father die on its banks."

"Then you will have no trouble finding the town you must go to."

"It must be the home of the Burgundians."

"That is where you will find the way to accomplish your task."

"But how?"

"It will be revealed to you in time. You will become part of this people's way of life and you will come to love them even though they must suffer destruction for the fulfillment of your mission. But remember! The events which have already unfolded and will lead you to your destiny would have taken place even without you. They were created by the very forces you must defeat. Do not let anything stand in the way of completing what you must do. Now you must leave Mallor immediately, before the gods find a way to destroy you."

"Won't they be able to follow us wherever we go?"

"They will. But the further away they get from the gateway to our world, the more feeble are their powers. Unless they can materialize their wishes through a willing subject."

"What about the giants?"

"It is the same with them. They are demiurges from the North. They can only extend their powers through human beings. If the Hun conquers all of the West, they will have complete dominion over human souls."

The image suddenly changed into a sprawling city made of tents and oriental buildings.

"Hungvar!" Hadrian exclaimed.

"What is that?" Ethrain asked, worried at his tone of voice.

"Attila's home. The command center of the Huns."

"You will have to travel there as well," Hyndla stated coldly.

"To Hungvar? That's impossible!" Hadrian cried out. "It's in the heart of their territories. They call it the Land of Phantoms!"

"Nothing is impossible, Roman. You should know that by now."

The image vanished and the reddish light quickly withdrew back into the crystal. Soon, the scarlet light was a tiny flame at the center of the prism, flickering like a candle dancing precariously in the wind. Then it vanished as though some invisible being had suddenly blown it out. The room was left in darkness.

They sat at the table, still as statues. Ulbrek's labored breathing and the rising howl of an angry wind brought them back to the present. As his eyes adapted to the darkness, Hadrian noticed that Hyndla's gaze had shifted to the window and a look of fear was creeping over her face. The howling wind was now swirling around the building like a raging storm. Hadrian turned toward the window. He saw instantly what was causing the turmoil in the witch's heart. Though the sound of the wind was growing to a deafening roar, not a branch was moving! The countryside was absolutely still. It was not the wind making that sound!

The wolf leaped up, ears perked, showing his fangs. Something out there was terrifying the beast. Hadrian turned to Ethrain and saw that she too was aware of the unnatural occurrence.

Suddenly, Hyndla wrapped her arms around the crystal and yanked it off the table. She raced toward the hearth and tore open a secret trap door. The weight of the crystal caused her to stumble and she fell to her side. Hadrian jumped from his chair and hurried to her.

"Hide the crystal!" she shouted.

Hadrian had never seen her strangled by such fear. He

lifted the crystal and was astounded to find it so heavy. Hyndla was stronger than he had imagined. He carried the object to the trap door. In the darkness, he could see moving waters. There was a deep well beneath the floor.

"Hook it to the rope!" Hyndla said breathlessly as she came to his side.

She picked up a heavy cord and tied it to a golden ring at the base of the crystal.

"Throw it in!" she exclaimed.

Hadrian dropped the great crystal. It fell with a mighty splash and sunk deep into the waters. Hyndla slammed the trap door shut and covered it with a large bear skin. Just then, the door blew open, flying off its hinges and crashing against the far wall.

Ethrain let out a scream as the wolf charged into the doorway. The animal let out a piercing yelp and then was silent. The howling sound had now reached a climactic noise which made the walls and ceiling shake. Hadrian grabbed a chair and threw it through a back window, smashing the wooden shutters.

"Get out! Get out!" he shouted.

Ethrain ran to the window. Hadrian helped her crawl out. Ulbrek followed close behind, tearing his way through the debris. Hadrian turned to Hyndla. She was standing in the center of the room, motionless.

"Hurry!" he yelled as the great logs began to creek and moan under the pressure of the immense force. "It's going to cave in!"

Hyndla shook her head. He ran up to her and grabbed her by the arm. She jerked it out of his hand.

"No!" she shouted over the deafening noise.

"Why?" Hadrian asked, horrified.

""My time has come. Let me go in peace."

Hadrian looked at her harsh features and saw for the first time the sensitive young woman she had once been. A deep emotion took hold of him. He felt in an instant all the pain of her solitary life. Involuntarily, he reached out and touched her cheek. A sad smile softened her eyes.

"Go now! Take care of my Ethrain! And save us from the demons!"

The beams upholding the ceiling cracked and the logs began to tumble down, crashing over the plants and talismans which filled the room.

"What about the crystal?" he cried out.

"It will be found by the right person at the right time."

Hadrian turned toward the window, but then hurried back and picked her up in his arms. She struggled with him but he held her tightly.

"I cannot let you die."

"You don't understand, Roman! The stars are aligned and these events are ordained!"

"No!"

He ran toward the window. A great log suddenly crashed down over him, falling on Hyndla's head. The blow knocked her out of his arms. At that moment, the whole ceiling tumbled down as the walls fell in. Hadrian dove out the window as all the logs fell in a cloud of dust, creating a giant tomb for the witch of Mallor.

They ran through the woods as the howling sound continued relentlessly.

"Where's Hyndla?" Ethrain called out.

"With Ubarra!"

Hadrian took her hand and guided her through the underbrush. He knew her sight was blinded by tears.

They came into a clearing broken by swampland.

"Wait!" Hadrian shouted as he slowed his pace. "We'll end up in quicksand!"

But it was too late. Ulbrek let out a shout as he sunk into the mire. Hadrian grabbed the giant's hand and pulled with all his might, but he was too heavy.

"Find a solid branch!" he called out to Ethrain.

Ulbrek was already sucked in to his chest. He looked at the Roman with terror in his eyes.

"Don't move! It will make it worse!"

Ethrain suddenly let out a frightful scream. Hadrian turned in time to see a strange formation of light swirl around her. It took on a human shape and within moments a little stocky man stood before her, laughing.

"Odin!" Ulbrek cried out.

He motioned for Hadrian to let him go and save Ethrain. The Roman hesitated. Ulbrek pushed his hand away and looked at him with great sadness.

"Save Ethrain!" he said in his deep, gravely voice.

Hadrian unfastened his belt and held it out to the giant.

"Hold onto it!" he ordered as he tied the other end to a tree trunk.

Ulbrek grabbed onto the belt and Hadrian ran over to Ethrain. The giant sank beneath the thick mud as he fumbled to keep hold of the belt. He cried out Ethrain's name as his head disappeared beneath the gurgling sands.

The translucent creature watched Hadrian approach.

"You will not longer interfere, Roman," the demiurge stated in an unearthly tone.

"He has no power over you!" Ethrain shouted. "They can only strike through a human form."

The little man laughed and sent out a ray of light across the clearing.

"You are powerless, human! We will destroy you and claim middle earth for ourselves!"

They heard a great roar and turned to see Ulbrek lifted out from the bowels of the swamp. His body glowed with the light released by Odin.

"We can free the earth from the power of the giants!" Ethrain exclaimed desperately.

"You cannot! And if you could, they would only possess other souls and ravage the world with their wickedness again!"

Ulbrek stumbled toward them. His eyes had rolled up into his head, leaving only the white stare of blind possession.

"I command you to kill the Roman!" Odin ordered as he drew Ulbrek toward them with his unworldly power.

"No, Ulbrek!" Ethrain cried out.

Her voice caused him to stop, though his eyes remained in their convulsed state.

"Do as I command!" Odin thundered.

The giant approached, sloshing in the mud that covered him from head to toe.

"Ulbrek!" Ethrain cried out again. But the man was no longer under her spell.

"How do you fight against the dead, Roman?" Odin asked with a sinister laugh.

Hadrian tried to evade the giant's grasp, but slipped. Ulbrek grabbed him by the throat.

"This world is ours!" Odin exclaimed triumphantly.

Ethrain took hold of Ulbrek's slime-covered arm and pulled at it frantically. The zombie wrapped his fingers tightly around Hadrian's neck.

"The stone! Use the stone!"

The voice was Ubarra's and echoed through Hadrian head like a clarion call. He took hold of the amulet and slammed it against Ulbrek's forehead. It sizzled against the mud-caked skin. The giant's eyes returned to their orbits. He let go of his victim.

"Kill him!" Odin commanded angrily.

The demiurge shot a flash of light into the giant, causing his whole body to shake. Ethrain wrapped her arms around Ulbrek's neck and kissed him on the cheek. His eyes widened and filled with tears.

"Ethrain . . . " he whispered.

He turned to Odin and fell upon him with a mighty shout. An ear-bursting squeal exploded from the little man as his form faded and returned to a swirl of light which vanished into the night. Ethrain hurried to the fallen giant and struggled to turn him on his back. The man's soul was slipping away quickly. He touched her golden hair and ran his big hand gently along her cheek. For the first time in his life, he smiled and peace radiated over his distorted features. He closed his eyes with a sigh.

Hadrian kneeled at Ethrain's side and put his arm around her. She caressed the giant's hair and wept silently.

"Love is greater than the power of the gods," Hadrian whispered. "And look . . . Ulbrek is smiling! You've given him happiness to take into the other world."

chapter twelve

The voyage across the North Sea was a calm one. The ocean was unusually peaceful, much as sailors knew her to be before the outbreak of a deadly storm. Hadrian and Ethrain first sailed to Britain on the very boat which Grundler would have taken. There they boarded a vessel for Gaul. The journey was their first experience of tranquility since their fateful meeting. For a brief time, they enjoyed the simple pleasures of two people in love. The further they got from the Isle of Mallor, the freer they felt and the more they forgot the weight of the task with which they had been charged.

Hadrian came to discover another side of his companion. The young woman was still full of playfulness despite the disasters that had marked her life and the dark forces she had encountered so often. He marvelled at her strength of spirit, and how she could return virtually unscathed from the tragedies they had shared together. The rugged sailors often smiled at their passengers who acted like young lovers discovering the mysteries of passion for the first time. In their few days together, Hadrian found the peace which had eluded him for so long and which he had travelled the world to find. Ethrain was indeed the woman he had longed for his entire life. She was so filled with courage and insight, sensuality and compassion. Her stamina seemed inexhaustible.

On the ship they met a man who exuded a rare serenity and radiated goodness to everyone he encountered. He was named Patrick and was one of the first to bring the new religion to the isles of the North Sea. He rejoiced at their love and spent many hours telling them of the God-man from Judea, the Holy One who had paved the way to an intimacy with the highest God, the Creator of all life.

He read to them from a book which he handled with great reverence for he told them that it contained the map to the salvation of humanity. Faced with the mission with which they had been charged, they listened with great interest. If they were to participate in a new beginning, surely such teaching would be vital in cleansing the world of dark forces.

The good man was deeply convincing, not only in telling the story of what he called "the good news," but through his actions, gestures, and the unconditional love gleaming in his eyes. How different a being he was from either the stoics or the druids. His gentle humility mixed with great strength of spirit, his constant joy rising out of a permanent sense of the nearness of Divinity, and his kindness to all were the most persuasive arguments for the power and truth of this new teaching.

By the end of the voyage, Patrick the Briton was prepared to baptize his two friends. But they were not ready for such a charge and asked only that he make them man and wife in the name of the God of Love.

They parted ways on the coast of Gaul. The monk blessed them and, seeing their poor means, insisted that they take a purse of coins to make their voyage to the Rhine. Though they had not told him anything of their mission, he sensed that a great task lay ahead for them, one which would benefit many. He also penned a letter to King Gunther, Lord of the Burgundians whom he had personally baptized some five years before. They promised to search for him in the wilds of Ireland if ever they returned across the North Sea.

"I'll be waiting for you," Patrick told them as he raised his hand in a final blessing.

They watched him walk along the dusty path until he was a small figure in the distance, knowing that they had come across a man who would also change history. With the money he had given them and the jewelry Ethrain carried with her, they purchased two horses from an old Norman farmer and headed toward their destiny.

IT WAS late fall along the banks of the Rhine. The noble Burgundian lords were making preparations for the long winter which would soon turn the mighty river to ice. King Gunther and his queen, Brunhild, a daughter of Iceland, had ordered the great gates of their fortress opened for the people to join them in the last feast of the hunting season.

The hunt had been bountiful. The king's brothers, Gernot and Giselher, were fine warriors who in peacetime turned their skills on wild boar and the great stags of the Alpine forests. They were assisted by the legendary abilities of Lord Hagen, the most famous knight in the land and a close adviser to the king. He was a brooding man whose strength had not waned though he was beyond the prime of life. Majestic in stature and bearing, he stood some two feet above his companions. But his features bore the scars of secret tragedy and he was always accompanied by some dark cloud which would one day burst over them all.

The Burgundians had not been at war for ten years, since the bloody victory over the Danes. They had been led into battle by the great Siegfried, Prince of the Nordic Isles, more myth than man. He was a stunning young warrior, with a musculature to rival any adversary and the features of a god. He had befriended King Gunther, become like a son to him and was to wed Kriemhild, the king's sister, merging kingdoms and families in a unity of great affection and territories. But King Gunther was a man easily fooled and though a strong and courageous warrior, his physical power hid a gentle heart which could not see through the masks of power-hungry men like Prince Siegfried. Lord Hagen, faithful watchdog for his weaker royal friend, had uncovered the true face of the prince and his efforts to betray the King. For Siegfried was not the kind of man to be satisfied with new alliances and vaster lands. His lust for glory and power had eroded even his natural sense of decency and, on a dark, moonless night, he had been seen sneaking into Queen Brunhild's private chambers. Out of loyalty to his king, and to revenge the terrible outrage, Hagen faced Siegfried in mortal combat.

These tormented lives would soon intertwine with those of Hadrian and Ethrain. The events which prepared the way for their fateful meeting had begun unfolding some ten years before. . . .

IT WAS dawn, a decade earlier, among the giant pines of the northern mountains. An autumn sunrise shimmered through the majestic trees of the Alpine forest. Winter would soon be here, covering the great peaks and lush valleys of the region with a mammoth white coat.

The serene peace of the mountain woods was suddenly shattered by the frantic scurrying of a wild boar. The beast crashed through the underbrush, weaving its way at amazing speed past the ancient pine trees. Three silhouettes appeared in the glow of the rising sun. They chased the boar with sure footing, circling it with the precision and teamwork of lifelong hunters.

The leader was dressed in the heavy furs of a Germanic warlord. His rough jewelry identified him as King Gunther, Lord of the Rhineland tribes. Towering over his companions, nearly the size of a grizzly bear, was Lord Hagen, the greatest warrior in the land, a living legend to his people.

The king heaved his huge spear at the boar and missed his mark by inches. The animal raced off in another direction, but was skillfully herded off by Hagen. The aging monarch retrieved his weapon and leaned against a tree to catch his breath. Smiling at the excitement of the hunt, he wiped the sweat from his windburned face and watched his loyal warrior continue the chase.

The third hunter suddenly leaped in front of the boar. His long blond hair and clean shaven face was a striking contrast to the flowing beards of his friends. The famed Siegfried moved with the speed and gracefulness of the great stags of the forest. He circled the beast as it descended into a little ravine. Racing down the steep hillside, Siegfried cut off the boar's path and plunged his spear into the creature.

The other hunters hurried up to him.

"Well done, Siegfried," the king said as he tried to catch his breath. "He'll make for a fine feast tonight."

The handsome prince kneeled by the dead animal and swiftly cut out its shiny tusks. He rose and presented them to the king.

"For you, my liege, as a sign of our friendship."

"And a symbol of our good fortune to have you among us."

Siegfried threw the animal over his powerful shoulders and walked toward a small stream making its way through a nearby clearing. King Gunther turned to his companion, Hagen of Trony, and noticed his gloomy gaze.

"As always, Hagen, you seem ready for battle. Do you fancy a stag leaping from the woods to impale you on its antlers?"

The jovial king laughed, but stopped abruptly upon noticing that the great knight's features had turned fierce. He knew that look well. It came over his faithful warrior in the moments before battle, and always foretold the demise of an adversary.

"Now is the time, Mylord," the big man muttered in a cold, guttural tone.

Gunther's face turned pale. He looked over at the blond prince kneeling by the water.

"Leave us, Sire."

The stoic knight suddenly unsheathed his great sword. Siegfried turned around in surprise at the deadly sound of the iron hiss. He looked at Hagen's cold, determined eyes. Then he turned to King Gunther who was nervously moving behind the trees.

Hagen's booming voice broke the tense silence.

"Stand, Prince Siegfried! And die by the sword of the Lord of Trony!"

Siegfried jumped to his feet, astounded. Hagen tightened his grip on the heavy weapon and aimed the huge blade in his direction. The prince drew his sword.

King Gunther watched on sadly as the two men circled each other. The peaceful dawn of this autumn morning suddenly crackled with tension. The birds stopped their melodious tunes as the two skilled warriors readied for the onslaught. The deep forest stillness exploded with the violent echo of sharp blades crashing together.

Despite Siegfried's strength and skill, Hagen's great bulk soon overwhelmed him. He fell under the massive blows from his adversary. Hagen grabbed his spear which he had planted in the ground nearby. As Siegfried rose, the old warrior mercilessly heaved the spear into his chest. The king buried his face in his hands as the prince shouted and tried to remain on his feet. But he soon dropped, falling onto the spear and remaining propped up like a broken puppet before slipping to his side.

The Lord of Trony stood over his fallen adversary and looked at him without a glimmer of pity. King Gunther, trembling with guilt and disgust, stumbled over to the warrior's side. Gasping for his last breath, Siegfried looked up at Gunther. The young man's eyes froze in a look of hatred as he moaned for the glory which would never be his. Hagen slipped his sword back into its scabbard. He picked up the dead boar and turned away from the corpse.

"Come, Mylord."

The king was too shaken to move. He stared with great sadness at the legendary hero who had been his friend and was to have become his sister's husband.

"It had to be, Mylord. Come."

"We mustn't leave him here . . . "

"The wolves will take care of him."

"No! I want him buried."

He kneeled beside the dead prince and touched his golden waves. Hagen shook his head, a profound sense of doom invading his soul.

THOUGH TEN years had gone by since this tragic incident, it was in an atmosphere of guilt and tension that Hadrian and Ethrain arrived among the Burgundians. Patrick's letter brought great joy to the melancholic King Gunther and he made them his honored guests. They were welcomed to stay as long as they desired and share in the life of the people of the Rhineland. They had no idea what the next step might be in the fulfillment of their destiny, and they watched patiently for Fate to manifest itself. It didn't take long.

The newlyweds had barely moved into their new home when the fateful events were set in motion. Over the horizon, the silhouettes of five horsemen galloped toward the primitive castle of the Rhineland tribe. As they came closer, a guard on the ramparts noticed that they were small, Asian, fierce. The guard hurried into the castle, the metallic jingle of his weapons echoing through the narrow hallways.

He came up to another soldier who stood by the massive doors of the king's chambers.

"Wake the king! Foreign warriors are approaching the gates. They look like Huns!"

"Huns?" the second guard whispered in horror. He quickly hurried into the chambers.

He stopped at a respectful distance from the huge royal bed. Two large dogs laying at the feet of the bed growled menacingly.

"Mylord! Mylord!" the guard exclaimed in a hushed tone.

A grunt came from the mountain of furs.

"Forgive the intrusion, Sire. There are strangers at the gates."

King Gunther turned over under the great furs.

"What is it?"

"Envoys are at the gates, Mylord. They appear to be Huns."

The king sat up as though his bed were on fire.

"Huns?"

"Yes, Mylord."

"My cloak! Where is my cloak?"

The guard hurried to the chair where the king's garment were strewn. He wrapped him in a large coat of fur.

The queen looked up from under the covers.

"Is it morning so soon?"

Gunther patted her disheveled mane of blond hair.

"It appears that there are Huns at the gates."

"Huns?" she cried out. "Cernunnos save us!"

Gunther caressed her long waves reassuringly.

"Only envoys, my dear. We are safe. Return to your dreams."

Queen Brunhild pulled the furs back over her head. Her doting husband quickly left the chamber, followed by his soldier. They hurried through the dark corridors as the castle came to life. An old, dignified woman, the Queen Mother, appeared from one of the chambers.

"Why this disturbance?" she asked angrily.

"Foreign warriors are desiring entry, Mother."

"Have you sent for the Roman? He has travelled far and may know of these people."

The king mumbled orders to his guard and continued his rush toward the ramparts. The old Queen Mother watched her son vanish into the shadows as an ominous dread tensed her features.

In the courtyard, servants and soldiers were gathering at the gates to peer out at the newcomers. When the king arrived on the ramparts, no one bothered to give him the honors due his rank. The savages riding up on their wild ponies were much more interesting. A powerful, stone-faced man in his middle years, Gernot, brother to the king, stepped out onto the fortress walls. His bearing was similar to that of the Lord of Trony, revealing the supreme confidence of a skilled warrior, veteran of many battles. Behind him came a young man of eighteen years, Giselher, the youngest brother of the royal family. Even at this time of the morning, he sparkled with vitality and youthful exuberance.

Hadrian soon appeared on the ramparts and joined the group staring down at the strangers. The Huns had halted at the foot of the great walls and were patiently awaiting entry as their horses nibbled the frozen grass.

"Are they Huns?" the king asked Hadrian.

"Yes, Mylord, I have seen them too many times to forget their features."

"I'm told those ponies are quick as lightning," Gernot stated with interest.

"Quicker than any mount I have ever ridden," the Roman responded.

King Gunther peered over the ramparts.

"Can you see their features?"

Hagen covered his eyes from the rising sun and looked down upon the men like an eagle studying its prey.

"Slanted eyes and scars running down each cheek."

"I hear they cut their infants' cheeks so they can taste pain before their mother's milk," Gernot muttered with disgust.

"They carry Attila's banners," Hadrian observed, unable to hide his excitement. He knew that they were here for his purposes.

"What would Attila want with us?" Giselher asked.

"Perhaps they bring news of your sister," Hagen stated grimly as he exchanged a glance with his king.

"We have not heard from her these ten years, since she wed that savage. Why would she call on us now?" King Gunther wondered with a tremble in his voice.

"I've never cared for the looks of those little men," Hagen grumbled as his hand instinctively went to rest on the hilt of his sword.

"They are only envoys," Gernot pointed out to his battle-ready friend. "They come in peace."

"I have yet to hear of peaceful Huns, Gernot," Hagen responded with suspicion.

He approached the edge of the ramparts, crossing his muscular arms.

"Speak!" he called out in a booming voice. "What is your purpose here?"

The Hun leader looked up at the men standing high above him. The long scars twisting down his cheeks distorted his sinister features in a permanent evil grin.

"We bring tidings to King Gunther from the mighty Attila and his queen, the king's sister!"

Hagen motioned for the guards to open the gates. The Huns entered the courtyard, holding back their spirited horses which became agitated by the pressing crowd. The Burgundians descended from the ramparts to greet them.

"King Gunther, ruler of the Rhineland tribes!" Hagen stated as he presented his liege to them.

The Huns immediately jumped off their horses and dropped to one knee.

"We bring tidings, King Gunther, from the great Attila, master over most of the earth and husband to your sister, Queen Kriemhild. It is their hope that these times find you in good health and prosperity. They send these small gifts as tokens of their esteem and affection."

The Hun unbuckled an elaborate sword from his saddle as one of his men took a small chest of gold from his satchel. They presented the gifts to Gunther who smiled at the honors.

"King Gunther, Mighty Attila and his Queen desire that you travel to their domain and celebrate your bonds of friendship."

A great murmur rose from the crowd. Hagen turned away to hide his displeasure while the king beamed with elation.

"You must be wearied from your long journey. We will speak more of this matter over a feast in the Great Hall."

He motioned for a servant to take them to their quarters. The Huns bowed and followed as the crowd parted before them. From a tower window, Ethrain watched the foreigners pass beneath her. The leader's face looked terribly familiar. She knew she would encounter him in the future in a land of terror and bloodshed. She looked over to where Hadrian was standing and they exchanged a glance which said everything. The oriental men were not only envoys of Attila but heralds of their destiny.

Young Giselher stepped up to Hadrian's side and the Roman quickly regained his composure from the dark introspection he had entered.

"These Huns don't seem so ferocious to me."

Hadrian turned to the young man and smiled at him sadly.

"You must never judge a man from his external actions. Pray that you never have to meet them on the battlefield. These are the most bloodthirsty warriors you will ever come upon."

A Burgundian knight, close to Giselher's age, approached them and examined the gifts. Though strong and agile like most of the young men of the tribe, his arrogance was tempered with dreamy eyes filled with some vague longing which he himself did not comprehend.

"Would you have thought that those savages could possess such treasures, Dankwart?" Gernot asked with a paternal smile.

The young man studied the sword in awe, amazed by the craftsmanship. Gernot patted the ponies and studied their musculature with an expert eye. As he stepped back, he bumped into a peasant girl who was making her way through the courtyard. She bowed in deference to his royalty.

"Please, Felicia, how many times must I tell you not to bow before me," Gernot told her with a gentle reproach.

They exchanged a glance which expressed secret, unspoken affection.

Hadrian watched on, fascinated by the irresistible love of life which he witnessed in these people. They were a far cry from the stern, isolated inhabitants of Mallor. He felt as though he had come back into humanity after a voyage to the underworld.

Ethrain joined her new husband in the banquet hall. She had discarded her rugged clothing for a gown which the queen had given her. Hadrian had never seen her look so enchanting, so feminine. It seemed to him an omen of their future, of peace and happiness, even in the presence of the fearsome Huns.

They sat side by side, enjoying the merriment of the Burgundians. Food was always plentiful at the king's court as the forests and meadows yielded abundant life, unlike the rocky shores of Mallor. The lovers' thoughts were far removed from the hideous events they had been through. Their love generated new life, new hope and the past was washed away in the flood of their great joy.

They watched the servants rush back and forth around the crude dais, shooing dogs and chickens away from the table. Felicia appeared from the kitchen, bringing a platter to the king's table. Ethrain studied her closely and felt a menacing premonition rise from the depths of her intuitive powers. How strange it was, she thought to herself, that in the midst of so much laughter and rejoicing, she felt the painful tugs of impending devastation.

Hadrian noticed her grim expression and took her hand.

"Live for the present," he whispered lovingly. "The future will come soon enough."

She turned to him and found herself immediately warmed by his great love. She gave him a sweet smile and released herself from the claws of her premonition.

Hadrian leaned forward and observed the king engrossed in conversation with his guests.

"Does my sister find happiness in your lands, with your people?" King Gunther asked the Hun commander.

"She is given much love from my people, and from my Lord Attila. He seemed so saddened after the death of his first queen. We worried greatly for him. But now he is happy."

"That is good," the king stated, sitting back with satisfaction in his great chair.

"What of his other wives? Does it not become confusing?" Gernot asked sarcastically. Beneath his grim exterior, there lurked a man of humor and a lover of life. Hadrian had taken an instant liking to him and sensed that they were kindred spirits.

His companions at the dais laughed but were quickly quieted by the Hun's cold glare.

"They are mostly state marriages to bring the many tribes together. Our Queen Kriemhild is his only marriage for love."

"We have heard that you marched on Rome itself and nearly conquered her," Giselher interjected. "Is this true?"

"It is. Were it not for sickness, we would have taken her and those weaklings they call soldiers. Next time we will!"

He slammed the table with anger. An uneasy silence fell over the listeners. Ethrain took hold of Hadrian's arm and squeezed it tightly to help him stay in control of his temper.

"Rome belongs to the Huns now. She is our inheritance."

Hadrian would have leapt from his chair and forgotten all his ideals concerning peace and harmony had the king not abruptly changed the subject. But the proud Roman also understood that his reactions might have ruined the purpose of their presence in this Alpine fortress. He felt a cold sweat run down the back of his tunic as he realized that the demons of Jotunheim were never far away and, in a gruesome pact with the gods, searched out every opportunity to destroy their mission.

"When is it that my sister and her King wish to see us? And for how long?"

"In the spring, when the travelling is easier and a warm sun lights the way. You are welcome to remain in our kingdom as long as you desire."

"That is most hospitable," the king stated merrily.

But his eyes fell on Hagen who watched on with great suspicion. The look of gloom in his eyes frightened the jovial king. He suddenly stood as though to express his royal authority in order to reassure himself.

"I will discuss this with my princes and knights. You will have my answer tomorrow. Now you shall be given warm beds and baths."

Giselher snickered at the thought of Huns taking a bath. The envoys rose from their seats, bowed and left the room, walking past the Burgundian warriors, back straights and chins raised with great pride. When the doors had closed behind them, Gunther turned to his men.

"What do you think, Hagen?"

"I think it is a trap."

"A trap? Do you believe that Attila wants to conquer us?"

"I believe that his queen seeks vengeance for a past sorrow."

The king's face turned scarlet. Hadrian studied the two men intently, sensing the terrible secret between them.

"I cannot believe that an event which took place some ten years ago could still be feeding my sister's wrath," he stated hoarsely. "However painful it may have been . . .

Hagen gazed at him with grim certainty, and the aging ruler turned to his brothers for support.

"Tell me, Gernot, what do you think?"

"My sister has never been a vengeful woman. It is true she did not accept that Prince Siegfried died in a hunting accident, but I cannot believe she would start a war between two peoples for revenge."

The king then looked at his youngest brother.

"What do you say, Giselher?"

"Well, I never really knew our sister. I was only eight when she left. But I would like to see the Hun court and the man who has brought an empire to its knees!"

A huge bear of man sitting next to Giselher slapped him on the back.

"And maybe a few Hun women as well, eh?" Ortwin said. "These Huns dress in furs. Wait until the ladies see our fine array!"

The heavy set man stood and clasped his large belt.

"We'll be the handsomest men they have ever seen!"

Everyone around the table laughed and cheered.

"And perhaps we'll have a few contests to see how the Hun sword fares against this!" Dankwart exclaimed as he unsheathed his weapon.

"You men speak like fools!" Hagen said in his brooding tone which immediately quieted the assembly. "Women, clothes, contests! Do you realize that you are talking of the Huns who rule half the earth! And at their helm, at the very seat of power, sits a woman who swore vengeance when she left. Should we walk into her clutches like foolish children?"

The men began to murmur among themselves. Hadrian and Ethrain exchanges glances. They both knew that some awful tragedy lay ahead.

"But she does not sit at the seat of power. Attila does," Dankwart pointed out, hoping to reignite the enthusiasm for the voyage which was fading fast.

"There may be wisdom in what Hagen says," Gernot responded with concern.

"Don't tell me, Gernot, that you fear your own sister!" the young warrior exclaimed.

A tense silence fell over the room as the Burgundian prince sat thoughtfully.

"No, I don't," he said at last. "She loved us all, as we loved her. And it is true that Attila is a man of his word. He must be to keep his tribes together. If he beckons us in peace, then it is so. If he wanted war, all he would need to do is swoop down upon us like those roving bands of nomads that disturb us now. His men number in the hundred thousands, like the leaves on the trees . . . No, he does not need to resort to trickery. I say we go!"

"Then it is agreed?" King Gunther called out with excitement.

A loud approval exploded around the dais. Hadrian's heartbeat pounded on a new rhythm as he realized that they were going to provide him the means to accomplish what he had to do. He looked around the table at the large, bearded men and noticed that Hagen remained cold and suspicious.

"We are making a mistake!"

"You need not come, Hagen. I will not resent it," the king stated.

Hagen turned to him indignantly.

"When, in twenty years, have I or my sword left your side, Mylord? I leave when you do, and return when you do!"

The king raised his goblet over the heads of his loyal men.

"To my sister and to new adventures! May God be with us!"

The men toasted cheerfully, except for the Lord of Trony who looked down at this powerful hands, the very hands which had killed the Nordic prince and placed the lords of the Rhine on this fateful course.

chapter thirteen

That afternoon, Gernot took Hadrian for a tour of the magnificent countryside which surrounded their castle. They rode through meadows thick with flowers and waves of grass, crossed green valleys sparkling with streams descending from the snows of the mountain peaks. Hadrian breathed in the cool, scented air and felt as though the power of the great Alps were filling his body. The glorious vistas spreading out before him, guarded by graceful pines taller than anything he had ever seen, seemed the very image of an earthly paradise.

The riders came to a halt on a ridge overlooking the vast greenery. Above them, and surrounding their world of forests and meadows, rose the jagged white teeth of the royal mountain chain.

They dismounted. Gernot sat on a fallen log while Hadrian walked to the edge of the ridge and looked out. Suddenly, the Burgundian lord slipped to his side and dove behind a tree, pulling out his large knife. Before Hadrian could do more than turn around, a huge woodsman stepped into the clearing. The Roman went for his sword as Gernot came out from behind the tree.

"It is I, Gernot," the man said with a grin.

"Well, we meet again, Thorin!"

They clasped forearms. Hadrian breathed a sigh of

relief. He knew it would have been difficult to overcome the man's great bulk.

"Few men hear my approach. You grow wiser with age," the woodsman said warmly.

"Not wiser, my friend. More cautious."

"You will live long with that caution."

"What has it been? Four winters? Where have you travelled these last years?"

"North. Where the seas turn to ice."

"The land of the Vikings? What took you there?"

"There are no Romans, Huns, or Franks to disturb us."

Gernot smiled and remembered there was a Roman behind them.

"Not all Romans are enemies. Meet Hadrian Aldius, a guest of our king."

Thorin looked at him suspiciously.

"Your people have caused us great troubles," he muttered.

"They have often caused me great troubles as well," Hadrian replied with a smile.

The men's laughter eased the tension.

"Tell me, Thorin, have the Saxon tribes not settled those regions?"

"The Saxons give me no concern. Those who do, I leave to the wolves."

Hadrian did not doubt the man's word.

"And you, Gernot, how have you fared?" the woodsman asked.

"I grow restless sometimes, Thorin. I am not made to live behind castle walls."

"You are a son of the great forests, as I am. We should join together on another journey, like those of our youth."

The friends both smiled at the memories of another time.

"I am bound to the life of the warrior now. I have chosen the welfare of my people over the woodsman's freedom. And what of your people? Are they still in the North?"

"I no longer travel alone."

Gernot looked at him in surprise as Thorin signaled and two young men appeared from the woods.

"These are my sons, Gernot."

They all greeted each other. Hadrian recognized in their features the characteristics of peoples he had often faced in battle. It was a good feeling to meet them on friendly terms.

"They do you honor, Thorin," Gernot stated as he studied them.

"They are good men. But they move through the forests like a wounded bear. Sons, you have heard me speak of Sir Gernot, mighty Prince of the Burgundians. Many times have we crossed paths in these mountains."

"And many hours have we spent learning each other's ways. You lads do well to learn from your father. He has taught me many things."

"We have heard tales of your deeds since we were children," Jeoffrey, the oldest son said with respect. "My brother and I long to become warriors and to follow in your path. We know the ways of the staff and the bow. Could you teach us the ways of the sword, Sire?"

"The training of a warrior is hard and tedious," Gernot responded.

Hadrian felt his heart sink at the thought of these young woodsmen turning into soldiers and leaving behind their more natural ways for the gore of battle. But he realized that young men of all times would seek to find "glory" in the madness of military exploits. He remembered how he had once been so proud to stand beneath the banner of the Empire and march before his troops. How foolish it all seemed now. Hadrian could see how men let themselves be taken over by the demons of violence and cruelty, becoming possessed by the giants of the underworld to fulfill purposes of which they knew nothing. The pageantry of war was no more than blind capitulation to dark forces and absurd self-destruction in the name of something meaningless.

"Will you take them along?" Thorin asked. "Will you make warriors of them?"

The young men awaited his answer with great anticipation.

"If you are like your father, I will be proud to have you among us, although you may learn more by staying at his side."

"No, I am a wanderer. That is no life for these young bucks."

"We will work hard," the woodsman's son assured Gernot.

"Then my people will welcome you with open arms."

"I am grateful, Gernot," Thorin said as he took his arm.

"Will you stay with us for a time, Thorin?" Gernot asked his old friend.

"No, I find comfort only in the heart of the forest. My people and I will go south for the winter. To the Wisigoth lands."

He turned to his sons, beaming with pride.

"When I return to these mountains, you will be warriors."

He embraced them with deep affection. Hadrian sensed that the man would never see his sons again. It caused him even greater agony as he realized that these young men were being swept up in a tidal wave created by his destiny and the mission which he had to fulfill.

"Until we meet again, old friend," Thorin said. "May the gods be with you."

"Farewell, Thorin," Gernot responded as the woodsman headed back into the forest.

"When shall we begin, Sire?" the younger brother asked.

"Today! Come along."

He turned to Hadrian.

"Would you care to see how we make warriors of boys?"

Hadrian nodded reluctantly, preferring to hide his thoughts from people who would never understand his revulsion with ways that they had pursued as far back as memory could take them.

THE BURGUNDIAN warriors practiced in a great barn-like building on the far side of the inner courtyard. A whirlwind of activity thundered in the vast room. Under the guidance of a aging, bald-headed master trainer, hundreds of young men were training for combat. Hadrian was flooded with memories as he watched the swordplay, wrestling, spear throwing, and all the skills he had learned from early youth. He could still taste the physical exhilaration which combat stimulated. But, as clear as a trumpet piercing the air with an urgent call to arms, he understood that his old habits were not merely the pleasures of his muscles and sinews, but the entryway for alien influences, for the puppet masters of the underworld.

Othmar, the trainer, motioned for Gernot, Hadrian and the woodsmen to join the group surrounding him.

"Many of you are familiar with the ways of the hunt, but those are not the ways of the warrior. Your bows and staffs are not much use against men armed like this."

He held up a shield and sword and motioned for one of the young men to approach.

"Come!"

The worried young man stepped forward. Othmar handed him a bow and several arrows.

"Notch an arrow," Othmar commanded as he backed away. "Tell me where your target is."

He held up the shield in front of his body, nearly covering it, and peered around the side.

"Where is your target?"

"I see only a small part of your head . . . and your feet."

"Release your arrow!"

"But Sire . . . " the boy pleaded.

"Release your arrow, I say!"

The young man raised his small bow and shot an arrow which Othmar easily deflected. Then the trainer rushed toward him with upraised sword as the youth frantically tried to re-notch another arrow. Othmar knocked him down and stood over him like a grizzly bear ready to deliver the fatal blow.

"You see, woodsmen, we have much to learn. That doesn't mean that your talents are lost, for we will also make use of the bow. So keep your eye sharp and your hand steady."

A commotion echoed in a corner of the room, disturbing the attention of the group. Prince Giselher, his entourage in tow, burst into the training hall, eyes glaring. Othmar's ears turned red with anger as he observed the arrogant young lord.

"The newest ones come with me, and you other lads work with each other by the wall while I train the beginners."

Giselher joined them as Othmar showed his students the rudimentary moves of swordsmanship. Hadrian watched on, his interest rising in spite of himself.

The trainer paired the young men off and studied their moves.

"No, no! You must return the sword to a guard position after you strike! Sir Giselher, come here and show these boys the importance of returning to guard."

Giselher snickered haughtily as he faced off with Martin, the younger son of Thorin. The woodsman swung high and then low as Giselher blocked and retreated. The boy swung again, and Giselher countered, striking him hard in the ribs.

The onlookers's faces turned grim as the arrogant prince struck the boy at every opportunity. Jeoffrey, the older brother, hurried to the trainer.

"Sire, may I take my turn now?"

"Yes. Try to recover quicker from your strike."

The powerful young man took up the sword and positioned himself. They circled each other as Giselher taunted him with supreme confidence. The boy was determined to hit the prince but showed more caution than his brother. He lunged several times and was soundly struck in the sides and on the head. Hadrian grimaced at the direct hits the young man was taking in his angry attempt to wipe the smug look from the Burgundian lord.

The more frustrated the woodsman became, the greater his mistakes and the harsher the blow he received. Finally, Othmar separated them.

"Enough for today. Do you lads understand what I mean about the guard position?"

He then glanced at Giselher and his adversary with a half-smile.

"Now, let's end today's training with a bit of staff work."

He took the wooden swords from them and handed them each a staff. Jeoffrey wrapped his hands eagerly around the familiar weapon. Once again, they circled each other. Before long, a downpour of snapping blows was falling on Giselher as he lost control of his staff and was knocked to his knees. Othmar intervened even though he was enjoying the thrashing.

"Enough! That will be all for now."

He helped the prince up from the dusty floor.

"Sir Giselher, you may return to the spear area."

The outraged young man hurried off, growling at his servants to follow him. He glanced back at the two brothers, threatening them with a furious look. Martin grabbed his brother's arm.

"Are you mad? Don't you know he is brother to the King?"

Jeoffrey jerked his arm away and walked off, still full of anger. Hadrian watched them disappear in the crowd of young warriors. It seemed to him that the demons were hovering over all of these youthful spirits, seeking entry. Gernot came up to him and suggested that they observe Hagen and his practice.

In a corner of the building, the Lord of Trony was smashing full-power blows with a wooden sword against a crude heavy-bag. The bag jumped and shuddered with each blow. Giselher stood nearby, in awe at Hagen's power. The blows echoed throughout the building, shaking the rafters.

Giselher took up a spear and threw it against a target hanging on the wall. With great skill, he drove several more into an area the size of a shield.

"Well, Hagen, did you see that?" he exclaimed, impressed with himself. He turned to Hadrian and pointed to the spears.

"Your best centurions cannot beat that, Roman!"

Hagen stopped beating the bag and wiped the sweat from his brow. He dropped his sword and approached the young prince. The mighty lord took a spear from the startled young man's hands. He positioned himself and proceeded to throw one spear after another into an area less than a foot in diameter. Then, without a word, he returned to the bag, picked up his sword, and proceeded to beat his monotonous tune.

Giselher looked at the target, astonished. Hadrian felt grateful that he had never confronted the great warrior in his many encounters with the Goths.

"How, Hagen? How do you do it?"

"Why did you not ask me that before?" Hagen muttered as he continued his practice.

"I . . . I thought I was doing well."

Hagen stopped beating the bag, leaned on his sword, and looked the young man square in the eye.

"You thought? Listen, boy, we deal with life and death here! There is no room here for arrogant thought!"

"Do you realize, Sire, that you speak to a Lord?" Giselher cried out, embarrassed.

"I speak to a boy. The brother of my friend, the King, but still a boy," Hagen stated as he struck the bag with a thundering blow.

"You speak to a Burgundian warrior!"

"A warrior? You are a whelp pup. And you will remain one until you see it for yourself and try to learn from those who can teach you. You have no privileges in this hall."

Vivid with rage, Giselher looked at the spears. He picked one up and prepared to throw it but held it back as he realized he could not possibly do has well as Hagen.

Like a dog with his tail between his legs, he returned to the old soldier.

"Then show me, Hagen."

The Lord of Trony took the spear from the young man's hand and approached the target.

"Stand with your forward foot facing the target. As if your forward foot were a tree, make your rear foot the earth, like this."

Hagen put his rear foot against his front foot, forming an L shape.

"Now step out until you are comfortable. When you throw, let your front foot go forward into a deep stance. But remain straight. Do not waver."

Giselher followed the instructions and prepared to throw the spear.

"Remember! The difference between what I do and

what you do is that I throw with my body. You throw with your arm."

Giselher threw with great concentration and hit the target. He cried out victoriously. Hagen returned to his practice without offering any sign of approval.

Gernot winked at Hadrian and they moved to the hand to hand fighting area. The Burgundian prince removed his belt and heavy fur jacket. He stretched his muscular arms and stepped into the fighting area.

"You Romans may have fine war strategies, but we have learned from the Greeks how to fight with bare hands. Watch and learn, centurion!"

Hadrian smiled and observed closely. Gernot's opponent rushed him and was swiftly thrown to the ground. The crowd surrounding them cheered. The young adversary tried again and was slammed on his back. Hagen looked over and motioned for Giselher to join him.

"Look at your brother. See how relaxed he is. Do you see his confidence? It is not false."

Hagen stepped into the ring area, carrying Giselher's spear.

"Gernot!"

He shook the spear at him. Gernot smiled and faced his friend. Hagen circled him, then made a quick thrust. Gernot blocked it and sidestepped. He jumped in to hit Hagen square on the jaw. The crowd roared. Laying in the dirt, Hagen rubbed his sore jaw and turned to Giselher.

"You see? Now what if you had lost your weapons in battle? Could you still fight?"

He rose and grabbed a sword from one of the men. Spinning around, he rushed toward Gernot. As the wooden sword came down, Gernot calmly sidestepped and, clasping his hands together, struck Hagen neatly below the ear.

"You must always be prepared," Hagen said as he shook his head.

He jumped toward Gernot who met his rush and attempted to throw him, but was suddenly lifted into the air and thrown against the spectators. The men cheered wildly. Hagen walked up to Giselher.

"You see? Always be prepared!"

His eyes went past the young prince and fell upon those of Hadrian. The Roman felt in that gaze a strange knowing, as though the Lord of Trony perceived that their guest had a secret purpose whose cost would be ruinous to his people.

"Why don't you show us how they teach soldiers of Rome?"

All eyes turned on Hadrian. He hesitated, attracted by the heat of competition, all the more intensified by Hagen's veiled challenge. The Roman had indeed rejected all violence and was daily seeking to enter the glow of peace and good will which he had witnessed in Patrick the Briton. He knew this was the only path to the life he craved. But here in this practice area, it seemed safe to unleash his old skills one last time.

A murmur rose in the crowd of men as he removed his shirt and stepped into the circle. The great Hagen awaited him like a snorting bull ready to charge. Hadrian had the strange impression that if he beat their mightiest warrior, he would win over these Burgundians and insure their assistance in his mission.

They circled each other slowly. Gernot and Giselher watched on with great interest. It had been a long time since Hadrian wrestled with an opponent without the intent of killing him and he felt uncomfortable in this playful competition for it carried with it the same lust for winning that had soiled his soul for so long.

A great arm flew toward his head. With lightning speed, the Roman pushed it aside and dove to Hagen's side, grabbing his leg. He slipped behind him, lifting the man's leg with a groan, and stepped in front of the other leg. Hadrian threw his weight against the massive body and Hagen fell flat on his face. But no one cheered. The Burgundians were stunned by the sudden defeat of their greatest warrior. Hagen reached for the Roman's foot, but Hadrian leaped in the air and landed on the man's back. His blood now rushed through him like a burning lake. He sensed that the playful competition had turned into survival now that honor was suddenly at stake.

The Lord of Trony roared like a wild beast and shook Hadrian from his back. He grabbed him with an iron grip and threw him down like a limp toy. Hadrian felt the giant arms wrap around his neck. He struggled but the man's bulk was so much greater than his that he was unable to move.

"Hagen!" Gernot shouted angrily.

The huge man stopped short of breaking Hadrian's neck. He lay over him, inches from his face. They looked at each other intensely.

"You're here to kill us all, aren't you, Roman!" he whispered for him alone to hear. "The fates have brought you here to collect their blood money."

For a moment, Hadrian thought the man would kill him and end his mission here on the dusty floor of the practice area.

"Hagen! What are you doing!" Gernot shouted again, this time smacking his friend on the shoulder to get his attention.

Hagen released Hadrian reluctantly and stood up, staring at him hatefully. The Roman rose and stepped up to him.

"I mean no harm to your people. We are caught in circumstances that none of us can control. It is for a better future that I am here."

He took his shirt from Gernot's hands and walked away quickly as the men made way for him. Hagen watched him disappear. Wet dust dripped down into his grey beard as though weeping for what was to come. He knew that even his great strength could not halt the course of events which would carry them all over the waterfall of Destiny.

chapter fourteen

ETHRAIN WANDERED through the village in the company of several young women who worked at the castle. She felt more comfortable with the simple people who toiled in the fields than with lords and royalty. She could not understand the concept of arbitrary importance, of wealth or poverty doled out according to one's birth. Only the wisdom of spiritual insight was a sign of true royalty to her. The rest was frightfully unjust.

Felicia had taken an immediate liking to the straightforward woman from the Nordic isles. They were the same age and born under the same stars. Ethrain was the first guest of the king to address her as an equal and this created a bond between them that nothing would ever sever.

"I want you to meet my parents," Felicia said as the other girls parted company.

The two friends entered a little cottage near the center of the village. Her parents greeted them with the warmth and hospitality characteristic of good-hearted people of the land. Their features were aged before their time from the rugged peasant life. But their eyes sparkled with affection for all things, especially for their daughter Felicia. Ethrain joined them at the table for a meal of stew and black bread.

"I have heard that there are Huns at the castle. Did

you see them?" William the peasant asked.

"Yes," his daughter answered. "They look like little demons. I didn't dare approach them."

"That is not like you, Felicia," her father responded with a twinkle. "I would have thought your curiosity would have gotten the best of you."

"They are savages!" the mother exclaimed, pleased that her child had the good sense of staying away from them.

"Their leader, Attila, is called the Scourge of God, the Dread of the World," William continued, proud of his worldly knowledge.

"The cook's helper told me that the King has been invited to the Hun court," Felicia stated with concern.

"They mustn't go!" her mother cried out.

"Lords of the Rhine fear no one, be he man or devil!" the father exclaimed.

"I've heard that they call the Hun territories the Land of Phantoms," Ethrain said softly.

"The King believes in that Christian God," William responded. "He is not afraid of spirits."

"The King is foolish then," Ethrain stated matter-of-factly.

"You mustn't say that!" Felicia scolded. "Our good King Gunther is the finest leader of the Burgundian tribes!"

"Even the great Roman general Aetius has expressed admiration for our warriors," William said solemnly.

"The Huns will massacre them," Ethrain said as she gazed inwardly, speaking from her mysterious intuition.

A tense silence spread out among them as though some dark cloud had entered the room. Ethrain wondered what had compelled her to share her vision of the future with them. Perhaps she felt responsible for what was taking place.

"I must hurry back to the castle," Felicia blurted out to break through the awkwardness of the moment. "It will soon be time to make preparations for the banquet."

"Another banquet?" Ethrain asked, still full from the previous one.

"We Burgundians like to celebrate!" the old peasant told her with a warm smile which chased away the tension of the previous moment.

Felicia and Ethrain left the cottage and walked silently through the village. Every step of the way, Ethrain felt a new wave of intuition crash upon the shores of her awareness. She knew that terrible tragedy awaited the gentle young woman who walked alongside her. But she also perceived that she had a special role to play for the future.

She stopped suddenly and took Felicia's arm.

"Whatever happens, Felicia, know this. You will bear one of the greatest kings ever to bless these lands!"

The peasant girl looked at her in utter astonishment. Then she laughed out loud.

"What strange magic is this?" she exclaimed. "See who is before you! A simple girl of the fields!"

"Remember my words," Ethrain said as her eyes pierced into the girl's soul. "Your pain will yield a precious gift for the people of the future."

Felicia was stunned and tears filled her eyes in spite of her mind's rejection of this prophecy. Ethrain put her arm in hers and guided her toward the castle, knowing that what she had foretold was too much for the girl to accept or understand.

HADRIAN SAT in the courtyard on the wooden steps leading to the ramparts. The golden light of an autumn sun fell on his face, warming his features and soothing the turmoil in his breast. Already, the sense of great danger made his blood rush through him. The thought of what he had to do was terrifying, even for a centurion of the great Roman legions. But the quietness of the day also foretold of a time to come when peace would reign over his life with Ethrain. How he longed for it and for the days when they could live by Nature's rhythms and rejoice at the sound of their own children playing in the meadows.

He smiled at the feeling of that longed for future, hearing it praised by bird songs and the gentle sound of farm animals grazing nearby. Just then, he saw the Hun commander step out into the courtyard with his companions. He called himself Magag and bore the looks of a man who had pillaged his way across many lands.

The Huns could not see Hadrian from where he sat and the Roman's blood turned cold upon hearing their muttered conversation in a language he had learned long ago when fighting alongside the legendary Aetius.

"Our Queen comes from fine stock," Magag said to his men as they examined the ramparts. "These Rhinelanders have good defenses and fine warriors."

"We could conquer them easily!"

"Certainly," the leader responded with a grin. "But we would lose many men. And what would be gained? These people are not rich. They are farmers. Attila will not waste his troops for wheat. He wants gold."

"The gold of Rome!"

"Some day. Some day we will be masters of that city!"

Their morbid conversation was interrupted by the jovial Ortwin who appeared on the steps of the ramparts, descending toward them. He saluted them coldly.

"We have heard that you Huns are great warriors. And good on horseback as well."

"We are the best horsemen in the world!" one of them growled.

"And I take it you have the best horses as well?" Ortwin asked with a twinkle.

"No one has ever questioned that," Magag responded coldly.

"What to you think of that horse over there?"

In the far end of the courtyard stood a beautiful black horse which Gernot was grooming with great care. The king's six year old daughter, Nisha, was feeding him bits of apples.

"A horse's coat does not make him a war horse," Magag observed cynically.

"Look how gentle he is," another Hun said. "He eats food out of the hands of children. That is no war horse!"

"Only the finest war horse in the realm!" Ortwin exclaimed.

"Is that not the King's brother grooming him?"

"Yes, that is Sir Gernot. A fine warrior, he is. You cannot separate the animal from his master. Like a hilt and a blade, together they make a mighty weapon."

"The two of them know how to fight, eh?" Magag asked with rising interest.

"There is no doubt," the heavy set Burgundian replied.

"Are you interested in some sort of contest?"

"For a little wager, perhaps?" Ortwin wondered with a smile.

"Do we wager gold?" Magag asked, a look of greed in his oriental eyes.

"What else?"

"How do we arrange for such a contest then?"

"Well, if it were me, and I were wanting to challenge Sir Gernot, I would offer a few unflattering remarks on that animal of his."

Magag snickered and headed toward Gernot. Ortwin rubbed his hands together and hurried off to gather a crowd. On the steps, behind the wall, Hadrian shook his head. The Burgundians were playing with fire!

Gernot saw Magag approach and instantly sensed a menace in the air.

"Find me that halter, Nisha," he told the little girl who scampered off toward the stables.

"This is a fine animal you have here," the Hun stated as he looked over the horse. "I'm told he is a war horse."

"That he is."

"But he seems so gentle."

"Do not judge an animal's spirit by his temperament. Nor a man's either."

"Do you Burgundians test your skills in contests?"

"I have never known a people who do not."

"Then perhaps you and I might try a little competition . . . with wooden swords."

"I have no need to test my skills, or to prove them."

Gernot turned to lead his horse away.

"Perhaps your horse becomes gentle with age and you do not wish to let it show. You could use one of our horses."

Gernot stopped and stroked his animal's neck.

"Bring my gear, boy," he called out to a stable hand. "This man wants to know how my horse handles himself."

Magag smiled devilishly as the boy hurried off.

Hagen and several other lords pushed their way through the crowd of villagers and soldiers gathering in the northern field behind the fortress walls. Hadrian came upon Ethrain and Felicia as they were virtually carried along by the tide of excited onlookers. The furious snort of prancing war horses sounded over the noise of the crowd. In the center of the field, Lord Gernot on his shining black stallion prepared to face Magag the Hun. The riders jockeyed for position and Ortwin called for them to begin.

Gernot noticed Felicia in the boisterous crowds and acknowledged her with a slight bow of the head. She responded with an irrepressible squeal of delight, rising on her toes to get a better view of him. Ethrain smiled at her unconcealed attraction for the Burgundian lord.

She took Felicia by the arm with the support and assurance of an older sister.

Thundering hooves raised clouds of dust in the lazy afternoon sun. The crash of wooden swords and grunts of power and rage shook the cool, quiet autumn air like demonic howls rising from the lower depths.

The well-experienced Burgundian prince maintained a striking calm throughout the chaos of weapons and animals, swinging arms, and kicking hooves while the Hun rushed for the kill with wild speed and ferocity. Hadrian watched Gernot's face closely as he sent hammer blows against his opponent, whirling his horse about with exceptional grace and assurance. An unexpected admiration stirred within him, sparked by the expert control of the battle-weary warrior. His soul had to be anchored in solid ground in order to remain unjarred by perilous outer circumstances. There was wisdom behind the man's abilities.

Magag fought with incredible speed. The northerners with their heavy weapons had never seen such flashing motion, such relentless, explosive charging. To the Hun's surprise, the black war horse, once unleashed, was as aggressive and accurate in its moves as its master. But their skills were well-matched and neither showed advantage over the other.

Finally, in a wild clash, both men were knocked to the ground. The Hun was the first on his feet, dashing toward Gernot. The black stallion suddenly intervened, rearing and kicking at the little man. Gernot jumped up, called his horse away, and showed clear superiority over the Hun whose skills rested on top of his pony. The Burgundian swept him off his feet and shoved the wooden sword against his throat. Magag acknowledged defeat and was let up.

Gathering his things, Gernot impassively mounted his horse and road away as the crowd cheered him. Felicia hugged Ethrain, filled with excitement and relief. Little Nisha hurried after Gernot and offered apple bits to his horse. The ferocious animal was now docile and ate from the girl's hand.

"Uncle Gernot, if I were just a little older, I would marry you."

"Oh?" he responded with a smile.

"Well, it would be very proper. The beautiful princess always marries the greatest warrior. Everyone says you are a great warrior and I am certainly a pretty princess."

Gernot patted her on the head. He looked up to see Magag dusting himself off, a savage anger raging within him. He stared at his victorious adversary as if to say "it will be different on the battlefield!"

The crowd dispersed with shouts and songs praising the valiant lords of the Rhine. Hadrian joined Ethrain and returned with her into the courtyard.

"They have no idea what they are dealing with," Hadrian whispered.

"I know," Ethrain agreed. "But what can we do? Surely, we cannot stand by and watch them be massacred."

"All we can do is accomplish what we have been given to do. The rest is merely foam in the ocean of Fate."

Ehtrain looked at him curiously.

"Your view of things has certainly changed, Roman!"

She still called him that despite the intimacy of being man and wife. But now she said it with affection rather than disdain.

"I have seen too much to cling to what I thought was reality," Hadrian murmured. "I now see some larger plan, and greater forces, involved in everything human."

"What do you see in this?" she asked as she took hold of his neck and bent his head down to kiss him warmly on the lips.

Hadrian laughed, somewhat embarrassed by his brazen young wife.

"I think that this is the mightiest force in the universe, just as the good Patrick told us!"

They hugged and headed through the chickens and pigs wandering about the edges of the courtyard.

The Queen Mother rested her tired limbs in the sun. She seemed in prayer as her son Gernot dismounted quietly and approached her. He gave her a soft kiss on the forehead and she looked up with radiant love in her eyes.

"I prayed for your safety, my son. Come sit beside me."

The powerful warrior sat by her with the eagerness of an obedient child.

"Do you spend much time speaking to this new God?"

"Yes, I do," she answered thoughtfully.

"This God hears you? He listens to you like I am now?"

"I believe so . . . I have felt His Holy Presence."

"How do you know? Where is your proof that this God hears you, or even exits?" Gernot asked with great longing in his voice.

"Oh, none that I can reveal. My proof is here," the Queen Mother responded as she touched her heart. "Here I know what Truth is."

"What is it that this God requires? What must I do to reach him?"

"He only requires one to trust Him and rely on Him concerning everything in this life and beyond. As for doing, imitate what you witness from Him. Goodness and care for all living things."

Gernot looked away, out toward the blue sky swallowing up the white mountain summits.

"I wish I could have such faith."

"You can, Gernot, you can," the old woman stated enthusiastically as she placed her arm around him. "But you must believe in a Being whom you cannot see or hear or feel. Yet, He is nearer to you than your own shadow. He is in the glow of the sun, the song of the birds, the beat of your heart."

"But what if this God is another legend like the tales of our ancient Kings?"

"We are creatures of Heaven, my child, not merely of Earth. We are not separate from the Divine breath in all of life. If we surrender ourselves to Him, we shall live in Eternity even now."

They sat in silence for a moment that seemed to blend with timelessness. The silence which spread around them seemed to make room for the sacred to manifest itself. Then the Burgundian prince stood, unable to bear the tension of unknowable mystery almost palpably present in the courtyard.

"Your words interest me, Mother. But it is hard to believe without seeing and to trust in anything but this sword. I will think on these things."

He hurried away as the dignified old woman watched him, saddened by his loneliness and desperate yearning. She whispered a few words on his behalf to the great forces she had come upon in the stillness of prayer.

HADRIAN WANDERED through the castle, searching for a place to be alone. The contest had once again stirred old memories within him which rose to the surface and threatened to sweep him into their currents like the ocean's undertow. He hurried through the empty hallways as though attempting to escape the nostalgia of his old ways. It was crystal clear in his mind that he could not hope for external peace as long as internally something still craved violence. The experience on the cliffs of Mallor beneath the great dolmen had revealed to him the interrelationship of all things, from the movement of the stars to the anger in a man's heart. He was particularly aware of the ease with which the forces of other worlds could take hold of the human spirit. Men like the Hun Magag were clearly shells emptied of their humanity and filled with the venom of the underworld. Such a man was a slave to every passing thought or passion without reference to a higher good. Therefore, he was capable of anything, no matter how dehumanizing. Despite all his bravery and prowess, he was a slave who didn't know that he was a slave!

Hadrian felt a shiver rush through him as he headed up a small stairway leading to the more private rooms of the castle. It wasn't the dampness that caused his tremble, but rather the terrible realization that virtually all people, including himself, were capable of becoming such passive servants to the purposes of other-worldly forces. Strong-willed men like Hagen or Gernot were no less subject to the domination of unknown powers playing with their lives like wooden pieces on a chessboard.

The Roman came out onto the ramparts and sat on a bench overlooking the grandiose landscape. The great mountain peaks in the distance and the sweeping forests of pine seemed to incarnate the qualities of the soul which alone could keep people from prostrating themselves before the dark forces of the cosmos.

There was a purity in the strength and grace of Nature, a purity which was especially visible in the way the earth gave itself to the harmonious whims of sun and wind and rain. Even the magnificent white summits rising above all life to the very threshold of heaven found their ultimate nobility in playing their part in the ebb and flow of creation.

As the witch of Mallor had told him, it all depended on which influences one became receptive to. Life in splendid isolation was a grotesque illusion from an ignorant mind. No matter how brilliant, powerful, or wealthy a person became, there was no escape from the tapestry of life in which all things were interconnected just like the weavings in the fabric. Hadrian received the mountain air into his lungs and smiled with gratitude at the regenerative power of the air currents that swirled about him in this high country. He was thankful to be so far from Mallor and its stifling mists which hovered over it like steam from a decaying corpse. Yet he never felt very far from the malefic isle, as though the strange world he had encountered there was following him and revealing itself in new forms every step of the way. He could no longer look at people and things without seeing more than was physically present. This was especially the case with human faces. They were no longer handsome or ugly, friendly or savage, but rather glowed with the life story of the individual as though a color which he alone could see emanated from the features.

Lord Hagen was a powerful example of this odd new sensitivity Hadrian was developing. Beyond the rugged wrinkles and bushy grey hairs, there was a bleak resignation to some anticipated gloom which took the light from his spirit. Even his eyes had dimmed, like people of advanced age, announcing that some part of himself had already died, or was buried alive beneath the ruins of his heart. Somehow, the old warrior knew that the death of Siegfried would set in motion events leading him relentlessly to destruction. It wasn't that he had committed such a horrid act, but that he perceived that his life had been thrown on a course utterly out of his control. And for a man of great will power, such awareness was devastating.

Hadrian turned around as he heard footsteps softly approaching him from behind. Their delicacy announced the presence of a woman and Hadrian assumed that it was Ethrain. But when a hand gently pressed upon his shoulder, he immediately realized that it was not his beloved who had come to find him in this isolated corner of the castle. He looked up to find the angular features of Queen Brunhild staring down at him.

"Am I disturbing you?" she asked with a pleasant smile.

The Roman shook his head reluctantly. He had really hoped for some time alone where he might reflect upon the events which were rushing him toward a future he was not eager to meet.

"May I sit by you?" the Nordic queen inquired as she sat next to him.

The bench was small and there was barely enough room for the two of them. The brazen woman took hold of his hand and sat, bringing him down next to her. The queen's long legs pressed against his, making him terribly uncomfortable.

"Stay a moment. I wish to speak with you."

He looked into her eyes and knew instantly what she wanted. Her feline eyes contrasted sharply with her cold, rigid face. They were afire with sensual hunger, as though desperately seeking a satisfaction which could not be found. Queen Brunhild was a beautiful woman despite the harshness of her features. She was big boned and tall, a healthy descendant of the strong peoples of the far north. But something had gone awry in her nature. The body she had been given to nurture new life was desecrated for the purposes of power and ambition. Her manner and lack of shame made it evident that she had known the company of many men, even after becoming the queen of the Burgundians. But she had found no one to ease the fires forever pushing her toward new conquests. Now she preyed upon her Roman guest and called upon all her skills to attract him into her arms.

"I am wedded to Ethrain," Hadrian stated in the event that such a declaration might make a difference. As he suspected, it did not.

"Yes, the girl from the western isles. She is sweet, isn't she?"

She placed her hand on his leg and squeezed his thigh muscle. Hadrian jumped to his feet.

"Mylady!" he exclaimed angrily.

"You are strong, Roman. I like strong men."

"Men like Siegfried?"

The words burst from him unexpectedly. Gernot had told him the story. The queen's features turned scarlet and her temptress eyes took on a bestial glare.

"What do you mean?" she cried out indignantly.

In the flash of an instant, he had perceived that the northern beauty was at the center of the fateful events which would lead him to the fulfillment of his mission. It was through her infernal lust that everything had been set in motion. A terrifying thought shot through him like an arrow finding its mark. This woman was from the land of Odin! Hadrian felt certain that she was a servant of the supernatural powers known to her people. But she seemed utterly unconscious of the true motivations governing her behavior. She was chained to her passions and those very chains were the channels through which the gods of Valhalla and the giants of Jotunheim were warring upon the people of earth.

Hadrian suddenly felt something hot against his chest and looked down to see the amulet which Hyndla had given him. He had nearly forgotten about it. He raised his eyes to find Queen Brunhild intently staring at the ancient stone. Her face took on the look of one who had come upon a ghost and she abruptly stood and hurried away. Hadrian sensed that trouble was on its way.

ANOTHER DAY broke through oncoming storm clouds as the squalid village on the outskirts of the castle came to life. Peasants headed out to the pastures with their animals as others left for the fields, tools in hand.

Several small children filled the air with joyful sounds, pulling a broken wagon toward old William's home. He sat on a stump, enjoying the fresh breeze of a new day.

The children surrounded him and begged that he fix their wagon.

"I can't fix a wagon like that. It's so big!" he said with a grin. "How would I lift it to put the wheel on?"

The children tugged on his clothes with shouts of "you can do it! you can do it!"

"All right, all right children. Let me see, what have we got here?"

Just then, Felicia's mother stepped out of the cottage.

"William, it's time to eat. If you wait any longer, this food won't be fit to feed the hogs."

"I'm coming. Well, children, I must go now. We'll fix your wagon later."

The children were displeased, but William pulled out a little treat from his pocket and gave one to each of them. He sent them on their way, playfully swatting them on the bottom as they ran down the dirt path. He entered the cottage and joined his wife and daughter at the table.

"William, I don't know what I am going to do with you. You spend too much time with those children."

He sniffed the air and detected the scent of cooking meat.

"What have we got here?" he asked excitedly.

"Felicia was given a chicken by our good king."

"You must have worked very hard yesterday."

Felicia smiled with a touch of pride.

"I think the royal family likes me. They have given me charge of our guests. I am their hostess."

"Isn't that wonderful, William?"

The old peasant shook his head sadly.

"I don't like seeing you work like this, Felicia," he said in a tired voice. "But with the crops the way they were this year, I don't know what we'd do if . . . "

"Oh, father," she interrupted, "I don't mind it at all. I enjoy it even. There is so much excitement at the castle."

"Enough of this," the mother scolded. "Eat now."

"I promised Dame Hausen that I would fetch some water for her this morning. It won't take long."

She rose from the table and took a piece of bread with her. They watched her leave, eyes brimming with affection for their only child.

"I'll dress the hog today," William stated to his wife. "You'll have to prepare the meat for the winter."

"I wish you didn't have to. I'd like some piglets this spring."

"Well, without crops . . . "

"I know, William, I know."

"Maybe in the spring we will be able to buy a brood sow . . . "

He was interrupted by a terrible scream that exploded at the far end of the village. In an instant, people were running wildly past their cottage.

"Barbarians!" William cried out.

He grabbed a pitchfork in the corner of the room.

"No, you're too old, William! We must hide!"

She hurried to his side and took him by the arm, pleading. The old man removed her hand.

"The children . . . " he said as he gently touched her cheek. "I do what I must do."

He walked toward the doorway. Thundering hooves rushed by, filling the cottage with dust. Just as William stepped outside, his body was hurled back into the room driven by a spear thrown into his chest. A shabby, long haired barbarian burst into the cottage. His eyes quickly scanned the room. Seeing the terrified old woman, he rushed toward her and cut her down mercilessly. Then he grabbed the food from the table, stuffing some into his mouth, while filling a sack at his side.

The gates of the fortress flew open and a group of warriors led by Hagen and Gernot galloped toward the village. Giselher followed quickly behind, eager to fight.

Hadrian rushed to the ramparts and came upon

Ethrain who was hurrying up the stairway to witness the struggle. The Burgundians swept down on the motley gang of roaming nomads. Gernot was the first to be surrounded by the fierce savages as they attempted to throw him from his horse. He deflected the blows as his horse reared and faced the enemy. Another barbarian charged him, swinging a giant ax. The horses collided, but the stallion managed to balance himself. The ax struck his black, glistening coat and he staggered, throwing Gernot to the ground.

As one of the savages readied to plunge his sword into the prince, Felicia appeared in the mele, brandishing her father's pitchfork. She had just come from the cottage and madness twisted her features in a horrid expression of rage. She struck the man solidly in the back with a great shout. He dropped his weapon, swirled around, and stumbled toward her, trying to grab hold of her. She beat him with her fists as he nearly fell on top of her, dead. Felicia struck the corpse over and over.

Gernot hurriedly pulled her away and lifted her in his arms. He dashed away from the fighting and laid her near the walls. Ethrain raced down the stairs to assist him.

Soon, the enemy was routed, pursued by many of the Rhinelanders who were not satisfied with the carnage. Hagen and Giselher rode up to Gernot who was kneeling beside Felicia. Ethrain covered the girl's forehead with a damp cloth and whispered for everyone to step back. Gernot turned to find his horse and felt his heart tighten when he saw him laying on his flank, seriously wounded. The animal was slowly kicking his feet, trying to rise. Giselher jumped off his mount and tried to help the stallion. Gernot's impassive mask wavered ever so slightly. He suddenly leaped onto Giselher's horse, motioned for Hagen to care for the stallion, and galloped off into the countryside.

From the top of the ramparts, Hadrian watched him vanish into the soothing shadows of the great Alpine forests. He closed his eyes and felt a prayer rise in his heart to ease his new friend's pain.

chapter fifteen

THE DARK stables were crowded as gloomy faces wandered about amidst the piles of manure and hay. Gernot was kneeling next to his horse, petting its sweat-covered neck. Ethrain sat on the other side of the animal, trying to ease its suffering with one of her healing remedies. Little Nisha rushed through the group and entered the stall. Ortwin took her by the arm.

"Come, Princess. Let me take you back to the castle."

"No! I won't go until Uncle Gernot comes out."

Gernot rose and approached Nisha. Hagen stepped forward and put his hand on his shoulder.

"Perhaps I should take care of this."

"No, Hagen. I must do it."

Nisha looked up at the two old warriors and suddenly realized what they were talking about.

"No, Uncle Gernot! No!"

Gernot gazed at her sadly. He motioned for the other men to leave. Kneeling by the little girl, he took her shoulders in his hands and looked deep into her large, innocent eyes.

"You don't want him to suffer, do you, Princess?"

"No," she answered as tears filled her eyes. "But you don't want to kill him, do you?"

"No, I don't."

"I don't understand! You don't want to, so you don't have to!"

"I must, Princess."

"He'll get better if you help him. I'll help too. I'll come every day. He'll get better!"

Gernot shook his head. He gave her a hug and motioned for Hagen to take her out of the stables. As she was lifted into the man's powerful arms, she lost all control and became hysterical.

"Don't do it! Don't kill him!"

Gernot closed his eyes in agony. Nisha's bitter weeping mixed with the sound of his sword leaving its scabbard.

A drizzle fell from the grey sky. Silent crowds gathered around the freshly dug graves. The king and Queen stood nearby, oblivious of the thick mud soiling their fine linen. An old man of great dignity, the Elder of those who had accepted the new faith, read from a scroll which a woman protected from the rain with her shawl.

The Queen Mother approached Felicia and put her arm around her. Hadrian and Ethrain stood nearby, deeply touched by the grief and the faith of the Burgundians. Other villagers and soldiers watched from a respectful distance, curious to see the unusual ritual of the religion that was changing their ancestral ways. Gernot moved forward to hear the words from Holy Scripture being read with great solemnity by the Elder.

On the hill above them, Hagen sat on his horse, watching the scene with grim melancholy. His soul seemed as grey as the day and the falling rain hid the tears crawling down his wrinkled, weather-beaten face.

Hadrian looked up at the silhouette overlooking them. The stillness of the day, the steady beat of the rain over the earth, and the weighty words from illumined souls who had seen the unutterable all combined to fill him with strange new insights. It was as though the simple life of these people had conspired with Fate to rewrite his understanding of the world. Gone were his prejudices against less "cultured" tribes, gone were the differences between citizens of Rome and barbarians, gone were his desires to escape earthly life in favor of some mystical spiritual existence free of human troubles. Standing in the mud, drenched by a soothing rain, hearing the quiet weeping of mourners and the glowing words of hope and faith despite the present evils, all gave birth to a new consciousness of life's purpose. It was at the heart of human trials that ultimate enlightenment and even happiness could be uncovered. The Divine could only be found through the human spirit and its daily trials, not in spite of them.

THE RAIN turned to snow and the rivers to ice. Winter's heavy mantle slowly covered the Alpine landscape, bringing with it a deep silence which caused thoughtful persons to turn within and commune with the invisible.

There was no one to be seen in the courtyard or the fields surrounding the castle. Soldiers stood guard on the ramparts beneath the tiny round roofs over the towers which alone protected them from the cold winds.

Felicia stood at the fountain in the center of the courtyard, breaking the ice in order to fill a bucket of water. She dipped the wooden bucket into the frosty waters and carried it off, trying to avoid splashing the freezing water. As she passed by the stables, Gernot appeared pulling along a young colt. She managed a weak smile and moved on. Gernot eyed the lonesome silhouette crossing the frozen courtyard.

"Felicia!"

The sound struck against the icy stones and reverberated through the empty spaces. She turned around.

"Yes, Sire?"

"Have you seen my new colt?"

The pretty peasant girl came up to the animal and caressed its main.

"He is beautiful."

"He'll make a fine war horse some day."

"War . . . Bloodshed . . . It is so senseless . . . " she murmured as she turned away.

"I've not seen you for days. Have you been staying in your room?"

"Yes, Sire."

Gernot studied her for a moment. He could see the signs of a nearly broken spirit.

"Will you help me a moment?" he asked. "Here, hold the reins."

He handed her the halter, picked up a brush and blanket, and headed into the stables. She followed him silently as the walked past the powerful horses snorting and kicking their stalls. They came to an empty area at the far end of the stables.

Gernot gathered some hay to feed the colt. As he moved behind it, the spirited animal kicked him in the leg. Gernot roared with pain as Felicia, in spite of herself, burst out laughing. She immediately tried to smother her laughter as Gernot reacted in anger, first at the colt and then at her outburst. Just as she regained her control, Gernot stepped forward with a humorous limp and she erupted with laughter again. His anger turned to delight as he watched her come out of her dark melancholy. He limped around the colt to gather some tackle. Felicia fell silent again. He turned around and their eyes met for the first time. Instinctively, almost involuntarily, he approached her and cradled her head on his chest.

In her room, looking out the window at the wintry scene, Ethrain smiled to herself. Her parents' skills were blossoming within her and opening her heart, mind and soul to new vistas. She could feel Gernot's love healing Felicia from her grief across the courtyard in the stables.

Down below, Lord Hagen and the jovial Ortwin were walking slowly over the hardened mud.

"The king will not leave until we are certain our people will be protected from future raids," Hagen said in his booming voice.

"I know you don't want to make this trip. Why do you help in the preparations, then?"

"My King wishes it. That is enough."

"He treats you like a brother, not a subject. You are not even of our people. Why must you obey him?"

"He is my friend. And I have sworn myself to his side until he dies."

Ethrain leaned forward, compelled to eavesdrop as the men stopped right beneath her window.

"You have not returned to your lands since the death of Prince Siegfried. Why is that, Hagen?"

"You ask too many questions, Ortwin."

He fell silent as his mind drifted into the secret recesses of his soul. Ethrain concentrated all her attention on him, aware that a revelation was about to take place. Slowly, like the thick, curling smoke of temple incense, images rose before her inner eye, images which she sensed did not come from her imagination, but from Hagen's memories.

The fluid shapes formed into a man running down a dark hallway toward a silhouette that could be none other than Hagen.

"Sire! Sire!" the man shouted in a voice that seemed as distant as some half-forgotten dream.

"Sire, there is a traitor among us! I have been approached to overthrow the King!"

"Who would dare such a thing? Speak, man!"

"Prince Siegfried, Mylord! He promises wealth and power to those who would help him."

"He takes our king to be a silly old fool!"

Ethrain could feel the sting of rage rush through her solar plexus like a hot blade thrusting from within.

"What are his plans?" Hagen's voice said in some obscure corner of her mind's labyrinth.

"He has made a pact with the Danes . . . "

The very people he defeated?"

"He would become a valuable ally to them if he allowed them to pursue their raids down the Rhine."

"How do I know you speak the truth? Siegried is like a brother to the king!"

"Come with me . . . "

The words were haunting as they echoed through the recesses of her telepathic sight. The dark images of mystic gold flowed before her as fluid as reflections of the moon on the dancing waters of the great river. A shadowed grove came into view. A barn rose on its edge and out of a small opening where the hay was stacked came the threatening movement of concealed light. Hagen and the informer hurried through the night. All was still and peaceful until they came to the side of the barn.

Armed silhouettes stood among the dim torches. Hagen slowly stepped against the wall and leaned forward to peer through a hole in the wood. As his eye came closer to the opening, he could see the blond mane of the prince's locks. His heart sank with the weight of a heavy anchor as he came to rest his cheek against the humid wall and saw, in the center of the room, Siegfried whispering with great energy as the men listened in terror and fascination.

Ethrain felt Hagen's lust for blood erupt like a tidal wave over her being and she shivered at the horrid sensation. In that very feeling, she thought she glimpsed an awareness of a presence which manifested itself as a sinister laugh, blending with the tingling rush of blood through her arteries. It was in these feelings of violence and hatred and revenge that the creatures of Jotunheim penetrated matter. Their power was not in miraculous exploits among the elements, but in the subtle manipulations of human emotion and thought. Every feeling, every opinion was subject to their poisoning and ultimate control. Every reaction was fertile soil for dark forces to plant their seeds of destruction.

Ethrain jolted out of her haze of insight and found herself trembling with cold at the windowsill. Beneath her, the two men were walking away.

"That prince may bring us down yet . . . " she heard Hagen mutter grimly.

IN ANOTHER part of the fortress, Hadrian sat next to the Queen Mother as she counselled young Giselher. She had called upon him for his experience of war and travel to offer wisdom to the prince's first great voyage.

"You are not sure of this journey, are you Giselher?" she said lovingly to her son. "The many months . . . The strange lands and peoples . . . All for a sister who is now a stranger to you."

Giselher lowered his head in shame. The old woman looked on him with compassion.

"Your father was always nervous before an important event. What a worried man he was when you were born."

The young man smiled and looked into her limpid eyes, searching for the warm rays of love he had never failed to find there.

"But somehow, he always managed to do what needed to be done. I have often wished that he might have lived to guide you in your early years. Your brothers have helped, but it is not the same."

"Have you missed Kriemhild these ten years, mother? You rarely speak of her."

"I miss her greatly. There is a special place in a mother's heart for a daughter. She was such a pure, innocent child."

Her gentle features darkened as her mind drifted back to sweet days which would never come again.

"But perhaps it made her love so strong that she could not see the truth. She never did believe that Siegfried died in a hunting accident. She had it in her mind that someone was responsible somehow . . . I don't know what happened to her. The tragedy certainly changed her."

Tears sparkled in her eyes as the memories flooded through her mind.

"Then one day she announced that she was leaving. And a year later we heard that she had wed this Attila . . ."

The thought still made her cringe, even now. She put her hand on Hadrian's arm who was respectfully listening.

"This Roman is a good man, Giselher. I can feel it in my heart. I have asked him to watch over you on the journey."

"You mean like some sort of nursemaid?" the young man cried out in anger.

"No," the Queen Mother pursued calmly, "like a friend and a veteran of such adventures. I need you to come back safely, Giselher."

"I will, mother!" he said in exasperation. "I can face a Hun sword!"

"You are not going there to fight," Hadrian observed, "but as a guest of the Kagan. Don't seek out trouble with them."

"I won't," he muttered, resenting his paternalism.

"Have you found a gift for your sister?" the Queen Mother asked, trying to ease the tension.

"No. I don't know what to bring her. I hardly remember her."

"She loved us all, but I think she loved you the most. It was almost as if you were her own baby."

"Do you think she will remember me after ten years?"

"Why, certainly."

The old woman leaned over to him and caressed his untamed mop of hair. Her eyes were full of love and concern. The youth felt a shiver rush through him as he sensed that she perceived great tragedy ahead. He turned to Hadrian and saw the same shadows etched on his features. For the first time, he realized that he would be voyaging into the jaws of Death itself!

THROUGH THE castle windows, a snow-covered countryside glistened in the moonlight. The snow fell softly, endlessly, disappearing in the fluffy white tapestry below. Great flames crackled in the hearth as a minstrel sang a Christmas melody.

At the dais, King Gunther and his Queen conversed in hushed tones with Hagen. Giselher and Dankwart contented themselves with mugs of steamy grog. Nisha played with several pups as the Queen Mother watched on, happy to witness this blessed moment.

Gernot stood by the window, staring at the falling snow, lost in some mysterious brooding. Hadrian and Ethrain sat together by the hearth, listening to the gentle, melodious voice of the minstrel. The peace of this wintry eve invaded each soul, chasing away their anguish and dread. It was one of those rare moments in which the human spirit was lulled into the vast movement of the Great Life, discovering bottomless joy and harmony rising out of the unfathomable source of all things.

The door in the far end of the hall opened and the Elder entered. He brushed the snow from his cloak and blew the graceful flakes from the scroll he was carrying. The servants brought out two large candles and placed them on the center table. The Queen Mother joined the Elder and they sat in the flickering candlelight. The minstrel stopped singing as everyone gathered around the old man who carefully unfolded his scroll.

Hadrian and Ethrain joined the group and were soon mesmerized by the rich voice reading with veneration the words of Holy Scripture. They fell upon the people's heart as the snowflakes upon the earth, silently, softly, and yet transforming the landscape.

It was on this intimate, quiet evening that Ethrain and Hadrian learned of the vital faith of their hosts. Especially through the efforts of the Queen Mother, a stream of higher understanding had pierced the mighty walls of barbaric ancestry. Above the warrior's code and the hunter's way, there shone a dim sense of the Unknown God's commandments. They had learned that this all powerful Deity was also a God of love. The Rhinelanders had no trouble with this paradox as they witnessed its truth every spring when the death of winter giving way to new life.

The old woman had shared the story of her soul's journey with the king's guests. It was on a winter's eve such as this one that a man had knocked at the gates seeking shelter from the cold. He had lost his way on his voyage from the Etruscan mountain passes. The stranger was ageless despite the long snow-white hair which cascaded to his shoulders. Before a bowl of warm stew, it became clear to the royal family that their unexpected guest was a man of great learning and rare piety.

Despite his obvious hunger, he sat in silence for a time before his meal and seemed to disappear into some hidden sanctuary within where he gave thanks to the mercy of his Maker. It was through his actions and the aura of calm benevolence that the Queen Mother first experienced the awesome realization that this faith was unlike any other religion that had drifted west from the centers of early civilizations. This teaching opened onto that greater life which whispered to her beneath the vast, swaying branches of the great pines.

Ethrain received every word from the soft-spoken old woman as precious gems. Just as it had in the presence of the kindly Patrick, her soul thrilled at this astonishing news from the desert lands she had only heard of in myths and legends. A king was born in a manger to free all peoples from the bonds of darkness! Could it be that the prophesied battle of Ragnarok in which the decisive struggle of good and evil would end all things, had been delayed for the arrival of this Emmanuel, this God-among-us? Had the battle already been won? Surely not, when the likes of Attila still ruled over the earth.

Ethrain perceived how great indeed was the mission that had been given them to accomplish. Could it be that the God-Man had appeared on the dusty roads of Palestine in order to empower individuals with the capacity to participate in the cosmic battle? Was it possible that all was not in the hands of demons and demiurges, but was dependent on the frailty of human wills?

Under the guidance of the Queen Mother, most of the royal family accepted the grand truths of the burgeoning religion. The stranger who had opened her eyes to the new vision of Eternity in the midst of time vanished as he had come, leaving seeds of goodness in his wake. Now the Queen Mother offered those seeds to her new friends. They were a far cry from the dark powers of the druids and the mysteries of the invisible regions. The forces tapped by this Faith were internal. There was no need for dolmens and lunar cycles to make contact with the Beyond.

Under the spell of the story of the Angel's visitation to the shepherds, the two lovers sat in a glow of deep inner peace whose roots went further than any sentiment they had ever known.

The snow continued its relentless descent for days,

muffling all the sounds of the forests and mountains. Ethrain had never seen such a royal mantle on Nature's children before. The Isle of Mallor was rarely covered with thick snow and when it fell, the white coat quickly turned brown as though some infernal furnace burned just beneath the ground. But here, the great pines doubled in size and the valleys sparkled with virgin white as far as the eye could see. Even the cold wintry breezes were bearable as there were enough furs to bundle up for everyone at the castle. Like the animals of the forests, the Burgundians made sure that they had all the necessary provisions to face the winter months which stilled virtually every activity in the kingdom.

One morning, after a warm breakfast, Hadrian wandered out into the deep snow toward the frozen river. He was surprised to come upon the sons of Thorin cutting a hole in the ice. Just as he was about to call to them, Giselher appeared on the other bank with two servants.

"Didn't Othmar tell you to stay within the outposts?"

His voice rang across the immobility of the landscape like the sound of lightning. Jeoffrey, the oldest brother, dipped a string in the water, paying no attention to the prince.

"Answer me!"

"He did not, Sir Giselher," the younger brother responded.

"Well, I'm telling you! Return to the courtyard."

Jeoffrey looked over at the grey silhouette standing with his hands on his hips, threatening them. Giselher stepped forward to better see the woodsman's face.

"No one as taught you manners yet, boy!"

"Do you wish to teach me manners?" Jeoffrey answered coldly.

Giselher turned red with anger and came forward, his hands closing into fists. Jeoffrey stood up.

"What are you doing, Jeoffrey?" his brother Martin asked with fear.

The older sibling walked through the icy fog toward his adversary, stepping into the thick snow.

"I don't want to hurt you, Sire. But we will not be pushed about like sheep."

"Hurt me? Why you lowly commoner, I'll show you who is going to be hurt!"

Giselher approached, tightening his gloves around his fingers. His servants followed closely behind.

"Jeoffrey!" Martin called out in fear.

"You cannot face me alone, Mylord?" the woodsman asked the prince in a taunting voice.

"Stay back!" Giselher barked to his servants. "I want this pleasure for myself."

He pulled out his dagger as Martin gasped. Jeoffrey watched calmly while Giselher circled him.

"You'll learn your manners now, boy!"

"I have no weapon."

Giselher continued to circle him, but hesitated to attack, realizing the cowardliness of his act. Hadrian watched on, insensed by the prince's action. There in the white mantle of peace and purity, he saw the fiendish grimace of the giants of Jotunheim present in the young lord's hatred.

Giselher recognized the cowardice of his action and slipped the dagger back into its sheath. He lunged at Jeoffrey, fists swinging. The virgin snow flew around them as they engaged in a brutal fist-fight. The Roman looked on grimly, feeling his adrenaline rush through him like some hot brew firing the body and its passions. The lust for blood was contagious. But he caught himself in time before the demon of violence overwhelmed him and took control of his mind and soul. He knew these raging sensations only too well, having given himself to them as a willing slave so often on the battlefield and at the Circus Maximus where blood soaked the arena's sands daily. This was the first time in his life that he was able to make a choice as the fumes of the enticing poison invaded his being. He resisted the urges and took a deep breath of icy air, clearing his mind. His heartbeat settled and he studied the fighters with detached concern. He knew he had won a skirmish with the invisible powers seeking to manipulate the human world.

The young woodsman knocked Giselher down again and again with blows that would crush a bear's skull. The more he fell, the more the prince's temper roared and the more frenzied and incompetent his fighting became.

Like two wild beasts, they wrestled and charged and struck each other. Hadrian could see in Jeoffrey's fierce energy the repressed humiliation he had suffered so long as a nomadic child treated like an outcast of "civilization." Giselher could not stand up to the onslaught of his indignation, and he soon fell in the snow, nose and lips a scarlet red against the white backdrop.

The prince rose, wiping the red stream away.

"Enough! You aren't worth my trouble. But I'll remember this, you mark my words!"

He motioned angrily for his servants to follow him. As he walked off, he slipped on the ice and fell soundly on his bottom. The domestics quickly helped him up, doing their best to conceal their pleasure. Hadrian turned back toward the fortress, satisfied that some small justice had taken place in this icy corner of the universe.

As Giselher hurried past him, Hadrian took hold of his sleeve and looked into his eyes.

"You are meant to be a king someday, boy. You must learn to have a noble spirit if you are to be worthy of such a destiny."

The young prince was stunned by his words.

"What do you mean, Roman? I am last in line for the throne!"

"Remember what I am telling you. If you do not prepare yourself within, you may lose the opportunity of serving Fate as a leader of your people."

The youth shrugged his shoulders and hurried away. Hadrian stood in the snow, amazed at what he had just said. This was perhaps the first time in his life that such a strong premonition had surged through his being and burst out into the reality of the moment. He felt uneasy about having spoken those words, but he had no doubt as to the truth that he had intuitively perceived.

AS THE sun timidly broke through the grey ceiling of winter clouds, people began to venture out into the frozen landscape. Ethrain and Felicia walked along the edge of the woods. They came upon Gernot and little Nisha exercising a young horse. He held her in front of him with one arm as he guided the nervous animal.

"Good day!" Nisha called out.

Gernot slowed the horse and came to a stop in front of them.

"What is your name?" the princess asked the pretty peasant girl.

"Felicia. And I know your name. You are Princess Nisha."

Nisha struggled to get off the horse. Gernot gently helped her down.

"I want to show you something," the little girl said.

She took Felicia by the hand and hurried her around a great pine. Nisha pointed to a tiny flower barely keeping its head above the snow.

"Look! Isn't it beautiful?"

Ethrain joined them as they kneeled down to examine it.

"Yes, it is," Felicia whispered in wonder. "Oh, here is another one beginning to bloom."

"Blue is my favorite color," Nisha stated in a joyful tone.

"This means that spring will soon be here," Ethrain observed. There was a slight tension in her voice as she realized that the fragile flower announced the approach of the terrible danger they would have to face.

"Blue is my favorite color as well," Felicia told Nisha, overlooking the disturbing silence that had followed Ethrain's words.

"Then which one of you will have it?"

The ladies turned around to find Gernot dismounting behind them. He came up to them with a bright smile and picked the flower with a grand gesture.

"Oh, no!" Felicia cried out. "Why did you do that?"

"Uncle Gernot! You picked it!"

"It's a flower. You're supposed to pick it," the warrior said, his smile quickly fading.

"Not the first one!" the little girl insisted.

"Now we cannot make a wish!" Felicia added with a pout.

"A wish?" Gernot questioned.

"Don't you men know anything?" the little girl shouted as she stomped off into the snow.

"I'm going back to my room to find a vase. Maybe I'll get a wish before it wilts!

Gernot looked at the two women staring at him with mock rebuke and shook his head.

"Women!" he cried out in exasperation.

The sound of a high-pitched bell rang out from the castle.

"It's time to eat," Gernot stated as he turned to Felicia. "Come, you eat with me today."

"Oh, I cannot eat at the King's table!" she responded in fear.

Gernot took her by the arm and led her to his horse.

"But, Sire . . . " she complained as he helped her up on the saddle.

"Don't worry, Felicia. Where I come from, there are no such distinctions. We are all just human. Brothers and sisters," Ethrain said reassuringly.

The Burgundian lord threw her a strange look. He was not willing to go that far.

They returned to the castle and soon approached the closed doors of the banquet hall. Felicia's heart was pounding with terror at this breach of centuries-old tradition. Nisha came scampering up to them, relieving the tension.

"I've put that flower in water!"

"I'm sorry I picked your flower, little princess," Gernot told her softly, picking her up in his arms.

"I forgive you," she said, curling her lip upward.

"I had better set you down so you can enter like a Princess," the aging soldier told her as he brought her to the floor like a feather.

"I wonder if Mother missed me."

"You did not tell her where you were going this morning?" Gernot exclaimed.

"Maybe she thinks a big dragon has gotten me. With teeth this big!"

She spread her arms out as far as they could reach. Felicia and Ethrain laughed while the child giggled sweetly.

"It might not be so funny when your father the King learns about this."

He opened the door and they were swept up in the joyous sounds of music, voices, clanging goblets and plates.

"Please, Gernot, I can't go in there! I'm only a peasant girl!"

"You will eat with me today and hold your head up. You are my guest."

Nisha took her arm.

"Yes, yes. Come along, I'm hungry."

They entered the banquet hall. Heads turned as they walked to the front of the dais. Ethrain went to sit by Hadrian and enjoyed the show as the lord and his maiden broke the rules of tribal society.

"Bring another chair," Gernot ordered to a servant. "Felicia will be dining with us today."

He faced his brother the king who was in a frozen stupor, mouth open, eyes wide.

"Good day, Gunther. Mylady," he added, turning to Queen Brunhild, "allow me to present Felicia."

The peasant girl bowed awkwardly as the haughty queen studied her with suspicion.

"We grieve with you for your parents, my child," the good king stated sadly. "Gernot has informed us. You are welcome at our side."

Gernot assisted Felicia as she sat by the royal couple. The queen turned to her husband.

"This is not proper! She is a peasant girl!"

Little Nisha leaned over toward her parents.

"What are you whispering about, mother? Is it something you don't you want me to know?"

She let out a loud giggle, and the dais roared with laughter. The queen's stern features turned red.

"Nisha! You must discipline her, Gunther!"

"Nisha!" the king said in reprobation, but his twinkling eyes gave away his appearance of anger.

"And where have you been all morning?" the queen exclaimed, still upset with her bold child.

But the king held up his hand and silenced his bride. He had enough of domestic quarreling at his table.

"Hagen tells me that the village will be well protected. What do you think, Gernot? I cannot leave my people until I am certain of their safety," the king announced.

"Hagen's plan is a good one. With a few posted guards

and the additional walls, there will be no more trouble. Those tribes want to steal, not fight."

"What does the Roman think?" Othmar asked in a guttural tone.

Hadrian did not look up at first. He was staring down at his bowl of victuals. But that was not what he was seeing. He was witnessing dismal visions of death and destruction. They flashed before him so vividly that the images interfered with his physical sight. Ethrain's elbow brought him out of his morbid reverie.

"What is it?" he asked in a daze.

"The castle, is it well protected for our journey?"

Hadrian hesitated to answer. He had seen the construction of wooden grills with ends as sharp as spears and the expanded ramparts protecting the village. The structures would do the job. But it was the oppressive feeling that few of these men would ever return to their homes that made him waver.

"The fortifications are in good order," he finally stammered.

Ethrain glanced at him through a loose strand of golden hair. She knew he was experiencing the same premonition that gripped her throat.

"Tell me, mother," Gernot blurted out to veil his new friend's odd behavior, "how is that mare of yours doing? She should be foaling soon."

"Yes, I am expecting a colt any day now. And it will be a fine one. Wait and see."

Nisha tugged on Felicia's sleeve.

"I like you," she told her sweetly.

Felicia smiled and patted her on the head.

"Uncle Gernot," Nisha called out in a loud voice, "why don't you marry Felicia?"

Everyone at the table was startled. Queen Brunhild nearly dropped her goblet. But King Gunther burst out in laughter and was quickly joined by the others. Felicia cowered in embarrassment while Gernot stuffed a piece of bread in the little girl's mouth. There was still time for joy and laughter, even as the storm clouds of destiny gathered on the horizon.

chapter sixteen

RUNNING WATERS from the mountain summits announced the return of spring to the valley. The soaked earth awakened in sparkling colors. Great hills of snow were soon vanishing beneath the warming sun.

Men's voices echoed somewhere in the forest, causing flocks of birds to rise into the sky. The frosty world carried the sound for miles. Dankwart and Giselher appeared from the woods, chasing a deer. Further down the hill, Hagen, Gernot and the king awaited on horseback for the animal's appearance.

The enthusiasm of the hunters exuded in a great release from the long, dark months of inactivity. The new life appearing in every corner of the landscape was also stirring within them. Spring dawned in their limbs and in their hearts.

The sons of Thorin appeared at the top of a rocky hill overlooking a clearing that the deer had just entered. Jeoffrey readied his bow. As they descended the side of the hill, the deer dashed across the open space. He released his arrow. The animal tumbled into the grass and everyone hurried toward it. King Gunther congratulated the brothers as Giselher turned away to hide his jealousy and hatred. The men tied the deer over a horse alongside several rabbits and headed off. Gernot came up to Giselher's side.

"If you had waited just a bit longer before releasing your shot, he would have been yours."

"If, if, if!" Giselher muttered in a bad mood.

"Tomorrow we'll have our first venison roast of the season, eh?" Gernot said as he galloped away from his temperamental little brother.

A YOUNG stable boy raced through the hallway toward the Queen Mother's rooms. The kind aged woman sat in a large, barren room weaving tapestries with her domestics. Ethrain sat among them, patiently learning their fine skills, fascinated by the ways of another culture. The boy burst through the doors, out of breath.

"Mylady! Mylady! Your mare . . . "

"Settle down, young man. What is it you have to say?"

"Your mare is foaling!"

"She is? Is there trouble?" she asked with concern.

The stable boy nodded in fear. The Queen Mother dropped her needles and hurried toward the door. Everyone followed her.

They rushed through the courtyard, evading the rummaging pigs.

"Where are the other stable boys?" she cried out as they walked quickly through the empty stables.

"In there, Mylady," the boy said sheepishly as he pointed to a stall. The ladies peered in and found the stable boys passed out on the ground, an overturned jug at their side.

The Queen Mother quickly searched out a bucket of ice water and threw it on them with full force. The boys moaned but were too drunk to move. The women hurried to the stall where the mare was foaling. The animal lay in the hay, wet with perspiration, struggling to give birth.

"She needs help!" the old woman cried out. "Come

here, Isabel!" she called to one of her servants.

"Oh. Mylady, I couldn't do that!"

"I'm too old and weak for this! I need your help!"

Ethrain hurried to the mare and immediately began to apply the sciences she had learned from the witch of Mallor. One of the domestics knelt by the struggling animal and screamed as it kicked.

"Get away!" the Queen Mother ordered angrily. "Boy! Boy!" she called out to the stable hand who had come to warn her.

He approached the mare and put his arms around its neck. But he quickly proved to be too small to hold the horse down. Just then, a silhouette appeared in the entryway. It stood for a moment in the golden winter sunbeam piercing into the barn like some supernatural shaft. The figure stepped forward. It was Felicia. She had grown thin and dark wrinkles surrounded her once bright eyes. Yet some new light glittered through her pupils as she quickened her way through the stable. The animal's moans were awakening her natural care for other beings that had been buried alive beneath the ruins of her tragedy.

She came to Ethrain's side and gently moved the stable boy out of the way.

"Stroke her neck like this," she instructed him.

Together, Felicia and Ethrain helped the new life make its way out onto the damp hay which would be its first experience of Mother Earth. The young women struggled in silence side by side, joined in a unity of purpose and action. They entered the same rhythm as the miraculous birth process taking place inches away from them. Both felt the unspeakable sensation of being swept into a great cosmic occurrence which reached all the way to the domain of the Almighty.

"It will live . . . " the old woman whispered in wonder through her tears.

The mare snorted loudly and the newborn appeared, bursting with life. A sigh of marvel rose from the onlookers as they peered at the being who had just arrived among them.

"The boy and I can take care of everything now, Mylady," Ethrain told the Queen Mother. "It is cold and you must be tired."

"Yes . . . I am very tired," the old woman acknowledged, showing her age as never before.

She took hold of Felicia's hands and looked deeply into her eyes. Her smile said everything. She then hurried off with her servants to the relative warmth of the castle hearth.

ROYAL HUES of violet stretched across the mountain peaks as though a princely cloak were being tossed over their shoulders. The Queen Mother lost herself in the magnificent display as she stared out the window of her chamber window. She felt a melancholic chill rise along her spine and wondered at its origin. The mysteries of Christmas were with her still and she was under the stirring influence of the story of the Creator making Himself known through a humble human child. Yet the promise of new, imperishable life in the presence of the Eternal was dimmed by the distant shadow of the horrid cross of torture that accompanied the baby on the Virgin's lap. The angel songs were distorted by the pounding of large, heavy nails into the desecrated tree of Judea.

The young woman of Mallor had questioned her on these matters, vitally interested in this strange tale of the Holy dwelling in humanity and transforming the history of the world for all time. But she was repulsed by the suffering that came with the irrepressible joy. Why did he have to go the way of agony? These questions were too difficult for the Queen Mother who had only been baptized into the new Faith less than a decade before. She could only know what she understood with her heart and this kind of knowledge could not be communicated with words.

Now that she looked out upon the dramatic sunset, dark fears rose from within, from those places where she had experienced intuitions of the future. She was certain that doom lingered not far away for her people, as though she had spotted vultures circling over their awaiting future. The Queen Mother also detected a feeling that this dread was linked to the Roman and his bride from the western isles. But she repressed it because she knew that they were victims themselves of this fateful hurricane which, though still undetected, threatened to destroy them all.

A knock pulled her out of her reveries.

"Who is there?" she called out, surprised.

"Felicia and Ethrain, Mylady."

The Queen Mother told them to enter and pointed to chairs in the center of the room. They sat in an awkward silence as the sun vanished behind the peaks and the sky turned black.

"Ethrain told me you wanted to see me," the peasant girl finally said.

The old woman looked at Ethrain with a mysterious smile.

"Our guest seems to know many things . . . even before they are manifested."

"It is the way of our ancestors," Ethrain said simply.

The Queen Mother turned to Felicia.

"Do you wish to work again?"

"Yes, Mylady! I don't like being idle."

"Then I wish you to be my handmaiden. I grow old and need help with many small chores. Would you like that?"

"Oh, yes, Mylady! That would be a great honor. But I know nothing of . . . "

"Don't worry, the others will teach you."

Felicia stood, thrilled by the offer. But she hesitated to leave, sensing that there was something else to be said.

"Do you find my son handsome, Felicia?" the Queen Mother suddenly asked.

"Which one do you mean?" she replied with great nervousness.

"Come now, don't treat me like an old fool! You know who I mean!"

"I'm . . . I'm only a peasant's daughter."

"But do you find him handsome?"

"Yes, Mylady," Felicia admitted as she lowered her eyes.

"What sort of man is he?" the old woman asked as she scrutinized Felicia.

"He is a great warrior, a noble lord . . . "

"There are many great men at court."

"Yes, Mylady . . . "

The Queen Mother smiled. She could see all she wanted to know written on the young woman's features.

"Sit by me, dear," she said softly.

Felicia approached obediently, but more nervous than ever. The old woman watched her pensively.

"You are pregnant, aren't you?"

Felicia's eyes filled with tears, but she did not answer. She had kept that secret to herself for a long time.

"Is it Gernot's child?" the Queen Mother asked softly.

"Sir Gernot has not . . . "

"Then it is someone else's baby?" the old woman queried indignantly.

"No, no one else's."

Ethrain hurried to the elderly woman as she clasped her breast and seemed unable to breath. But she recovered and took Felicia's face in her hands.

"Does anyone know?"

The peasant girl shook her head negatively.

"Not even Gernot?"

Felicia looked away in shame.

"I do not want to tell anyone for now. Especially Gernot," the young woman whispered.

"Do you think that he would leave with the men if he knew?"

"I don't know . . . " Felicia said fearfully.

"Then you do not know my son very well yet. Are you aware of the court gossip over the two of you? What do you suppose would happen now if he remained home from this journey? The men would despise him. What would he be like to live with then, when the men he had led and fought alongside all these years now despised him . . . all because of you."

She caressed Felicia's long hair with motherly affection.

"In my heart, I feel you would be good for my son. But we must consider this carefully."

Ethrain took Felicia's trembling hand and eased her fears.

"This child will have a great destiny, Felicia. He will help to mold the future for new generations. You should be proud to be picked as his mother for his entry into the world."

Felicia smiled through her tears at the mysterious words. She did not see the painful look in Ethrain's eyes, even as she spoke of the wonderful destiny awaiting her child. She knew that its mother would not be so fortunate.

DOWN IN the courtyard, Hadrian approached the stables in the company of Gernot and Hagen as the servants lit torches to break through the thick darkness of the night.

"This girl," Hagen muttered to his old friend, "she's costing you your respect among the men. You are seen too much with her."

"I'll be seen with whom I please!" Gernot responded defiantly.

"You've never been like this before."

Hadrian felt uncomfortable as he found himself between the two men, caught up in this intimate subject matter. He was beginning to tire of this life among the Burgundians and was eager to get on with the work at hand. For a time, he had rejoiced at witnessing the ways of these people of the Rhineland who were such a welcome relief from the grim experiences on Mallor. But it all had a mesmerizing effect on his soul, as though tempting him to turn away from what he had to do for the sake of a life of tranquility. Did he care if the world fell into the hands of dark forces as long as he was left in peace to bring up a family in the heart of protective Nature? Without realizing it, he had begun to seep into a disinterest for the vaster needs of humankind as he participated in the life of his hosts. But the end of winter had thawed his apathy and he was rediscovering the call to complete his work.

They approached the stables and heard voices coming from the steaming building.

"Who will you take to the feast, or will any wench be seen with you?" a voice inquired.

"I'll have my woman, you'll see."

"I wonder if Sir Gernot will bring that peasant wench with him."

"First, she'll have to slop the hogs!"

The men laughed as Hagen and Gernot entered the stables. One of them noticed the newcomers and suddenly became still.

"Mylord! We . . . "

Gernot calmly walked up to him and stared at him for a moment. The man turned pale with terror and the others held their breath.

"Weapons or empty hands?" Gernot asked slowly.

The men stood like statues in the shadows, their fear becoming palpable.

"I said, weapons or empty hands?"

This time, Gernot started to unsheathe his sword.

"Empty hands!" the man cried out in despair.

Hagen shook his head and stepped outside, rejoining Hadrian. A wild commotion exploded in the stables. Hagen smiled at the Roman, knowing full well what was going on. Two of the soldiers came flying through the doorway, landing with a great splash into the mud. They jumped to their feet and started back in but the bear-like figure of the Lord of Trony stood before them, wagging his finger.

The men froze in their tracks, not one of them willing to go up against the massive bulk of the legendary warrior. As they stood there, the crashing noise in the barn continued until, all of a sudden, there was utter silence. Gernot came out of the stable and walked off without a word to anyone. Hagen followed him, shrugging his shoulders at the amazed Roman.

From her window in the highest turret, Queen Brunhild watched the three men intently. Her passion for the Roman had turned to vicious dislike. The sight of the amulet around his neck had stirred terrible ideas in her mind. She knew that it was a druidic object and, in her ignorance, that could only mean that her guests had made some demonic pact with the underworld. As she watched Hadrian enter the castle, she suddenly tore her tunic from her shoulder and shook her locks into a tangle.

It wasn't long before the court was brimming over with news of the scandal. The king was in a fury. His queen had come to him in tears with her gown ripped and her voluptuous flesh indecently exposed. She told him, in the throes of well-acted hysterics, that their Roman guest had assaulted her.

Hadrian had just entered his chambers for the night when the doors burst open and a dozen warriors surrounded him. Spears and swords were aimed at his body and some might have sunk into his limbs had King Gunther not burst into the room.

"Don't touch him!" he ordered.

The angry king pushed his soldiers aside and approached Hadrian. His ferocious grimace only intensified when he looked into the Roman's eyes.

"You have abused my hospitality, Roman! I opened my gates to you and offered you my friendship. You have betrayed me in the worst way!"

"I don't understand, Mylord!" Hadrian protested.

"Do you take me for such a fool?"

The old monarch unsheathed his dagger and raised it with a terrible roar. Hadrian stared at him, unblinking. If his moment to die had come, it would be with the dignity of a free man.

"My King!"

The voice was Hagen's. Gunther flinched and his rage suddenly seemed to melt into some strange inner disturbance. He stood still, holding the blade in midair.

"Mylord," Hagen said softly as he put his hand on his shoulder. "Must we make this mistake twice?"

The king turned to his old friend, eyes wild with sorrow. He could not bear the thought that his queen was the real traitor and that she had tempted Siegfried long ago, destroying the king's peace forever. But Hagen's intense gaze forced him to see what he had refused to look at those many years past. The Lord of Trony waved the soldiers away and embraced his king as the man began to weep. He accompanied him out of the chambers and turned back to glance at Hadrian. For the first time, the Roman saw the terrible agony which had marred the lives of these men and which was sending them headlong on a path of no return.

ETHRAIN HURRIED through the halls, looking over her

shoulder. No one had seen her enter into the upper rooms. She came to the queen's private chambers and listened at the door. She knocked softly.

"Go away!" the queen called out angrily.

Ethrain opened the door and entered. Queen Brunhild was sitting by the hearth, staring into the fire.

"What do you think you're doing?" she cried out. "Begone!"

Ethrain closed the door behind her and approached without a trace of intimidation.

"I must have a word with you, Mylady."

"How dare you disobey me! I'll call the guards!"

The young woman from the forests of Mallor could hardly be frightened by the queen's temper. She stopped near the hearth and defiantly put her hands on her hips.

"What are you trying to do to my husband?" she asked coldly.

Queen Brunhild's handsome features turned to ice. Her lips remained clasped together.

"I know he would never do what you have accused him of!"

"No man is to be trusted," the queen muttered hatefully.

"This man is!"

"You are a naive girl then. But that is no surprise considering where you come from."

"What do you mean?" Ethrain asked as her blood boiled within.

"You're from a primitive world. He is from the center of civilization. There are some things you may not know about him."

Ethrain felt the cold winds of doubt howl within. But she knew that if she let herself go with those feelings, she might plunge into the misery of mistrust and jealousy. It that instant, she understood that these fumes within were powerful dark magic, the kind that could consume her utterly and destroy all that the future held for them. She peered at the queen and saw the woman as a pawn in the hands of Odin and his treacherous ways.

"I know that he could never desecrate his honor with such as you!"

Queen Brunhild turned a deep shade of red.

"What do you know about me?" she cried out.

Before Ethrain could answer, the queen began to sob bitterly. Her efforts to fill Ethrain with uncertainty had failed and she was left with her sordid loneliness.

"We are sisters of the North, you and I," she managed to say. "I have not seen my people or my homeland for longer than I can remember. These Burgundians are a decent people, but it is not the same. Their ways are different, their gods are strange, and they know nothing of our Nordic arts."

She wept for her isolation and painful yearning for the places she called home. Ethrain relaxed her aggressive posture and took pity on the lonely woman.

"What has my Hadrian to do with any of this?"

The unhappy queen rose from her seat and leaned against the stone mantle. Her luscious blond hair was in tangles and her face was streaked with tears, dissipating the royal haughtiness that she had adopted long ago. Ethrain saw before her a desolate soul, longing for something she mistook as lust.

"I care for Gunther . . . " she said in a whispered confession. "I love him even, but more as an uncle than a husband. I've begged Odin to bring me someone else . . . Someone like Siegfried."

"You pray to Odin?" Ethrain asked as her heart began to pound faster.

"They've tried to make me a follower of the new faith but I cannot let go of what I have always known. Odin has been good to me . . . "

"He has?"

"Yes! It was because of him that I first met Siegfried. I carried out all the rituals for several years before he granted me my wish. But then I found that there were two sides to these gifts."

"What do you mean?" Ethrain questioned, deeply interested.

"Siegfried came to me to convince me to wed Gunther and consolidate a new kingdom. So the outcome of my prayers was not what I had asked for even though I was given the pleasure I had desired. The gods are not predictable."

"No, they are not," Ethrain agreed. "Tell me, have you continued to worship Odin all these years?"

"Certainly. That is why I was so sure that Hadrian had come for me. Why else would a Roman centurion travel to this faraway place?"

"Have you ever seen Odin?" Ethrain asked with trepidation.

"Of course not! No one ever sees the gods."

"Then how do you know it is he who answers your prayers and not some other deity?"

"I have dreams . . . "

"What sort of dreams?"

"Special dreams where I feel the presence of the warrior gods of Valhalla and worship them."

Ethrain was suddenly struck with the realization that the woman was one of those willing subjects manipulated by the forces of Valhalla. She had been placed in this distant land to create the circumstances that had led to this moment. It was as though everything had been planned outside of time and stretched out over the years, giving the impression of being disconnected events without purpose or reason. But it was clear to the daughter of Mallor that everything had purpose, everything was interconnected, everything was part of a vaster reality.

Ethrain knew she had to act quickly before the queen

again became a submissive agent of the gods, unaware of the cause and effect of her actions. An assassin brandishing a cutlass could not be more dangerous. Queen Brunhild's ignorance of the motives behind her choices was the perfect soil for the activity of supernatural beings, both gods and giants alike.

She took a small amulet from the satchel which never left her side. It was the last gift from her mother and was made of a rough but brilliant crystal set in a rock said to come from the mystic isle of Avalon. It was one of her most precious gifts, but she knew that it was very powerful and could ward off negative other-worldly influences. Ethrain understood that if she did not block the entryway through Queen Brunhild which the gods and giants fought over, some other catastrophe would occur before they could move on to the land of the Huns.

She gently placed it around the queen's neck. The lonely woman studied it and her eyes lit up with gratitude.

"I've never seen such a sparkling stone! How can you give this to me, especially after what I've tried to do?"

"I give it to you in the name of the future," Ethrain stated with a forgiving smile.

As she left the queen's chambers, she had the queer sensation that it was not so much the stone that would heal the woman from the darkness in her soul, but the forgiveness that Ethrain had offered her. It was her first glimpse of the magical powers of simple human kindness.

THE VERY next morning, before the castle came to life, Gernot and Felicia rode out alongside a waterfall deep in the Burgundian domain. They dismounted and sat in the warm sunshine.

"What a glorious day!" Felicia sighed as she looked around at the bright, clear sky. She leaned her head against him. The Burgundian prince buried his face in her fresh, forest-scented hair.

"I love you, Felicia," he whispered in spite of himself.

"Don't say that," she responded, placing a finger on his lips.

"You don't want me to love you?"

"I am yours. You know that. But you are a nobleman. You will lose face."

The hard, mask-like face of the warlord softened beneath the light of an emotion he had never felt before.

"I want you forever, Felicia."

"They will shame you . . . "

"Damn them!" Gernot shouted fiercely. "I would take you over a thousand royal women!"

A look of concern suddenly tensed his features again.

"Don't you care for me?"

"When we've made love, each time seemed like the final time," she murmured, placing a warm hand on his cheek, "because I knew I could not keep you. I am the child of peasants. And it will always be so."

"The Roman says that he has seen slaves become generals in his land! The world is changing, Felicia. Besides, I know that I have what I desire. That is enough."

"If you come to me secretly . . . "

"No! I will make you my wife and I will kill any man who breathes a word against you!"

He kissed her passionately, as though defying all the laws men had established to obstruct the natural way of love. They embraced in near frenzy.

A horse's snorting suddenly pulled them apart. Felicia gasped as she saw three barbarians from the nomadic tribes in the nearby field, seated on their horses and gazing at them intently.

"Don't move," Gernot whispered. "Maybe they'll take our horses and leave."

The barbarians bolted toward them at full speed.

"Get to the woods!" he cried out as he unsheathed his sword. He grabbed her hand and they raced across the patch of meadow leading to the trees. One of the barbarians, faster than the others, led his horse between Gernot and the forest.

"Get behind me!" the Burgundian lord shouted out.

His adversary wheeled his horse around and galloped directly upon him. Gernot awaited his attacker, spinning out of the way at the last moment and catching the horse's hind legs with his sword. The animal fell, sending its rider into the tall grass. Gernot cut him down with a single blow.

The other two men circled him. He fought viciously to keep them in front of him, but one of the barbarians slipped past. Felicia leaped in front of his horse, causing it to rear. As it rose, one of its hooves hit the young woman in the head. Gernot sliced his attacker's leg, skillfully parried his sword, and struck him in the ribs. Before the man's body hit the ground, he had turned to face his final adversary. The man charged him, raising a spear over his head. Gernot stood calmly, his steel gaze awaiting the right instant. He parried the spear and plunged his sword to the hilt into the man's chest.

The Burgundian lord whirled around to find Felicia. She lay face down in the field. He hurried to her and lifted her gently. A weak, muffled "No!" rose from the depths of his being. As he examined the head wound, a great moan rose from him and tore across the meadows like the roar of a jungle beast.

His powerful body quivered with agony. Then something broke through his grief and caught his attention.

"She breathes!"

He rushed to his horse and mounted it while holding her limp body in one arm. He galloped frantically across the quiet countryside toward the castle.

She was placed on a bed of furs and Ethrain was summoned to apply her rare skills. As she cleaned the gash, she knew that the beings of Valhalla and Jotunheim were teaching her a fearful lesson: there were countless ways for them to manifest in the physical realm and no one could fully block their entrance. No one except the prophet from a little town in the hot sands of Judea and the disciples who followed his harsh and lonely path. But such persons were more than rare. They were transfigured beings, living in the breath of the Almighty and freed from the devastating fears that forever washed up on the banks of the human psyche.

It was not long before she came out of the room to speak with Gernot.

"She lives, but I cannot say for how long or if she will ever be the same."

Gernot hurried away down the hall, hoping to escape his agony. He stopped at a window which overlooked the courtyard. It bustled with activity as the departure for the journey was underway. Wagons, horses, crowds of soldiers packed the yard and filled the spring air with joyful noise and excitement. Gernot heard Othmar call out "All is ready!"

The king would be leaving within the hour. Gernot was torn. He could not bring himself to leave his beloved in such condition nor could he watch his brothers and friends ride off into the unknown without him. Just then, Hadrian came up to him and put his hand on his shoulder with brotherly affection.

"What should I do, Hadrian? She needs me . . . Perhaps I should not go on this journey."

"She is beyond your help now, my friend. Her mind is gone. She recognizes no one."

A look of despair flooded the crusty fighter's dark eyes.

"This is hard what God has dealt me . . . "

"The mysteries of destiny are too great for us to comprehend, Gernot. But remember that she still carries your child. Ethrain says it will be safe. It will be here to come after you and carry your legacy to another generation."

"I've never known love before. Not like this. And it vanished out there in that meadow in one blow. There is nothing left for me . . . Nothing!"

"Your brothers, your men, they need you now, Gernot. What lies ahead will be very difficult and without you, the dangers awaiting them will be all the greater."

"Hagen can take care of them. And you can devise strategies for . . . "

"No one can replace Lord Gernot, brother to the King! You must come with us."

Gernot looked at him with great sadness. A glow returned to his sunken eyes as his friend's words resonated within him. He too felt that there was some mighty task to be accomplished. As he had done when physically wounded, Gernot seemed to grit his teeth against the leather strap which kept warriors from screaming when their cuts were sown. He was a man who was no stranger to pain and to the relentless obligation to push forward, to survive.

chapter seventeen

HUNGVAR WAS a vast, exotic conglomeration of Asian buildings and nomadic tents infested with peoples and animals from all parts of the known world. It was from this chaotic jumble of fragmented civilizations that the Scourge of God unleashed his merciless devastation of the earth. Ornaments from the great cities of the world, now pillaged and humiliated, hung about like the displayed corpses of the vanquished.

The largest building, sculptured by the peerless hands of Chinese craftsmen, was the residence of Attila and his Queen. In the luxurious chambers of the Kagan's bride, Kriemhild the Burgundian princess, was searching through her jewelry absentmindedly. Her magnificent brown hair fell loosely to the middle of her back and complemented her melancholic, dark eyes. Her features bore the imprint of the Germanic peoples: strong, noble, austere.

She found a necklace to her liking and tried it on before a great mirror. Satisfied, she approached her bed on which lay several silk gowns. She chose one and then wandered over to the window. The queen gazed out at the noisy court. She seemed to be impatiently awaiting for some great event to take place. A knock at the door brought her out of her introspection.

"Enter!"

A pretty young Asian girl floated into the room.

"My Queen, Lord Attila desires your presence at the feast he is holding for his generals."

Kriemhild's striking bearing suddenly transformed into that of a furious caged beast as she whirled around.

"The dog! Does he take me for one of his slave girls to show to his horde of wild tribesmen? I am not his concubine! I am his Queen!"

"Oh, you must, my Queen!" the servant-girl said in terror. "It would be a great insult to disobey him! Who knows what he might do!"

Kriemhild was silent, her grim expression hardening into the desperate resignation she had lived with these past ten years. Through the window, the echo of raucous merriment drifted in, warning of the humiliation and disgust she would have to endure. She had never learned to tolerate the brutality and savagery of men who lived by pillaging. Yet she had called this fate upon herself in her desperate search for the power to avenge the deed which had so crushed her soul.

In the Hun banquet hall, belly dancers moved gracefully around the vast room as the leaders of the most terrifying armies known to humanity laughed and drank. In every corner, against every wall stood sinister guards always alert and ready to strike. At the far end of the crowded room sat Attila. Even from a distance, he emanated a malefic magnetism which turned the blood cold. He was powerful of body and of mind. His eyes had the piercing but faraway look of one compelled to fulfill inner urges that influenced the very movement of history.

Next to him sat Magag, the Hun leader who had visited the Burgundians. He watched the scene with the eagerness of a coiled snake. Big events were about to take place and he felt himself an intricate part of what lay ahead. He awaited Kriemhild impatiently, knowing that she too was longing for the time when her pain would finally be eased. Magag was not interested in her vengeful motives, but he had been searching for an opportunity to shift the balances of power. Attila was aging, and had accepted his first great defeat when he pulled back from Italy. His sons and his brother Bleda were hovering around him like hungry vultures waiting for a corpse.

Magag alone knew of the sad queen's intentions and recognized that the intensity of her passion was nothing less than madness. But it was the kind of madness which changed the course of events. It had that relentless, bottomless quality which would let nothing interfere with its desire. The cunning warlord had found his murder weapon in Attila's very bed. The storm this woman was prepared to stir up could quite possibly send the Hun empire into civil war. And that was exactly what the ambitious commander was hoping for.

KRIEMHILD MADE her entrance into the hall, proud and defiant. A smile split the Kagan's features into a grimace more terrifying than his usual deadly glare.

"Tell me, my valiant warriors! Have you ever seen a more beautiful woman, a more worthy queen?"

The men cheered as Kriemhild turned scarlet, feeling the lusting eyes of three hundred thieves and killers. She walked slowly down the aisle between the tables and cushions separating her from her king. At every step, her humiliation left her as the thrill of power shot through her entire body. Her feline sensuality and desperate need for a love she knew she had lost forever created fire in the least of her gestures. Though she felt herself fondled and raped in the presence of these men, awareness of the mesmerizing control she exerted over them all was a healing balm to her suffering.

She had long ago lost the qualities of innocence that

had been the hallmark of her beauty. Her face had turned hard and bitter, and deep wrinkles were beginning to scar her features with the marks of a hopeless soul. Kriemhild had sold herself like a common prostitute, but she had tasted a sweet victory when sheer coincidence, or so it seemed, had tossed her in the arms of Attila the Hun. She satisfied him as no woman ever had because of the repressed frenzy which accompanied all her actions. It was as though she lived daily with the death of her beloved Siegfried and was impaled on Hagen's spear.

Only one thought, one god, filled her mind and soul. Vengeance. Once she saw the dead body of her lover's killer laid out before her in all its helplessness and weakness, she would find satisfaction. That is how she had seen Siegfried's corpse, the man who had become her joy and her very life.

On an icy, moonlit night, she was awakened by an owl's plaintive cry. She had been dreaming a dreadful nightmare, the kind that brought demonic fear to the surface and held its victim in a breathless grip. She wasn't sure whether the screech of the night creature had echoed in her dream or in the outside world. The bird's cry seemed to carry a message, a warning of impending doom.

Then she heard the faint sound of hooves passing beneath her window. She was flooded with the certainty that some unspeakable tragedy had taken place. Kriemhild hesitated before going to the window, as though something within refused to look upon the horror awaiting her. Yet she was urged on by a compelling need to face the onslaught of the future.

The princess rushed to her balcony but stopped in time to remain hidden from the gloomy figures gliding beneath her. The obscure shadows which enveloped them seemed to veil in mourning cloth a deed too hideous for the eye to view. The very darkness howled in shame at the horrid crime. The young woman peered over the stones separating her from the sight that would devastate her soul forever. She felt the shiver of the icy night, its blackness and omnipresence penetrating beyond the marrow of her bones into the recesses of her spirit.

Then she saw them. The blond locks of her lover made blue in the ghostly moonlight. They dangled at the side of his horse like the strands of a broken puppet wrecked beyond repair. All that life, so abundant and overflowing, so lusting to carve a place for itself in the sagas of history, was drained out like the precious liquid from some forsaken golden jar. A thick, black substance trailed behind it, leaking from the corpse of the man she loved more than herself.

Here in Hungvar she could still hear the owl's screech that had never stopped echoing in the smoldering ruins of her spirit. Even the night haunted her as the other witness of the odious vision. It possessed and throttled her like some slow devil's garrot, and she was convinced that only the exorcism of vengeance would free her. She had sold everything to the demons for the sake of striking back at those who had caused her such inconsolable grief.

She stood before the emperor of slaughter, her husband. She would willingly undergo this degradation knowing that the day was approaching, the day for which she had given herself as bride to the dark forces that played upon humans as living flutes in their battle song against the powers of the higher realms.

Her mind's eye saw the scene she had created through her scheming: a long file of men, horses and wagons in an Alpine landscape headed by her brother the King and his closest friend Hagen, Lord of Trony, murderer of the man who was to be her husband. She knew that what she was seeing was no weavings of the imagination, but the clairvoyant perception of a real event. As she rejoiced over the fulfillment of the desire that had consumed her, she sensed the oppressive, frightful presence of a vaster world at the door of her soul, forcing her into actions precipitating events completely unknown to her. It was a dizzying, heart-pounding experience to feel the cold shadow of an all-powerful force seeking entrance into the world through her own festering inner wounds. But she had gone too far, wept too often and hated too long. There was not turning back now. There was not even the time for a last glimpse at the sweet life and happy home that she knew before the appearance of the Nordic prince. She had taken a demon's hand in the bleakness of her desolation and would follow her destiny blindly to the very end.

THE GLORIOUS colors of pristine nature were a striking contrast to the dark currents carrying events to their ultimate encounter. The Burgundians found great excitement in their journey of discovery, their great adventure into new territories. Only two solitary figures who kept to themselves and wandered on the outskirts of the caravan were aware of the fateful winds hurling them onward. Hadrian and Ethrain traveled with the resignation and solemnity of visionaries heading to their own funerals. Neither knew the details of what lay ahead, but they both understood that whatever was to come would manifest itself in a cataclysmic way. The lovers were especially conscious of the fact that their happiness hung in the balance. Either they would be destroyed or a future of great promise awaited them.

They too thrilled at the sweeping grandeur of Nature as they crossed the mountain passes. But the very magnificence of what they saw reminded them that greater forces than they were in command of life. It would take more than a Roman's courage and the mysterious gifts of a druid's child to accomplish the act that would decide the course of history's next stage.

Beneath a panorama of scintillating stars, celestial beings were present to honor the nobility of these men who were voyaging to their doom. The Burgundians sat around great campfires, huddled close together for warmth and telling of past glories.

"Speak of your victory over the Danes!" Martin, the son of Thorin, called out.

"That is a tale! How we showed them what Burgundians were made of! Our armies were led by Siegfried who later married my sister," Giselher cried out.

"We would have won, boy!" Hagen stated emphatically in a booming voice that rang through the night.

Silence fell over the men. It was commonly known that Hagen hated the legendary prince and it was quietly assumed that only the great knight could have overcome the legendary prince.

"Tomorrow, we cross into Aleman land so we had better rest," he finally added to break the unease which wailed louder than the whistling mountain chill.

THE SUN rose over the snow-capped mountains as the travelers came upon a great river. They halted and let their horses ease their thirst as a strategy was determined for the crossing.

Dankwart trotted upstream away from the group and heard a splashing sound at the bend in the river. He dismounted and crawled through the rocks and foliage. Flat on his stomach, he parted the bushes and found himself staring at a young woman bathing in the shallow waters. He turned away, ashamed of invading her privacy, in time to see a huge silhouette standing over him and raising a heavy ax.

Dankwart jumped up but slipped on the mossy rock

and fell on his back. The ax came smashing down. He evaded it by inches and felt the burn of sparks flying from the impact of blade and stone. Dankwart grabbed the man's leg and wrestled him to the ground. The big woodsman easily rolled over him and grabbed him by the neck. Dankwart shouted for help as he took hold of the huge hands blocking the air from his lungs. Just as he drifted out of consciousness, he heard the crashing footsteps of a powerful oncomer.

Hagen swung the man around and crashed his fist against his face. The burly man fell back and rolled down a small hill, landing in the river. Hagen rushed down after him, lifted him up in his arms and hurled him against the rocks. The man fell to his knees, but still attempted to struggle. Hagen pulled out his sword.

"Don't kill him, Hagen!" Dankwart cried out. "It was my fault."

He pointed to the girl hurrying out of the water, trying to cover herself. Hagen looked back at the man and relaxed his warrior's stance.

"Can you help us cross the river?" he growled.

"I am a boatman . . . But this is the land of Lord Gelfrat. Strangers are not welcomed."

"Take us across, boatman!" the Lord of Trony roared.

"Believe me, my Lords, you will bring the wrath of a monster upon yourselves."

"If this monster rouses our anger, he will find himself floating face down in this river!"

Gernot galloped up to them, sword in hand.

"What is it, Hagen?"

"We have found ourselves a boatman, Gernot. He tells us the lord of these mountains does not like strangers."

"We shall have to teach him the manners of hospitality!"

"That is just what I was explaining to this man," Hagen responded.

They followed the boatman to the edge of the water where a long raft lay hidden in the reeds. He untied it and rowed the barge toward them. The Burgundians splashed about in the water as they sought to get their horses onto the platform. Giselher was one of the first on the boat and hurried to its far side to get a good look at this unknown land. He was eager to prove himself as a warrior.

They reached the other side as the boatman fought the currents and kept a worried eye on the banks. The men galloped off the barge to the muddy edge of the new territory.

"Tell the men to keep their helmets tightened and their swords ready," Hagen whispered to Othmar as they headed into the thick woods.

King Gunther removed his horned helmet and wiped his brow. He carefully placed it back on his head and readied it for combat, a mechanical action repeated many times before battle. The advance group moved deeper into the forest. Even the bird cries increased the tension as they moved forward. They were strange sounds from unfamiliar creatures. Such alien surroundings filled them with a dread they had not known before.

"Something moved behind those trees, Hagen!" King Gunther whispered hoarsely.

Hagen glanced toward the trees. A shadow disappeared into the woods.

"They're here! Make ready!" Hagen muttered to Gernot who passed the word back.

"I have a feeling we are being surrounded," King Gunther told his friend as he unsheathed his sword.

Giselher rode up beside them. This was his first smell of battle and his nerves were responding differently than he had expected. The silence of the forest suddenly erupted with thundering hooves.

"Here they come!" Hagen shouted as he raised his great sword.

From all directions, ragged men crashed through the brush and hurled themselves upon them. Their attackers looked more animal than human with their crude weapons, thick beards and heavy fur clothing. Howls and groans mixed with the sharp clash of steel. The Burgundians swung their heavy swords and charged their adversaries fearlessly in the narrow spaces of the forest path.

Horses stumbled and reared, sparks flew from shields as hatchets crashed against them. Giselher fell and scrambled away from his attacker. But he was forced to turn and face the man who towered over him. He fought frantically, trying to apply all that he had learned. The beast-like man soon overpowered him and cut him across the face. A club smashed into Giselher's helmet and dented it. The prince dropped against the rocky ground and watched his attacker raise his heavy weapon over his head.

Out of nowhere, Jeoffrey appeared before him and swung wildly at the barbarian, opening a deep gash in his head. The man stumbled backward as the son of Thorin cut him down with a vicious blow. He helped Giselher to his feet. They gazed at each other for a split second. The roar of battle and blur of action seemed to stop, making way for a sudden cleansing of all animosity and the birth of a new friendship.

Gelfrat, the commander of the mountain men, charged Hagen and furiously swung his ax at him. Hagen's shield cracked under the blows and he dove away to evade a fatal swing, falling from his horse. He managed to get away from the tramping hooves, but could not find his sword. Gelfrat, an evil grin on his face, swung his hatchet and knocked Hagen's helmet off. With lightning speed, Hagen grabbed his adversary's leg and threw him from his mount. They wrestled and tumbled into a little ravine. Gelfrat got away from him and grabbed a heavy branch from the ground. He beat Hagen as hard as he could. But the Lord of Trony kept approaching, barely protecting himself from the blows. He finally grabbed the branch as it struck at him and tore it out of Gelfrat's hands.

The two men looked for their swords. They faced each other for the final onslaught, knowing that one of them would not walk away from this encounter. Using all his legendary might, Hagen attacked and showered him with blows that would kill an ox. The barbaric lord was soon overwhelmed and fell on his face, lifeless.

A mountain man rushed up behind Hagen and was about to avenge his fallen leader when Gernot cut him down. He handed Hagen his helmet and hurried off. The Lord of Trony adjusted his headgear and looked back at the bloody corpse of his enemy. There was a tiredness in his eyes, a grey cloud of weariness which had witnessed too many seasons of bloodshed. Somehow, in the dust of the embattled clearing, he knew that his end was not far, and he longed for it and the peace that he would find someday.

Finally, the mountain men were routed, leaving many dead behind. King Gunther's warriors, drenched in blood and sweat, gathered together. As they bandaged their wounds and counted their dead, Hagen called out in a loud voice:

"We must reach Polcharn on the other side of these mountains. Our friend Lord Ruedeger will let us rest there."

Hadrian rode up to them, having heard the skirmish from the river bank where he was supervising the crossing. The forest path was carpeted with bodies. It was a sight with which he was all too familiar. But the gruesome vision vividly revealed that they were getting nearer to the source of greatest evil, the dark outpost that the forces of the underworld had made their own. He knew that Polcharn would be the last rest these valiant men would ever find.

chapter eighteen

"WE'VE ARRIVED! Lord Ruedeger's court is just beyond those trees!"

A ripple of excitement ran through the ranks of the tired, hungry men.

"Polcharn is the last outpost before entering the land of the Huns," King Gunther announced.

"No more of this!" Ortwin shouted as he pulled out a sack of dried meat from his saddle bag and held it up in disgust.

"And we can sleep in soft beds for a change!" Dankward added joyfully.

"I hope my old friend Ruedeger is as happy to see us as we are to see him," the king observed.

They descended into a meadow leading toward the small fortress lost in a maze of forest. A number of the lord's men rode out to escort them to the court. The gates were covered with the curious as the visitors entered into the courtyard. They had seldom seen the noble features of these western warriors. Lord Ruedeger hurried up to greet them. He was a rotund little man, gone soft after years of living under the shadow of his conquerors.

"Welcome, King Gunther! It gives me great pleasure to see you again."

"Greetings, Lord Ruedeger!" the king replied with a beaming face. "How have you fared these past ten years?"

"As you can see, this is a peaceful country. My only struggle has been with boredom."

The Burgundians dismounted as their hosts hurried to assist them.

"Sir Hagen, it is an honor to have you as my guest. Word has already reached us of Gelfrat's death at your hands."

Hagen acknowledged the acclaim with a disinterested nod of the head.

"And Sir Gernot! You have not changed since our last meeting."

"A few more scars," Gernot pointed out.

"I would rather have them than this barrel I now carry," the jovial host stated as he patted himself on his protruding shape.

"And who might this be? Not little Giselher?" he exclaimed.

"Himself, Mylord," the young prince said with pride.

"You were but an infant when I last saw you. You have grown into quite a handsome lad."

"A lad?" Ortwin cried out. "He fancies himself a man already just because he faced a few beasts with clubs!"

Lord Ruedeger's daughter appeared at the top of the steps. The Burgundians quieted at her sight.

"My daughter, Helen, the emerald of my treasures."

The men bowed. Giselher was mesmerized by her graceful air and soft features.

"You must hunger after such a voyage," the host exclaimed as he looked over his dusty guests.

"You have guessed correctly, Lord Ruedeger!" Ortwin shouted with glee.

"Well, let us lose no more time! If your men will follow my servants, they will show them baths and quarters. I will see to it that your animals are cared for."

He put his arm around King Gunther.

"Come, my noble friend. Let us enjoy together the fine offerings of these forests."

The banquet hall was filled with exotic oriental decor that had been given to Lord Ruedeger from the Huns. The Burgundians were astonished with the fineries which were so foreign to their rugged, simple ways.

"You have seen the world, Lord Ruedeger," Dankwart stated as they feasted.

"Not all of it, unfortunately. I have yet to see the Holy lands."

"The Holy lands?" King Gunther questioned, surprised. "Have you become a follower of the new religion?"

"No, it would not be wise for a close vassal and hunting companion of the Scourge of God to become a disciple of another Master."

"Attila has never shown anger toward my faith. The Huns believe in nothing, so nothing worries them."

"Everything worries them," Lord Ruedeger responded. "When the wind howls, they think they hear the cry of phantoms and demons. They even build little huts to lodge the spirits of their ancestors."

"How interesting . . . " Dankwart murmured aloud.

"Dankwart is still a pagan," King Gunther retorted apologetically. "Not all of my people have come out of darkness."

"Well, these matters are too complicated for me," their host stated as he chewed on a large chunk of meat.

"Have you seen our sister these past ten years?" Gernot asked, uncertain that he wanted an answer.

"Only twice, although I have visited Attila many times. She rarely leaves her chambers. It is said that she prefers solitude to festivities."

"This is not like the sister I knew. Does Attila not make her happy?" Gernot inquired with concern.

"Her wish is his command! He truly loves her, to the

extant that such a man can have feelings. And I can tell you that his love has not diminished these ten years."

He turned to King Gunther, eyes shining with a sense of loyalty.

"If you'll remember, I swore to you when I presented her to the Kagan that I would make certain everything she wanted was hers. I have kept my oath."

"Has she ever asked for news of her brothers?" the king wondered with deep sadness seeping from his tired eyes.

"I cannot say," his old friend told him honestly. "But if she asks that you travel all this way to see her, I would think that she has missed you."

An awkward silence warned the host that something was amiss and he quickly changed the subject.

"Will you grace me with your presence for more than a day, Mylords? Perhaps we might arrange for a hunt."

"We will accept your hospitality, Lord Ruedeger. We need to repair our wagons. It has been a strenuous journey over your mountains," the king said.

"Then let us toast to the merry times awaiting us. And to your sister."

Everyone toasted. Hagen did not raise his goblet. Hadrian had the strange sensation that the old warrior was wishing he had been cut down by the mountain men and that his journey was over.

That afternoon, the Burgundians rested at the home of their host. King Gunther and his friend stood on the ramparts overlooking the peaceful scene. By a pond in the distance, they could see Giselher and Helen walking side by side, followed by her governess.

"You have a beautiful daughter," the king observed with a smile.

"There are few noblemen here to court her. I sometimes fear that she will grow old with no one to love in these lands so far from civilization."

"It seems that my little brother has found her to be interesting company."

"It would be a great honor to be tied in marriage to your valorous people."

"You are hasty, Ruedeger. Although, they do make a fine couple."

"My lands are rich. The dowry would be a handsome one."

"It would be, indeed. But that will be Giselher's decision, not mine."

"Certainly," the rotund host was quick to add, barely capable of concealing his hope.

The king leaned on the ramparts and watched his men down below. Hagen was off riding by himself. Ortwin sat under a tree, digesting the feast. On another ridge, Hadrian and Gernot rode slowly through the countryside.

"Quiet country," Gernot stated.

"We are on the edge of wilderness. To the North of these forests live only wild beasts, scattered barbarians, and perhaps a few holy men," Hadrian mused as he peered at the horizon.

"The Romans have never come this far east?"

"No, our legions could not maneuver in such forests. This is no man's land, between two empires. "

"How is it that Lord Ruedeger came to live here?"

"I've heard it said that Attila himself commanded him to establish his court here. A resting place between Hungvar and the rest of the world."

"All the lands to the east belong to the Huns?"

"If not to them, then to demons."

The companions came into a clearing overlooking a small field where a woman and two children toiled. As they approached, the children ran to their mother who picked up a large pitchfork.

"We won't harm you," Gernot called out.

"You're crushing my crops!"

The Burgundian prince looked down and moved his horse away.

"We are guests of Lord Ruedeger. Have you any water for thirsty travellers?"

The woman stared at them suspiciously. Hadrian's horse began to chew on her vegetables.

"Pull your horse back, Hadrian. She'll cut his nuzzle off. Come, woman! Is there no hospitality in these regions?"

"Where do you come from?" she asked, still holding up her sharp tool.

"Far to the west of those mountains. Do we look so frightening?"

The woman hesitated, then finally lowered her weapon.

"Not many men travel through here unless they are thieves or . . . "

"We are noblemen," Gernot interrupted, "loyal warriors of King Gunther, Lord of the Burgundians."

She hugged her children close to her and turned toward the hut partly hidden in the woods.

"Come," she said quietly.

They dismounted and followed her. The children studied them with great curiosity.

"What is your name, boy?" Gernot asked gently.

The boy hurried to catch up with his mother. Inside the two children huddled in a corner of the small, dark room as the mother poured a jug of water into two wooden cups. She placed the goblets before them and remained standing as they sat at the crude table.

"Where is your man?" Gernot inquired.

"He left me," she answered coldly.

"How long ago?"

"I have stopped counting."

"So you live here alone in this wilderness?"

"I have my children."

Hadrian looked over at the children and smiled at them. The little girl smiled back.

"Who hunts for your food?"

"My son is learning to use the bow."

"Did you catch that rabbit?" Hadrian asked, pointing to a rabbit skin on the wall.

The boy nodded shyly.

"With that bow?"

Hadrian gestured to a crude little bow in a corner of the room.

"You must have a sharp eye. Did your father teach you?"

"I did," the woman responded solemnly.

"You are a strong woman," Gernot observed.

"What is your name?" she asked with new interest.

"They call me Gernot. And this is my friend, Hadrian Aldius, a Roman citizen."

He extended his hand toward the children.

"Don't be afraid. We'll not eat you."

The boy approached. Gernot placed his hand on his shoulder.

"You're a strong lad. You'll make a fine warrior. Would he not, Hadrian?"

"Certainly," the Roman responded warmly.

"Perhaps I can show you a few things. So that you can better protect your mother and sister. Would you like that?"

"Yes!" the boy answered excitedly.

"Ah! He does have a tongue!" Gernot exclaimed with a smile. "Have you a staff, boy?"

The child hurried into the shadows and returned with a long branch.

"Oak wood. The best. With a bit of knowledge, you can fend off several men at a time with this weapon."

Gernot looked up at the boy's mother with a questioning look. She nodded, trying not to show appreciation.

"Come along," Gernot said to the boy as he left the hut.

Hadrian sat at the table and studied the mother and daughter.

"Where are you headed?" she finally asked.

"Hungvar."

"You are friends of the Huns?"

"No one is friend of the Huns. Attila's bride is the King's sister. We go to see her."

"Do you trust those devils?"

"Huns are men as we are. They die as easily."

Hadrian seemed to drift off for a moment as he reflected on what lay ahead. The sweet peacefulness of the surroundings was like an ominous silence before a terrible storm.

"There will be no trouble. We are guests of the Kagan," he added to reassure himself. "You have a pretty daughter."

"Her father was a Saxon," the mother said with pride.

"Can you not send her to Lord Ruedeger's court? She will be safer there."

"I need her to work the field. There is so much to be done if we are to eat every day."

Their conversation was suddenly interrupted by the boy's cries.

"Mother! Mother!"

They hurried outside to find the boy and Gernot facing each other.

"Look! Look at what I can do!"

Gernot prepared to charge him.

"Hold the staff further down," he advised.

The boy readied for the attack. Gernot rushed him and he jumped to the side, hitting the Burgundian prince in the stomach and back of the head with a quick motion. The boy turned to his mother, beaming.

"He learns quickly!" Gernot muttered as he rubbed his head.

The mother smiled, perhaps for the first time in years.

"Now I'll show you how to fight two men," Gernot said with enthusiasm.

"We had better return to court. They'll be waiting for us," Hadrian reminded him.

"Wait!" the boy cried out. "I want to learn!"

Gernot looked into the child's pleading eyes and felt an ache in his heart.

"I'll come back in the morning. If your mother will allow it."

They both turned to the woman who nodded with deep gratitude.

"I want you to practice those moves. Tomorrow, we'll spend more time together."

"You promise?" the boy asked in near desperation.

"You have the word of a Burgundian prince."

The little girl approached Hadrian and tugged on his clothing.

"Will you return also?"

"You've made a friend, Roman," Gernot observed with a smile. "If I teach you to ride my horse, will you be my friend as well?"

"Oh yes, I love horses!" she exclaimed with glee.

"Very well. We shall do it then!"

They mounted their horses. Hadrian noticed the longing in the veteran warrior's eyes. The children waved and the mother's eyes filled with tears of thankfulness. Gernot could hardly bring himself to turn his back on them. He yearned for a family life that had always eluded him.

Accompanied by her three ladies in waiting and her old governess, Helen made her way through the peaceful countryside to a crystal-clear lake where Giselher and the two brothers were fishing. The girls giggled as they whispered over the looks of their handsome guests.

On an agreed upon signal, the young ladies moved away and Helen approached Giselher. The old governess' features took on a stern expression as she watched her closely. Martin was the first to notice her.

"It's Lady Helen!"

Giselher turned discreetly as he continued fishing.

"That old woman is with her again. I'll never be able to speak with her alone."

The two brothers glanced at each other with the same idea in mind. Helen came up to them, followed by the governess.

"Good day," Giselher said awkwardly, feeling his heart aflame as his gaze fell on the beautiful young woman.

"Good day, Prince Giselher."

"We have been fishing today."

"You have?" Helen responded, surprised that he would say such an obvious thing. She was thrilled at his awkwardness.

"Have you caught anything?"

"No . . . " the prince answered as though it were a blow to his manhood.

Helen realized that it would be up to her to take control of the situation. She turned to her governess.

"We are going to walk along the lake shore."

"Stay in my sight," the grim old woman stated coldly.

Giselher leaped to his feet and followed the ravishing woman as she headed away from the group. The brothers winked at each other and Martin jumped in the water.

The governess let out a scream of terror and hurried to them. Giselher turned around and was about to rush to their aid when Helen took his arm.

"Can't your friends swim?" she asked with a twinkle.

"Certainly, they can!" he responded, realizing what they were up to.

They hurried off as the governess took hold of a branch to help the brothers. They pulled and yelled and in the chaos the old woman fell in the water with them. The sons of Thorin quickly helped her out onto the bank.

"You must change, Mylady," Jeoffrey said with great concern. "You'll catch your death of cold."

"But Helen . . . "

"She's be well cared for. She's in royal hands, you know."

The brothers smiled at each other as they accompanied the woman back to the castle.

From the ramparts, Ethrain looked on, delighted by the scene. She knew the two young people would discover the secrets of love that evening and establish a relationship that would have lasting consequences. Nearby, Hagen stared at the horizon in silence. He felt her gaze and turned to her.

"Beyond those hills lies Hungvar, Attila's court," he mumbled.

"Are you worried, Sir Hagen?" she asked as she studied his deep, tense wrinkles.

"I worry for my friends . . . "

The gloomy man turned away and looked back at the darkening sky. Ethrain could sense that he had resigned himself to his fate, accepting the punishment his crime required. He had understood long ago that the legendary prince marked them with some frightful future from the very day his destiny became intertwined with theirs.

KING GUNTHER and his men mounted their horses, preparing for departure. Servants offered them gifts from their lord.

"I hope to see you shortly, King Gunther. We'll have festivities ready for your return."

"You are very kind, Lord Ruedeger. We'll stay longer on the journey homeward."

Ethrain watched Giselher and Helen gaze at each other longingly. She looked away to hide her tears, knowing they would not be coming back this way. With a last farewell, the king and his men rode out of the courtyard.

They entered the woods that would lead them to the other side of the mountains.

"Giselher has not said a word since our departure. Might he be ill?" Ortwin asked with a wink to Gernot.

"Would you not be ill as well if you left behind such a charming creature?" Gernot pointed out.

"I've never seen him under the spell of a woman before."

"He's only known . . . "

The words stuck in Gernot's throat as his eyes fell upon a small building whose roof was shaped in the sloping oriental style.

"What is that?" he exclaimed.

"A temple," Hadrian observed.

"A temple to whom?"

"To a god they call Buddha. Their ceremonies consist in sitting in deep trances. I've never understood it."

"Did you ever try?" Ethrain asked him with a slight reproach. She remembered only too well how difficult it had been for him to accept the teachings of Mallor.

"Might we stop to look inside?" Gernot asked breathlessly, as though some great revelation awaited his seeking spirit.

"Why?" Ortwin called out angrily. "We have no use for their gods."

"Gernot wants to speak to those eastern spirits," King Gunther said with a smile. "Go on, brother. Beware of demons with slanted eyes."

The men moved on as Gernot headed toward the temple. Hadrian and Ethrain pulled their horses out of the caravan and watched the prince approach the building. He dismounted and examined the intricately sculptured walls and the exotic, frightful statues guarding the entrance. He eyed the wooden guards suspiciously, but they did not hamper his curiosity.

He entered and was astounded by the sight. The walls were covered with highly detailed frescos of demons and gods. A dim sunlight filtered through the cracks in the wood and revealed to him dream images of Asian myths.

He moved further into the dark temple and came upon a huge golden statue of the Buddha. A mist of incense burned before it, rising like the prayers of believers. Gernot instinctively dropped to his knees. The half-closed eyes of the meditating statue hypnotized him with their other-worldly calm.

He noticed food by the foot of the statue and came closer to examine the ornaments. Then he saw the silhouette standing as still as a statue in the shadows of the room. It was a monk, head shaved and wearing a strange toga. Gernot did not dare move, feeling as though he were intruding on the sacred ground of another people. He finally stepped backward, hoping to slip out of the temple and get away from the mysterious universe contained in these walls.

"Are you a Goth?" the monk asked unexpectedly.

"Burgundian."

The man in cloth stepped into the dim light. In his hand, he held burning incense. Through the scented smoke, Gernot could perceive eyes filled with peace.

"What brings you to my temple?"

"I . . . I am on my way to Hungvar. I was curious."

The monk came closer and studied his face.

"You are thirsting for spiritual knowledge."

Gernot did not respond, but his expression revealed the truth of the man's statement.

"You are far from your homeland. If you stay, I can show you the way to great tranquility and ecstasy in communion with Atman."

"I am a warrior, not a priest," Gernot said with anger.

But then his voice softened. "Who is Atman?"

"He is the life force behind all things."

The good man smiled at Gernot and gently put his hand on his shoulder.

"I see an unhappy future for you, mighty warrior. I offer you the choice of staying here where you will find peace and understanding far beyond anything in your primitive world. I can see that you are a man of thought. Why live by the sword?"

"You can foretell the future, holy man?"

"You must not return to your friends. They are heading for their doom."

Gernot was shaken by his words. He took a step backward.

"Stay, friend," the monk said softly. "Only here will you find peace with yourself."

"I cannot leave my friends. If they are to die, then I will die with them!"

He hurried out of the dark temple and found himself face to face with Hadrian and Ethrain. They were solemn, knowing what the monk had told him. Gernot could hardly contain his emotion as the monk's prophecy reverberated in his soul. Looking at the grim foreigners, he was suddenly struck by a new insight.

"What have you brought down upon us?"

They stared at him silently as he mounted his horse.

"Why don't you stay?" Ethrain asked him.

"If we are to walk into the jaws of death, then I will be the first to sacrifice my life!"

"But you don't know why this must be," Hadrian said.

"I don't want to know! I just want to be with my companions when they will need me most!" he cried out as he kicked his horse into a gallop and vanished in the woods.

chapter nineteen

A HERALD quickly made his way through the bustling crowd, his pony bumping into haggling merchants and warriors in the market place of Attila's court. He leaped from his mount before it came to a stop at the steps of the largest structure in the camp. Its sharply sloping roof resembled claws from a preying beast aimed at the heads of the passersby. Ancient gods and demons from half-forgotten religions surrounded the vast city as though seeking to ward off the forces of light that resisted the onslaught of the Huns. This was Attila's domain.

The herald raced up the stairs and through the giant red doors, passed a legion of armed Hun warriors, the best in an empire of naturally skilled fighters. Monkeys screeched as they nervously watched on from the shoulders of massive statues.

At the top of an inner stairway, the herald came upon the sinister figure of Magag, the Hun commander. He observed the message-bearer with great interest. The man hurried down a corridor and knocked at a chamber door. A female voice allowed entrance and the herald dashed into the room.

Kriemhild was having her thick locks braided in the fashion of the Germanic peoples by three oriental domestics.

"Speak!" she let out with intense anticipation.

"My Queen, your brothers will soon be at the gates!"

The square features of the sad queen flushed red with the heat of excitement. Some demonic furnace had been lit in the recesses of her spirit. The time had come!

"Hurry, Cyra, fetch my tunic! I must look my best!"

The colossal gates opened and the caravan of Burgundian warriors entered in clouds of dust. They gazed silently at the strange eastern architecture and the alien faces of peoples they had never seen before. In the ocean of movement, structures, tents, statues, stables, they could detect Roman tunics and Visigoth dress. The world was here in this sprawling, chaotic mass of humanity. This was the gathering storm of the future, the molten lava from some demonic volcano threatening to inundate and cover the earth for all time.

An awesome silence descended like some monstrous shadow and quieted every person for as far as the eye could see. Everyone stared at the foreign warlords riding into their innermost sanctuary.

Hagen glared at the hordes around him with dark suspicion as the slow processional meandered toward the giant building squatting at the center of the human waves. A heavy man dressed in the simple gear of the Hun soldier came out of the building to greet them.

"Welcome to Hungvar, Mylords! I am Bleda, brother of the Kagan. I trust your journey was a pleasant one."

King Gunther made some ceremonial reply, seeking to maintain his composure in the ear-piercing tension that stretched across the vast courtyards.

"My brother is eager to greet you, Mylords. But I must ask you to leave your swords with the servants. No weapons are allowed in the Hall."

"We will not be without our swords!"

Hagen's mighty voice exploded with defiance. The Burgundian lords looked at their longtime companion in stunned surprise.

"You need not worry," the oriental man said with a diplomatic smile. "There is nothing to fear, Sires. It is our custom not to carry weapons in the Hall."

King Gunther unbuckled his sword.

"We must respect their custom, Hagen."

"I will not, Mylord," the gloomy warrior mumbled as he heard the crash of future battles already pounding in his ears.

"We must comply!" Gernot counseled urgently. "We're just a bit outnumbered, don't you think, Hagen?"

"Then I will wait outside, on these steps!" Hagen announced for all to hear.

"Why such hostility, Sire?" the Hun leader asked with a deadly look in his almond eyes.

Dankwart rode up next to Hagen, fierce determination frozen on his face. He had the expression of one who accepted that he would die young.

"I will wait with you, Sire," he said proudly to the old warrior.

"The Lord of Trony cannot be without his sword. It is his custom. He means no disrespect," King Gunther announced loudly to his angry host.

On his signal, the Burgundian lords dismounted and unbuckled their great swords, handing them to servants who bowed as they took the weapons. Hagen and Dankwart stood aside as their friends headed up the stairs toward their encounter with the conqueror of continents.

High up in the exotic and graceful curves of the building, from a window hidden beneath the slopes of the gigantic roof, Kriemhild watched the arrival. She spotted Hagen immediately and kept her gaze on him throughout. This was the man whose death she had wished for every day and every night for ten agonizing years. His demise would absolve her of all the humiliations she had willingly accepted.

"Mylords!" Bleda announced in the Hall where guests were received.

Curtains were drawn back across a magnificent carpet.

"Descendant of the great Nimrod, King of the Huns, Goths, Alans, Itimari, Medes, and countless smaller tribes, ruler over most of the earth, our mighty Kagan—Attila!"

From the shadows of the antechamber, a great bull of a man stepped forward. His black, unkempt locks were turning grey and his large muscles were beginning to sag beneath the weight of years, but his almond-shaped eyes pierced across space like a striking serpent and penetrated their prey with rare power.

Hadrain stood in the back of the room, holding Ethrain's hand. It wasn't that he lacked courage now that the mission was to be completed, but the shock of finding himself in the den of Rome's ultimate enemy shook him to the core. He had to force himself to accept the reality before him. Saved from a fateful shipwreck on the other side of the world, he had been hurled back from those desolate rocks among the very people he had sought to escape.

His dreams and the witch's crystal had foretold this moment when he would look upon the Scourge of God. The noble features of his friend and mentor, General Aetius, entered his mind. The great soldier had given his life to defeat the Huns. He had understood their danger to the world, having been brought up among them as a kidnapped child only to become their mightiest nemesis. Now Hadrian was called upon to accomplish what no legion had been able to do.

Ethrain stood close to him. After all they had been through, she knew that this was the final obstacle to their happiness. To kill the lion in his lair and to escape alive was the price of their freedom! But she was certain that the great Attila was made of flesh and blood despite his awesome power. The demons used him as a common slave to fulfill their purposes on earth. The man who was striking death blows on the Roman Empire could be stopped with six inches of sharp steel.

"And his queen, Kriemhild!"

Kriemhild entered solemnly and came to her master's side, taking his arm. Her brothers gasped with joy but restrained themselves to follow the ceremonial requirements.

"My people welcome you and your companions, King Gunther," Attila stated with cool detachment.

"I am honored to stand in your presence, noble Attila," the Burgundian king responded with sincerity.

He turned to his sister and his eyes glowed with tears. "Kriemhild . . . "

Ethrain studied the stoic woman closely and saw with horror that her heart was dead.

"My brothers," she said with a faint, forced smile.

She approached them as they reached for her awkwardly.

"Can this be Giselher?" she wondered as she looked upon the young prince.

He smiled with embarrassment, not recognizing anything familiar in her gaze.

"You haven't changed much, Kriemhild," Gernot said with the pride of an older brother.

"I thank the gods that I've been in good health."

Their eyes crossed for a moment and they both felt the icy discomfort of recognizing that they had grown far apart.

"Your beard is turning white, Gunther!" she exclaimed with artificial excitement as she turned to her favorite brother.

"The worries of a king," he said with a sad smile.

"How fares our mother?"

"She still has her strength," Gernot stated gratefully.

"She sends you her love and regrets that she cannot

have the pleasure of seeing you again," the king added dutifully.

"I have missed her so," Kriemhild murmured more to herself than to her brothers, as a mist of deep melancholy gleamed in her eyes.

"Were there not others in your party?"

Attila's commanding voice fell on them like a menacing storm.

"They fell ill during the journey and are unable to join us on this happy occasion."

King Gunther did his best to make his way through the lie. Bleda said nothing, unwilling to stir the wrath of his all powerful brother.

"I'm certain that you have much to talk of with your sister. You have my leave to remain at Hungvar as long as you wish. We will feast this evening in your honor. I must now return to more pressing matters."

With that, Attila vanished behind the curtains leading to his private chambers. The king hugged his sister with greater freedom now that the fearsome conqueror was gone.

"Our mother has made this cloak for you," Gernot said as he handed her a beautiful garment in the style of their people. She grasped it with frantic emotion, holding it as though it contained her mother's soul. Here was the last refuge of her humanity, of her feelings for others.

"Her fingers have not lost their magic," she whispered as a tear escaped her control.

The brothers sadly contemplated her, witnessing the terrible pain that lay just beneath the surface of their sister's queenly appearance.

"You must be tired from your long journey," she stated abruptly, seeking to release herself from the bottomless emotion she felt for the mother she would never see again. "You must rest now."

She hurried away, not looking back. Gernot turned to

his older brother to seek out in his face that which he felt in his heart. But the aging king seemed lost in the sweet agony of nostalgia and the innocent hope that all could be made well again. The thought that some demonic maelstrom was about to be unleashed over him was furthest from his mind.

WASHED AND dressed in their finest clothes, the Burgundians gathered around the gigantic dais where Attila presided. Kriemhild's gaze had turned into a haunting stare as she precipitated herself into the void of unavoidable fate. She felt the presence of Hagen who sat several chairs away, and she looked at him with a malefic glare that only Hadrian and Ethrain noticed.

The feasting and ceremonies began with great commotion. Several warriors in colorful attire came to the center of the room and put on an exhibition of oriental sword fighting with incredible speed and skill. The Burgundians were greatly impressed and all the more eager to return to their homeland.

"This is truly amazing. I've never seen such speed!" King Gunther exclaimed.

"All my warriors train in such a manner," Attila grumbled. "That is one reason why the Roman legions have never overcome us."

Hadrian bit his lip, remembering the hideous massacre he had witnessed only a few years before. It was there that he had finally recognized the utter waste and madness of war. But his mind was quickly taken away from the shadows of the past as he felt Ethrain grow tense. He looked up in time to see the dark-eyed queen address the lord of Trony.

"Tell me, Sir Hagen, how many men would you say you've killed in your time?"

The king choked on his food. Hagen ate calmly.

"I cannot answer that, Mylady. I have never bothered to count."

"Surely, you must remember some," she insisted, her voice becoming more angry.

"No, in the heat of battle, one hardly notices."

"What of those whom you kill with their backs to you?"

Attila turned to her in surprise. The Burgundians all froze in shock, except for Hagen who continued to eat as though nothing was taking place.

"I don't know what you mean, Lady Kriemhild."

"I mean when you murdered my husband, Prince Siegfried!"

Her harsh tone exploded across the Hall. A hundred scarred Asian faces looked up. Hagen did not flinch and waited for the gasps to die down.

He put his bowl aside and wiped his beard and mustache as though dining by his own hearth. He then looked out at the sea of eyes peering at him. This was the moment he had anticipated for ten years, since the instant he released his spear and ended the life of the Nordic prince. As though the planets had aligned in one straight, clear path, the old warrior knew that his time had come.

"Yes, I slew Prince Siegfried. I slew him for the wrong he had done my King!"

The room was utterly silent. Giselher's eyes filled with tears. This was the revelation he hoped never to hear. He had eagerly accepted the story of the hunting accident. The king let his head drop in his hands. His judgment day had come as well.

Kriemhild began to shake uncontrollably. Hagen's defiant confession had torn out the last shred of sanity from her tormented mind. She let out a shriek that would not stop. Attila made a quick motion and Magag and several domestics took her out of the hall. A savage commotion took hold of the Huns, each of whom was religiously loyal to their queen. Attila held up his hand and they fell silent again.

"Whatever happened then does not concern us now. But I do not want you to come in sight of my Queen ever again, or I will have you torn limb from limb!"

Attila peered viciously into Hagen's eyes. The warrior held his gaze, undaunted. No man had ever looked back at the Kagan that way, not since his last encounter with the Roman general Aetius. Attila rose and left the room, choosing not to have the proud lord destroyed because he had given his word of hospitality.

Hagen also stood and walked off, followed by staring eyes. Gernot turned to his older brother, deeply hurt. He too had avoided the truth all these years. King Gunther closed his eyes and whispered a prayer.

OUTSIDE, THE lord of Trony adjusted his heavy sword and readied for combat. He was surrounded by the Burgundians who watched him in grim silence.

"I warned you that she sent for us to tear open those old wounds. They have never healed. Your sister will see us dead before her hatred is appeased. It would be best if we left at dawn. I will stand guard."

"Kriemhild will not murder her brothers!" Gernot cried out angrily. "We had nothing to do with Siegfried's death."

"This is not caused by one event," Hadrian announced solemnly. "I urge you to leave as soon as possible."

Gernot hurried up to him and defiantly faced the Roman.

"So tell us, why were we brought here?"

"To bring me here," Hadrian said impassively.

Gernot abruptly turned away from him, unwilling to accept his answer. Then he looked back as he brought his anger under control.

"So you will not be returning with us?"

"No," Hadrian said sadly.

Gernot was struck by the melancholy in the Roman's eyes. He suddenly understood that he was not the only one who might not be making the voyage home.

NIGHT FELL and the creatures of darkness roamed the world. Kriemhild sat at the window and stared out at the eerie moonlight. Her features drooped, weighed down by great fatigue and sorrow. Her loyal servant, Cyra, stood nearby, frightened by her queen's gloomy state.

A pounding knock at the door caused her to jump in terror. She opened the door and found herself staring into the yellow, menacing eyes of Magag.

"She wishes to be alone," the pretty Asian maid stated.

Magag paid no attention to her and pushed her out of the way.

"Forgive me, My Queen, but I must speak to you."

"Leave me, Magag!" she cried out in despair.

The Hun commander quickened his step and soon reached the end of her chambers where she sat.

"It concerns Hagen of Trony."

Kriemhild turned to him, suddenly alert.

"Attila will keep his word and not touch his guests. That is his way. But the murderer must not go free."

She stood and approached him.

"You'll help me, Magag?"

"Whosoever hurts my Queen must not live!"

She put her hand on his powerful shoulder.

"My loyal friend . . . What can we do?"

"I have a thousand men under my command."

"Attila would not allow it."

"Attila need not know. If it is your wish, I will bring you Hagen's head on a golden tray!"

"That evil man has caused me great torment. I will

reward you for this!" she said passionately.

"Your favor will be my greatest reward," the cunning leader whispered.

"I do not want my brothers harmed," she said with only mild concern.

"They will return to the Rhine in safety."

"Then go, Magag, and may the gods be with you."

"I am your faithful servant, Mylady," he said as he backed away.

As he disappeared from her chambers, the queen let out a hoarse cry of victory which sent her little maid shivering into the corner. A demonic howl from some monster of the underworld would not have terrified her more.

THE BURGUNDIANS rode out with the first lights of dawn and slowly retraced their steps. No one spoke for a long while. Gernot finally moved his horse next to King Gunther who was lost in a haze of regret.

"Was Hagen just in his act?" Gernot asked his brother.

"The Lord of Trony slew a traitor!" the king muttered.

They rode in silence. Ahead of them, Hagen trotted his horse in grim isolation. The sons of Thorin and their friend Giselher were greatly distressed by the desecration of the legends in which they had placed men like Hagen and Siegfried. Dankwart fell behind the group, lost in his own sense of doom. His horse stumbled and he dismounted to check the animal's hooves. He found a little stone and brushed it out.

As he prepared to remount, something caught his eye in the distance. He strained to distinguish the movement. A cloud of dust rose from the other side of the hill like the fumes from some angry dragon. Dankwart quickly put his ear to the ground. The deep pounding of many horses echoed beneath him. He leaped onto his horse and kicked him into a wild gallop.

Crashing through he brush, he rejoined the Burgundian troop. Hagen reeled his horse around at the sound of Dankwart's frantic gallop, knowing that something was about to fall upon them.

"What is it, boy?" he yelled.

"Huns! Hundreds of them! They're coming after us!"

"That cannot be!" King Gunther cried out. "We have the word of Attila!"

"Look! I see the gleam of their spears!" Giselher shouted. Swords flew from their sheaths as the men suddenly became battle-ready.

"We must get to the river!" Gernot ordered.

"Which way?" Ortwin called back.

"South!" Hagen commanded, galloping off through the underbrush.

A roar exploded from the men as they threw their horses into a mad rush across the fields. Already, hordes of Huns could be seen racing toward them.

Approaching the crest of a hill, the Burgundians reined in their animals.

"We're closed in!" Dankwart shouted out as he peered over the slopes that led into a valley cut off by sheer cliffs.

"Back to the forest!" Gernot roared.

"No time!" Hagen responded. "Behind those rocks! To the caves!"

The men raced off for the protection of a field of boulders at the base of the desolate hill. Moments later, Magag and his warriors swarmed across the field. But the Burgundians reached the cliffs where Hun ponies could not climb. They left their horses below and gathered on a small plateau in the mountainside.

Magag halted his troops and rode alone toward them.

"Men of the Rhineland! Surrender Lord Hagen and you will return alive to your lands!"

Before anyone could react, Hagen threw down his sword and stepped out from behind the rocks. Gernot leaped at his legs as Dankwart and the king pulled him back.

"Bind him!" the king cried out with fierce loyalty.

Gernot fastened leather straps around his arms and feet while the others held him down. King Gunther pulled his knife from its sheath and sliced off a chunk of his friend's hair. He stood before the Hun commander and brandished it defiantly.

"Hun! You will have to walk over our corpses to touch a hair on the head of the Lord of Trony!"

Magag sat straight on his vicious pony and smiled. Any respect for the Burgundian king vanished and he relished the thought of destroying him. But he noticed that the old king had a new glow about him. Valiant courage confronted him and there was no question of weakness or vacillation in this man. The Hun commander also knew that every warrior there radiated the same fierce determination. It would be a bloody struggle.

Magag remembered the peaceful slopes and Alpine ridges that were home to his enemies. He imagined the faces of the women of the castle when they would learn of the demise of their noble men. Then he recalled the promise of glory awaiting him as he broke through the first weak link in mighty Attila's armor.

He reeled his pony around and raced back across the rugged terrain to his awaiting warriors. The Burgundians gathered around their king in this final hour. Everyone was silent except for Hagen's moans. King Gunther looked down at his old friend and they exchange a glance of common understanding. He would not let his friend be a helpless witness in his last battle. He motioned for Gernot to release him. Hagen leaped to his feet as Gernot handed him his great sword.

"If one dies, we all die," the king announced. "Our

time has come, my children, to face the ultimate battle. This is not a time for heroes and great feats of battle. Each one here must face his death with nobility alone before his Maker."

He looked upon every one of his men. His old companions, his young warriors, his beloved brothers. Giselher was so hungry for life, yet he had taken the king's words to heart and a new radiance of dignity and nobility of spirit broke over his youthful features.

"Perhaps the Roman is right!" Hagen called out so that all could hear. "Perhaps we die for some greater purpose that we cannot understand. There are mysteries in the events around us and our actions may be rooted in a vaster plan. But we do know one thing! We do know how to fight!"

The men roared as they raised their swords to the sky, touching the sharp blades in a final salute to each other.

Then there was silence. The sound of sheep grazing above them could be heard, carried by the spring breeze gently ruffling their clothing. An old shepherd appeared on the edge of the cliff and looked down upon them, unaware of the violence about to take place. The sons of Thorin embraced Giselher quietly and prepared to die. Gernot kissed the hilt of his sword, giving his farewell to all earthly things.

The ponies' hooves struck the dirt path like the crash of drumbeats pounding at battle speed. The Burgundians watched on from behind the rocks as countless Huns appeared before them from every nook and ravine, woodland and hillside. They were forced to dismount in order to approach the Rhinelanders as the ponies were unable to dash up the steep inclines. An explosion of gutteral roars shook the countryside. The first wave of Huns were met with an overwhelming assault by the Burgundians, and they tumbled back in chaos beneath their blows.

Magag studied the action closely. He barked orders

to circle around to the top of the hill. Then he sent another wave of warriors against the rocks.

The Burgundians fought like madmen, holding off four or five attackers each. Martin was the first to fall beneath the Asian swords. Dankwart slipped on the rocks and was struck with a mortal wound. Giselher fought in a frenzied state, terrified by the wild yells of his savage adversaries. The Huns swarmed over them, descending the hillside to strike from behind.

King Gunther found himself surrounded. He was cut several times as he sought to evade the thrusts of his attackers. Gernot tore his way into the warriors assaulting his brother and came to stand at his side. Dozens of Huns pressed against them, and the two brothers were dragged under the swell of blades and spears. A Hun came up behind Gernot who was still fighting relentlessly and stuck his sword into his back. The prince swirled around, killed his assailant and slowly sunk to his knees. Another Hun rushed to him and struck him with a fatal blow. Felicia's features, beaming with life and love, appeared to him in a flash of light. Then all went dark.

Magag appeared on the plateau, thirsting for blood. Jeoffrey stood before him and fought him ferociously. The Hun toyed with him and finally cut him down.

The powerful Lord of Trony charged his enemies with thunderous rage. He mowed them down like weeds as he stood over the bodies of his friends. Every swing was meant to cut down the cruel gods who had turned his life into such hell. In the midst of his ultimate struggle, he remembered what the Elder had once told him: "One who lives from the sword will die by the sword."

Giselher appeared at his side, now fighting with the courage of a true warrior. He had been hurled through the gates of death and was giving himself over to his fate. They stood by a path that led to another hillside which the Huns had not reached.

"Run, boy!" Hagen shouted in his gravelly voice. "You can reach our horses from here."

"No, Hagen! I will die with you!"

"Your people need a king! Do it for your brothers!"

Hagen blocked the narrow corner from which Giselher could escape. The young prince fought valiantly at the side of the great warrior.

"This is not your battle, boy! I order you in the name of our King! Go back!"

The Huns were unable to crowd into the narrow passage. Hagen savagely cut them down.

"We will meet in another kingdom, Lord of Trony!"

Giselher dashed up the rocks toward the other hill while Hagen doubled the power of his mighty blows. The young man jumped on a horse and turned back for a last look. Sir Hagen, bloodied but still standing, was surrounded by Huns. Giselher kicked his horse into a wild gallop, tears streaming down his cheeks. He galloped to the top of the hill and dashed through the herd of sheep. The old shepherd watched him sadly as the sounds of fighting echoed from below. The Burgundian prince disappeared into the woods that would lead him back to Helen, his mother, and an awaiting throne.

The gore of battle, the presence of death, and the tragic loss of all the men he held dear was transforming him. It was as a new man that Giselher would face the future and the great events of history heading his way.

A lone rider suddenly appeared ahead, like a demon coming to claim its victims. Giselher drew his sword as he approached the silhouette. His whole being trembled with rage when he saw that it was Kriemhild. The queen had a vacant look in her eyes, as though her soul had been torn out of her. The prince reined in his horse.

"Woman! See what you have done!"

He forcibly halted her horse. She turned a dazed look upon him.

"You've destroyed the finest lords of the Rhineland!"

A high-pitched, wrenching laughter erupted from her broken spirit.

"I have avenged Prince Siegfried!" she cried.

"You've murdered your family! The demons have taken hold of you, Kriemhild!"

"Yes, the demons possess me!" she shrieked with a wicked glare in the eyes. "The Lord of Trony thought a frail young woman would be powerless to call justice down upon his head!"

Giselher's rage quieted as he witnessed the insanity in his sister's features.

"Are you satisfied, sister? Are your demons appeased?"

"No . . . " she whispered as tears filled her desperate eyes.

She suddenly grabbed her brother's arm in a frenzy.

"Kill me, Giselher! Free me from my pain!"

The young man looked at her in disgust and pulled her hand from his arm.

"I beg of you, brother! Run your sword through my heart in the name of your dying friends!"

Giselher tightened his hand around the hilt of his sword. He raised it with a dreadful yell of anger and pain. Kriemhild closed her eyes, longing for release.

"I am coming to you at last, Siegfried, my love!"

The prince suddenly stopped his motion as he was about to bring the sword down upon her.

"No! I will not feed the demons anymore blood. There will be no more vengeance! The madness stops here. I . . . I forgive you in the name of the new God."

Kriemhild opened her eyes in horror.

"Please, brother, kill me! Don't let me live with what I have done!"

Giselher reared his horse as he prepared to kick it into a gallop.

"You're already dead!" he yelled.

With a great shout, he sent his horse into a furious run. She let out a terrible scream as he disappeared over the hillside. Another rider appeared from the woods. It was Ethrain. She had been following Kriemhild at a distance, leaving Hadrian in the banquet hall to await the moment to strike. She had seen Magag and his men secretly ready themselves for the pursuit of the Burgundians. They had left Hungvar as the festivities turned into an orgy of drunkenness. But it wouldn't be long before Attila learned of what had happened.

Ethrain hurried over to Kriemhild and took her by the hand.

"Come with me, Princess. I'll take you home."

The woman didn't seem to hear her. She followed in a daze, broken by the horrid events she had instigated. Ethrain took the reins of both animals and had hardly turned around when a group of Hun warriors galloped up to them, lead by Bleda, the Kagan's brother.

"The Queen is coming with us!" he said, barely concealing his ferocious anger.

"Whose orders are those?" Ethrain asked defiantly, sensing that they were lusting for blood.

"The Kagan's."

"I don't believe you!" Ethrain shouted. She knew that Bleda would not forgive Kriemhild for causing so much death.

She tried to kick her horse into a gallop but the men surrounded her and separated her from Kriemhild. She struggled with them and managed to push her way through. A scream exploded behind her and she turned in time to see Kriemhild fall from her horse. Bleda held his dripping sword over her.

"Too many good warriors have died because of you!" he yelled. "The Kagan will forgive me."

He swung his horse around to face Ethrain, but she was already in the distance, galloping at full speed.

Hadrian road up to the gates of Hungvar, filled with disgust. He was utterly confused and horrified. He knew that beyond those hills his Burgundian friends were being cut to pieces. What was the purpose of all this carnage? He had hoped that this would have been his opportunity to strike Attila. But the mayhem of celebration in the hall had not slowed since the departure of King Gunther and his men. Today was the Kagan's birthday, and Attila himself was filling the empty spaces of his soul with the wine of forgetfulness.

He dismounted and leaned against the wooden walls. Despair slowly crept through his heart, spreading its heavy darkness over his soul. If he could not complete his mission now that he had reached Hungvar, then perhaps it was not to be after all. The massacre that was ripping his heart as painfully as a dagger clearly revealed to him the presence of the Jotunheim demons. He understood that one man's death, however cruel he might be, would not end the bloodshed or quell the spirit of war in humankind. Yet he also knew that the expansion of Attila's reign would decimate civilization for generations.

"The time has come!"

Hadrian reacted with a jolt. He looked around but saw no one there. But he had distinctly heard a voice address him. Something familiar about it struck a deep chord within. Again, he turned in all directions. The outskirts of Hungvar were desolate. A gnawing feeling rose within, generating a new energy that broke through his despair like the morning sun through a cloud bank. Then it hit him. The voice was that of Ubarra!

Suddenly, he saw a rider thundering down a hill at breakneck speed. The sun illumined the rider with a glow of golden light, creating the impression of some unleashed spirit escaping the flames of the underworld. Hadrian was about to draw his sword, responding to his warrior's sense of imminent danger, when he recognized the outline of Ethrain's wavy hair.

He leaped on his horse and raced toward her. They met in the middle of the plain.

"Bleda's killed Kriemhild!" she shouted.

"Attila will tear him to pieces! He'll be looking for her any moment now."

"We've got to get away from here! They'll turn on each other and we'll be caught in the middle."

"Follow me!"

Hadrian whirled his horse southward and was about to kick it into a gallop when Ethrain grabbed his reins.

"Wait! We must finish what we came for."

"It's impossible now! We'd be walking into a den of wild beasts. As soon as he hears of Kriemhild's death, he'll turn into a madman!"

"Where is he now?"

"In the great hall. He'll be returning to his chambers where he thinks his queen awaits him."

"That is our chance! Come!"

She turned her horse toward the gates of Hungvar.

"What do you think you're going to do?"

"I'll be in his bed, under the covers. He'll think I'm Kriemhild until I cut his throat."

"No! It's too dangerous!"

"Not as dangerous as letting him take over the world!"

"Ethrain! I won't let you soil yourself with such violence. Let me do the butchering."

They galloped through the gates.

Attila was still at the table, drinking one mug after another. He rarely indulged himself so, but this day he was in that sort of a mood. He knew that Kriemhild would be waiting him in his chambers, enticing as always in her sheer gowns of finest silk brought from the land of the Chinese emperors.

His queen's fiery temperament had especially aroused

him. He thought that perhaps she would act out her aggression in their love making. The Kagan rose from his chair and stumbled over his drunken men, heading back to his chambers.

He entered the large dark room that had been his private retreat for so long. True to his nature, it was sparsely decorated, though every object was a trophy from some distant land he had plundered.

He leaned against a post. The wine made him dizzy for a moment. He regretted having lost control, betraying his usual disgust for such slothfulness. Perhaps it was to drown the dim but growing feeling that his life was coming to a close and that his rivaling sons would break up the empire he had created. He looked over at the great bed in the corner of the room. A feminine shape covered over with sheets awaited him. He smiled as a surge of lust rushed through his body and he removed his great leather belt. He stumbled over to the bed, taking off his vest of fur and throwing it in a corner by the velvet curtains brought back from the destruction of Milan. The vest fell on a hard shape beneath the curtains. Hadrian's heart leaped as he felt the clothing fall over his foot. He parted the curtains slightly and peered at the massive frame getting into the bed. His hand tightened around the hilt of his sword as a hot burst of energy shot through his veins. But he restrained himself, awaiting the fateful moment.

Attila caressed the curves outlined under the sheets and let out a moan of pleasure.

"Wake, my butterfly. Your master wants you."

He kissed the motionless shape. Just as he was about to pull the covers back, he noticed a yellow strand of hair laying on the pillow.

Attila sat up and yanked the sheets back, revealing Ethrain.

"What is this?" he roared.

Ethrain turned to him and hid her terror beneath a sensual smile.

"Your queen has offered me as a present to you."

"What?"

"For your birthday."

Attila's ugly features broke into a hungry smile.

"She is always full of surprises," he said, gazing at Ethrain's youthful form. "Why are you clothed, then?"

"So that you may have the pleasure of undressing me," Ethrain responded, unable to hide a tremble in her voice.

"Has the queen told you of my secret pleasures?"

Ethrain nodded as her heart pounded to the point of choking off her breath. Attila leaned over and began to untie her leather vest.

"Let me feast my eyes on you."

The curtains parted and Hadrian stepped forward. Attila heard a sound and would have turned around but Ethrain took his face in her hands.

"The queen is here to watch your pleasure."

Attila's slanted eyes suddenly turned fierce.

"What nonsense is this?"

He violently pulled her hands away. At that moment, a Roman sword flashed over him. Ethrain rolled away and fell off the bed as the Kagan's blood gushed across the sheets. He let out a gurgling sound and fell heavily on the bed. Hadrian stood over him, ready to strike again. Attila's body shook briefly and then turned rigid.

"It is done!" Hadrian cried out victoriously.

Ethrain jumped to her feet.

"Hurry!"

But Hadrian remained standing over the Hun, eyes glazed.

"Hadrian! We must leave immediately!"

"I've never killed a man with his back to me . . . "

She grabbed his hand and pulled him away.

"Come!"

Hadrian stumbled behind her, disgusted with himself.

"It had to be done!" Ethrain exclaimed.

Hadrian dropped his bloody sword.

"I'll never kill another human being . . . "

"Now is not the time to become a man of peace!"

She slapped his face.

"Come to your senses or we'll be roasted alive!"

She picked up his sword and they hurried through the small corridor leading to the stables.

They mounted their horses and galloped toward the gates. One of Attila's lieutenants appeared before them.

"Stop! Bleda has ordered all foreigners to remain in Hungvar!"

"We are doomed," Hadrian whispered hoarsely. "But our work is accomplished."

"No, it is not!" Ethrain shouted as she charged the warrior and cut him down with the sword.

Hadrian looked at her, astonished. Her horse reared as she pulled in the reins.

"Don't you remember? There is a new world to create! Follow me!"

She kicked her horse and headed toward the gates. Several warriors were pushing the giant doors shut. They bolted the lock just as Ethrain was about to go through them. She reared her horse to kick the guards aside. Hadrian pulled on the reins to avoid crashing into her. His horse slipped and fell. Hadrian tried to rise but his leg was trapped. Ethrain swung her weapon at the Huns as they circled her. One of them jumped up and pulled her off her horse. She plunged the sword into his chest and he dropped to his knees, taking the weapon with him.

"Hadrian!" she screamed as the two other warriors approached her.

Hadrian struggled frantically to move his horse. He watched on helplessly as they tried to strike her. She jumped back, barely avoiding the sharp blades.

"Ethrain!" Hadrian cried out. He heard himself from deep within beg the higher powers that had led them to this dreadful moment. To witness his beloved cut down before his eyes was a fate worse than the most hideous death.

Just as his horse rose to its feet, the mighty doors exploded, sending logs in all directions. The warriors were struck by the flying debris and fell to the ground. Hadrian leaped on his horse and grabbed Ethrain's hand. He helped her onto his mount and they bolted through the opening.

As they galloped away, he glanced back and saw a tall, gaunt figure in flowing robes standing by the smashed gates. Next to him stood the silhouette of the witch of Mallor.

"Look!" he cried out.

Ethrain turned and saw her mother and father. Their hands were raised in the ancient blessing of her people. Then they vanished in the dust clouds rising from the debris.

HADRIAN AND Ethrain journeyed back across the hills and valleys of Gaul. They were headed for the shores of Brittany.

Across the North Sea, on the barren Isle of Mallor, a new life awaited them. Perhaps the crystal would tell them what lay ahead. They knew that both the gods of Valhalla and the giants of Jotunheim had been defeated, at least for now. Perhaps Ragnarok would be postponed, and a new civilization would be born from their efforts, one built on goodness and peace. Already, a child stirred in Ethrain's womb, a child destined to carry their mission into the future.

They rejoiced at the thought of joining forces with the saintly Patrick, knowing that their adventures had served to prepare them for an even greater task, one which only the luminous Briton understood. He would surely bless them with his guidance and, in turn, they would assist him in bringing a new light into the darkness of human strife regardless of the cost. Hadrian and Ethrain both sensed a foreboding turbulence ahead of them, but for now they had each other, and the time had come to let themselves be carried into a new day on the mighty wings of their love.

Part Two

The Day of Destruction

chapter twenty

THE CELTS of the western isles were terrified of the Fomorian king of the underworld—Balor of the Baleful Eye who was said to bring instant death to any human he looked upon. Only one being inspired more dread than the one-eyed demon of Tory island. But this fearsome creature was no legend invoked by keepers of the past knowledge. This monster was a man.

Coroticus was the ruler of Dumbarton, in the isles of Scotland. He was called "King of the Rock" and his fortress stood high on the Firth of Clyde. There he had gathered a savage army of mercenary Saxon and Picts to increase the source of his wealth—slave trading. Relentless raids on the Irish shores were decimating the Celtic population and ravaging the last of signs of the proud culture that once honored the rocks of the North Sea.

The tyrant was hated with greater zeal than the Roman emperor and his dying civilization. The man was a Briton and a Roman citizen who had butchered his way to power. The Celts feared him more than they did the warriors of the far north who travelled their waters when the seas of ice melted.

Enslavement was the worst of fates for the descendants of the Tuatha de Danaan, the children of the goddess Danu. Handed down through the tradition of the great seers and druids, every child of Celtic origin knew of the curse of the ninth wave. To go beyond the ninth wave, across the boundary of their beloved world, was to fall into the abyss of foreign waters from which no one could be saved, even with the help of the Maiden of the Waters. For generations, the greatest punishment inflicted on those who betrayed the ways of their people was to be sent beyond the ninth wave, adrift on a boat without roars or rudder. To the people of the Celtic isles, the evil Coroticus impersonated that ultimate horror without hope of return.

But the darkness of this brigand ruler needed no comparison to the people's ancient stories. The man's cruelty could not be equalled in any myth of the Otherworld. The size of a great bear, with features distorted by his corrupted soul, the King of the Rock was as ugly as he was ferocious. He lived in lavish splendor, decorating his fortress with the skulls of countless victims. His appetites were voracious and never satisfied. Women feared his tempestuous passions and men trembled before his thunderous rage.

It was known that the despot had committed his first murder at ten years of age. Without father or mother, Coroticus was said to be the perverse product of the Otherworld, a child from the caves of Cruachan, gateway to the land of the dead and the dark gods of the North.

For the fisherman of Ireland, the bloodletting of Caesar's legions and the pillaging of Attila's Huns paled before the hideous ways of the slave trader. Every new raid upon the isles left name of Coroticus signed in gore. It was whispered that he killed for pleasure and relished the sight of human pain. The few who escaped his grasp told of his terrifying black eyes that sparkled with some unnatural joy while witnessing unspeakable brutality.

The greatest warriors in the land, the sons of Mil who

first conquered the isle from the gods, stayed far from him.

Coroticus had only one real enemy. A young man, recently returned to Ireland, who was called Patrick. He fearlessly denounced the ruler's evil. Yet this monk of a new faith was alone, rejected by many, and utterly unprotected. Coroticus eagerly awaited his next opportunity to sail across the channel and find the bold holy man. He had already prepared a place for his skull.

A SHIP SAILING from Gaul appeared in the waters near the breakers of Ireland's eastern shores. On deck, Hadrian Aldius studied the boat's approach to the coastline. He tightened the red and gold cape of the emperor's legions around his broad shoulders and placed his right hand on the thick hilt of the cutlass strapped to his side.

He took a deep breath and recognized the scent of the island's oaks and meadows of darkly green grasses. He loved these rocks now, even though they held mysteries that had nearly killed him. But they were also the home of his new bride.

He closed his eyes to remember their first encounter in the woods of the mysterious isle of Mallor. He had immediately seen her mysterious powers simmering behind a wild mane of golden hair and striking blue eyes. She was the light of his life. He had left the rotting corpse of Rome forever to find a new existence. Ethrain embodied it in every way. Sensuous and secretive, steeped in knowledge foreign to him despite his high learning, she surprised and delighted him daily. Though he could not conceive what Fate held in store for them, he accepted it all as long as he could live it out with his beloved.

Ethrain's hand gently touched his shoulder. His pensive face lit up and he turned around. She was a sight to behold. She was strong as a man. Yet she beamed with feminine wisdom and sensitivity. Ethrain could read into the depths of the human heart on the most rigid of faces.

Now this child of Celtic lore was Hadrian's spouse. Their love grew deeper with every passing day. They were bonded by a strange sense of destiny, knowing somehow that they were from all eternity meant to find each other.

"What do you see?" Ethrain asked with a sweet smile.

"Home . . . " he whispered as he gently kissed her warm lips.

"Truly? You don't long for Rome and your palaces?"

"There is no more Rome. Visigoths wander the halls where Cicero once spoke. The emperor dissipates in drink and madness. There is nothing left for me."

"So you belong to us now?" she asked, eyes sparkling with pleasure.

"I belong to you, Ethrain. You and your land of mysteries and enchantments."

They kissed passionately as the sea breeze enveloped them. Hadrian hugged her in his soldier's arms.

"Do you think we will live in peace now that we have accomplished what the druid required?" Hadrian questioned as he caressed her hair.

"Peace? Is there such a thing for anyone in this realm?"

"Surely, there must be. I'm so tired of bloodshed and misery. Who will bother us among these rocks? Seagulls and squalls rising off the North Sea?"

Ethrain ran her hand along the contours of his aquiline features. She loved the smoothness of his skin and the olive tint of his ancestry. The black curls cropped short in Roman style intensified his dark, brown eyes and their glare of intelligence and inner strength.

"My love, our peace is here between us. Don't search for it anywhere else. It cannot be found in a world ruled by men."

"Will it be war and savagery to the bitter end? Can we not find someplace free from these evils?"

She smiled at his idealism, knowing that his soul was tired by the horrors he had witnessed on the battlefield and filled with dreams of a quiet home.

"We cannot escape from what the gods require of us."

Ethrain's smile faded as she watched a cloud of sorrow dim the light in Hadrian's eyes. Her battle-weary soulmate foresaw a future of relentless danger for them.

"Perhaps we should have stayed in Gaul," he whispered.

"And do what? Raise chicken and take the cows out to pasture?"

"Why not?" Hadrian wondered as he embraced her.

"Look at the age we live in! Darkness may consume us all. Nothing stands in the way of the forces of evil!"

"What can we do but be destroyed? I want to grow old with you."

"There is someone else."

"You mean the holy man?"

"Yes, Patrick."

He pictured to himself the monk who had joined them together forever on board the ship that was taking them to the land of the Burgundians. Beaming with youthful vigor and utter self-abandonment to a mystic cause that towered over him at every moment, Patrick had traversed the boundaries of the physical and penetrated deeply into the realm of the spiritual. Among all of Hadrian's fellow centurions, each of whom was a shining example of courage, obedience, and loyalty, there was none to match the simple Briton's willpower. In the very poverty of his humble submission to a higher power, Patrick manifested monumental strength and commitment. That amazing contradiction fascinated Hadrian who had never encountered this combination of opposites.

Yet Hadrian believed that the man was walking into the abyss of annihilation, undertaking an impossible mission. How could the teaching that he carried with him ever be accepted by the worshipers of Agrona, goddess of slaughter? Yet, he knew in some way that if any human being could achieve such a miracle it would be this unassuming man with eyes aflame with devotion to his cause.

"We are not alone. How can you not know that by now?" Ethrain asked.

Hadrian tightened his arm around her and looked out at the North Sea. Sunlight glistened across the quiet waves as though smiling at Ethrain's words.

"Yes, I have seen your Celtic wonders. My mind has yet to make sense of what my eyes have witnessed on these isles."

"Don't even try, Hadrian. It doesn't matter how brilliant your teacher was back in Rome. There are things that your mind is not capable of apprehending. Let your heart do the knowing."

"What are you saying? My heart cannot think!"

Ethrain took his face in her hands and pulled him toward her. She kissed him passionately, a warm, wet kiss brimming with the lovegift of herself. Hadrian felt his centurion's control waver as he was drawn into her powerful passion. He had to pull back and catch his breath. Never had he loved a woman in this way. Her aroma alone stirred overwhelming desire to melt into her being.

"Your heart can know," she murmured to him. "Your heart knows that our togetherness is our destiny. If this is right, then we can be sure that we are on the path we were born to travel."

She pulled him to her again.

"Tell me that this moment is the only place you want to be."

The Roman felt his love for Ethrain rush through his veins like the burning wine of his homeland.

"Of course, Ethrain. This is where I have always wanted to be. In your arms."

An ocean wind circled them and caused a cold shiver to bring them closer to each other. Hadrian pulled his cape around his shoulders and tried to wish away the ominous feeling passing through his soul.

"Look! There are the moors!"

Hadrian followed Ethrain's excited gesture and spotted the soft hills at the top of jagged cliffs. The coast of the Celtic lands was a grandiose sight even for one who had stood before the Sphinx of Egypt.

"How beautiful!" he stated in awe. "Who would dream that such a glorious landscape was home to so many terrible beings?"

"The Dark Ones are everywhere," Ethrain responded with irritation. She loved her birthplace too much to hear its demeaning.

Hadrian smiled at his young wife's quick temper. As quick as it came, so did it vanish. From the cauldron of that fire also came his beloved's passion for him. So he accepted her ways, all of them, with joy and gratitude.

THEY LANDED in a quiet alcove, disembarked and prepared to journey toward Armagh where they had heard the saintly Patrick was toiling. Ethrain was thrilled to be back in the isles of her birth. What she had seen of the world of the East on her journey with Hadrian could not compare with the sweet blend of ocean and forest unique to this lost corner of the world. It was good to stand on the hard earth of Ireland where her ancestors had struggled so valiantly to create a home in this wilderness.

Tears of joy streamed down her cheeks. She wanted to embrace the meadows, vales, and cliffs of her homeland. She wanted to fill herself with the spirits of the land and bask in mystic unity with the elements. They journeyed side by side, astride horses given to them by the Burgundian princes whose friendship would linger with them to the end of their days, followed by a third animal carrying their few earthly goods. With every breath, they absorbed all the scents and sounds of the isle. Soft rain greeted them from the skies, soothing their windburned faces and welcoming them home.

As they neared the first village on their way to Armagh, Hadrian's soldier instincts suddenly awoke. He caught sight of a cloud of smoke rising over the next hill. He knew instantly that it was no campfire or cottage chimney releasing this black, acrid sign of death and destruction.

"Rein in your horse," he said to Ethrain.

She looked at him, aware that danger was at hand.

"What is it?" she asked anxiously, her hand grasping the dagger in her leather belt.

"Over there."

"It's only smoke, Hadrian. Perhaps a forest fire."

"No, there is more than wood burning there. Believe me, I know the sight."

Before his mind's eye flashed the grisly scenes of his last battle with the Goths on the banks of the Danube. The legions had massacred an entire tribe—men, women and children. They had dared to disobey the emperor's edicts. Trotting through a village of corpses, he knew then that his days as a centurion were over.

"We must cross over that hill. There is no other way to get to Armagh," Ethrain stated.

"Wait here while I see what is ahead."

"No!" she cried out. "I am not some lady from the King's court. You know I can fight."

"I don't want you to be hurt."

"Nor do I want to see you hurt. I will be by your side and protect you as you protect me."

Hadrian loved her in that moment more than ever.

"Then let us proceed slowly. Keep your horse quiet."

As they approached the top of the hill, Hadrian gestured for them to dismount. They tied down their animals and walked over the ridge. Sprawled out before them, in a small valley, lay a scene of unspeakable horror. Even the riverbanks of eastern Gaul were not as drenched in blood as this gentle vale. Everywhere they looked, there was beastly desecration of life.

Ethrain let out a scream of revulsion and fell to her knees. Hadrian rushed over to her and held her tightly as she shook uncontrollably. Never had her eyes beheld anything of the sort. Mutilated bodies lay along the road, across the field, in doorways. None of the bloody cadavers had weapons, all were helplessly butchered.

"Gods of my forefathers! What evil is this?"

"Don't look anymore," Hadrian ordered gently as he turned her face away. "They are at peace now. There is no more pain."

He hoped she had not seen the dead children and the old women viciously cut down. As he studied the sight, he became aware of his own reaction to the awful scene. His heart was beating fast, and the blood had rushed to his face in the heat of outrage.

"Who could do such atrocities?" he heard himself mutter.

"Are they all dead?" Ethrain asked, hugging her beloved in an effort to gain control of her grief.

"Everyone. Even the animals. Whoever did this was very efficient. They know how to kill."

"We must be sure, Hadrian. Will you go down there?"

The Roman hesitated. But he knew that she was right.

"Wait for me here."

He hurried down the hill and into the village. He went from body to body, quickly determining the state of the butchered victim. It had been years since he had seen such gore. He looked into innocent faces that stared at him through gashes and blood and caused his rage to rise. It reached a fever pitch when he turned over a small corpse and looked into the angelic features of a child of the island.

"I'll bring vengeance down on your murderers!" he cried out, looking up at the clouded heavens. A stream of raindrops mingled with his tears as he shouted out for the gods to hear.

He took the child in his arms and rocked it as though it were his own.

"I'll avenge you, little one! I'll avenge you!"

In that moment, Hadrian felt himself the father of this dead child, the father of every child in every land. Righteous anger mixed with deep sorrow for the agony of the innocent filled him to the brim and he let himself weep freely for the first time.

Hadrian Aldius knew in his heart that he must resist such darkness. He had to take a stand on the side of light, against the forces that could do such evil. His fantasy of a peaceful life hidden away from the troubles of the age caused a wave of guilt to wash over him. How could he even consider seeking his own comfort when there were men who could raise their swords against helpless people? He knew then that his knowledge of warfare, perfected in the hard schools of the Roman legions, held a higher purpose. He had not been trained to fight the enemies of Rome, but the enemies of humanity. There was good to be found in what he had learned and his past could be redeemed by putting his skills to such use.

He returned to the top of the hill and found Ethrain sitting quietly in the tall grass. A mist of rain and fog enveloped her and she seemed in a trance, staring at the slowly moving clouds so oblivious to human misery. He kneeled at her side.

"What do we do?" she asked without expression.

Hadrian did not respond but instead placed a broken

spear in front of her. She stared at it for a moment, then looked up a him.

"Why did you bring me this?"

"Do you recognize it?"

She picked it up, avoiding the blood on one end, and examined the carvings along the side.

"This is from across the waters. The land of the Picts."

"Why would they be raiding these shores? Don't they fight the Britons?"

"They fight everyone. Especially the weak and defenseless."

Hadrian took the spear and examined the decorations carved and painted on the wooden shaft. The images were primitive and grotesque, the work of barbarians still living in a dark age.

"Do you know who leads these people?"

Ethrain looked at him, her sorrow turning to anger.

"Why? Are you going to go after him?"

Hadrian said nothing, which made clear what he was thinking.

"What is the matter with you, Roman?" she shouted in outrage. "Does the sight of blood make you yearn for more?"

"The sight of wrong makes me want to right it."

She stood up and her composure changed again, like a rainbow appearing after a storm.

"Well, then, Hadrian Aldius, you have confirmed your purpose."

"What do you mean?"

"The man who wanted to escape from the world is losing to the man who needs to care for the world. You have to choose which one will receive your loyalty."

Hadrian was irritated by her blunt perception of his vacillation. He still had plenty of Roman pride.

"The choice must be made once and for all," she continued. "There is no more time for uncertainty."

"Why do you push me, Ethrain?" he asked in exasperation. "I will know in my own good time."

She took him by the arm and forced him to face the massacre below them.

"Look closely. It is too late for those poor people. How many more must suffer such a horrid fate before the hero arises in you?"

"I cannot be responsible for all the evils in this barbaric wilderness. And I never claimed to be a hero."

"You don't have to claim it. I am telling you that you are such. I knew it the first moment I saw you."

"Maybe you were victim of a young girl's fantasies."

She pulled away from him, her face turning red beneath the blond locks made wet by the light rain.

"How dare you insult me? I don't live in a world of fantasy. I've seen too much, suffered too much for such indulgences. I've had a hard life too, Hadrian. My battlefields were different than yours, but just as painful."

Hadrian felt ashamed of his patronizing attitude.

"I'm sorry . . . "

"You still don't recognize the powers within this Celtic woman, do you? You think you've wedded some orphan child of the wilderness, without proper training."

Hadrian tried to protest, but she would not be interrupted.

"I was trained, Hadrian. Not by some Greek philosopher, but by the wise ones of my people. The greatest druids in the land taught me from my earliest years. I've been taught to see in ways that you cannot. It is my inner sight that saw the hero in you, not my eyes of flesh."

Hadrian approached her and took her hands in his.

"Forgive me, Ethrain. I will never belittle your insights again."

"I am not only your wife, Roman. I have been chosen to be your finder," she said in a softer voice.

"My finder?"

"I have tried to tell you this before. Your people read the entrails of small animals in search of omens that will reveal the future. I am your omen of the future. Through me, your destiny will appear, whether we like it or not."

He marvelled at the confidence with which she spoke. She was so certain of her mysterious knowledge.

"I don't speak out of pride," she went on as though reading his thoughts. "I simply know, that is all. Believe me, there are times I would rather not have this gift. This is one of those times."

"What do you mean?"

She turned again toward the gory sight in the valley and shook her head.

"I know what our encounter with this terrible event means. Just as you do."

"All I know is my rage at this horror!"

"And it spoke to you, didn't it? It told you what you must be, and therefore what you must do."

"What must I be?"

Ethrain looked deeply into his eyes. He had the strange sensation that it was no longer his beloved staring at him longingly, but a wisewoman, a prophetess like the priestess of Delphi, one who saw into his soul and spoke words with supernatural authority.

"You must be a warrior of Light."

Thunder exploded above them and the rains fell heavy into the mud, splattering the two lovers and the corpses below. The wind howled in the nearby woods, with a warning of impending danger.

chapter twenty-one

AMARGH WAS a bustling town nestled in woodlands atop high cliffs overlooking the North Sea's turbulent waves. The wealth of the ocean and commerce with the Franks brought the town out of the wretchedness that characterized most of the fishing villages on the islands. A beginning of civilization and culture rose around the hamlets and marketplaces built over the jagged rocks.

Statues of the ancient Celtic gods stood aside more recent arrivals like Zeus and Minerva. The Roman deities were sculpted in greater detail but lacked the striking presence of the simpler stones. The Celtic spirits were very much alive in the stark faces of the carved boulders.

This was a land teeming with the company of the Otherworld. Human beings were merely passersby in a realm that did not belong to them. Their short lives could not compare with the eternal myths and legends of the Celtic pantheon. Most of the inhabitants of Armagh considered themselves servants of these great forces and worshiped the stones in fear and reverence.

It was here that Patrick the Briton came to bring the teaching that had so transformed his own life. As a boy of sixteen, he had been kidnapped by Irish slave traders and lived six years in captivity on the isles. Now, a bishop in the new Faith, he had chosen to return to the peoples who once knew him as a slave. A dream-vision had called him back to Ireland.

In the misty images of an extraordinary dream, a man appeared to him traveling from the isles and bearing many letters. These letters the dreamer understood to be the voice of the Irish. As he opened one of them, he heard thousands of voices coming from the Wood of Volcut, near the Irish Sea on the eastern coast of the isles. They cried out to him: "We ask thee, boy, come and walk among us once more."

There was despair in these voices that united uncounted cries of young and old, born and unborn. The dreamer wept at the sound and could read no further. But he knew that the forests of Volcut represented Dalaradia where he had lived out his captivity.

A second dream came to him soon afterward. The Celtic voices called to him again, though he could not understand them. The dreamer felt a presence praying within him. At the close of the mysterious prayer, the presence said to him: "He that has laid down His life for thee, it is He that speaks in thee." The dreamer experienced himself transported out of his body, summoned by a Spirit before whom he could only surrender his life, knowing that it belonged to Him. Patrick had no desire to return to the land of his captors, nor to leave his family, but the power of his dreams forged in him an indomitable will that nothing could deter.

THE HIGH KING of the isles, Laoghaire of Tara, would have nothing to do with him and would remain pagan to the end of his days. But the chieftains of the tuatha, the smaller states of the kingdom, were willing to hear his eloquent and fiery words. With his small entourage given to him by Pope Celestine, Patrick had settled for a time in Armagh because another strange dream had convinced him to do so. The young bishop had learned to pay close attention to the messages of his nightly visitations.

The swirling images of the dream brought back from the recesses of his memory two faces that he had forgotten in the intensity of his missionary activities on the isles. A beautiful and mysterious young woman and a powerful, serene Roman aristocrat. He saw again the day that he consecrated their union aboard the ship taking them to Gaul where he would prepare with the help of the great Germanicus for his fateful mission to the Celts.

He remembered how they impressed him even then with their own power of will and determination to follow a dangerous mission required of them by the spirit world. His determination to follow his inner calling had strengthened them in their uncertain journey. He had even shared with them something of his faith. In fact, the young woman would be the first from the land of Ireland to hear his words.

Now, a year into his mighty call, Patrick dreamt of them again. He knew that it could only mean one thing: they would be reappearing in his life soon. So he waited for them while undertaking his colossal self-imposed chores. Having surrendered everything to divine wisdom, it was a simple matter to wait in trust for the next sign of guidance.

Patrick did not have to wait long. Hadrain and Ethrain entered Armagh within a week of his dream. They had no trouble finding their way to his home. They were meant by an older man of massive build, Macc Cairthinn who was Patrick's loyal protector and traveling companion. He took them to the garden behind the humble cottage.

Ethrain's heart raced as she saw the small silhouette of the humble man whose goodness of spirit had so marked itself in her memory. He was standing among the flowers and vegetables, silently contemplating the dance of sunshine upon colorful petals. Dressed in a white robe, his hair tonsured in the way of the monks—shaved at the top and cut around his head in vivid symbolism of his total devotion to his Master, the Crucified One—he was the very image of a being rooted in another world.

Hadrain took his beloved's hand, reliving the sacred moment when the kind man blessed their wedding. The Roman had never experienced such authentic spiritual power as the prayer of young Patrick. He knew that the man's words were a true blessing, bringing upon their lives the protection and attention of divine forces.

Patrick turned around, a broad smile filling his features with light.

"My friends! I have been awaiting you."

Hadrian was taken aback by the man's lack of surprise at their arrival, but Ethrain knew better. She understood that this was a man whose heart knowledge was of the highest order. They greeted each other warmly.

"Have you come to stay with me awhile?" the unassuming man asked softly.

"To speak honestly," Hadrian responded, "We're not certain why we are here, and what we are to do."

"Ah, that is a good thing, dear Hadrian," Patrick said with delight. "A sure sign that you are following His instructions."

"Whose instructions?" the centurion inquired, still unable to grasp the idea of invisible presences.

Patrick and Ethrain exchanged a knowing glance.

"These Romans are so . . . earthbound. Like the apostle Thomas, they must see and touch before believing. Even your emperor knows to whom I am referring. Surely, you are not that unaware of these things."

"You mean the Anointed One, the man from Judea that you told us about?"

"Of course," Patrick replied, eyes sparkling with faith.

"So he is here as well."

"Sometimes I think he is hopeless," Ethrain said with a sigh. "But I am helping him along."

Patrick laughed with the joy and innocence of a child.

"I wish you well in your efforts, Ethrain. It will be easier for me to convert the people of this isle than to teach this Roman to understand with more than his logical mind."

Hadrian was flushed with embarrassment. They were mocking him as though he were some dull fool. Patrick placed his hand on his shoulder. The Roman felt a heat as warm as the sun's rays radiate from the man's palm.

"All in good time, all in good time," the holy man said with patient understanding. "Your empire lasted a thousand years and that cannot be displaced from your mind in only one. But you must be hungry after your journey. Let us share a meal together."

EYES WIDE open in wonder, Ethrain watched as the little man broke bread and past it to them. His every move carried with it the weight of a sacred ritual. He seemed to move in rhythm with some unheard divine melody that captured his attention and heart in every moment. He then made a sign with his hand, gracefully moving from his forehead to his chest and across his shoulders. She had never seen such a gesture but she knew that it invoked a palpable power unlike anything she had ever felt. Not even the magic of the druids could beckon such a wondrous presence into their midst. She looked at Hadrian who also watched Patrick's mysterious behavior with great interest. There was so much for them to learn about the great mysteries.

After a time of eating in silence, Patrick relaxed his inner attention to unseen forces and turned to them with a childlike expression.

"Tell me of your latest adventures."

"What makes you think that we have any tales for you other than the hardships of travel?" Ethrain asked, seeking to discover some secret to his insight.

Patrick gazed into her eyes. His penetrating look carried with it a mist that seemed to rise from some secret abyss of knowledge that encompassed past, present, and future. His look was ageless as though caught in the fishnets of eternity.

"I know that you have seen something terrible," he said simply.

"Indeed we have," Hadrian responded. He too was amazed at the man's great powers which seemed so strangely out of place in his small, humble frame.

"Tell me," Patrick said with unexpected authority.

"We came across a village on the way to Armagh," Ethrain stated solemnly. "Everyone was dead."

Patrick's face darkened with sadness. Hadrian recognized in his compassion the same sense of universal responsibility for the welfare of life that he had experienced holding the dead child.

"No one left alive?" the young priest asked.

"No one," Hadrian answered. "They killed everything that had breath. I've never seen such a monstrosity. Not even Attila's people destroy sheep and cattle."

"Did you see any men and young women among the dead?"

"I believe so . . . " Hadrian replied. Then he caught himself. His mind pictured the gruesome sight despite his reluctance to view it again.

"All the dead were the elderly and the very young. I cannot remember seeing anyone else."

"Then this is the work of the slave traders," Patrick observed grimly. "They've taken the men and women and sold them off to foreign lands."

"We found a Pict spear," Ethrain stated angrily.

"I'm sure you did," Patrick responded. "I know the beast behind this atrocity. It's happened before."

"You know who is responsible?" Hadrian cried, almost rising out of his chair.

Patrick studied him, reading into his reaction the lust for revenge. "I have dealt with him before," he said quietly. "He has destroyed dozens of villages in this way. The people fear him more than the demons of their ancestors."

"What is his name and where do I find him?"

The words came from the centurion with a determination that nothing would obstruct.

"I don't believe you want to find this man, Hadrian."

"I must!"

"Why is that?"

"I held his victims in my arms. He is not only their enemy, but mine now. I cannot live in peace until I end this evil."

Patrick smiled sadly.

"You have come to the right place for this task, friend. The monster is searching for me now and when he finds me, you will find him as well."

"He is searching for you?" Ethrain asked in horror.

"I have spoken against him and his soldiers and he has expressed his displeasure. He has sent word to me that parts of my body would decorate his home soon."

The two lovers were astonished at Patrick's calm demeanor. How could any man not fear such cruelty aimed directly at him? What secret in the depths of his spirit allowed him to find this utter detachment from the terrors of this world?

Hadrian realized that there was something more to this man's religion than a good story. And he knew that someday he would have to search out and discover the source of that inner strength.

"How can you not fear such a creature?" Ethrain asked.

"My friends, I have already died to this world. I belong to the Almighty God who created us all. I have given Him my all to do with as He wishes. I know that He directs the events of my life, and if it is His will that I suffer such an end then I will do it with joy."

These were disturbing words for the couple. No druid, no philosopher had ever spoken such ideas to them.

"How can you be so certain?" Hadrian wondered.

"Because I do not merely believe in something, Hadrian. I know that which I believe."

"You have met the originating powers of the universe?"

Patrick nodded affirmatively to their great shock.

"They call him the Word, the Son of God. Yes, I have encountered Him. He is with us now."

Hadrian couldn't keep from looking around the room. He caught himself, embarrassed. Patrick smiled at his confusion.

"Not out there, but within. The spirit knows. Doesn't it, Ethrain?"

She was surprised by his statement and wasn't sure how to take it. She realized that the remarkable man perceived her own powers of intuition even though she was far from any knowledge of the holy being he called the Son of God.

Hadrian was overcome with the need to change the subject because an ache in his soul threatened to invade him with a yearning he could not understand.

"What is the slave trader's name?" he asked with impatience.

"He is called Coroticus, ruler of the Firth of Clyde and all Dumbarton."

"I know this man!" Ethrain shouted out in surprise. "He was a merchant from the British isles long ago. He once came to my mother, Hyndla of Mallor, to find the crystal."

She bit her lip, having said more than she wanted.

"The crystal?" Patrick asked with concern.

"Just a talisman of our people."

"Really?"

Ethrain blushed with shame for lying to a man who could see through the human soul so clearly.

"You know this man?" Hadrian asked with horror.

"I saw him once," she said, straining to remember. "I was a child. He made a terrible impression on me, as though he incarnated the worst of human degradation. I remember that I was left alone with him briefly, and he tried to touch me. But I ran out of the cottage."

Hadrian could barely contain himself. He couldn't stand the thought that his beloved had come across such a beast.

"Where is he now?" he shouted as he rose to his feet and clasped his cutlass.

Patrick stood as well and took hold of Hadrian's arm. "I don't doubt your skills of war, friend. But you will not help anyone by getting yourself cut to pieces."

Hadrian was beside himself with anger. He had to pace the room to release the surge of energy possessing his body.

"We have dealt with such a man before, Patrick. And we vanquished him."

"Is this your plan? To rid the world of tyrants by personally murdering them all?"

"Do you have a better one?" the centurion asked as a challenge.

"I do indeed. But mine seeks to avoid violence."

"Then I wish you the best of luck. Evil has only been overcome with this!"

He pulled out his heavy Roman sword and held the blade high. He was surprised at himself to find relief for his rage in merely unsheathing his weapon. His lifelong training was in his very sinews.

"I do not believe that, Hadrian. There is another way.

One that has been revealed and that is all-powerful."

"You refer to your God-man from Galillee? It seems to me that his way destroyed him mercilessly."

Patrick step closer to Hadrian and placed his hand on the sword. The centurion felt the urge to kill evaporate from him, as though pulled out through the weapon by the hand of the priest. He lowered the sword, unable to resist the peacemaking feeling that eased his passion.

"You are wrong, Hadrian. And until you know how wrong you are, you will live in misery and restlessness."

Hadrian sensed that those words rang true. But his mind refused them entry and he pulled away, seeking to free himself from the magnetic effect of this most unusual man.

Patrick turned to Ethrain and seemed to beg her with his look to save her beloved from the fate he had prophesied.

"My Master said that if you live by the sword, you shall most surely die by the sword. I do not want to see your heart wrenched from you when that takes place."

Ethrain hurried to Hadrian and wrapped her arms around him.

"I could not bare it if I lost you!"

"That is all you would accomplish, Hadrian," Patrick observed gently. "If you charge into the tyrant's camp sword raised, you will only create a young widow forever lost in melancholy."

Hadrian returned his sword to its sheath and caressed Ethrain's golden locks. He was at a loss. How could he contain his feelings and do what he knew he must without causing more sorrow in the world?

"If you are called to save us from Coroticus, then the Almighty will give you a way. But it will not be at the price of Ethrain's inconsolable pain. After all, it was before Him that you were joined together. And it is also because of His will that you are here."

Hadrian had enough of talk that he could not understand. He took his wife's hand and faced Patrick.

"I know nothing of this god of yours. Never before have I been told of this one Power who knows and guides all things. I am not ready to accept such ideas, Patrick. I come from a world of multiplicity and conflict. My gods, the lords of Mount Olympus, have never spoken of peace. They have been the source of human strife, not the source of harmony. It is the same here on these strange isles. There are countless beings from beyond, few of which seek our happiness. I cannot understand how your one god can overcome all the harpies, demons, demiurges, and guardians of darkness that are on the threshold of taking control of our world!"

Patrick's eyes shimmered with compassion. He did not want to convince the Roman warrior of something he was not ready to grasp. He knew it would come in its own time, in a way no one could expect. But his visionary powers perceived that this troubled man was destined to be an instrument of the God of light. Somehow, the day would come when Hadrian Aldius would indeed confront the evil Coroticus against all odds.

chapter twenty-two

"Show me the letter!"

The deep voice shook the air with its brutal power. Two guards standing before the chamber doors looked at each other in fear. When the anger of Coroticus was stirred, someone was going to be hurt.

"Show me the letter, I said!"

Lupita, the tyrant's latest Celtic slave girl, hurried to his bed, trembling from head to foot. She handed him a scroll which he snatched from her and tore open. He laid back against the mounds of fur covering his huge bed. His ratlike eyes scurried through the scratches on the parchment. His large body, hanging through a silk tunic, shook with anger. He read out loud.

"The riches which he has gathered unjustly shall be vomited up from his belly; the angel of death drags him away, by the fury of dragons he shall be tormented, the viper's tongue shall kill him, unquenchable fire devours him."

The huge man let out a yell of rage and threw the scroll toward the flames in the vast hearth. He leaped from the bed with agility despite his size and took hold of the young woman. She shrunk back in terror.

"How is that miserable fool going to stop me? He can't save you, can he? It's just words! Words that mark him for death! Am I not right, Celtic girl?"

"Yes, master, yes."

He kissed her as though he would devour her. Every move he made was filled with violence. He tore at her clothing as his lust took hold of him. Lupita closed her eyes and burst into tears. She thought of her homeland as he molested her, trying to escape the nightmare in which she was caught.

OUTSIDE THE FORTRESS walls overlooking the North Sea, a rider galloped at full speed toward the dark castle. He was quickly given entrance and he pulled in his mount below the window of the ruler's chambers.

The frantic soldier hurried into the living quarters.

"Is Lord Coroticus in his chambers?" he called out as the guards prepared to keep him from approaching the doors.

"I have an urgent message for him!"

"He will see no one at this time," one of the guards answered sternly, knowing what awaited anyone who disobeyed.

The messenger, covered in mud and torn by bushes and tree limbs, was not about to be stopped after riding for so long.

"This message is from the High King's druid."

"Show me."

He held the scroll before his face.

"It bears the signature of the mighty Lochru," the guard said to his companion.

"Even the great magician will have to wait. If we disturb our master, he will feed us to the wolves."

"I come directly from Tara! When have you known the High King of Eire to send word to Coroticus? Call your master now!"

" Can you not show it to his advisers? They will present it to him in the morning."

"Look man!" the herald shouted in frustration, pointing to the royal seal. "There is to be a gathering on the hill of Slane by the graves of the Men of Fecc."

"And why should our king be interested in these affairs?"

The messenger looked about to insure that no one was overhearing them. Then he said in a low voice:

"The monk Patrick will be there."

The soldiers looked at each other and knew that their chieftain would cut their heads off right there in the corridor if they did not provide him with this information. His desire for Patrick's blood was greater than his lust for the flesh of his slaves.

HADRIAN AND ETHRAIN cuddled by a small fireplace. It was their first night in Ireland after an absence of more than a year. The events of the day had worn them out, but now that they basked in the heat of the burning wood, the joy and passion of their togetherness returned with zeal.

Here was a sparkle of the bliss Hadrian's soul longed for. His stoic teachers, among them the great Epictetus whose wisdom would ring down through the ages, taught him that such ecstacy could be found even in this brief passage through time. Other teachers told him the same as well: the sunsets that entranced him as a child on the marble patio of his home in the hills above Rome; the glimpse of some vaster reality in the crystal waters of a softly singing stream; the moments of mortal danger when he was strangely freed from his terror.

Now before this dying fire, pressed against Ethrain's warm and inviting skin, he entered into that blessed contentment, that alignment with the harmony of the spheres, and was flooded with a gratitude that filled his heart with peace.

They would be making love this night, leaving far behind the hardships of life and finding joy in an oasis of pure oneness of being. As he slowly ran his fingers through her flowing locks, he wondered whether this feeling of liberation was a key to the path the holy Patrick had found. Yet in his effort to reach the shores of a greater life, the monk had turned away from the life-giving union that Hadrian shared with Ethrain. For the Roman, there was no question that the mutual gift to each other which came from the depths of their love was at the heart of the mysteries of the universe.

The daughter of the druid Ubarra was freeing his soul from the narrow prison where he had lived most of his four decades in this world. Not only had she introduced him to the mysteries and enchantments of her ancient people, but she also released him from the chains of his past. The son of a general, no young Roman ever received better or more severe training to be a man of war. To become the soldier admired by his imperial culture, Hadrian left behind his capacity to be sensitive and therefore vulnerable. Though the development of his body was balanced with that of his mind, the central part of himself was left aside.

By the warm hearth, encircled with the soothing aroma of crackling logs, he sensed a thawing of his inner glaciers. They were close together, and could feel each other along every inch of their bodies. There was security in this exotic sensation. The desperate loneliness in the cave of his soul that seemed buried alive forever was able to take its first steps into the light of togetherness. In that brightness, the Roman warrior could finally lay down his weapons. A new strength was found, not in muscle and steel, but in self-surrender to the power of love.

The more he let himself love Ethrain, the more the hard pieces of his former self broke off and revealed new vistas of meaning and purpose. The Roman way was always aimed in the opposite direction. Self-mastery through a wretched amputation of human gentleness. And with that loss, so did the spirit's inner vision dim, making the world a desolate place of raw survival. Hadrian was learning that all of his culture's ideas were distorted by this formation of its men.

From the blood-soaked arenas where people cheered the ripping apart of men and women, to the oppression of most of the tribes across the known world, there was something hopelessly wrong in the very nature of the empire.

Hadrian kissed Ethrain's cheek and made his way to her lips. Her woman's softness beckoned forth his deepest humanity, beyond the soldier's inner shield and unlocked the doors of his childhood. The boy who loved the colorful butterflies fluttering in the meadows of Italy came face to face with the embittered man who had sunk iron blades into the bodies of his adversaries.

From the recesses of his mind echoed the songs of his early youth, with sweet harmony of flutes and lyres along with the dreamy sound of children's voices. His mother stirred in his memory, with her unrelenting care that could be trusted like the sun's daily rise and fall. Then he saw the woods of his youth and heard the whistle of countless birds singing through the trees. All this had been lost and forgotten for some twenty-five years. Instead had come the mask of merciless power.

He had learned to give and take pain by cutting off its source. Nothing could truly hurt without the heart. The slash of swords and spears, the agony of an arrow's piercing point, were easy to sustain. But the surfacing of deep feeling was another matter. Hadrian recognized that the courage of this vulnerability was precisely what made Patrick such an extraordinary being. Never had the Roman encountered such a man. His Greek teachers, learned men that they were and versed in the spiritual wisdom of Pythagoras and Plato, had nothing of the radiance seeping through the features of the young monk.

Patrick was Hadrian's very opposite. The man from Briton looked with love upon all things, while the centurion always carried suspicion in his glance and recognized enemies in all men. Patrick freely lived his every breath in a stunning humility, as though he were forever in the presence of some awesome divinity. Hadrian lived by the surges of energy racing through his tense body, and was perpetually ready to strike.

The Roman buried his face in Ethrain's shoulder. Soon, he would be lost in an ocean of passion. But as he vanished into the bliss of lovemaking, he heard a voice far in the labyrinth of his mind say clearly: "You will follow Patrick and protect him for me."

SHORTLY BEFORE sunrise, Ethrain opened her eyes. It was dark and for a moment she could see nothing. In the distance, the monotonous crash of waves on the rocks of Ireland echoed in a never-ending rhythm. She thrilled at the sound of the sea welcoming her back to her native shores. Then she felt her lover's arm at her side and remembered the hot embrace that kept them close far into the night.

In this twilight between sleep and waking, she let her thoughts wander and mix with her dreams. In the past, such moments had regularly revealed to her what lay ahead. But the swirl of images before her mind's eye would not release their secrets to her on this quiet morning.

Among the faces, wooded glens, and chanting rituals that wandered across the stillness of her mind, she caught sight of a shining triangular object. It stood out from the rainfall of forms and colors. Ethrain focused her attention and recognized the great crystal that belonged to the druids and had been kept by her mother, the witch Hyndla, until her death.

The magical treasure came down from great antiquity. Ethrain heard over the years that the crystal was fashioned by another civilization that had sunk to the bottom of the sea before the gods came to the Irish isles. Kingly priests of a desert land that fashioned its shape with giant stones were its later guardians. The very first druids had carried it to these western shores.

No one knew of the crystal's location, except for Ethrain. It was all but forgotten since the massacres of the druids by the Roman legions. Hadrian had seen it once and been exposed to its magic, but he did not understand what it truly was. Gazing upon the magnificent object through the mists of her inner sight, Ethrain realized that they must recover it and save it from complete obliteration. Too much of her people's ways had already been destroyed.

The first glimmers of dawn stretched across the North Sea and penetrated the cottage where they slept. Ethrain rose up and walked over to the window in her flowing robe. The sky was filling with rich hues of violet and orange. A golden haze moved across the horizon and illumined the windswept cliffs. The light caught in Ethrain's hair and glowed around her like the hallow of a divine being.

Suddenly, the glow disappeared. It took Ethrain a moment to realize what had happened. A silhouette stepped between her and the first colors of dawn. She quickly kneeled, but it was too late. Strong hands grabbed hold of her and covered her mouth. Other hands pulled her through the open window and wrapped her in a heavy blanket.

An owl's cry awoke Hadrian from a deep sleep. He stretched his arm over his beloved, only to find a void.

He opened his eyes and looked into the shadows of the room.

The centurion sensed trouble and jumped to his feet. He saw instantly that the window was damaged. He hurried to it and found a shred of Ethrain's tunic shivering in the breeze.

Hadrian shouted from the core of his being and tore out of the cottage. Everywhere in the mud were signs of rushing men. Hadrian ran toward the cliffs and frantically looked out toward the rising sun. Then he ran toward the other cottages, desperation burning through his soul. He finally ran toward Patrick's home, on an instinct that the good man could help him.

He found the monk sitting under a tree, at prayer before the glorious mantle of the dawning sun.

"Patrick!" he cried out.

Hadrian slowed his pace as he came up to him. The man was in some sort of trance. His eyes were partly open, yet he was not looking outward. A soft smile rendered his face profoundly peaceful. Hadrian had only seen such a look on the death mask of his wise Greek tutor. For an instant, the Roman was lifted out of the hurricane of dread howling through his being. A deep silence washed over him and he lost track of himself in the presence of the beatific serenity of the monk.

Patrick turned toward him, his peace unruffled by the disturbance.

"God be with you, friend. What troubles you?"

"Ethrain! She's been taken from me!"

Patrick stood and took Hadrian by the shoulders, revealing unexpected strength.

"Show me where this happened!"

Hadrian led him back to his cottage. Patrick examined the disturbed grass near the window. He kneeled and pointed to the form of a boot's heel encrusted in the dirt.

"See the shape. It's a soldier's boot."

"A soldier? Where is an army encamped in these hills?"

"Nowhere. Not between here and the valley of Boyne where the High King resides."

"Why would his men come to this coast?"

"I don't know. But I am traveling to Tara this very day. I have been granted an audience with King Laoghaire. I will ask for his help. You may be sure that his men will not harm someone who comes under the High King's protection. They know the penalty too well."

"I must save her now!"

"Listen to me! The king has done this before. He has kidnapped my friends and fellow workers in order to negotiate with me. Today he wants to confront me again and prove that his gods are greater than mine. He believes I will be sure to appear at his court despite the dangers if he holds someone dear to me in captivity."

"What kind of a king behaves in that manner?"

"Why, a barbarian king, of course. Don't forget where we are."

"Will they harm her?"

"No. The High King knows better than to rouse my wrath. He has seen the results of my curses."

Hadrian was too overwrought to inquire further into his strange statement and he hurried into the cottage to dress and arm himself.

"Patrick!" he called out as he strapped on his sword. "I will not be so gracious when I find the men who did this."

"I tell you they will not harm a daughter of the isles. They reserve their brutality for foreigners."

"It seems they have already brutalized her. She will not follow them passively."

"I assure you, Hadrian, you'll find her at the King's court. The crafty old chief knows he can have control over me in no other way. I do not obey his demands unless I must. So now we travel to the royal castle at Tara."

SOON THEY were mounted and hurrying their horses over the plain of Meath toward the hill of Slane claimed by the Irish High Kings from time immemorial. Across the channel, a boat filled with armed men was headed toward the same hill. On deck, a huge figure paced like a caged beast. Coroticus could not wait to get hold of the monk who dared to defy him.

Hadrian and Patrick travelled across fertile valleys, over low hills and ridges, through meandering streams. The deep green pastures of ancient Ulidia, the silver sparkle of landlocked salt waters of the lough of Stangford, the dark summits of the Mountains of Mourne -- all past by in a blur of brilliant colors and sweet aromas.

Hadrian saw nothing of the serene landscape around him. He was flushed with anger and remorse as he forced his horse into a relentless gallop. How could his beloved have been taken from his side while he slept like a child? Was he becoming old and losing his skills and instincts? He had never feared death, but neither had he imagined living long enough to watch himself slowly disintegrate with age. Yet he knew his body was still taut and agile, capable of taking on any man.

The humiliation of sleeping through Ethrain's kidnapping ate at him as much as his fear for her safety. His pride had always been founded on his power to protect and be counted on in times of danger. As he galloped alongside the monk, he felt stripped not only of his dignity but of his very identity as the mighty centurion, hero of many battles.

He found himself doubting the sanity of returning to these barbaric isles. Why had he not listened to his reason? He had let himself fall under the sensuous spell of the Celtic beauty who mesmerized him as no woman had ever done.

"Fool!" he cried out involuntarily. The wind carried the sound to Patrick's ears.

"Don't blame yourself, Hadrian! The King's men are masters of such things."

"How soon will we be in Tara?" Hadrian yelled out, unable to shift his mind from the single purpose that consumed him so painfully.

"Midday. But we'll have to rest the horses."

"No!"

Patrick brought his mount next to the Roman and they galloped side by side.

"Keep your wits about you, friend! If we run these animals into the ground, we'll have to walk the rest of the way. The King awaits me at the great hall for the noon meal. He will not stand for anymore delays."

Hadrian wished more than ever that they had stayed in Gaul where remnants of his Roman world could still be found.

Perhaps they could have settled in Massilia by the warm waters of the Mediterranean. He remembered how the first sight of the troubled waters of the North Sea gave him an ominous feeling of their future, as though they were entering a realm poisoned by the presence of demons.

A group of men in horned helmets appeared ahead of them. Patrick slowed his horse and ordered Hadrian to do the same.

"That is the ruler of this province."

The five men, dressed in heavy furs and armed with axes and spears rode toward them followed by a pack of hunting dogs.

"Rein in your horse!" Patrick shouted as he came to a stop. Hadrian pulled sharply on the reins and came to a halt.

"Dismount!" Patrick insisted as he slipped off the side of his animal.

"Why?" the Roman asked angrily. He wanted to maintain his position of strength. Never had he dismounted in the face of adversaries.

"Get off your horse or they will attack us!"

"Let them. I'll kill them all!"

Patrick hurried over to Hadrian, grabbed his foot and threw him off his horse. Hadrian jumped up and barely refrained from pulling his sword on the vivacious monk.

"Trust me," Patrick said gently, knowing that the soldier had never done so with anyone.

The Celtic warriors reined in their mounts at a short distance from them. A whistle caused the dogs to come to a standstill. Tension filled the air as the men gazed at each other. One of the Celts wore a large helmet decorated with huge metal wings. He was clearly the chieftain and the others awaited his orders.

Seeing the travelers dismounted momentarily confused the men who would have otherwise charged them without a second thought. But their unexpected act of submission held them back from immediate attack. Hadrian stood frozen as a statue, feeling more humiliated than ever. No Roman centurion would stand for such passivity in the face of other warriors. They would rather be torn to bits than submit without a fight. Nevertheless, Hadrian sensed that he must trust the monk if he was to be reunited with Ethrain. Even his rigid pride could not get in the way of that purpose.

One of the men whispered to the chieftain and gestured toward Hadrian. The warlord turned his hunter's gaze upon him. Beneath the thick hairs of his beard and heavy eyebrows, a scarlet shade darkened his weather-beaten features. He recognized the cape and sword of a soldier of the hated empire.

The chieftain let out a high-pitched whistle. From behind the horses came a great wolfhound. The Celt gave another whistle and the beast rushed toward Hadrian.

Just as the Roman reached for his weapon, Patrick stepped in front of him. The monk raised his hands and began singing a psalm. The melodious sound seemed utterly out of place as the savage wolfhound raced across the meadow, preparing for a kill.

Hadrian hesitated. His companion's bizarre behavior took him aback. Every fiber of his being cried out to draw his cutlass as the creature approached. But the sound of Patrick's gentle voice, in the cadence of an angelic prayer, disoriented his senses. Hadrian felt out of control for the first time in his life, even though his instincts were ordering him to defend himself. The monk's song interfered not only with common sense, but with the reality of the moment, displacing the sense of danger in some incomprehensible way. The man's unshakable faith was contagious.

The wolfhound abruptly stopped before Patrick and stared at him. He was no longer baring his sharp teeth, but now bore the look of a loyal dog awaiting his master's command. The beast sat and let out a soft whine as Patrick continued to sing his prayer. The monk caressed his thickly matted head, still wet from the blood of a recent kill. The creature's tail wagged with joy.

Eyes wide with shock, the Celtic warriors watched the scene in disbelief. Their amazement quickly turned to fear as they recognized the supernatural quality of what was taking place before them. The chieftain dismounted and approached Patrick. The two men studied each other while Patrick continued his melodious chant. The barbarian warrior's fierce gaze melted before the goodness emanating from the young monk. Like his wolfhound, the savagery of his nature gave way to a hidden decency in the recesses of his nature.

"I am called Dichu, lord of Sabhall."

Patrick stopped his unearthly chanting. A broad smile filled his face with light.

"I am Patrick, a bishop of the true Faith."

The chieftain's eyes suddenly brimmed with tears as he gazed into the face of such resplendent goodness. He fell to his knees and took Patrick's hand.

"Teach me your magic, holy man!"

Hadrian's jaw dropped in astonishment. What he saw was inexplicable and yet utterly beautiful.

"I pledge to do so, my good man," Patrick stated with serenity. "I will build my first church in the name of the one God here on your lands."

The man wept with a strange joy that came from the very roots of his soul. He pointed to a barn near the banks of a river.

"I give you that barn for your purpose. Please accept it."

Patrick looked at the simple structure by the Slane river. He raised his hand in blessing and said in a loud, clear voice.

"God's blessing on Dichu who gave me the barn! May he have afterwards a heavenly home, bright, pure, and great! God's blessing on Dichu and all his children. No child, grand-child or descendant shall die but after a long life."

The warlord kissed Patrick's hand, weeping like a child. The monk helped him to his feet and embraced him.

"This is the place I will come to end my days. It will be a sacred place for all time."

Accompanied by their new friends, the companions reached the domain of the High King without further trouble.

Hadrian glanced at Patrick many times during the journey, realizing that he was in the presence of a man with exceptional powers despite his simple appearance. He felt a new sense of peace settling within, believing that as long as he was in the company of this man, everything would come to a good end. He was beginning to trust in Patrick's unseen force of light even in the uncertain and dangerous circumstances surrounding them.

chapter twenty-three

THE COURT of the High King of Eire was a vast wooden complex teeming with soldiers, royal family, cattle, druids and bards. The palace at Tara on the hill of Slane overlooked the lush valley of the Boyne and the plain of Meath. A forest of great oaks surrounded the fortress.

Great beamed halls had witnessed the passage of Celtic heroes and kings, the island's most beautiful maidens, and the magic of its mightiest druids. Tara was also home to the stone called the Lia Fail or Stone of Destiny upon which the High Kings of Ireland stood when they were crowned. Legend had it that the magical stone would release a great roar when the rightful monarch placed himself upon it.

Here also men more godlike than human had made their mark. Midir the Proud, Lugh the son of Kian, Sun-God of all Celtica, Nuada of the Silver Hand, and the mightiest hero of the Celtic race Cuchulain, the Hound of Ulster whose head and hand were buried in the mounds of Tara.

This day King Laoghaire sat with his druid magi in the great hall, eagerly awaiting the arrival of Patrick the Briton. He was an aging warrior, secure in his power and yet worried by the new religion the monk had brought to his isles. Beneath the long grey beard and snow white hair falling to his shoulders, the High King pondered the greatest enemy he had to face in a lifetime of war. Neither the Vikings nor the Angles ever confronted him with such a threat. The little solitary man in the white robe who wandered his provinces carried with him the power to annihilate the very spirit of his ancestors. The king had no fear when he sent his great warriors into the fray, but now he was faced with the struggle of magicians whose weapons were invisible and of supernatural power. Could he send his druids against this man as he had done with his armies? What kind of magic did this servant of the Most High possess?

At the king's side stood the druid Lochru. He was the chief magi and was nearly as revered as the king himself. An eagle's glare burned in his piercing eyes, and his demeanor emanated with a lofty dignity. The very name of his position—druid, from the Welsh Drywn meaning "knowledge of the oak" and "deep knowledge"—was reflected in the power of his presence. The mighty oak was the symbol of deity, and those who possessed such knowledge were said to be in direct communication with supernatural forces.

It took twenty years of deepening study to enter the inner circle of the druids. Lochru had started like all the chosen ones as a bard, studying recitation of tales, philosophy, and verse form. This was followed by seven years of learning the poets' secret language where, through poetic form, he memorized the oral tradition of his people's deepest wisdom. He learned the art of soothsaying and the secrets of the Otherworld beyond death. He reaped mistletoe with a golden cycle on the sixth night of the moon, while in its full strength though not yet in mid-course, and sacrificed two white bulls to the gods. He sat in judgement and applied the law to his people. Lochru the druid was as powerful as his king.

The chief magi to the High King awaited patiently for the moment he had so skillfully arranged. His daily counsel to the king offered him the perfect strategy to bring Patrick to Tara. He had known of this man's arrival from the very first day. The elder sage had seen visions for many years of what was to come. A disturbance in the spiritual realm was occurring, one which the greatest of the seers had prophesied for centuries.

He remembered how the most powerful druids from Gaul, Iberia, and the Isles came together in the oak groves of Carnutes. Deep in the dense forest, far from all uninitiated eyes, the mystic masters gathered in a circle under a gigantic oak shimmering with silver bundles of mistletoe. In flowing white robes they performed the secrets of their rituals and beckoned forth powers known only to them. Then they spoke to each other of their fears.

"I have seen it for myself," Lochru said to the stern faces made a ghostly blue in the moonlight. "There is a new power manifesting in the spirit realms. It cannot be controlled."

"How do you mean, wise Lochru?" asked the elder Uthidor of Connacht, whose knowledge was beyond compare.

"Odin has appeared to me."

"The being from the North? Why would the gods of Valhalla commune with the druid of Tara?"

"There is a shift in the Age. The nexus of power is moving. A great force is interfering with their entrance into Middle Earth."

"I have noticed that our sacrifices are less fruitful," the magi of Gaul observed with great concern. "Tell us what the Norse spirits have spoken."

Lochru hesitated. The circle of white-bearded men came closer to him, moving forward as one body.

"The tides are shifting. The ancients are leaving us."

"That cannot be!" the druid of Connacht shouted out for the heavens to hear.

"The stars have pointed to this for many cycles."

"What will the gods have us do?" Ulthidor asked with a deep tremor in his voice.

"Our western isles will be the place of confrontation. Gaul has already lost to the power of the holy man Germanicus. But we will fall even further and be lost forever if a battle is not waged."

"We druids do not battle!" a seer who had lived more than a century whispered hoarsely.

"There will be no more druids if we do not act now!" Lochru shouted for all to hear. "The enemy will be coming to my shores where the spirits have given us an entryway to their world. If we are destroyed in Ireland, there will be no place left for us."

"You forget that we survived the Romans!" Ulthidor said forcefully. "They massacred us and desecrated our holy places, but our teaching lives, and we pass it on to the future."

"If Odin and his demiurges are fearful," Lochru roared, "we must be in dread! This power is like the scorching sun of Egypt. We will vanish like shadows. As will the ancient ones."

"This is impossible!" a Gothic druid called out. "We have ruled these lands from the earliest days. No armies can overcome us."

"It will only take one man to change everything. The gods tell me that there is more than one. They are appearing in every land."

"Let us invoke the spirits from the kingdom of Donn!"

"Fom the Annwn?" Lochru asked gravely.

"It is forbidden!" Ulthidor insisted.

"But nothing will be as it once was!" The druid of Gaul added in fear. "Not only is the sky descending upon us, but the earth is opening up underneath our feet! Our world is at an end!"

Ulthidor stepped into the center of the circle. He was

taller than most of the other druids and was charged with energies that flowed from him in torrents. He was the Master of masters.

"Hear me, brothers! Let no one believe that our knowledge will be lost, even if every last one of us is cut down! Even if the bard is silenced and our verses of truth forgotten until the sun turns cold, there will arise new channels for the gods to speak to us. There was a time once when all was lost to the great waters, but we stand here filled with the mysteries passed on despite utter annihilation. Lochru speaks to us of the druid's power among the people, not the power of which we are the gatekeepers."

Lochru approached his fellow Celt and aimed a glare as sharp as a spear into his pupils.

"Ulthidor of Connacht! You forget yourself among your brethren! I stand here before you as druid of the High King. You insult the King himself!"

"No, Lochru of Eire, I speak only of you. You worship the palace and the armies of the King. Not the gods of our ancestors."

Lochru's glare burned with the heat of the evil eye itself. He turned to the assembly of wisemen and addressed them.

"Brothers of the teaching, how many gatherings under this very oak have we shared together? I am one of you. I have faithfully served our sacred ways, just as I faithfully serve my people's King. I warn you of things to come that will curse us all. Though we have great respect for the wisdom of Ulthidor, we also know that he speaks in riddles and dreams. I speak to you as a man who lives in this world. The day will come when there will be no more druids sitting by the thrones of our kings. What then, my brothers? Will we be reduced to the rank of the silversmith or the merchant? Or perhaps we may be so forgotten that we sleep among beggars and drink from the wells of the peasants."

The assembly murmured in agreement. Lochru looked at Ulthidor with a sparkle of defiance. He had finally vanquished the man who diminished his own importance. He saw in his visionary's mind a bird of prey picking at the body of its victim. He conveyed that image to the mind of Ulthidor and smiled with the satisfaction of conquest.

The sage of Conchract shook his head. He did not fear the druid of Tara though he recognized the meaning of the picture flashed before his inner sight. It could only suggest that Lochru would kill him some day. Ulthidor perceived the mysterious irony that his adversary was bringing down on them the very destruction that he feared.

IN THE HIGH King's great hall, the druid was becoming more impatient. The king sat at his table, chewing on the wing of a recent hunt. His eyes were vacant, and Lochru recognized the dimming of age and the shadow of final consummation already present in the monarch.

"He's fought his last battle," he thought to himself. He would have to act quickly before King Lagohaire was buried on the plains of Breg. He had seen in the flames of his hearth the release of a new faith all across the isles and the utter collapse of the spirit world he frequented so obsessively.

Lochru did not merely find amazement in the encounter with the disembodied ones, but he also lusted for the dark powers they possessed. His life was spent acquiring them for his own purposes. So many full moons witnessed his incantations, rituals, and bloody sacrifices as he stretched his soul to merge with the breath of another realm.

He achieved great feats in front of his people, stirring the forces of magic and controlling them with the might of his will. No seer or sorcerer in any land, except perhaps for the miracles in the sands of Judea, could harness the elements and manifest them in the outer world as he did.

Lochru looked out the window toward the ridges in the distance. "Will he not come?" he wondered. He was so eager to gaze upon the face of the man who claimed to be the messenger and instrument of this disturbance of cosmic proportions. Already, he had encountered his courage and heard of his strange conversations with uncreated power.

But he wanted to see the man behind the magic, the individual who dared to attempt the overthrow of his almighty role among his people.

The druid stepped into an antechamber and gestured for his apprentice, Lucetmael, to approach him. The young man, also dressed in druidic robes, hurried to him.

"How is our guest fairing?"

"She is very displeased, sire."

"As wild as an unbroken beast, is she?" the druid whispered with amusement. "A rare woman, that one. Perhaps I ought to keep her."

"No, I beg of you, good master. Release her as soon as it can be done. She will break everything in the palace."

"Then tie her down! "

"No one will approach her. She has a weapon and threatens to cut the throat of the first man who steps forward," Lucetmael said fearfully.

"How did she get possession of a weapon?" the druid asked in anger.

"One of the soldiers was careless and turned his back on her. I believe he is recovering well, however."

"Fools! How can a woman be such trouble? We have

captured others before. They did not make all this commotion."

"She is not like other women, mighty Lochru. I fear she will never stop fighting."

"Then I'll sell her into slavery if she does not comply. That will teach her."

The druid dismissed his assistant and wandered the long hallways of the castle. He came to another window that opened onto the sea. On the horizon, the sails of a ship caught the wind and sped toward the shores. The druid smiled wickedly. He was starting the battle with Patrick from a position of strength. Lochru had long ago decided that the greatest power of all was his own ability to take control. The mystic knowledge of which he was a vessel was second to his own well-being. Unlike the monk Patrick, he was not prepared to die for his gods. They were there to serve him, not the other way around. It had always worked well for him.

THE SUN WAS descending from its zenith when Patrick and Hadrian arrived before the giant doors of the High King's fortress. They were brought into the great hall where the court awaited them. A heavy silence fell over the vast room as they walked toward the throne. The old warrior king watched them intently and Lochru, who stood beside him, was visibly stunned. He knew the tall man could not be Patrick. He was obviously a Roman with the gait of a centurion.

His companion was short of stature, thin and pale with an odd tonsure that took away any dignity to his appearance. He wore a white robe that was brown with mud from top to bottom. His eyes contained none of the impressive glare so often seen among his fellow druids. Patrick was the least likely adversary the druid had ever come across. A wave of arrogance comforted the seer who was now certain that he would win any contest of magic with such a wretched and ignoble being.

"So you are Patrick the Briton?" King Laoghaire inquired. "I've heard much about you."

Patrick bowed before the king and Hadrian mimicked his motion without conviction.

"It is an honor to come before you, King Laoghaire of Eire and all Ireland. I too know about you."

The old man frowned, sensing that there was some hidden meaning in those words.

"Who is your companion?"

"A Roman from the heart of the empire. Hadrian Aldius, a former centurion and tribune."

"I have done battle with your armies many times, Roman," the king exclaimed. "I have even won a few."

He laughed, recalling an old man's past glories.

Hadrian tried on an amicable face and searched the features of the sovereign. He wore a great fur mantle, and at his side hung a long, iron sword—wide, flat and double-edged. The Roman was struck by the realization that this weapon may well have cut down his dearest friends in the days of his youth. The king was old enough to have fought Hadrian's father.

Hadrian studied the men standing at the king's side.

Immediately, he was drawn to the powerful presence of the man in robes with a white beard falling below his belt. He found the eyes of the druid locked on him, seeking to penetrate his mind and perceive his mission.

"What brings you this far north?" the king wondered. "Rome has long pulled away from this most distant corner of its realm."

"I am a friend of this man," Hadrian stated, gesturing to Patrick.

"Are you a follower of the crucified god, then?" the monarch asked suspiciously.

"I am not. I owe allegiance to the gods of my people

and know nothing about this new mystery religion."

"Nor do I," the king muttered. "But I do know that it is invading my domain like an advancing enemy army."

"If I may be so bold," said Patrick in his direct and honest voice. "I am not here to threaten your reign, Sire. I deal with the souls of men and women, and I give witness to the eternal One."

"Why do you bother us with all this?"

"I was a captive in this land, a slave for six years in my youth. I came to know your people and to feel their need for the light."

"What light?" the old king asked, confused.

"The light of the Holy Trinity that gives us freedom from ignorance."

The king turned to his druid.

"Do you know anything of these things, Lochru?"

"Indeed, I do, your majesty. This strange teaching is utter nonsense, filling the simple with foolishness."

Patrick's face turned bright red. Hadrian could see his body fill with the heat of outrage.

"They tell of one god who is three persons. Yet they say that these three beings are manifestations of one being. Even the Greek philosophers have trouble understanding their fantasies."

"Blasphemer!" Patrick shouted with full force. "How dare you mock the Almighty so lightly!"

The druid looked at him with disdain.

"You have no power," he proclaimed with contempt. "Our gods will destroy you like a worm trampled underfoot."

"Despite all your learning, druid, you are ignorant and your soul will be flung into outer darkness!"

Lochru shook with rage. He charged toward him.

"Will you be the one to do so, miserable wretch?"

"If it is my God's will!" Patrick answered with absolute confidence.

The druid was struck by the look of unbreakable certainty that radiated from the little man. No wiseman had ever been more anchored in the ground of his belief. But he composed himself and raised his hand high.

"Behold the magic of the druids!"

He shouted out an incantation in a strange language and twisted his hand in the air. A great flash filled the room and blinded everyone. The banquet hall went dark despite the brightness of day because of the intensity of the flash.

A roar of terror exploded among the nobles and soldiers in the great hall. An acrid smell filled the room. Eerie moans echoed all around. A swirl of light, like a small cyclone, descended into the middle of the room. In this cloud of light, a hundred faces appeared, each more tortured than the other.

The king jumped to his feet and drew his sword.

"Druid, what have you done?"

Lochru cried out another incantation and the room was suddenly empty of the supernatural sight. The druid turned a haughty gaze upon Patrick and dared him to do better. Astounded by the wizard's skill in the magic arts, Hadrian had the sinking feeling that their cause was lost.

"Remember that we must save Ethrain," he whispered to Patrick.

The monk looked into his eyes and smiled sadly.

"Do you fear that I cannot match this sorcerer's power? Are you still that far from me, Hadrian?"

The Roman stepped back, uncertain as to why he felt such remorse for doubting his friend.

"King Laoghaire of Eire, behold the presence of the Almighty!"

Patrick crossed himself slowly.

"In the name of the Father, and of the Son, and of the Holy Spirit," he said quietly. Then he spread out his arms.

"Have mercy on us who trust in your word. Reveal to the unbelievers what you have granted us to know."

The crowd looked around and saw nothing. Hadrian became worried. Lochru the druid smiled triumphantly. Then a queer sensation took hold of the wizard. He looked down and noticed that his feet were no longer touching the ground. He began rising up into the air, above the heads of the king and his court.

Lochru struggled but found that he could not move any part of his body. Terror burst from his eyes as he felt himself utterly helpless in the grips of an unknown force.

The crowd screamed as he was lifted all the way to the beams supporting the great structure.

Lochru looked down and was dizzied by the distance between his old bones and the stone floor below. He looked at Patrick, desperate and pleading for his safety. The one thing he had sought throughout his life was gone. He was utterly without control, a puppet in the hands of an infinite power.

Hadrian watched this unnatural phenomenon in awe. He pulled himself out of his trance and realized that if harm came to the old sage, they would both be destroyed instantly.

"Patrick!" he whispered. "Don't kill him. Remember Ethrain."

The monk's face was knotted in a look of anger that Hadrian had never seen on him before.

"This creature blasphemed against the Holy Spirit! The sin that cannot be forgiven!"

"They will butcher us if you kill him!"

"I will smash his skull on the steps of the throne like cheap pottery!"

"I thought you were a man of peace, Patrick."

The monk turned to him, fuming.

"There is a time for peace and a time for war. I fight the darkness that he serves!"

"In the name of the holy man of Judea, don't kill him!" Hadrian insisted, thinking only of his beloved hidden somewhere in the castle.

Patrick calmed himself with a deep breath and looked up at the terrified sorcerer, completely stripped of the arrogance that had been a permanent feature of his character. Patrick crossed himself.

"Forgive me, Father, for my passion."

The invisible force slowly lowered the druid from the heights of the ceiling. He dropped onto the floor like a sack and remained in fetal position, shivering like a leaf.

"Thank you, friend," Patrick said to Hadrian. "I must work on that temper."

Everyone was frozen in fear. The old king's mouth was wide open, eyes bugged out like a giant insect. No one dared make a move.

"Mylord, shall I call upon my God and His angels for more displays of power?"

"What do you want?" the old monarch managed to state in a trembling voice as he looked upon the crumbled old man who was once his high priest and chief druid, his kingdom's very source of power.

"I want your permission to share my teaching among your people without hindrance."

"Granted!" the old king muttered as he wiped the sweat from his wrinkled brow.

"I also want you to release the young woman whom your soldiers took from us this morning."

"I don't know what you mean," the king said angrily.

"Ask your druid then," Patrick insisted.

The king gestured for one of the nobles to assist the druid to his feet. When they picked him up, Lochru was wet with terror and unable to stand on his own.

"The King addresses you," the guard whispered as he held him up.

Lochru saw that the entire court was staring at him. He did his best to regain his composure.

"Druid!" the king cried in disgust at the weakness revealed by Patrick. "What is this about a captive woman who belongs to the Briton?"

Lochru's eyes turned red with venom and he peered at his nemesis.

"I know of no such woman."

"Someone gave orders to kidnap her!" Hadrian shouted, his hand on his cutlass. "Bring her to us now!"

The king's guards levelled their spears at the Roman.

"What woman is this?" the king inquired.

"She is my wife, Sire, a daughter of your isles, and I demand to have her released immediately!"

Lucetmael, the druid's assistant, looked at his master in search of instructions.

"Who knows of this?" the king ordered. "Speak now or die by my own hand!"

"I know where she is, Mylord," Lucetmael said fearfully.

Lochru grit his teeth with rage.

"Where is she then?" the king shouted.

"In Lochru's chambers, My King."

"What is this foolishness, druid?" the king asked his old wizard angrily.

"Merely insuring that the Briton would obey your command, Mylord," Lochru stated as he boiled with humiliation and anger.

"Give her back to them now!"

"Yes, Mylord," the druid said submissively as he stepped into the corridor.

"She'd better not be harmed!" Hadrian cried out.

"Silence, Roman! Our people are not as primitive as you think," the king said. He slapped his hands together, ordering the servants to bring food to the table. "Let us commence the feast we have prepared for this day.

This is the great feis, gathering our nobles from every tuatha in the land. My chieftains are hungry. Join us!"

Hadrian reluctantly followed Patrick to the dais and sat near the king. The regal old warrior tore off a leg of venison and chewed on it angrily. His hunter's eyes glanced over at Patrick. He could not hide his suspicion and anger. Hadrian observed this exchange and knew that treachery was in the air. Patrick accepted the food like a grateful child, full of the joy of the manifestation that had been granted for him.

Queen Ethne, a tall, serene woman who had watched the events with great attention, nodded to the monk. She recognized in him the authentic signs of a true holy man.

AFTER A SHORT while, Hadrian lost all patience.

"Why is she not here?"

The king looked up from his dish of victuals and put down his goblet. He motioned for Lucetmael to go find the druid. Hadrian rose and followed him.

They hurried down the corridor. As they past by a window cut out of the wall, Hadrian caught sight of the dock below. Instinctively, he stopped and peered out in time to see his beloved Ethrain, ropes around her hands and ankles, quickly carried onto the boat by mercenary soldiers.

On the dock stood Lochru with a giant of a man, Coroticus, the King of the Rock. Hadrian's warrior blood hurled through his body and he shouted to the young druid.

"Show me the way to the docks!"

The apprentice magician pointed to the stairs. Hadrian drew his sword and rushed down the steep stairway. He ran through narrow stone halls and lost his way in servant quarters. Finally, he discovered the doors leading to the docks.

He appeared in the midday sun only to find that the boat had raised its anchor and was moving out to sea. The druid stood on the dock alone. Lochru turned around to find Hadrian rushing at him with a great war cry. The sorcerer raised his hand. A force field shook Hadrian's body so violently that he dropped his sword. With a wild look in his eyes, the druid called out an incantation and circled his hand in the air, preparing to strike like a serpent. He caught himself and an evil smile darkened his features.

"I'll let you live, Roman. It will be much more painful than death. You'll have to live with the knowledge that your loved one is a slave girl, abused by her masters as a plaything and servant for the rest of her life!"

Hadrian fell to his knees and shouted.

"No!"

The druid laughed and returned into the palace, leaving the Roman in despair on the empty dock.

chapter twenty-four

AN OCEAN WIND howled through the cracks in the dungeon wall. The North Sea waves crashed against the ancient stones, furious that an obstacle rose in their path. The sound of clanging chains and sorrowful moaning echoed in the darkness.

Ethrain returned to consciousness and found herself laying on a wet and slimy stone floor. Her head ached from a soldier's blow. She had resisted to the very end and her captors struck her with the blunt end of a spear. She opened her eyes and instantly wished herself back into the blissful unconsciousness that had veiled the reality in which she found herself.

A dim streak of grey light fell into a corner of the dark room. She could hear the waves bellowing just on the other side of her prison walls and she realized that the floor on which she lay was below sea level. It seemed to her for a moment that she was in the belly of a monster from the depths of the ocean and that she would never again see the light of day or the face of her Roman lover.

Ethrain moved her arms and discovered that they were locked in heavy chains that came out of a massive pillar upholding the fortress above. She took a deep breath and almost fainted at the smell of filth and rot hovering in the dungeon. Something moved by her feet and let out a shrill squeak. It was a huge rat sniffing around her. She kicked at it in horror and it scurried away.

"You are awake?"

A hoarse voice echoed over the crashing waves. Ethrain turned toward the sound. At first, she could see nothing but shadows. Then she heard the rattle of chains. A silhouette detached itself from the obscurity and leaned toward her. A woman's features came into the light. She had been beautiful once, but her plight had emaciated her body and much of her hair had fallen away. She was still young, although illness and confinement had carved wrinkles of despair upon her flesh.

"I was once called Maev. What is your name?"

"Ethrain . . . "

"You are one of us?"

"I am Celt, from the isle of Mallor."

The woman crawled toward her, revealing the horrid rags that barely covered her from the winds of the North Sea.

"Mallor? Praise be to the Danaan Faeries! The spirits have heard my cries!"

Ethrain sat up and leaned against the mossy wall. She was still disoriented by the blow to her head.

"You know of my home?"

"All of us do, child. It is the mighty gateway to . . . "

The woman interrupted herself and covered her mouth with hands scarred by wounds and sores. Fear brought a mist to her melancholic eyes. But then she showed her brown and broken teeth in a wide grin as the joy of a new companion came back to her.

"Never you mind that. I'm so happy to have someone to talk with. I've been alone for a long time."

"What is this place?" Ethrain asked as she squinted in the darkness to see what was around her.

"Don't look too closely, my dear. There are things that

are best left unseen. You are in the dungeon of the Master of Dumbarton. A place of death. Don't ask me why I'm still alive. The gods must have a reason."

"Who has taken me here?"

"The slave-trader, the evil one from the depths of Annwn, the abyss of Chaos."

"Not Corroticus!" Ethrain gasped.

"This is his home, child. You are his slave now."

Ethrain frantically pulled on her chains. The wretched woman let out a frightening, high-pitched laugh that sounded more like a shriek of despair.

"You cannot free yourself. You are doomed, as I am. Your only hope is that he forgets you are here and leaves you to the rats rather than to his hordes of criminals."

"No! Hadrian will find me! I know he will! He is on his way now!"

"Hadrian?" the woman asked with interest.

"My husband. He is a centurion and he will know how to free me."

"Does he have the emperor's legions at his command?"

"No . . . "

"How many soldiers does he have, then?"

"None," Ethrain whispered as tears filled her eyes.

Maev laughed again.

"No man can save you from here on his own. The beast will cut him to pieces and place his head in his collection."

"I cannot die here!"

"That would be the easy way, child."

"How long have you been in this horrible place?"

"Three winters have gone by. I know that by the toes I have lost to the frost at the coming of the cold."

She ran her fingers through the greasy mat that was left on her head.

"I was beautiful then. Even more beautiful than you. The beast knows how to torture his victims. He left me to slowly decompose with just enough food to feel the agony of it."

"Why would he do this to you?" Ethrain asked in horror.

Maev slid toward her, close enough for Ethrain to see the tragic condition of her body.

"Because I dared to resist him. I had power once and I used it against him."

"What kind of power?"

"You are from our isles. You know what power is possible for our womankind, the sort that makes us stronger than kings."

"You are a witch?" Ethrain asked breathlessly.

"More than that. I am the keeper of the Crystal!"

A great wave crashed against the dungeon wall, sending foam through the slit that served as window. The salty spray fell on the two women as though the elements were reaching out to them. Ethrain stared at the woman before her and searched through the misery of her condition to see what she had been.

"The Crystal of the Dagda?"

"You know of it?"

"My mother was an initiate. As was my father."

"Well, then, you know that it came to us from the realm of the Danaans. Have you heard the tale?"

Maev closed her eyes and lifted her haggard face toward the streak of light coming into the room. For a moment, Ethrain could recognize the outline of a once noble face, brimming with beauty and intelligence.

"Am I not a candidate for fame," Maev recited with joy,

> "to be heard in song in the Castle of Pwyll?
> The first word from the Crystal, when was it spoken?
> By the breath of nine maidens it was gently warmed.
> Is it not the crystal of the chief of Annwn?

What is its fashion?
A rim of pearls is round its edge.
A sword flashing bright will be raised to him,
And left in the hand of Lleminawg."

Maev was no longer in the cold and smell of the dungeon. Her soul rose into the sunlit realm of the spirit world and left her misery far below. Ethrain did not dare bring her out of her brief escape.

A sparkle of sunshine broke through the clouds and penetrated the dank chamber. It fell on Maev's features like a compassionate kiss for her plight. A smile made her face graceful again and she spoke in a gentle whisper.

"The Crystal is one of the treasures of the Danaans who came out of heaven down to our shores. With them they brought the Stone of Destiny, the sword of Lugh of the Long Arm, a magic spear, and the Crystal."

Maev open her eyes and looked into the sun, as though gazing into the face of her lover.

"The King of the Danaans is Dagda, the Mighty One of Great Knowledge, who brings his children to life again. He cares for the daughters of Branwen who are born to suffer."

Maev turned her glazed eyes upon Ethrain.

"You too are a daughter of the goddesses. We share the same Fate."

"Never! I will not die in this dungeon! I will find my freedom!"

The ragged woman joined her in the shadows and tried to put her arm around her. Ethrain instinctively pulled away.

"I will not hurt you, my dear. Is my smell repugnant to you? Are you better than I, that you will not receive my care?"

Ethrain shook her head, unable to talk. She feared

becoming contaminated with the same misery that was destroying the poor woman.

"Do you know what you must do to avoid this living death? I will tell you."

Maev grabbed Ethrain's clothing and tore at them.

"Let go of me!" she cried out as she pushed her arms away.

"That's what you must give the beast if you don't wish to wallow in this festering hole, child."

Maev took hold of Ethrain's leg. The young woman kicked her hand away.

"And this you must give to him and his soldiers. Is freedom found at that price? I would rather die here with the North Sea waves as my companions, then become a toy for the lust of these brutish men!"

"They will not touch me!"

"So what power do you possess besides satisfying a man's lust? Are you skilled in the magic arts?"

"I learned from the greatest of the druids and from the most powerful witch of Mallor."

"Did they initiate you?"

"They are both dead now."

"Then you need another teacher. I, Maev of Llyr, can teach you."

"I just want to get out of this place."

Maev stood and moved through the shadows in a slow dance as her chains rattled behind her.

"This is where they lock away those who will never come out. The rest are sent to the deserts of the tent-dwellers. But I can show you another way out, a magical one."

"Will it take me back to my beloved?"

"It will lead you to the Morrhigan, the great goddess who is mother to us all."

"I don't want to go anywhere but into the arms of the man I love!"

Ethrain moved further into the shadows, frightened by the strange woman.

"If you learn from me, I will tell you the secret place where the Crystal is buried."

"Why should that interest me?"

Maev looked at her in amazement. She let out an insane shout, frightening several rats away.

"How can you say such a thing, daughter of Mallor? These are the sacred things of our people! They come from the divine ones and are full of power."

"I don't want power."

"What do you want, then?"

"I want to find happiness with the man I love."

"What childishness! A man's affection is not the purpose of your life."

"Maybe not, but affection itself surely is. I was an abandoned child. I was alone for many years. I've learned what is important. And it isn't gold and palaces."

"This is not the power I speak of, Ethrain. I am offering you mystical power that will fill your life with meaning and infinite joy."

"Is that what it has done for you?"

Maev held up her rags and chains and dangled them like musical instruments.

"I chose this destiny. The gods have given me all the joy I could hope for. And without them, this fate would be all the worse."

"How could it possibly be worse?"

Maev approached Ethrain again, who turned away from her to hide her revulsion

"I am not all that you see here, child. I live in other realms besides this dungeon. I spend my days with the faeries and their friends. I rarely notice the stench and filth of this place. It is not my home. I live in here."

She pointed to the center of her forehead.

"You see, the mighty Coroticus never captured me after

all. He believes he has ruined me, but the truth is that I have ruined him! He will pay for his crime, I'm sure of it. And the Crystal of Dagda will never belong to him. I will leave this world free and at peace. He will suffer torments unspeakable."

Ethrain did not want to contradict her. Better that she find a way to live in this wretchedness, no matter what fantasies she must invoke. Ethrain's fear of Maev subsided, melting beneath the warmth of sympathy. She reached out and touched her cheek. The woman took her hand and held it tightly against her face.

"The feel of another human being! Not even the gods can give me that! Thank you! Thank you, Ethrain!"

She wept as Ethrain caressed her stained cheek, trying to ease the pain of her terrible burden.

LUCETMAEL STOOD on the high cliff overlooking the tormented waters of the North Sea. They reflected his own anguish as he pondered the events of the day. For ten years, his master Lochru had been his teacher and mentor. Young Lucetmael was one of those chosen for the initiation and he was on his way to becoming a full-fledged druid himself, keeper of the knowledge and secrets of his people.

The events of the day threw him into a frenzy of confusion. Was it possible that there existed a power greater than that of the ancient druids? How could his master have been so humiliated by the little man from the British isles? What was this force that could overcome the greatest magic in the world? After a decade of study and initiation, he knew that the mysteries tended by the druids were a link to the Otherworld. From the furthest mountains in the East to the deserts of the nomad tribes, the sages of all times and places culled together the treasures that were now in the possession of the druids. And he was next to receive them all.

Yet he stood on this windswept cliff in great distress. Was he sacrificing himself to fading powers that did not come from the ultimate Source, the One that called to him from the depths of his being? It was not only the duel of magical skills that shook Lucetmael to his core, but also the fact that his master Lochru revealed such a low, earthly side of himself. His behavior with the Celtic girl was no better than that of a barbaric warlord. Lucetmael recognized that much of his master's behavior was motivated by the plotting of a seeker of position and influence rather than by that of a true sage. Surely one who possessed the deep knowledge that the druids inherited ought to rise above the commonplace depravity of other men.

Then there was this man Patrick whose eyes shown with a purity that Lucetmael had never seen in anyone before. Here was a grown man with the face of a child and the will of a mighty soldier. Yet his devotion to his god was unmatched. No druid ever manifested such humble adoration as he had seen this day in the great hall of the High King.

He cringed at the thought of Ethrain's fate. When he first saw her, bound and gagged in the antechambers of his master, the youth was mesmerized. Never had he seen such female beauty so close to him. When the soldiers brought her into the room, she fought like a tiger, with greater strength than Lucetmael could ever muster. Ethrain enchanted him instantly. Her bronze skin showing through the thin tunic in which she was captured, her fiery eyes aimed like spears at her assailants reminded him of the stories of the goddesses told to him in his childhood. Medhbh of Connacht who led her armies against the Ulstermen, Scathach the Shadowy One who trained young heroes, Buannan the Lasting One, and the

Phantom Queen Morrhigan the fearsome battle fury all commingled in the teeming passion shimmering throughout Ethrain's body. Here was a goddess incarnated in living flesh, hot to the touch, palpitating with life and the scent of vitality.

Ethrain was no mystic fantasy. The young druid felt attracted to her with a zeal that he had never experienced in the rituals under the oak trees. He wanted to feel her breath on his face, to quench his lips on her mouth. In that corner of the room where she crouched defiantly, he saw the glory of the elements, the fruit of the fertile land, and the inspiration of heroes. His head swooned with the aroma of her presence and the sight of her sun-drenched hair. For the first time in his life, he lost all sense of purpose. His attachments to the things he loved—the ancient tales, the great wisdom, the wizards gathered under moonlight, the thrill of ritual sacrifice—faded like a forgotten dream. This woman, more than woman, put to shame all of his ideals of what he must do with his life. What gods and goddesses could claim more attention than this daughter of the isles?

Lucetmael heard the sea breeze whisper in his ears. It sounded like the voice of the Maiden of the Sea singing softly to him—"Save her, save her." The druid shook his head to clear his mind. Had he heard a voice or was it his fantasies gone wild? He stood in deep silence, letting the wind flutter in his garments. On the horizon he could see the outline of the island where Ethrain was taken.

He knew the fate that awaited the victims of Coroticus. He had seen the raiders before and witnessed the abduction of enemies of Lochru. At the time, he was under such a spell of awe toward the old sorcerer that he did not question the demonic inhumanity of those events. He remembered the kidnapping of the witch Maev who dared to withhold sacred knowledge from the king's chief druid. Never before in the long history of the race had magic been hidden from the appointed keepers of Celtic lore. But Maev was different, a true daughter of the Morrhigan. She would not bent to the threats of the angry druid. She considered herself a druidess on equal footing with Lochru. Such a novel idea was the worst of heresies among the old men who searched for mistletoe, antidote to all poisons of soul and body.

"She must be long dead now," he thought to himself, recalling the magnificent bearing of the powerful woman, so courageous and defiant just like Ethrain. He did not dare contemplate the tortures and horrors that occurred to her. But he could not allow it to happen again, not when he was partly to blame. Something had to be done before Ethrain's body was desecrated by the King of the Rock and his band of killers.

Again he heard a voice in the wind—"The Roman, the Roman!" This time it came in loud and clear and he knew that he was hearing the voice of a goddess in the cold breeze of the North Sea. He turned away from the ocean and saw Hadrian Aldius and his companion Patrick come out on the moors. They too were here to gaze upon the horizon and seek a way to save Ethrain.

Lucetmael approached them in shame.

"I know where you will find her," he said softly.

Hadrian grabbed him by the shoulders.

"You will help us, druid?"

The young man pulled away from him.

"Please, he mustn't see us together or he will tear me to pieces!"

"Who?" Hadrian asked.

"Lochru and his followers."

"Are you not one of them?"

"I am his first assistant."

"Then why do you choose to help us?" Hadrian asked suspiciously.

"I don't want to see her sent off to the heathens across the seas."

"What is she to you?"

Lucetmael was at a loss for words, knowing that he stood before the woman's husband, a great warrior eager to use his sword.

"A sister," he answered with a tremor.

"What do you mean?"

"She is one of my people and I cannot let her be destroyed."

"Are you not loyal to the chief druid?" Hadrian asked, still suspicious.

"I am loyal to Truth."

Patrick's eyes brightened and he approached the young man.

"Are you now? Does your heart tell you that the way of the druids is not the royal way to union with the eternal One?"

"All I know is the teaching I have received. I see what it has done for Lochru."

"And what is that?" Patrick questioned with interest.

"Nothing. It has done nothing for him but made him a bitter old man, full of envy. There is not wisdom in that."

"You speak rightly. What is your name?" the monk asked.

"Lucetmael."

"How long have you studied the secret traditions?"

"Some ten years. I was to be initiated on the next full moon."

"Were you now? And you have doubts?"

"Tell me," the youth responded, "where does your power come from?"

Patrick held out his hands, embracing the sky and the

ocean. "It is not my power. It comes from He who is everywhere, in all things, but not bound by any."

"How do you know that there is only one God? I have seen so many manifestations."

"You've heard of the Dagba, Eochaid Ollathair, Father of All, also known as Ruadh Rofessa, the Red One of Knowledge, King of the Tuatha de Danaan."

"Certainly, Dagba the Good God is the foremost of our gods."

"Indeed. Do you remember how, on the eve of the Battle of Mag Tuiread, he rose before the council of your gods and declared -- All that you promise to do I shall do myself alone?"

"Yes . . . " the apprentice druid answered, amazed to hear of the monk's knowledge of his people's secrets.

"Well, then, you have in your god the dim reflection of the Holy One, the One Who Is, the God of Abraham, Isaac, and Jacob."

"I've never heard of this god."

"That is why I am here, my son!"

Lucetmael felt his whole body melt like candle wax in the heat of a great flame.

"Will you share your teaching with me, Patrick?"

"It would be my greatest joy, friend," the monk answered as he took the young man's hand. "Fear not. You have come upon the greatest force in the world. All It asks is that you surrender to it in complete trust."

"That is not an easy request."

"All or nothing, Lucetmael. That has forever been the key to entering upon the Path."

"Let us leave these philosophies for another time," Hadrian grumbled. "My Ethrain suffers."

"It will take many men to free her," the young man observed fearfully.

"Boy, I can fight like many men!" the centurion assured him.

"Coroticus commands the greatest army outside that of the High King."

"I have walked into Attila's camp. I can enter this demon's home as well. Show us the way."

"I have a boat."

"Will you risk your life with me, Lucetmael?" the Roman wondered.

"As the Briton says, it is all or nothing. I would rather be nothing than lose all."

Hadrian peered into his eyes, sensing that he was referring to his Ethrain more than to the mysteries of Patrick's teachings. He turned to the monk.

"This is not your battle, Patrick."

"Friend, where there is evil, it is my battle. Besides, Ethrain is a prisoner because of me."

"Let us draw up a plan," Hadrian ordered vigorously.

The three men descended down a narrow pathway, seeking shelter among the rocks where no one would see them prepare for their assault. But it was too late. High up in a tower of the king's fortress, the shinning eyes of Lochru the druid watched them vanish along the ridge. His white beard surrounded a face scarlet with hate.

chapter twenty-five

A DOZEN corpses lay twisted and grotesque in an empty mote on the edge of the ramparts. They were left there to instill fear in anyone who dared disobey the King of the Rock, Coroticus the merciless.

Naked and scarred by beatings, the cadavers were also a stark reminder to the captured that there was no escape from their dark fate. The people of the islands, nobles and peasants alike, who found themselves overlooking the Firth of Clyde were forced to accept their new identities as vile slaves, human refuse used by their masters according to any passing whim.

The slaves were led past the mote filled with their decaying companions on the way to the ships that would take them to distant shores. Brutality, endless labor, and pestilence awaited them. Men more primitive than the Fomorians of the highlands were to be their owners. The corpses were a final image of their destroyed lives. There would be no more hope for them.

The slaves were made to stand in long lines, surrounded by spears whose sharp points were inches from their flesh. Coroticus himself inspected his cargo of broken souls. He treated them all as animals, prying open their jaws to note the condition of their teeth, surveying them from head to foot, and fondling their bodies for his amusement. Not only did the beast enjoy touching his helpless prisoners, but he especially thrilled at the absolute power he held over them. He could do anything to anyone and nothing in the world would inhibit his desires. At times, he ordered them stripped, men and women, merely to snicker at their desperate humiliation.

Coroticus had a commander, who was always at his side, named Folchern. He had small, glassy eyes full of violence. Long blond hair and a drooping mustache in the Viking manner framed a square face whose nose had been broken countless times. A scar ran down the length of his face where a sword had sliced the flesh open.

His Hun-like eyes held a hunter's intensity. The man was always on the alert. His loyalty to Coroticus was only for his own purposes. He was not a follower. The King of the Rock gave him a portion of the spoils of his pillaging to keep him content, for he knew that his second in command was a very dangerous man and he had no faith in him whatever. But the man knew how to kill and was fearless in battle. He also knew how to be as cruel as his master.

When Coroticus brought Maev ought of the dungeon to amuse himself with her, Folchern was always present for he enjoyed the horrors of human agony as much as the King of the Rock. His own men feared him. They had seen many a time when he killed one of his soldiers for not obeying him to his liking. He was a beast in human form, always in search of more power over his fellow humans.

COROTICUS REVELLED in the exhilaration of domination over his victims. His lust increased over the years as his degradation found no limits. He thought himself the happiest man in the world, spending his days drinking, raping, eating, torturing, pillaging. It had been years since he confronted any sort of resistance. His savage men faced the uncertainties of combat for him and he waited for the swords to stop their flaying before stepping foot on the battlefield. His victims knew his reputation and were as children in his hands.

No one had resisted him in twenty years of pillaging except for Maev the witch. She was one of the many enemies of Lochru whom the druid betrayed into the hands of the slave trader. But no abuse could break her spirit. Coroticus has given long hours to the task. Finally, he abandoned her to the lower dungeon and its rats, worn out by her will of steel.

Maev's ordeal could not be matched. The beast's lust for her shapely body and for the secret she held fast to led him to new heights of cruelty. But he found his limits before discovering hers. The vicious man was still irritated over his inability to break her and he swore to himself that no one would ever put him in that position again. The guards who witnessed his final days of abuse were put to death so that the tale would not be told.

Coroticus remembered this rare defeat all too vividly.

The witch was hanging on his wall, her wrists and ankles chained. She was covered with blood that streamed from everywhere. The beast sat in a throne-like chair, staring at her hatefully. He wanted to rape her but her impassive eyes diminished his lust like a torrent of ice water. She seemed unreachable, no longer present to her body. Yet her eyes were very much alive and penetrated him with a condemnation that stirred even his dark soul. She was his to do with as he wished and yet she was ungraspable, untouchable in her inner being.

The tyrant had tried all his evil tricks to break her and none could do the job. The druid assured him that she knew the location of the magic crystal brought to the isles by the Tuatha de Danaan of Faeryland. Its power was said to renew life even among the dead. Coroticus yearned for the magic to stay alive forever so that he might satisfy his never-quenched vices.

"I'll cut off your head and place it on my shelf!"

"Do it!" Maev challenged him defiantly.

He stood on legs weakened by his efforts to break her, and approached her one more time.

"May the Morrhigan take your manhood and feed it to the wolves!" she said in a voice as hard as steel.

"Your curses don't worry me, witch!" he shouted, masking the shadow of fear creeping into his wretched being.

"You have no power over me!"

Maev let out an incantation in a foreign tongue. The despot felt a current of energy shoot through his body and his blood ran cold. He kicked her in the stomach but she continued.

"Silence, woman! I'll rip your heart out!"

She finished her incantation and laughed at him.

"Never again will you give your poisonous seed to another. You will languish in frustration until your final breath!"

She laughed again. The man grabbed a club and struck her until she lost consciousness. But the curse was fulfilled. Coroticus turned upon the two soldiers who stood by the great doors. They trembled with terror, knowing that any witness of his weakness was doomed.

The tyrant unsheathed a long Gaelic sword and approached his men.

"What have you seen?"

"Nothing, Mylord!"

"You speak the truth. Nothing happened here," he muttered, glaring at them.

"Nothing but the babble of a mad witch, Mylord."

"Yes, my loyal guards. That is all you saw."

Sweat poured from beneath the men's helmets. They were petrified before the snarling beast who lived to kill.

He turned away from them and they breathed out in relief. But the huge man suddenly swung his sword around and cut both of them down with one great blow.

SINCE THAT DAY, the evil slave trader became more hideous in his behavior, haunted by his impotence and forever in a rage at the witch's curse. But the moment his eyes fell on Ethrain, he felt himself freed from Maev's revenge and he eagerly awaited his first opportunity to satisfy his vile yearnings.

The door of the dungeon opened and the humid shadows were invaded with the light of day. Maev looked up, horrified. The door had not been opened in years. The prisoners who had come and gone from this hole of decay were tossed in through an interior window high up on the inside wall. The sound of keys and the grinding of rust could only mean one thing. Coroticus had come for Ethrain.

"The goddess be with you, child," she whispered to her companion. "Don't give in! Don't let him touch your spirit!"

"You there! Come to the stairs!" the guard barked at Ethrain.

She turned to Maev, sensing that she was looking at her for the last time. The witch took her hands.

"Remember what I have told you. This is no mad woman's fantasy. The crystal is there to be found by the worthy ones. Keep it safe from the unholy."

"I will," Ethrain said solemnly.

"Hurry up!" the guard shouted.

Maev tightened her hold on Ethrain's hands.

"I may not have done you a favor by giving you this secret. The gods will be watching you now. I know that you were meant to come to me so that the knowledge does not die with me."

"I wish you peace," Ethrain said, her throat tightening with pain for the witch's plight.

"Do not concern yourself with me, Ethrain. I am the true victor, even here in this horrid place."

"If I escape, I will come back and free you."

"It is too late for me. Save yourself. Not only for your own sake and that of your beloved, but for our people. Do not let our wisdom perish with the last of the druids. I'll tell you another secret. The fatal error of our wisemen was to keep us from becoming guardians of the tales as well. The gods will not forgive them this terrible mistake."

"And who will forgive the gods for what they have let happen to you, Maev?"

"It will take a greater god to do such a thing, like the Old Veiled One of the legends, who is Mother to us all."

"Come along, now!" the guard called out. "The master awaits you."

Maev pulled her closer and whispered. "Remember, child, the stories of our people are only the beginning of the secret. They are the doorway to the Otherworld where there is no such suffering as this. Find your way to that place."

"I need to be there now," Ethrain said with a tremor.

"You can be," Maev assured her. "It is not only after this life that we can enter it. You need only find a gateway."

"Is there one between me and the monster's castle?"

"There may well be."

"Where?"

"Within you. Start there and you will find guidance."

Ethrain caressed Maev's disfigured face. Her fingers burned with affection and compassion for her sister. Maev smiled.

"Find the crystal for me."

The guard descended into the dungeon and grabbed

hold of Ethrain's hair, pulling her away from her companion. The two women stared at each other until the moment when the soldier, having unchained her from the wall, pushed her out into the hallway.

As Ethrain fell to her knees, she sensed that some part of Maev's spirit was being freed from the dungeon with her. She understood that her liberation would be the witch's as well.

The guard lifted her up and shoved her forward. Ethrain spun around and struck the man in the face with her heavily shackled hands. He fell back against the wall and she kicked him with the force of a wild stallion. He dropped to the floor, calling to the other guards.

Ethrain grabbed the pummel of his sword and unsheathed it, turning to face three soldiers running toward her. They stopped as she swung the weapon with skill and accuracy.

"Drop the sword, woman. You cannot fight three of us!"

"Come and find out," she said as she thrust forward and nearly reached the soldier's chest.

"Someone has taught her well," one of the guards said jokingly. "Let's see what else she knows."

He lunged at her with his spear. She blocked it and came back at him with a downward blow that cut deep into his shoulder. The man screamed and fell face first, blood inundating the floor. She aimed her wet blade at the others.

"Who's next?" she cried out.

The men stepped back into defensive positions.

"Attack me, you creatures of darkness! I'll enjoy killing you!"

She moved forward and they scurried further down the hallway.

"Cowards!" she yelled.

The guard she had struck earlier rose up quietly behind

her as she intently faced the other two men, seeking to penetrate their defenses with her weapon. The soldiers distracted her as the third one came within reach of her.

"What kind of warriors are you?" she shouted mockingly.

Suddenly, the third man fell on her back, grabbing both of her arms and pulled her to the ground. The others rushed forward and shoved their blades against her skin.

"Don't kill her!" the man ordered as he held her arms down. "Get the sword from her!"

One of the guards stamped on her hand with his boot. She let out a cry of pain as they pulled the sword away.

"What kind of a woman is it that fights like a man?"

"Cut her throat now so she doesn't tell others what happened!"

"No! The master will have our heads nailed to his doors!"

"Let's enjoy her, then!" one of the men said as his hand patted her thigh.

She kicked upwards at him, striking his groin. He fell backwards, moaning.

"The witch will not give in! Chain her!"

The men wrapped her arms and legs with heavy chains hanging on the wall until she could no longer move a muscle.

"You'll pay for this, wench. When Coroticus is finished with you, we'll have our turn!"

They carried her off to the upper chambers of the fortress.

THE TYRANT took a long drink from a goblet as he lay in a tub of steaming water. He thought of what Lochru told him concerning Ethrain. The druid's spies had seen the daughter of Mallor with her Roman lover journey to

Patrick's home. The reason for their arrival on the isles was not known, but Lochru was certain of one thing. If they were allies of the monk, they were his enemies. The druid believed that if they captured Ethrain, the Briton would walk right into their hands. They could then destroy him in such a way that his followers would never find his trace.

Coroticus stepped out of his tub, dripping water on the floor like a great walrus. His servants dried him and covered him with a tunic of the finest silk brought from the distant East, undoubtedly payment for human cargo.

"Where is she?" he bellowed.

"The guards are bringing her now, sire."

The despot walked into his chambers and inspected them. They needed to be ready for the pleasure he so anticipated. The moment his eyes fell on his latest captive, he knew the curse of the witch Maev would be overcome.

The room was scented with flowers and oils. A strange aroma rose from an incense holder, the gift of some foreign king. No merchant had ever reached the level of wealth commanded by the gargantuan man. He had come a long way from the desolate childhood on the barren rocks of Mallor.

Orphaned in early childhood, stolen by barbarians who raided his village and massacred his family, he was raised in drudgery and isolation. As an innocent child, he witnessed the gruesome life of primitive thieves. Whatever decency he had been born with was long dead. He was left to grow up on his own, wild and struggling to survive each day.

Molested and beaten by his captors, he never learned of love between human beings, but only saw power and abuse. His first victim was a boy of his age, struggling to stay alive as he was. They fought for the leftovers of the camp's roast. Hunger drove them to fight to the death.

When the barbarians saw his ability, they made him one of their own. By his fifteenth year, he was skilled in the art of destruction and joined their raids against his own people. He hated the Celts and their ways, remembering them as the ones who had abandoned and forgotten him as a little boy. Why had no one come to save him? The rest of his life he would reek vengeance upon them for the child who was left in the hands of foreigners.

One day while leading a party of marauders along the shores of Mallor in search of victims, they came across a druid dressed in black. Young Coroticus rode up to him, sword in hand, ready to strike him down. The wizard merely glanced at him and the horse fell to its knees, toppling the rider.

Before the other warriors could come to his aid, the druid surrounded him with a field of bluish light.

"You dare to raise your weapon upon the wizard of Mallor, fool?"

"What kind of sorcery is this?" Coroticus cried out as the strange light took on the shape of demonic beings.

"You have come upon the Otherworld which cannot be conquered by the likes of you and your pitiful weapons."

The druid raised his hand, preparing to release forces that would devour him alive.

"Wait!" Coroticus shouted. "I am from this island."

"Then why do you seek to kill a druid?"

"I mistook you for a fisherman."

The stern man with the long white beard looked at him oddly.

"I know your face," he said as he peered at him.

By now the other pillagers had vanished, terrified by the supernatural creatures surrounding their fallen companion. Coroticus accepted whatever horrid death awaited him. He always knew that his wretched life would end as it had been lived. Alone and abandoned once again, surrounded by the jaws of cruelty, he felt strangely at home. This was all he knew.

"Who was your father?"

"I don't remember. He was killed when I was very young."

"Your mother?"

"She died at his side. But I know that she had scarlet hair."

The wizard waved his hand and the blue demons invoked from the Otherworld vanished at his command.

"Your mother was Taliesen."

"You knew her?" the brigand asked with a surge of emotion.

"There was only one person on this isle with such hair who perished at a young age. The sister of a chieftain in this province."

"I come from a noble family?" Coroticus asked in astonishment.

"Indeed. You are related to the High King."

Coroticus stood, shivering with the shock of this new identity. He had only thought of himself as a half-animal creature, the rejected refuse of his people.

"I am of royal blood?"

The wizard approached him and said in a softer voice,

"We all are . . . But if you mean the lineage of Eire, then you are that as well."

From that day forth, Coroticus strove to turn his life into the royal bearing that he had inherited. He would do it his way—through destruction. He no longer sought merely to stay alive, but to create for himself his own kingdom that he felt the world owed him. He offered the wizard who had revealed his true nature to him a part in the treasures he intended to amass. The sage refused and instead gave him a prophecy.

"There will come a day when you will face a child of this isle. You will be given a choice. Take the high road or you will lose everything that you seek."

COROTICUS HAD long forgotten those words through the years of zealous raiding and murder. His lust for possession knew no bounds and could not be satisfied. But this day, awaiting the wench they had brought from Tara, he felt that his hunger would be appeased at last. She would free him from the curse that inhibited his appetites and he would again revel in the indulgences that had become the only meaning of his existence.

In his lust for conquest, nothing was sacred to him, except for the memory of the red-haired mother whose face he saw to this day leaning over him and shining with love. Such affection he would never know again, and beneath all the fires of his passions lay the wound that could not be healed. If he could not have such life-giving warmth, he would take it by force.

He sprawled out on his bed awaiting the young woman whose enchanting features would help him forget the icy loneliness in the recesses of his tortured soul. He looked up at the wooden beams above him. His eyes grew wide. He thought he saw a face staring back at him, hanging in midair. The man who feared nothing felt his heart beat like the wild drum of war. He focused his gaze on the shadows above him and again he saw a pair of eyes. They were familiar to him, but he could not quite recognize them.

"What is this?" he cried out. "Who are you?"

The eyes vanished. Coroticus sat up and looked about the room, shaken by the unnatural appearance.

"Who goes there?" he shouted.

Only the silence responded with its mysterious knowing. He looked up again, but there was nothing. A knock at the door caused his heart to leap.

"Enter!"

The guards appeared in the doorway, holding Ethrain.

The sight of the young woman made him forget the ghastly fear that had crashed upon him like a tidal wave.

"Bring her to me."

The soldiers entered, pushing Ethrain to the foot of the bed.

"Unchain her."

"She is dangerous, Mylord."

"Do you think I fear a woman?"

"No, Sire," the guard responded, horrified at having raised his wrath. "But she has the skills of a warrior."

"Does she now?" He looked at her with hunger in his eyes. "Leave us!" he ordered his men.

The soldiers departed and he approached Ethrain who was tightly bound by her chains. He studied her closely. She stared back at him, unblinking.

"Aren't you afraid of me?"

"No."

"That is a foolish answer."

"Beasts of the field do not frighten me."

"A beast? Is that what you take me for?"

"That's what you are, Coroticus!"

"Do you know me?"

She looked away. He studied her intently. "I've seen you before. Where?"

She clenched her jaws and he slapped her across the face. "Answer me! Have I seen you before?"

She would not speak.

"Do you know what I do to people who disobey me?"

"You cannot frighten me, monster, no matter what you do!"

"Really? We shall see about that. You are from the

isles, that is evident. How do you know the Briton?"
"Our paths crossed on the way to Gaul."
"Why did you come back to see him?"
"This is my native land."
"Are you one of his followers?"
"No, only a friend."
"How can you be a friend to a man who seeks to destroy our gods?"
"What do you care about the gods?"
"You're right, I don't. But I am still a Celt and that man wants to take away our heritage."
"What do you think you're doing by enslaving our people?"
"That is only business. Nothing more."
"Some day you will pay for what you have done."
"Look around you, woman. I am paid very well for what I do. Even the High King doesn't have my wealth. And I began with nothing. Believe me, no one is going to take this away from me."
"Death will."
"Then it won't matter anymore."
"Yes, it will! You will have to account for your ways in the Otherworld."
"Ah, the Otherworld. I've heard wizards speak of such a place. Have you been there?"
Ethrain did not answer.
"Old men's fantasies, I tell you. There's only one world and I own it, just as I own you now."
"You cannot own me."
He ripped her clothes. "I can do with you whatever I want."
"But you cannot own me. My spirit is free."
"I will be content with your body," he said with a snicker as he looked her over and ran his hand down her back. She quivered with disgust.
"You will do as I tell you or I'll break you and hear

you cry for mercy."

"I know there is no mercy from you."

"You will cry for it nevertheless."

He pushed her onto the bed and removed his tunic.

"You are mine and after I have used you, I will throw you aside and cast you off beyond the ninth wave from where you will never return."

"They will come for you," Ethrain said fearlessly. "And when Hadrian Aldius finds you, he will cut you to pieces!"

"I want them to find me. Don't you understand? You are merely bait. It's Patrick I want. And while I wait I will have your body for distraction."

He sat on the bed and placed his hand on her leg. He unlocked the chains around her ankles and ran his hands along her calves, admiring the bulge of muscle beneath the soft skin.

Then he heard a whisper. "Coroticus!"

"What did you say?" he asked, thinking that Ethrain had spoken. Again, a soft voice whispered to him—

"Coroticus!"

A cold shill ran through his body. He felt the urge to cover his shame. For the first time in his life, he experienced a sense of wrongdoing. He looked around, sensing a presence. Instinctively, he covered himself.

Suddenly, the pair of eyes appeared before him, inches from his face. He let out a shrill scream. Ethrain turned around.

"Do you see that?" he cried out, unable to control his terror.

"I see nothing."

"Right there!" He pointed at the violet eyes looking at him with fury.

"Nothing," she said again, realizing that the spirit world was coming to her aid.

The outline of a face began to form around the eyes. The face of a woman. Long hair appeared in a red halo around her.

"Who are you?" Coroticus cried out. He pulled the blankets over his exposed body.

"You know me," a ghostly voice responded.

"No, I don't!"

"Don't you remember?"

"No!"

"You were taken from me."

"You no longer exist!"

"I remember you, Coroticus, my child."

Great tears burst from his eyes. He shivered like a leaf.

"Why do you come to me now?"

"She is the daughter of Mallor."

The words of the wizard on the barren coast of the isle of Mallor came back to him with the power of a massive blow. The woman's face began to fade.

"Mother! Don't leave!"

"I'm not yours anymore. Beware the wrath of the gods, my child."

"Don't leave me again!"

"Beware!" the face whispered as it vanished.

As the ghostly disembodied visage evaporated before them, Ethrain felt a tug in the chains holding her hands behind her back. An invisible force loosened her bonds.

"Come back! Come back to me!" the tyrant shouted frantically.

He leaped from the bed, waving his arms in the room like a madman, attempting to grab hold of the vision. Ethrain quietly rolled across the bed and stood up. She moved toward the door as the King of the Rock cried like a baby, flailing at the emptiness.

Ethrain slipped out of the room and ran at full speed down the corridor.

As she headed down a stairway, she heard the voice of Coroticus boom across the fortress.

"Guards! Catch her!"

She raced through a labyrinth of hallways and spiral staircases trying to find her way out. Lost and disoriented, she found herself in a narrow passageway leading to a low, wooden door. She hurried to it and put her ear against it. Then she opened it. The room was full of spears and swords. In the wall, a narrow slit of a window opened onto the waves of the North Sea.

Ethrain took hold of a large sword and tested it for its weight and balance. She put her finger to the blade and found it sharp and ready for use. She looked out the window and saw a small boat heading toward the fortress.

"Hadrian!" she whispered. "Hadrian, save me!"

Running footsteps echoed in the hallway.

"Hurry! Hurry!" she cried.

She turned around to see a dozen soldiers rushing toward her.

chapter twenty-six

HADRIAN TIED the moorings down and splashed through the waters onto the island's rocks. Patrick and Lucetmael followed him.

"That's the creature's lair," the young druid said, trying to conceal the fear in his voice.

Hadrian threw his cape back to reveal his sword. "Let's go then!"

"Wait," Patrick said gently. "He wants me. Let us follow my plan."

"I will not have you killed uselessly, Patrick"

"I'm not afraid of facing the sons of darkness."

"I know that. But if you will not wear a sword, we must try it my way."

"Very well. Remember... Don't kill more than you must."

Hadrian shook his head. He would never understand this man of peace. The three companions headed for the cliffs leading to the great walls of the somber castle. At the top of the ridge, several guards sat with their backs to the sea. They had long ceased to fear that someone would dare attack the King of the Rock and his mercenaries.

Hadrian motioned for the others to wait behind a boulder as he moved forward up the hill. He pulled out his sword and held it in a tight grip, ready to do battle.

He came up behind the guards as quiet as a night creature hunting his prey. He moved out of the shadows and ran at them. The men jumped to their feet but before either one could pull out their weapons, he was upon them.

The first soldier fell immediately, virtually split in half. Hadrian chopped at the other guard as he attempted to protect himself with his shield and spear. But he was helpless against the brutal force of the Roman centurion.

Within moments, he fell on top of his fellow soldier, motionless. Nostrils flaring like a raging bull, Hadrian felt the heat of combat fill his veins with delirious intoxication. It had been a long time since he had fought and killed another man. He had forgotten the thrilling sensation of triumph that accompanied the savagery.

He motioned for his companions to join him and headed toward the castle. Nothing would interfere with his finding Ethrain, even if he had to kill every soldier in the fortress. He pounded with the hilt of his sword on a small door built into the side of the wall. A square in the middle of the door opened and a guard looked out to see who was there. Hadrian thrust his sword into the man's cheek and held it there.

"Open up or I'll thrust it through!"

Unable to do otherwise, the man unlocked the door. Hadrian swiftly removed the blade from his face and threw open the door. He kicked the man in the chest and he fell over like a broken puppet. One blow put him out of his misery.

Patrick and Lucetmael entered.

"What did I tell you about butchery?" Patrick said angrily as he stepped in the blood covering the floor.

"What would you have me do? Ask him to let us in for dinner? I warned you this would not be a pretty sight. There's no time to lose! Come along!"

He headed up the stairs, followed by the others. Hadrian felt his rage growing with each step. He couldn't wait to meet the man who had taken his loved one from him.

He looked into a hallway and again motioned for his friends to wait for him in the shadows. He hurried down the corridor and heard voices coming from an adjacent room.

He kicked the door open. Five soldiers sat around a table, drinking. Hadrian rushed in and killed two of them instantly. The others went for their swords but he was on them like a wild beast and overwhelmed them with his fierce assault. A third soldier was quickly wounded and dropped to the floor. He fought the other two, backing them against the wall with exceptional skill, blocking and counterattacking with incredible agility. Another soldier went down, his hand badly cut. The last one hurried to the back of the room and prepared to face him. Hadrian whipped his blade through the air and approached him fearlessly. He didn't even try to protect himself. His only intent was to conquer.

The man thrust at him. Hadrian blocked it with a swing of such force that the other man's sword quivered in his hand as though lightning had struck it. He dropped his weapon.

"Don't kill me!"

"Stand over there!" Hadrian ordered, gesturing for the man to move next to the wounded soldier.

The wounded guard attempted to pick up his weapon. Hadrian saw him out of the corner of his eye and leaped sideways, kicking him in the head and knocking him against the wall, unconscious. He thrust his sword up against the other soldier's throat.

"Breathe loud and I'll take your head off. Tell me this. Where is the Celtic woman who was brought here today?"

The man could hardly speak with the point of the blade pressed so forcefully against his throat.

"She's with the master."

"Where is he? Show me or die!"

"Down this corridor, to the left. Take the first stairs you come upon," the man said with great difficulty.

"Take me there! And lock this door from the outside."

He led the soldier out of the room. As he passed by the wounded soldiers, he struck a fatal blow to insure their silence. In the corridor, he forced the man to lock the doors. He whistled softly and his companions came around the corner.

"Good, you've kept one alive," Patrick said, looking over the prisoner.

"We need him to show us the way."

"The way to where?"

"The chambers of Coroticus."

A look of horror twisted the young druid's features.

"We can't simply walk into the monster's room!"

"Certainly, we can. And we will!"

He pushed the soldier forward, his sword pressed against the man's back. They quietly made their way up the stairs leading to the chambers. When the great doors came into view, the soldier pointed at them with a trembling finger.

"There."

Hadrian turned to Patrick. "Don't look," he whispered.

Then he crashed the pummel of his weapon against the soldier's head. The man crumpled to the ground. Hadrian pushed him into a dark corner.

"You wait for me here and keep an eye out for soldiers," he told Lucetmael. "Patrick, come with me."

They approached the doors. Hadrian tried the brass doorknobs and found them unlocked. He quietly pushed them open, peering through the crack. The room was empty. He entered, followed by the monk.

A shape lay under the covers in the huge bed. In the hearth a fire crackled peacefully. The last colors of the sunset streaked into the room, filling it with an aura of deceptive serenity. Hadrian came to the edge of the bed. He raised his sword and prepared to throw back the covers. Patrick crossed himself and watched nervously.

The Roman pulled back the blankets. They revealed a mound of pillows. He threw them aside and confirmed that no one was in the bed. Alarmed, he looked around the room.

"It's a trap! Run, Patrick!"

But it was too late. From behind the furniture and the curtains surrounding the room came a horde of armed soldiers. Patrick was quickly overpowered. Hadrian attacked the guards with great fury. A dozen men converged around him. Despite his skill, the blades of his attackers found their mark. Hadrian was wounded in the shoulder, arm, and leg. Blood burst from his wounds like fountains, but he fought on, killing several soldiers.

Finally, he was overwhelmed and one of the men struck him from behind. With a cry that was more anger than pain, Hadrian fell. The men crowded around him and held him down.

"Don't kill him" a voice shouted out. "He's mine!"

Into the room came Coroticus, his face lit up with the ecstacy of victory. Behind him, his guards carried Lucetmael who was bloodied and unconscious.

The tyrant stood over Hadrian who lay panting on the floor.

"So this is the Roman I've heard about. Did you really think you could enter my domain and overcome my armies? What arrogance! You won't be so proud when I'm finished with you!"

He walked over to Patrick who was held down by several guards. Coroticus placed his hands on his hips and smiled with evil pleasure.

"Patrick the Briton! I've been eager to make your acquaintance. Quite a little man for such a big mouth, aren't you?"

"I am under the High King's protection," Patrick said calmly.

"I am the only king here! There is no law but mine on these rocks."

"You're mistaken, Coroticus. There is a greater King than all rulers of earth, and He watches us now."

"I've heard tell of your almighty god. So He is here in my chambers, is He?"

"He is! And you are powerless before Him!"

Coroticus laughed and turned to his men.

"The fool tells me that I'm powerless! Even with a spear at his throat!"

The soldiers laughed and tightened their grip on the prisoners.

"You must be insane, monk! And you should never have written that letter condemning me. That was your fatal mistake. Besides entering my fortress, which proves that you're demented."

Coroticus kneeled beside Patrick and looked into his face.

"I've matched wits with you and won! I wagered that you were stupid enough to come within my reach, and I was right. This is almost too easy, monk. And as for your great god of gods, I'll be sending you to him very shortly."

"What have you done with Ethrain?" Patrick asked, utterly unconcerned with his fate. Coroticus was surprised by the man's lack of fear.

"What does it matter to you now, monk?"

"Release her and my companions. I'm the one you want."

"You're in no position to give me orders. I'll do whatever I wish. And what I wish is to kill all of you. Slowly!"

Coroticus stood up and looked over at Hadrian. The Roman's blood was spreading across the floor, staining the lavish furs decorating the chamber.

"Get him out of here and clean up that mess! I want him kept alive, for now."

The soldiers lifted Hadrian to his feet. His face was turning ghostly white from the loss of blood but it had lost none of its determination.

"You still have some fight left in you, eh? That's good. You'll need it."

He turned to his soldiers, a hateful look darkening his features.

"Take them away!"

ETHRAIN WAS HANGING from the ceiling, dangling from chains wrapped around her writs. She slowly turned in circles, hanging in midair. The sound of keys rattling echoed behind the walls and the doors opened with a loud screech.

Lucetmael was thrown into the icy room and the doors slammed shut after him. He moaned and shivered with fear. But the instant he saw Ethrain, his vitality returned and he jumped to his feet. He approached with the veneration offered to the gods. As her body circled around, she looked down at him and recognized him.

"What are doing here?

"I came with the Roman and the monk to free you."

"They're in the castle?" she asked with new hope.

"Yes, but we are his prisoners now."

"Is Hadrian hurt?"

"He has been wounded."

"How badly?" she asked anxiously.

"I didn't see. But there was a lot of blood."

Ethrain tugged at her chains.

"I must help him! Can you release my chains?"

Lucetmael approached. His body leaned against hers as he tried to reach the chains. He felt a wave of excitement rush through him. He realized that he could have her at this moment and no one would stop him. She was within his grasp and utterly helpless. She watched him closely as he tried to resist the urge to touch her. His head pounded with the madness of lust. His mouth turned dry and he felt himself adrift on an ocean of sensation that he had never known before.

"Why would you help us?" she asked sternly, pulling him out of his trance.

He came to himself. The bitter cold of the dark room reminded him of their deadly circumstances. He felt ashamed at the temptation that nearly plunged him into the same evil as the beast of this fortress.

"I . . . I cannot stand by and allow you . . . and the others to be destroyed."

"Are you with us, then?"

His hesitation angered her. "It seems too late to be so uncertain! They will not let you leave this place alive."

"I am with you," he said fearfully. "But . . . "

"But what?"

"What will be my reward for trying to save you?"

"What do you want?"

"A kiss from you, Ethrain," the young man stated with new courage. If he was going to die, then there was nothing more to lose and he was willing to reveal his true feelings.

She was stunned. They stared at each other in silence.

"Untie me."

He reached for the chains and pulled on them. They loosened and, with several more tugs, he was able to release her. Ethrain rubbed her wrists and shook the blood back in to her arms. Lucetmael stood in the shadows, waiting for her decision.

"I cannot kiss you," she said finally.

The young man's passion suddenly turned sour. His intense attraction for her transformed into humiliation, followed by rage.

"Why not?" he managed to grumble.

"Because I am the wife of Hadrian Aldius."

"He is not here. He may even be dead. I have given my life to save you. Isn't that worth something?"

"Can you not do good merely because it is the right thing to do?"

"I want you, Ethrain!"

"Well, you cannot have me."

"I have never loved another woman."

Ethrain walked through the shadows, looking for a way out.

"Do you hear me? I love you as I have never loved. From the moment I saw you, everything I cared for was eclipsed by your beauty."

She paid no attention to him as she searched through the debris in the corners of the room. He came up behind her, his face contorted by the poisonous mixture of love and anger.

"Listen to me, Ethrain! I will do anything for you."

She turned and faced him.

"Then save my beloved."

"How?"

"Help me escape from here. See that window? It is large enough to slip through if we can reach it. We're on the ground floor."

"What will you do for me if I help you?"

"Nothing!" she cried out impatiently. "Help us because we need your help or don't help us at all."

Lucetmael felt his spirit shatter. He had lost everything to no purpose. His attraction to her had blinded him. It was her fault that he had thrown away his powerful future as a druid to the High King and she was not even grateful. He knew now that she despised him.

Ethrain tried to climb the wall to reach the window. He watched her, still enthralled by her feminine shape. But now he understood that she would never respond to him. He tore at her garments and pressed himself against her. His weight held her against the wall. She cried out in anger as he hugged her tightly. In a frenzy, he kissed the back of her neck and shoulders, seeking to taste the sweetness of her skin. She tried to pull away, but his wild lust gave him a strength she could not overcome.

"Let me go!" she shouted, trying to regain her balance and turn to face him.

"Love me, Ethrain! Love me!" the young man yelled, nearly insane with desire.

She managed to slip to the side and take hold of his arm. With a great burst of power, she pushed away from him and threw him into the wall. His head hit the stone with a loud crack and he slumped to the floor. She stood over him ready to fight him bare-fisted, but the youth began to whimper pathetically and curled up on the floor like a helpless child.

"You're going to help us, whether you like it or not!" she said in a rage. His desperate sobs only grew louder.

She suddenly stepped on his back and leaped up to the window, grabbing hold of the rim. She pulled herself up and looked out. The window stood over an inner courtyard of the fortress. She turned back to Lucetmael who was weeping uncontrollably.

"If we meet again and you lay your hands on me, I'll kill you!"

She leaped out of the window and landed on the hard dirt of the atrium. She dashed across the small alcove and found a door on the other side. With the same daring courage with which Hadrian had sought her, Ethrain now hurried into the fortress to save him. She would fight with teeth and nails if she must. Nothing would get in her way.

PATRICK KNEELED at Hadrian's side and tried to stop the flow of blood. But even the healing hands of the monk could not help the severe wounds. The Roman's face was covered in cold perspiration and had lost all color.

"Am I dying, Patrick?" he managed to whisper.

The monk blessed him with the strange sign of his faith and placed his hand on his friend's forehead.

"I am praying for you."

"I must see Ethrain. If I can be with her one last time, I will die in peace."

"You are not going to die."

"I've seen such wounds before. Men don't recover from cuts like these."

"You are still needed here, Hadrian. You cannot leave us so easily."

"We may all be dead soon."

"No, I don't believe that is the will of the Almighty."

"How do you know?"

"He did not save me from the sins of my youth and give me a vision of my destiny only to turn me over to the likes of Coroticus."

"He will not release us."

"Coroticus has no power, I tell you. When the time is right, my God will send legions of His angels to protect us. Even this awful fortress is His domain. Coroticus is merely a caretaker who has failed his Master miserably."

The doors opened and Coroticus appeared with several soldiers. He approached them and snickered.

"Not dead yet, eh Roman? What are you waiting for?"

"Will you let him see his wife before he departs?" Patrick asked.

"Why should I do this man any favors? He came to kill me."

"How can it harm you to give this man his dying wish?"

"This could be fine entertainment, now that I think of it. He can see her in chains and die knowing that she will be mine and live a slave for the rest of her days. You've asked for your own torture, Roman!"

He gestured for his men to bring Ethrain.

"This is will hurt more than a hot iron. Maybe I'll have my guards amuse themselves with her while you watch on. That would be better fare than the games your people enjoy in the arenas. We can be creative too in this far corner of the empire!"

Patrick shook his head and stood to face the tyrant.

"Why are you so evil, Coroticus? What has the world done to you to cause such darkness in your soul?"

"Silence, monk!" the man shouted, disturbed by his words.

He abruptly hurried away, and grumbled over his shoulder: "I'll be back with the girl! We'll see what you have to say then!"

Patrick returned to Hadrian and held his hands over him.

"Holy one," he said in reverent tones as he closed his eyes. "Reveal your power and mercy to us by healing your child, Hadrian. Bring his strength back to him that he might serve you according to your divine providence."

The monk moved his hands over Hadrian's torso where most of the wounds were inflicted. The Roman breathed with difficulty, trying to stay conscious. Several guards stood nearby, watching the Briton's bizarre activity.

"Look!" one of the guards shouted out in amazement.

Hadrian turned his head and saw the soldiers approach, their faces awed by the sight. The monk continued to pray silently, moving his hands above the wounds. He was not aware of what the others were seeing. The red streams dripping onto the cobblestone had suddenly stopped.

"What demon's magic is this?" one of the men cried out in fear.

Patrick opened his eyes and saw the sign of the miracle. His eyes filled with tears as a smile of great joy spread across his face.

"Thank you, Father, Source of all goodness! Thank you for the love you have for your creation. Thank you, Holy Christ of the Most High, for opening the way to infinite Mercy."

Color returned to the Roman's face. He looked up at Patrick.

"What have you done?"

"Nothing, friend. I have done nothing. Only the Holy Trinity accomplishes miracles of love."

"The pain is fading . . . "

"Lay there quietly, Hadrian. Receive the mercy of your Maker with peace and gladness."

The Roman centurion, covered in his blood and the gore of others he had killed, turned his face to the high ceiling. A deep stirring shook his soul to its foundations. An unfamiliar feeling surfaced in his heart, one that he could not understand. He felt unworthy.

"Why would your God concern himself with me?"

"You are His child as much as I am, Hadrian," Patrick said warmly. "He has always cared for you."

"You said His Son was a man of peace . . . "

"Truly."

"I am a man of war."

"His goodness shines upon all, like the sun."

"I have never seen someone healed like this. Why should I receive such a blessing?"

"You ask many questions for a man who ought to simply be thankful. Put your mind aside and let your heart do the knowing."

Hadrian grimaced with pain.

"Someone else told me that once."

"Who would be so close to the Truth?"

"Ethrain . . . "

Coroticus suddenly burst into the room, followed with a group of soldiers who surrounded Lucetmael. They pushed him toward the other prisoners. He tumbled and fell next to Hadrian.

"She's escaped again!" Coroticus yelled. "She's a spry one, Roman! You've wedded yourself to a stubborn creature! The druid boy helped her out the window. But we'll catch her and, when we do, she'll never run again!"

He kicked Lucetmael in the ribs with such furor that he lifted him off the floor.

"I'll teach you to defy Coroticus! You'll wish you'd never betrayed your people, boy!"

One of the guards whispered in the tyrant's ear. The big man hurried over to Hadrian, pushing Patrick out of the way. He examined the Roman's wounds.

"So your magic works, monk! Mine does as well!"

He pulled out a huge dagger and raised it over Hadrian.

"Wait!" Patrick cried out.

"Why? Don't you trust your god's powers?"

"Do not tempt the Lord your God!"

"He's not my god. But I'll keep the Roman alive for now. Only for the pleasure of watching him suffer all the more when we find the woman!"

He left the room. Patrick turned to the young man who was recovering from the blow.

"Tell us what happened!"

"It was as he said. I helped her escape through the window," lucetmael said with a strange light in his eyes.

"How is she?" Hadrian asked eagerly.

"She was unhurt."

"They have not beaten her?:"

"I saw no wounds."

Hadrian sighed with relief. "What did she say to you?" he asked, crawling over to the young man.

"Only that she is concerned for your welfare."

Patrick noticed a darkness in the young man's eyes that he had not seen before.

"What is it, Lucetmael? What is wrong?"

"That is an odd question, monk!" he responded angrily. "We are on the threshold of horrid deaths and you ask me what is wrong?"

"Do you regret your decision to join us?"

"It is too late for that!"

Patrick placed his hand on the lad's soldier. Lucetmael pulled away.

"As long as we live, there is hope, my son. We may escape from this hell."

"There is no hope! The Otherworld rules us and does with us whatever it wills. We have no power, no future except to serve the whim of the gods."

"How wrong you are, young man. We have been given free will by our Creator to make the choices that determine our destiny."

"We have no choices, I tell you! We are worthless slaves of the unseen ones!"

"There are greater forces than us, indeed," Patrick said softly. "But we can choose, we *must* choose. Light or darkness. They both need our decision to manifest in this world."

"They don't need us. They merely use us! There is nothing to decide."

"You made a choice, friend, when you came with us."

Lucetmael turned upon him, his face purple with inner turmoil.

"What do you know of me, monk?"

"I know that you had the courage to turn away from evil and seek to save Ethrain."

The youth looked away in shame. Patrick sensed that he was hiding something.

"What happened in that cell with Ethrain?"

"I told you!" Lucetmael shouted angrily. "Leave me alone!"

Hadrian managed to sit up against the wall. His wounds were beginning to close.

"Did you do something to Ethrain?" he asked as his vitality returned.

"I helped her escape! Why do you look at me that way?"

"He is not speaking the truth, Patrick," Hadrian said angrily. "What are you keeping from us, boy?"

Lucetmael jumped to his feet, losing control of himself.

"I've ruined my life for you foreigners! How dare you turn against me?"

"We are not turning against you, friend," Patrick said, seeking to soothe his torment.

"Speak for yourself!" Hadrian yelled. "If you have done anything to Ethrain, I'll spill your insides in the dirt!"

Patrick held the Roman back as he tried to stand.

"You still need time to recover, Hadrian. Be at peace or your wounds will open again. Don't abuse the gift that has been given to you."

Patrick approached the young man and placed his hands on his shoulders, seeking to appease him. Lucetmael violently pushed him away. Patrick fell to the floor.

"What is the matter with you, boy?" Hadrian shouted.

"I should never have listened to you, monk! Your magic is foul! The Ancient Ones warned us of your deceptive ways!"

"My teaching is the true way, Lucetmael. Your gods will vanish before the light that speaks through me."

"How can gods vanish? They've been among us from the beginning of my people! Do you think you can lock them up in the Sidh."

"What is the Sidh?"

"Don't you know? A child of five knows about the Sidh. Yet you come among us to change our ways and you don't even know what you're dealing with? Lochru was right! You're a destroyer of our heritage."

He moved toward Patrick, filled with the pride of his Celtic knowledge and the haughtiness of the elite priesthood for which he was trained.

"The Sidh are the sacred places where the Otherworld makes entrance into ours."

"They are merely tales from long ago, aren't they?"

"I have seen with own eyes the appearance of the radiant ones during our rituals. I've also known men who have travelled into the Otherworld."

"Have they returned?" Patrick asked with interest.

"I can prove the existence of other realms by sending you there myself!"

Hadrian moved his hand down to his ankle where a small dagger was hidden.

"Are you proposing to kill me?" Patrick questioned sadly.

"The magic of my people is greater than yours, I know that now! You have only caused me trouble."

"I have caused you no trouble. You've caused yourself trouble. Haven't you?"

"I challenge you to match your power with mine!" Lucetmael said defiantly.

"Did you see what happened to your master?"

"He wanted glory. I only want revenge!"

"Revenge for what?"

"I can never go back now. I lost everything when I joined with you. And you must pay for that!"

Hadrian grabbed the hilt of his dagger and prepared to remove it.

"Don't move, Hadrian!" Patrick ordered. "This is my battle, not yours."

He turned to Lucetmael.

"What is it that you wish to prove?"

"I've learned things from the Fomorians that cannot be overcome by any other magic!" the youth cried out, insane with rage.

"I've heard of these people. They come from the dark world. How would you have come upon them?"

"I have met their leader. You don't have to be an old man to conjure up the forces that seek to manifest."

"You have encountered Balor of the Baleful Eye?"

"I have!" the tortured youth said arrogantly. "I can beckon him forth from the in-between world. He can destroy you through me."

"You can bring such a devil into your own body?"

"This is mighty magic, monk, far beyond anything you know. I could have been the greatest druid of them all. And you have ruined me!"

"No, you have done this to yourself. Because of your weakness."

"What weakness?"

"You know what I mean," Patrick stated solemnly as he looked deeply into the young man's soul.

Lucetmael suddenly began to yell in a language never heard before by the uninitiated. His face turned dark hues of violet. He raised his hand and aimed it at Patrick. A vile smell filled the air as another dimension broke through the veil of matter.

"Patrick!" Hadrian shouted out, alarmed. "Don't let him hurt you." He pulled out his dagger, ready to throw it into the young man's back.

"No, Hadrian!" Patrick shouted back. "I beg of you."

"I cannot watch you die!"

Lucetmael opened his mouth and a roar came out in a gravely voice.

"I have come to destroy your ways!"

The youth's body shook with the possession of an evil being. His eyes glazed and turned black. Patrick crossed himself and spread out his arms.

"In the name of the Father and of the Son and of the Holy Spirit!"

Intense heat poured out of the young man's body and his veins seemed ready to burst from the side of his temples. Again the deep voice rang from him.

"I will turn you to ashes!"

A beam of reddish light tore out of Lucetmael's left eye and struck Patrick in the chest. He was thrown backward against the door of the room and slid to the floor. Hadrian rose to his knees, and with the last bit of strength left in him, he hurled the dagger at Lucetmael who was now more beast than man.

The knife penetrated his back with a loud thud. Already in convulsions and foaming at the mouth as though his innards were boiling hot, the youth turned around and faced Hadrian. The wounded centurion had never before faced such an enemy. The lad's eyes were now blood red and his skin was cracking from the pressure of the forces taking possession of him. He stepped toward Hadrian, holding out his arms to grab him by the throat.

Still disabled by the cuts in his arm, the Roman could not protect himself. He watched the fearsome creature approach and awaited his death with dignity. He knew that the power within the young man's body would overcome him with no difficulty.

Suddenly the door of the cell swung open and several guards appeared with Ethrain. Lucetmael turned around, revealing a face smoldering with an unnatural heat that consumed him from within. Blood poured from his reddish black eyes but something could still see through them. He roared at the guards, releasing a dark-colored foam that sizzled as it fell to the floor. The soldiers backed out of the room, utterly terrorized and quickly locked the door.

Ethrain was paralyzed at the sight of the young man so disfigured by the violent possession. He approached her slowly, his entire body shivering with grotesque convulsions. He reached out to her as his fingers split from the inner tension of the evil force. A last glimmer of the young man surfaced, and for a moment the eyes lost their reddish glare and became those of the lovestruck apprentice druid.

"Ethrain . . . " he moaned desperately.

She fell back against the door as he came closer, not to strangle her but to kiss her. She screamed before this apparition from the underworld. Patrick stepped between her and what was left of Lucetmael, holding up his hand in a sign of blessing.

"In the Name of the Father and of the Son and of the Holy Spirit . . . Begone!!"

He made the sign of the cross just as the possessed boy reached for him. A great burst of wind filled the room and Lucetmael was thrown back with incredible force. The blast sent his body through the fortress wall in a violent explosion of stone and flesh. As the dust settled, a large hole was revealed that opened onto the peaceful countryside.

"Help me with Hadrian!" Patrick shouted to Ethrain and he ran to the Roman to lift him up.

Hadrian cried out in pain as Patrick raised his arm and placed it around his neck for support. Ethrain took Hadrian's other arm and they hurried through the opening, stepping onto the grassy knoll outside. Lucetmael's corpse lay several feet away, broken by the force that had thrown him through the wall. His face had regained its youthful features, and now that the Fomorian spirit had left him, he seemed strangely at peace. His blue eyes looked up at the heavens that had so inspired him. But they were empty of life, except for a trace of melancholy that tore at Patrick's heart as he hurried past the bloody cadaver.

The monk knew that Lucetmael might have lived to become a fine man and a co-servant of the Light, rather than a victim of darkness.

chapter twenty-seven

THE DRUID LOCHRU stood in the center of an oak grove lit by the pale light of a full moon. The ghostly illumination barely lifted the darkness in the forest. Only the gleam of the old man's ferocious eyes sparkled in the night. A dozen of his fellow druids formed a large circle at the edge of the clearing. Another group formed a smaller, inner circle.

In a vat surrounded by huge candles lay the remains of Lucetmael. The handsome lad who had obeyed the wishes of his master for so long was now a soup of gore.

Lochru raised his arms to the heavens.

"Let the four directions be honored that power and radiance might enter our circle!"

An old man in the inner circle raised his frail hands toward the stars.

"With the blessing of the great bear of the starry heavens and the deep and fruitful earth, we call upon the powers of the North."

Another druid in the inner circle followed made the same movements.

"With the blessing of the great stag in the heat of the chase and the inner fire of the sun, we call upon the powers of the South."

A younger priest eagerly raised his hands.

"With the blessing of the salmon of wisdom who

dwells within the sacred waters of the pool, we call upon the powers of the West."

"With the blessing of the hawk of dawn soaring in the clear pure air, we call upon the powers of the East," another druid cried out.

"May the harmony of our circle be complete," Lochru said as he solemnly circled the vat.

He proceeded to light the candles as the other druids chanted in a strange language.

"Lucetmael, our brother!" he called out. "Your first candle lit is your sunrise birth: the flame of your house reaching Ceugant' brow. Second is the spark of your union with Bress, son of Elathan. Third is the pillar of fire, as you took the veil, rising high and clear."

An apprentice stepped forward and assisted the druid as the wind fluttered through the flames of his torch. They waited for the breath of Nature to die down.

"Fourth are brothers, Dagda the father, Broadb the Red, Medar, Ogma and Aenghus. Fifth is eternal life's spring that sings your name Lucetmael, in crystal gaze. Sixth is the flame on your Altar, that never dies!"

The apprentice wiped his eyes as they filled with tears.

"Seventh," Lochru continued as he lit another candle, "is the grove at Llandwynwn, on Mona's shore. Eigth is the strength of the oxen of Dil—Fea and Fernea, the red and the black. Ninth is the sigh of your breath, as new life grows from old, your bridge of truth."

He came to the last unlit candle and stopped for a moment. He looked into the vat and his lips trembled with sorrow and anger. "The last is your first, the beginning of the turning sea, the ending of the three, the dancing sun in the hearts of all. The candle that never dies!"

He lit the large candle as the chanting rose to a high pitch, echoing far into the woods. With all the skills of a lifetime of magical incantation, Lochru then conjured the forces that would give him ultimate power.

Lochru sought the powers of the gods as he never had before. He called forth not only the spirits of his people, but also the gods of the far north, Odin and his warriors of Valhalla. He knew that in the Otherworld he would find beings with the same purpose as his—the destruction of Patrick and his companions.

A light form swirled into the clearing, called into manifestation by the bitter old man. Soon the grove was filled with unworldly sounds and voices. The cloud of light turned into the shape of a little one-eyed man, Odin the god of the North.

"Why do you call me, human? What business have I to do with you?"

"A new force is at hand, seeking our destruction," Lochru responded. "It threatens to destroy even you and your warrior spirits of the far North."

"Another druid once invoked me for the same purpose. Is there a Roman among those you seek to punish?"

"Yes, Lord of the North, there is."

"I have been told of this man before. He is the sign of the end. Who else is with him?"

"A woman of our isles, and a monk from the southern isles. He is the one who brings the new power."

"Three humans? You cannot deal with them in your own manner?" the apparition snarled in a voice that sounded like thunder.

"The monk has mighty powers. He prays to an unknown god."

"What do you seek from me?"

"The magic to overcome him."

"There is only one way to achieve this. You must place them in our realm where their powers are submitted to ours."

"Which sidh must they enter?"

"Find the crystal first, druid! It will show you what must take place."

"The crystal of the gods, on Mallor?" Lochru asked with a tremor.

"Yes, the very one."

"It was lost forever, great one, in the days of Ubarra."

"Then you must find it. It cannot fall into the hands of those who do not do our will."

The translucent form approached the druid, leaving in its wake a stream of greenish light.

"We will assist you. There are many in your world who comply to our orders. But there is a price to pay, druid, for calling me into Middle Earth."

"What is that?" Lochru asked, a knot tightening in his chest like a fist squeezing his heart.

"If you do not succeed, we will take you to us. No one invokes us without coming under our rule."

"I understand," Lochru said, feeling the blood rush to his face. He had heard of the fate of humans taken into the Otherworld.

"We both seek the same thing, great one."

"Do we?" the fearsome spirit shouted. "How would you know what we seek, human? I am here before you only because we know that our time is short. The Day of Reckoning is at hand."

"Ragnarok, from the ancient legends?" Lochru responded in fear.

"The very one. This is the Age where the decisive battle will take place. And you have chosen our camp against the new god. We must succeed at any cost or this world will no longer be ours."

"I commit myself to this take, mighty one."

"Then prepare yourself for the greatest challenge of your life, druid. Mightier ones than you have journeyed on this path and failed. We will demand your all."

"It is yours, Odin of the North! But what do I receive in return?"

The creature from beyond cackled knowingly.

"The power you always wanted, Lochru."

He laughed again and suddenly vanished as quickly as he had come. The oak grove turned dark, lit only by the distant orb. A cold wind shivered through the trees and the druid Lochru felt a strange terror rise in his bones. He had wagered everything on this invocation. He knew that the Nordic spirits were merciless with those who failed them.

A GOLDEN sunrise spread across the North Sea as a little boat made its way toward the shores of the Isle of Mallor.

On board, Ethrain slept alongside her beloved Hadrian, healing him with her love. Patrick sat at the helm of the boat, lost in the magnificence of the solar birth taking place before him. He looked over at the couple whom he had united and smiled at their bonds of love visible even in sleep. He could see how deeply their souls were wedded. It was for such goodness of heart that he had come to the isles, and even though the two lovers were far from accepting the Faith he brought with him, he knew that they had stepped onto the path that could only lead to his God—the Loving One. For His power transformed brutish humanity into incarnate angels. Such magic was still unknown in this wilderness, but Patrick understood that he would live to see a new day among these Celtic peoples -- just as the sun's light broke through the darkness, so would his mission fill the isles with the wisdom of new understanding. He hoped that someday men like Coroticus would be seen for what they were and be rejected by humanity, rendered incapable of holding such power over them.

His contemplation led him into spheres beyond thought where visions appear for only the few to witness. He glimpsed a distant future, where all was strange and foreign to him. Yet he knew that his presence in this day would make a difference even to those generations yet to be born. And though he would not live to see his victory wholly manifest, he knew that Providence would make could use of his efforts in the name of the Holy One.

The outline of barren rocks appeared in the morning mist. Patrick turned his attention to the harsh silhouette of the Isle of Mallor. He had been told of this place. These rocks were seeped in the magic of the Ancient Ones more than any other. The entire island was a gateway to the Otherworld, a Sidh as the druids called it. But unlike the dolmens and other sacred places that littered the isles, these shores were particularly haunted by darker forces.

Patrick breathed in the cool ocean breeze and overcame his fatigue somewhat. He wondered at the events that had brought him to this place. Long ago he learned that nothing was coincidence, and that all events were part of a greater plan. His continual remembrance of the Most High kept him focused on the mystery of divine activity in the midst of seeming chaos. But he also knew that coming to Mallor meant that a decisive encounter would take place, one that would determine his mission throughout these isles. If he could survive what was to happen here, then the other isles would be more open to receive him.

He looked over at Ethrain, mindful that she was a daughter of this dark isle. Her soft features belied the powers that she had acquired in her short life. Clearly she knew something of her people's deepest secrets. She told him once of her father Ubarra, the great wizard, and of her mother Hyndla, the witch of Mallor. He marveled at the natural goodness in her soul despite the harsh influences of her past. Now she was in his company in search of a magical crystal that would reveal their future to them.

The monk crossed himself as the morning spread out across the heavens in royal colors. Celtic magic was indeed potent. He would need all his faith and strength to deal with what lay ahead.

Ethrain opened her eyes and was struck by the sight of the holy man outlined in the golden dawn. She watched him in the intimacy of his prayer with the sacred forces of the cosmos. An extraordinary presence radiated from this man, even with his back to her. She could tell that he was in touch with a silence deeper than the ocean itself and that he united with it in a way that no magical incantation had ever linked spirit and matter.

Her attraction to the mysteries of the unknown sent a thrill through her body as she witnessed this new religion incarnated in the simple man before her. He began to chant softly a beautiful melody the like of which she had never heard. It seemed to be in harmony with the rising sun and the lapping of waves against the boat. His music manifested the oneness of his heart with the awesome Spirit of creation. She sat up quietly, not wanting to disturb him.

Hadrian awoke and looked up at her. She smiled and held a finger to her lips, pointing to Patrick. The Roman heard the sweet rhythmic voice and turned to his friend. The golden orb had now risen directly across from his head and the rays shot through his hair, turning him into the unnatural sight of a heavenly creature. His chanting entered their being with the dawning of the day, filling them with a mysterious peace and contentment. What was this glorious connection with life that Patrick the Briton had acquired? How far it was from the bloody sacrifices of the druids and the wretched dissolution of the Roman gods.

He needed no idols, no temples, no priests or vestal virgins. In simplicity and poverty, he had crossed the threshold to the ultimate mystery of existence. Hadrian recognized in that moment that the little man was more advanced than his great tutors from Greece, students of the most famous philosophers of their day. In his humility, Patrick revealed a greater knowledge, one that seemed so profound and yet so utterly simple. In that very humility seemed to lie the secret of his teaching.

The sun rose over Patrick's head, casting a shimmering halo around his silhouette. He ended his chanting and crossed himself again. He turned away from the sun. On his face was a serenity of such beauty and peace that the two lovers perceived the fruits of the wisdom that he carried with him in a way that no words could transmit. He became aware of their observation and turned with a gentle smile.

"Good morning to you friends, and a beautiful morning it is."

"Good morning, Patrick," Ethrain replied, still enchanted by his prayerful state.

"Did you sleep well?"

"Never better," Hadrian replied.

"How are your wounds?"

The Roman looked down. They were now only reddish scars and had closed of themselves.

"The Lord has been good to you, friend," Patrick stated joyfully. Hadrian did not know what to answer. The proof was carved on his own body. Something miraculous had taken place.

"What does your god want from me?"

"He will let you know in time."

Ethrain stood up and pointed at the rocks on the horizon.

"There's my home."

They looked over at Mallor which seemed to be heading their way like the carcass of a dead sea monster. Its very presence was a dark omen.

Upon landing, they made their way to the foothills of Mount Elkar where Ethrain had lived out her early youth. The trees and bushes on this isle were permanently bent by harsh winds blasting down from the north, off the seas of ice. They resembled twisted statues of terrified beings forever cringing before the violent hand of some colossal master. Hadrian had noticed this strange vegetation on his first trip to the isle, but had not recognized the unearthly nature of their contortions. It was not merely the wind that created such disfigured woodlands. Some other force, even more powerful than the howling gales of the North Sea, was responsible for this look of horror in every branch.

"Has it always been so barren?" Patrick asked as they journeyed through the forlorn countryside.

"Always," Ethrain answered. "Our isle is said to be the home of the Old Veiled One, so it has been visited by invisible forces from ancient times. See that oak tree by the stream?"

The others looked in the direction she was pointing. A gigantic tree stood in the middle of a clearing, split in half all the way to its roots.

"That was no lightning strike. The giants of Jotunheim warred with the warrior gods of Valhalla on that spot."

"Who are these giants you speak of?" Patrick asked with some concern.

"They come from the underworld and are in covenant with the Fomorians who seek to take control of Middle Earth."

"Middle Earth?"

"This is Middle Earth," she went on, surprised that the monk was not familiar with the legends. "Supernatural powers have sought control of our world since the beginning."

"So why have we come to this forbidding place? It doesn't seem very safe."

"It's safer than the fortress of Coroticus or the High King's castle. They will be looking for us, along with the druid and his followers. The last place they will search is Mallor. Not even pirates comes upon these shores."

"Did the Vikings not land here at some time?" Hadrian wondered as he caught sight of the carvings of human heads buried in the ground like warning signs.

"They did," Ethrain stated. "But they soon learned that this land was cursed. It does not belong to humans, but to the Otherworld."

"Why would such a desolate place interest the spirit realm?" Patrick asked.

"Precisely because it is at the outermost edges of the civilized world. The further away from the affairs of men, the better. Not only for gods, but for the wise ones as well."

"Well said," Patrick added approvingly. Despite his missionary efforts, he valued solitude as an entryway into the deepest mysteries.

"When I was here last," Hadrian offered, "I was forced to recognize another reality that had nothing to do with the one I had known previously. This is a place like no other."

"Then we shall have to tame it in the name of the Almighty," Patrick proclaimed confidently.

"That may not be so easy," Ethrain warned.

The companions travelled throughout the day, across grim moors and through forests whose trees were leafless, though it was summertime. Battered by immense forces, the woods bore the scars of eerie wars that no human could have waged.

They reached a plateau overlooking the valley of Ethrain's birth. Tired by the long day's journey, they rested on fallen trees and studied the vistas before them.

Worry tightened Ethrain's sun-colored features.

"Something is different. It was not like this before."

"How do you mean?" Hadrian asked.

"Don't you remember? The woods were thicker to the south and the land below us was green. This is the meadow I played in as a child. There were flowers everywhere. Now there is only dirt."

They looked down at the bald spot that was once Ethrain's meadow. A giant hand seemed to have torn the greenery out of the earth by its roots.

"And look there. In those woods near the shore. That was Hyndla's home."

"I remember now," the Roman said, reliving the gruesome experiences of the past. Ghostly forces had destroyed the witch's home and buried her in the rubble along with the sacred crystal.

"How could the landscape change so much in a year's time?" Ethrain wondered, the shadow of fear clouding her eyes.

"Maybe your giants came forth from the depths and wrestled along these ridges," Patrick said, trying to lighten his friends' darkening mood.

"We must find the crystal!" Ethrain said with a burst of new energy. "There is no more time to lose!"

She stood up. Her companions studied her with surprise. "Right now?" Hadrian asked.

"Before sunset," she insisted. "If we don't find it first, it will fall into the wrong hands."

"What makes you say that?"

"Look at the destruction out there. It follows a path around Hyndla's land and ends on this side of the ridge. Whatever did this was looking for something that has yet to be found! And Maev told me that daylight was required to locate the crystal."

"You need more rest, Ethrain," Hadrian said calmly.

"See the earth where the meadow was. It is nearly turned over, as though plowed. They were searching for something buried."

"And why must we find it?" Patrick wondered, confused.

"Because it will tell us what we must know."

"How do we know we need to know it if we don't know it?" the monk asked playfully.

"With all due respect, Patrick, you shouldn't mock these things. There are powerful forces here."

"You're right, Ethrain. But this crystal you seek, how will it save us from Coroticus and his men?"

"The crystal reveals the future. And when it does, it attracts forces that will both help and hinder the effort to make it come to pass."

"Must we know the future in order to live rightly this moment?" the monk wonders.

"All things are drawing together now like never before. This is the Age of Ragnarok."

"I have heard of this tale. They also call it the Day of Destruction, yes?" Patrick asked, eyes widening.

"The very one. It is near and the two of you are its heralds."

"I have not come to the isles for destruction, but to bring new life." the Briton stated emphatically.

"New life often comes out of death," Hadrian observed.

"Indeed! But what sort of death would Ragnarok bring?"

"The end of this world," Ethrain said as she gestured to the island. "The end of the ancient gods and their mingling with humans."

"To make room for a new God?" Patrick thought out loud, his eyes shining with excitement.

"Maybe," Ethrain continued. "Or to overtake us completely and make us slaves to the Otherworld. Then the whole earth would be under the rule of men like Coroticus."

"The King of the Rock cannot be ruler of the world!" Patrick shouted with outrage. "That beast must be laid low. He is a servant of the darkness that keeps the Light from freeing us of our misery!"

"Consider this moment, then!" Hadrian cried out with sudden insight. "Here you are, the bringer of Light, on the very isle that is home to the forces of darkness. And Coroticus is undoubtedly in pursuit of us. If he steps onto Mallor, the two servants of the forces at war will have gathered in the land of dead!"

"Just like the legend says!" Ethrain added with enthusiasm. "Don't you see? We have been brought here, not to escape him, but to confront him! This is where the battle must take place. At the very gateway to the Otherworld."

"And the crystal?" Patrick asked with great solemnity.

"It will tell us how we can be victorious."

"Let us lose no more time!" Patrick ordered as he headed down the hill. "Show me the way!"

The companions rushed toward the landscape that was scarred with the wounds of unearthly warfare, hearts beating in unison with an urgency none had known before.

chapter twenty-eight

KING LAOGHAIRE angrily paced the castle floor. His chief druid and closest advisor, Lochru, stood silently at the side of the throne, arms folded in upon himself awaiting the royal response. Next to the throne sat Queen Ethne, greatly concerned with her husband's indecision.

"My King, there is no more time," the druid said sternly. "The Briton may already have his hands on the treasures of our people."

"So you want me to chase him down and kill him like a wild boar? What would my people think of me then? This man has done nothing criminal."

"He is a threat to all of us, my liege. Your very rule even." the druid grumbled.

"That is ridiculous!" the queen stated loudly. "The man is not out for power, unlike so many others."

Lochru glanced angrily at her. There had never been any warmth between them.

"The Queen seems to have taken a liking to this monk and his new religion."

"Yes, I have," she said as she rose in anger. "This man has spoken words of great beauty that have touched my heart. And we've all seen his power, have we not, Lochru? The King himself has given him his protection."

King Laoghaire shrugged, giving his counselor a guilty look.

"But he is still dangerous," Lochru insisted. "It is possible that he will wipe out everything we know and leave us without our true heritage and destiny."

"How can any one man do that?" the queen said in a challenging voice. "Or will you admit that he has a special power with him that can indeed change the world? Perhaps for the better."

"I will admit no such thing, my Queen. He meddles in our lives because he is a fanatic. He should have gone to the Visigoths. Any land would have done for him."

"That is not true. He came back here even though he had been enslaved in his youth because he loves our people."

"Enough of this!" the king ordered. "What is it that you propose, Lochru?"

"Give me a hundred men and I will find him and bring him back to you."

"Alive?"

"If that is your wish."

"It is," the king said unconvincingly.

The queen turned to him in outrage.

"You must tell him clearly! Do not let him do this. He wants to hunt down a good man. If you fight the forces of good, you will lose!"

"Since when has the good been a force of power?" the king asked.

"This is greater than anything we have seen before."

"You've always been so easily swayed by new things, my dear."

"The people will never forgive you if you kill Patrick the Briton."

"Will they forgive us if he destroys our ancient ways?" Lochru asked in a thundering voice.

"Perhaps it is time for our ways to change, druid."

He looked at her in horror. "Impossible! The gods have always accompanied us on our journey."

"Do you mean when we were brutes and head hunters, less worthy than animals?"

"We were great warriors conquering all the land across the continents!"

"That is long ago and far away, Lochru. This is a new day and you must awaken to it and recognize the signs."

Lochru turned his back on her. "My King, this is a time for the decision of men."

"Nonsense!" she cried out. "It is the heritage of our people that women are equal to you. How dare you suggest otherwise?"

"Laoghaire of Eire, this is the greatest battle you will ever have to face!" the druid insisted.

"Against one man?" the queen retorted.

"Silence! I cannot think," the old king shouted. He pulled on his beard and approached his chief druid. "Take a hundred men, Lochru, and bring him back to me. We will consider our next move when we have him safely at Tara."

"What about the Roman and his woman?"

"I am not interested in them. They have betrayed us by joining with the monk."

Lochru smiled victoriously.

"Then you will allow me to avenge Lucetmael?"

"Do what you need to do."

Lochru bowed and left the room. The queen hurried to her husband.

"Don't be a fool, Laoghaire. There is something holy about this Patrick. He is not like others. Those with him are under his protection. Do not take the wrong side, not this time! There will be no return from this defeat."

"Are you trying to frighten this old warrior?" the king said as he took her in his arms.

"I know that you are a man of courage and I have always loved you for it. Be a man of vision now. The future belongs to men like Patrick, not to the likes of Lochru."

"How do you know these things, wife?"

"My heart tells me."

"Has the Briton made you a follower in so short a time?"

"I don't know. But I like what I have seen in his eyes. There is such goodness there."

"The world is not controlled by goodness. I certainly have learned that in my day."

"What if we changed and a new Spirit ruled among us? Would you not enjoy the peace of such a golden time?"

"No, I will die in my armor fighting my enemies. That is who I am and who I will always be."

"But you can allow your people to discover new wisdom that will free them from the sword and the spear."

King Laoghaire embraced his queen, but as he leaned his grey hair upon her cheek, his eyes turned to the hallway where he could hear the rush of armed men gathering to hunt down the holy man who dared to challenge their ways.

HADRIAN STOOD on a mound of rotting wood that had once been home to the witch of Mallor. The entire structure was torn to shreds, leaving little that resembled a building. He searched through the rubble with a heavy branch. Patrick and Ethrain did the same further down the hill.

As he stepped through the debris, he lost his footing and with a shout fell into a hole beneath the piles of wood.

Ethrain looked up in time to see him vanish. She hurried to him, followed by Patrick. They quickly removed some of the logs and saw that he had fallen into a deep, empty well that opened onto a chamber below.

Hadrian lay on the dirt floor, motionless.

"Hadrian, are you hurt?" Ethrain called out.

He tried to move his legs. "I twisted something," he said painfully.

"We must find some kind of rope," Patrick said. "I'll go down there and bring him back up."

They searched about for a way to descend to the chamber.

"There must be another entrance somewhere around here," Ethrain stated. "I remember that she had a fireplace in this area. Maev told me to look for a trap door beneath it. It was often the way of the witches here, in order to escape their enemies."

They removed the shattered wood.

"Over here!" Patrick called out as he came upon a stairwell that led down into the ground.

"Be careful!" Ethrain cried out seeing him head down the rotting stairs. "There's no telling where it leads."

She pulled out her dagger and followed him. They descended under the earth into the blackness below. The stairway opened onto a narrow corridor of packed mud. Dripping water could be heard coming from somewhere nearby.

They wandered in the dark, making their way blindly.

"This must open onto the chamber where Hadrian fell," Ethrain said. "Maev mentioned a secret labyrinth. The druids designed them in spirals around sacred places. All the chambers must connect at some point."

A dim light appeared around a corner. They headed toward it. Patrick let out an involuntary shout as he turned the corner and came upon a grotesque statue that stared at him fiercely. It was an ancient god from people long past.

"Who is this?" Patrick asked, recovering quickly.

"The Old Veiled One. We must be on the right path. This is an ancient place, a perfect sidh for sacred objects."

They turned another corner and came upon the chamber where Hadrian lay. It was a small room with several entrances leading to other corridors.

They hurried to the Roman and helped him up.

"Careful," Patrick said. "There might be something else hurt as well."

"Just the leg," Hadrian muttered, embarrassed to find himself in a condition of weakness once again. One of his wounds had reopened and blood trickled down his arm.

Ethrain tore a piece of her tunic and wrapped it around his limb.

"I'll be all right. The two of you need to keep looking. We cannot stay here. This place may collapse at any moment."

"What makes you say that?" Patrick asked.

"Look!"

They turned to where he was pointing. The beams above them holding the giant pile of debris were creaking and sagging. The humid earthen walls leaked with water coming from within the ground.

"There must be a river nearby trying to break through. These places are often constructed near subterranean streams. They are a juncture of power in the earth." Ethrain stated.

"What else can you tell us of these places?" Patrick asked. "Is this some kind of sanctuary?"

"Yes. Through those doors must be the way to the inner chamber."

"Ethrain, you try this door. I'll go through that one. Let us not take long being apart," Patrick ordered.

"Over there! Torches on the wall!" Hadrian called out.

Several wooden torches were propped up along the wall.

"How do we light them?" Patrick wondered.

"I know how," Ethrain answered as she went over to the torches. "There are some things my people know that even you do not, holy man."

She took one of the torches.

"If this is unsettling to you, do not watch."

She let out a high-pitched incantation and aimed an intense glare at the torch. Little sparks appeared on the edges and a bluish haze surrounded the top of the torch. In a moment, it flared into a fire.

"How do you do that?" Patrick asked in amazement.

"Magic," she said simply and handed the flaming torch to him. Then she lit another one and gave it to Hadrian. She created a third one for herself.

They headed into the small corridors. Ethrain found herself in a narrow passageway that barely had room for her. It opened onto another chamber, larger than the one Hadrian had fallen into. She entered, and her eyes widened in awe. In the center of the room stood a huge dolmen, unseen for generations.

She approached it reverently. On its sides were carved spirals, representing the mysteries of the cosmos. She placed her hand on the smooth stone. An electric shock threw her back. She cried out in pain, shaking her injured limb.

Ethrain walked around the megalith, looking it over with the light of her torch. She could see that its lower part had turned brown with an unnatural heat that once burned from within. She came to its other side and let out a loud cry.

A skeleton, dressed in white robes, sat in a throne-like chair behind the obelisk. A long white beard fell from its slackened jaw. Brown, mummified skin lay in patches on the exposed bones. The skull was bent forward as though reflecting on some imponderable mystery. On one of the hands was a huge brass ring, with a dragon's head finely sculpted upon it.

The skeleton was tall. This mighty druid had been a large man, taller than most Celts in the region. Ethrain knew of only one such man—Ubarra, the wizard. She fell to her knees and burst into tears.

"Father! Oh, father!"

She took hold of the dusty robe and kissed it.

"Why must I find you like this?"

She looked up through her tears at the eerie figure before her. The teeth seemed to smile sadly at her and the empty sockets appeared to be watching her.

"I loved you so, father. Why did you abandon me? Why did you leave me to fend for myself so that you could follow your secret ways? I needed you so much. Wasn't I as precious as your mysteries? What good do they do you now? I could have cared for you in your old age."

Patrick entered the room quietly and came to kneel beside her. She wept as he put his arm around her.

"He is at peace now, among the mysteries he sought to discover. What was his name?"

"Ubarra."

"Was he a good man?"

"He did not seek to harm anyone."

Patrick crossed himself and blessed the skeleton.

"May your soul be accepted in the Kingdom of the Almighty."

He approached the skeleton and removed the ring from the hand. He turned to Ethrain.

"This must be yours, now."

He took her hand and placed the ring on her finger. Though large, it fit her finger. A red glow appeared in the eyes of the dragon head. Patrick marvelled at the sight.

"What is this?"

"An ancient ring belonging to the early kings of the isles. It is rumored that it was past on only to the high priests. Ubarra was the last of the lineage. I am not worthy to wear it."

"You are not worthy? I tell you, the Almighty considers you His precious child. That makes you worthier than kings because of your good heart. Your father would be proud. You will take it to a new level of wisdom undreamt of by the magicians of the past."

He held her head up and looked into her eyes.

"For you, Ethrain of Mallor, will be the first among your people to know the true God, the Source of all life."

He helped her stand.

"You begin where he left off."

"What makes you say these things, Patrick?"

"There is magic that you know not of. It requires no stones or crystals, but a heart that is cleansed in order to see."

"But you condemn our magic. Is this ring not vile to you?"

"Child, I know that you will use it for good. Transform it into a blessed gift, rather than a cursed one. Such is the power of love, the greatest magic of all."

"What shall we do with him?" she asked in a trembling voice, pointing to the skeleton.

"There is no time to bury him properly. He belongs here for all time, before his shrine contemplating the mysteries that tugged at his heart. Besides," Patrick said as he put his arm around Ethrain, "he is not there. This is merely a shell. His immortal soul has moved on to greater realms."

"Is there anything I can do for him?"

"Say a prayer for his soul that he may continue his pilgrimage even beyond this life and find the truth that escaped him here."

"There is truth here," she insisted. "This dolmen has

powers. If you touch it, it will cause you pain."

"That may be," Patrick said, "but it is blind power. The power that I speak of is one that knows from whence it comes and whither it goes."

They walked out of the chamber and it fell back into the darkness that would occupy it forever.

"The crystal cannot be far away," she said as they entered the tunnel.

They came into an adjacent chamber. It was a small room. In the center of it was a well.

"I remember now!" she cried out. "Hyndla brought it up from a well when we came to see her last. And Maev said that it would be in the chamber where the water was found."

They hurried to it. At that moment, the beams shook above their heads and a loud crack echoed through the labyrinth. The walls oozed with liquid. The sound of rushing water made itself heard. A subterranean river was angrily seeking to invade these ancient chambers.

"Hurry!" she said. They threw a torch down into the well. It fell onto an object twenty feet below. They looked in and a gleam came up from the bottom of the well.

"That must be it!" she said.

"Is it tied to anything?" Patrick asked impatiently.

With torch in hand, she searched around the walls of the well.

"A rope!"

Patrick pulled on it.

"It's heavy!" he cried out.

She put her torch down and joined him. It took all their strength to bring it up. As it rose to the top of the well, it filled the room with light, reflected from the torch. They moved it out onto the floor. The sparkling object was triangular, three feet in height.

Patrick looked at it with great interest, running his hand across its shimmering surface.

"Extraordinary," he said. "I've never seen the likes of it. Not even in the palace of kings."

"It's older than the land," Ethrain stated, awed by the magical object. "It is said to be a gift of the Tuatha De Danann, brought with them from the Otherworld."

Patrick put the rope over his shoulder and lifted it. It was heavier than his own body.

"We'll have to drag it along the ground."

"It will not crack," she said. "This is pure crystal."

She pushed with all her strength as he pulled it through the corridors back into the chamber where Hadrian awaited them.

"We must hurry!" Hadrian shouted as he saw the flickering torch announcing their approach. "The walls are going to break in on us at any moment!"

Upon seeing the crystal, the Roman let out a gasp.

"How will we get it up the stairs?"

"We'll have to find a way."

Patrick pulled as the other two pushed it. In spite of his pain, the Roman gave it his full might. He glanced at the beams. Several of them began to split and the walls bulged with pressure from the other side. A muffled roar came from beyond the chambers. The companions struggled up the stairs, stumbling several times.

Suddenly, a loud crash was heard in the chamber where the dolmen stood and a gush of waters echoed through the corridors.

"Here it comes! Push!" Hadrian shouted.

Water spilled into the chamber with the force of a tidal wave, bringing down the beams that held up the underground rooms. Patrick made it to the top of the stairway just as the labyrinth caved in upon itself. Ethrain and Hadrian narrowly avoided being crushed in the collapse of the structure. Just as Ethrain made it to the top of the stairway, water filled the chamber and shot up the stairs behind them, reaching their waists.

Patrick helped them to solid ground. They looked back to see muddied waters rise out of the hole and spill onto the debris around them. The chamber and its mysteries were sealed forever. They hurried away, pulling the giant crystal behind them.

"Look!" Hadrian cried out as he pointed to the coast.

A battleship was throwing anchor offshore and soldiers were quickly disembarking. On board, the huge silhouette of Coroticus stood next to the white robes of the druid Lochru which fluttered in a rising breeze.

chapter twenty-nine

"We must use the crystal now!" Ethrain said as she approached the sacred object.

"Right here?" Hadrian asked.

"There's no more time to lose."

"But they'll see us! We've got no protection."

"It's now or never. If they catch us before we can use it, there'll be no hope."

"So what must we do?" Hadrian asked anxiously.

"Gather around the crystal," Ethrain responded. "Place your hands on it."

"I cannot do that," Patrick said. "I cannot participate in your magic."

"It is not mine, Patrick. It belongs to all of us."

"I will not be part of that world. I belong to another one."

"Then keep watch over the soldiers while we proceed."

Patrick hurried to the boulders overlooking the shore and kneeled behind them.

They placed their hands on the clear glass-like stone. Within moments, a pinkish color radiated at its core. Then a rainbow of colors filled the triangle, as Ethrain chanted an incantation.

The colors swirled within the crystal, their glow reflecting on the faces of Ethrain and Hadrian. She stopped her incantation and watched in wonder.

"Your ring!" Hadrian whispered, noticing that the eyes of the dragonhead were mirroring the colors within the crystal.

"Quiet," she said gently as she observed in awe.

The shape of a face, formed by the colors, appeared in the crystal -- a long, bony face covered with a white beard of great length. It was Ubarra, the mighty wizard. Ethrain began to tremble and did her best to control her emotions.

"My daughter . . . " a ghostly voice said from within the crystal. "My daughter . . . "

"Father!" she whispered back.

"I am here to do for you what I did not do in life. Will you ever forgive me?"

She could not respond as her throat knotted in agony.

"Ragnarok is here, child," the ghostly image continued. "The time has come. Prepare yourself and listen carefully . . .

"The dark forces have learned to enter the hearts and minds of human beings. What you take as your thoughts and motives are not always your own. The Otherworld has cast a spell on the children of Earth and made them believe that they are in control of themselves, captains of their ships. But this is not the case! The Fomorians are no longer in need of manifesting physically. They can enter the world of matter through human souls who become their slaves without knowing it. The feelings and thoughts that come to them are mixed with the suggestions of the Otherworld. Only the vigilant, those who remain on the alert, will be able to recognize the difference. All others will be passive victims to this evil enchantment. Men will become puppets to forces they know nothing about and will be used for purposes they do not understand, all the while imagining that they are making their own decisions."

Ethrain and Hadrian listened in stunned silence. The

gaunt face, fading in and out like a candle flame blown by the wind, continued its revelation with great melancholy.

"The Day of Destruction is not only a battle for control over the plane of matter, child. We who sought powers in this world, wishing to conquer the elements, failed to perceive that the greatest conquest is within ourselves! The inner force to exist beyond the confines of our thoughts is the true wisdom, the great secret of the gods. This is the power that cannot be overcome. Ragnarok will be fought in the spirit realms as well. Humans who live only for their own satisfaction will have no means of avoiding enslavement. They will become miserable servants who think they are kings. It is the worst of spells. Beware, my children. Remember your true selves! Avoid the tyranny of your own passing thoughts. Be on guard against what seeks to enter your heart and conquer your spirit!"

On the ridge, Patrick peered out at the shoreline. The soldiers were heading across the beach toward the hills, led by Coroticus and the druid. They moved quickly, eager to find them. Patrick looked back at his friends. The crystal emanated an intense beam of colored light that spread out beyond them like a mysterious campfire. He crossed himself and looked back at the shore.

"What must we do with the crystal, father?" Ethrain asked the lightform.

"Send it to the bottom of the ocean."

"No!"

"If it falls into evil hands, it will become destructive. The Northern gods have gathered here and they will use the men who seek you as their servants for this battle. Tell the holy man to call for his forces. He will need them."

"Do we not have forces from our world to help us, father?"

"No, my child. The gods of the Celts are fading before the onslaught of the forces of darkness that control the underworld. The Fomorians are victorious in this realm."

"How is that possible? How could they defeat the radiant ones?"

"It is the fault of human beings, child. Men have chosen to serve their ways and have given them the power in Middle Earth. If they achieve victory this day, there will be no turning back. Your world will be an evil one forever."

The image began to fade.

"Father, what else can you tell us?"

"Help the holy man. He is the only one who can overcome the oncoming darkness. I love you, child. Forgive my mistakes. Forgive me!"

The image faded away.

"Father! Come back! Speak to me!"

The light within the crystal dimmed and slowly vanished.

"Father, tell me more! I want to know about your realm! I want to know the mysteries!"

"Forgive me, my child . . . "

With those final words, the light disappeared completely from the crystal.

"Father!" she cried out.

Hadrian took hold of her and embraced her.

"We must do as he says now! Come along."

He called to Patrick. The monk hurried to them.

"The soldiers are on their way. We must leave here immediately!" Patrick insisted.

"We were told to destroy the crystal. It must not fall into their hands," Hadrian stated anxiously.

"How shall we do that?"

"We must throw it in the ocean."

"There is a cliff to the north," Ethrain said. "Can we make it there?"

"They're on their way. We have no time. We must run now!"

"We cannot leave the crystal!" Ethrain insisted.

"They will kill us where we stand!" Hadrian shouted back. He pulled out his sword. "The two of you must take the crystal to the cliff. I'll fight them off."

"You cannot fight all those men!" Patrick said.

"What else do you propose?"

"Take the crystal into the woods. That will gain us a few moments."

They dragged the heavy object into the nearby woods.

"Stay there!" Patrick told them as they hid behind the trees.

He hurried off into a little clearing. They watched him fall on his knees and raise his hands to the skies.

Hadrian looked over at the ridge. The soldiers appeared like demons, swords gleaming in the sunlight. They could hear their voices.

"Look! Fresh tracks! They can't be far!"

"Find them!" the gruesome voice of Coroticus bellowed across the woodland.

The soldiers dispersed as the slave trader and the druid studied the tracks in the mud.

"They're dragging something with them. It's heavy."

"That must be the crystal!" Lochru cried out. "They've got the crystal! We must get it back!"

"We will, druid, don't you fear. They're mine now."

A number of soldiers approached the woods. Hadrian prepared to fight. Ethrain held her dagger tightly. Two soldiers came near the trees behind which they hid. Hadrian knew he could not wait any longer. He looked back at Patrick. A shaft of light fell upon him. The Roman couldn't tell if it was the sun's rays or some unnatural glow from another dimension.

The soldiers came within a few feet. Hadrian had to act. Just as they were about to step into the woods, he jumped out in front of them and slashed one of them across the stomach. The man fell to the ground as Hadrian attacked the other soldier. He struck a fatal blow but the man was able to shout before he died. The other soldiers turned to see Hadrian rush back into the woods.

"Over there!"

"Kill them!" Coroticus ordered.

"The King wants the Briton alive," Lochru reminded him.

"I am King here!" he said fiercely. "He can have his head, but that is all."

The soldiers raced toward the woods. Hadrian turned to Ethrain.

"You must run! Run like the wind! Find a hiding place. You know this island."

"I will not leave you, Hadrian."

"You must! They'll kill you, or worse!"

"I will not leave your side!"

"They must not get their hands on you!"

"Hadrian, I love you."

"And I love you, Ethrain," the Roman said as he took her in his arms and prepared to face his final battle.

"I carry your child within me."

A glow of joy beamed across Hadrian's face.

"You are with child?"

"Yes."

"How do you know this?"

"I know."

"All the more reason for you to run. Go! This is my last wish. If you love me, save our child."

She kissed him passionately and ran off into the woods.

Hadrian stepped out from behind the trees with a great war cry. He attacked the soldiers like a madman. Several men fell instantly at his side. With great swings of his sword, he fought the soldiers, keeping them from entering the woods. He cut them down with savage blows, strengthened by his love for Ethrain and the news she had given him.

Soon he was surrounded by many men. But they could not approach him, for his sword hit its mark with incredible precision. He was cut several times but nothing slowed him down. A semicircle of soldiers stood around him, trying to break through his defense. The Roman's every move was an assault and every blow was fatal. The mercenaries had never encountered such a warrior.

Coroticus appeared in the midst of his men.

"Step back, he's mine!"

The gargantuan man stood before the bloody Roman and pulled out a huge saber.

"Prepare to die, Roman!"

Panting for breath, Hadrian held up his sword.

"Morituri te saluant!" he cried out, aiming his dripping sword at Coroticus.

"What have you said?"

"The dead salute you!"

"The words of the gladiators in the arenas before the emperor," one of the soldiers said.

Coroticus laughed. "Indeed, I am the emperor of death."

He attacked. Hadrian blocked the first blow, but the man's great weapon knocked his sword from his hand. It found its mark with the second blow as he cut the Roman across the ribs. Hadrian fell to one knee. Coroticus raised his saber, preparing to decapitate him with a vicious blow.

Suddenly Patrick appeared in the clearing.

"Stop, Coroticus!"

The tyrant looked up, holding his saber over his head.

"It is I you want. Here I am."

Coroticus smiled an evil grin. "You're next, monk!"

"Do not kill him!" Patrick held his hand up in the form of a trinity. "You will not murder anymore, Coroticus."

"Watch me!" he said as he took a deep breath to come down upon the Roman. But he couldn't move his hand. An invisible force held his arms up in the air. He grunted loudly as he tried to pull his sword down upon Hadrian.

"Coroticus, you have defied the Almighty One too often!"

"What have you done, monk?" he shouted, unable to move his arms.

"Behold, the power of my God!"

The saber turned red with heat, sizzling the tyrant's flesh. He dropped it with a yell.

"Get him!" he cried to his men.

Patrick crossed himself and a wall of bright light appeared before him. The soldiers jumped back in terror.

"I said kill him!" Coroticus cried out.

Several soldiers moved forward. Their bodies caught fire the instant they stepped into the light. The men fell back in agony and were consumed by the supernatural flames.

One of the men threw his spear at the monk. As it entered into the wall of light, it exploded into fragments.

The soldiers shouted in fear.

"Lochru!" Coroticus shouted. "Use your magic!"

The druid stepped forward and faced Patrick. He aimed his hand at him.

"I have waited for this moment, monk. Now you will see the magic of the druids."

He let out an incantation. A blue light shot out from his hand and penetrated the wall of light. Colors sparkled between the two men and the wall suddenly vanished. Lochru smiled triumphantly.

"Die now, Patrick! Odin, take him!"

A swirl of green light appeared in the clearing and

voices of a thousand warrior-spirits echoed all around them.

Patrick stood calmly while the soldiers shouted in horror at the appearance of supernatural beings all around them. The gods of the north filled the clearing.

A great howling sound deafened everyone in the clearing as the Otherworld broke through into space and time. Thousands of beings, of all shapes and sizes, translucent and only partly visible, broke through into the world of matter. The mercenaries fell to the ground in unbearable terror. Even Coroticus was covered in a fearful perspiration.

"What have you done, druid?" he shouted.

"This is the moment I have lived for! Welcome to Ragnarok, the Day of Destruction!"

He waved his arms and shrieked an incantation as layer upon layer of spirit-beings faded in and out in great traces of colors sweeping through the air.

"What will you do now, monk, against such forces?" the druid roared victoriously. He aimed his crooked finger at Patrick and yelled fiercely.

"Destroy him!"

The armies of beings appearing everywhere across the landscape converged toward the solitary man. Fearless, Patrick held out his hands and whispered for his God alone to hear. As the beings approached, the ground trembled and cracked. Great crevasses opened up around them, engulfing whatever was on the surface. A number of soldiers fell into the abysses, screaming in horror. Smoke and flame rose up from beneath the earth as the entire island shivered in the merging of different worlds.

"Kill him!" the druid cried out again.

As the armies of giants, dwarfs, and creatures only partially formed swept down toward Patrick, he shouted in a loud voice.

"In the Name of the Father and the Son and the Holy Spirit!"

A great thunderclap erupted and a brilliant light expanded across the clearing from out of nowhere. Legions of angelic beings suddenly formed from within the light, radiant creatures of extraordinary beauty and power. Luminous rays streamed all about them. They charged into the clouds of creatures called forth by the druid. A massive burst of multicolored lights blasted over the landscape, shattering everything standing in the way.

Lochru was caught in the ring of light shooting across the air like a tidal wave. His body turned dark red as he screamed in agony. He exploded from head to foot, splattering across the clearing. Nothing solid remained of the druid's form.

In utter terror, Coroticus ran toward Patrick. He grabbed his saber and swung at the holy man who watched him in deep serenity. The saber flew out of his hand and traveled through the air toward a gigantic lightform. An archangel stood before Coroticus, holding the saber. His eyes were like the sun and he looked at the evil man with unearthly intensity.

"Live by the sword and die by the sword," a voice said, booming from the colossal form. He tossed the saber toward Coroticus. It sped through the air and tore into his flesh, exiting on the other side. The beast fell backward, shrieking in agony. He dropped at Patrick's feet. His dying eyes turned toward the holy man and their hate vanished, giving way for the frightened child that he once was.

"Help me!" he cried.

"God have mercy on your wretched soul, Coroticus."

Patrick made the sign of the cross. The dying man screamed as his inner sight perceived where his soul was headed as it left his body. His corpse turned rigid, freezing the look of terror on his face.

The angelic lightform changed shape and merged with the bright light that was entering into the chaotic combat with the underworld creatures. Fires broke out all across the ridge. The entire island was engulfed in this unearthly battle. The tyrant's soldiers ran for their lives, but the expanding turmoil of warring spirits swallowed them up. Their bodies caught fire and melted in the heat of the clash of the spirit worlds.

A rumbling sound rose out of the vortex of the battle as the armies of light and darkness encountered each other. A hurricane-force wind tore across the landscape, born out of the intensity the supernatural warfare. Patrick hurried to Hadrian and helped him stand. He had lost a great deal of blood.

"Where's Ethrain?" Patrick shouted over the terrible roar.

"She ran off into the woods."

"We must find her! We have to get off the island!"

"I can't go anywhere, Patrick. Go without me."

He slumped to the ground. Patrick pulled Hadrian toward the woods in the downpour of lightforms struggling with each other and the hurling winds emanating from their combat. The trees were bending to the ground, many ripped up by their roots. They flew about like great spears. Patrick peered into the maelstrom, searching for Ethrain.

Suddenly, he heard a shout from Hadrian and turned around. The corpse of Coroticus was standing up. On his face was an evil grin.

"Do you know who I am?" cried a voice resounding from within the cadaver.

"No!" Patrick said as he crossed himself.

"We have met before! I am the King of the Fomorians. Balor of the Baleful Eye! You escaped me once before."

The corpse stumbled over to Patrick and grabbed him by the neck.

"These dead hands will work for me one last time!"

He squeezed tightly and Patrick choked. Hadrian grabbed the creature's leg but was kicked away.

"Look at me!" the demon shouted as he strangled Patrick. "Look into my eye!"

The corpse's head turned to one side. Its left eye radiated a reddish light that caused it to bulge outward.

Patrick gazed into it as he tried to catch his breath.

"You have no power over me!" the monk shouted.

A freakish laughter came out of the corpse. "Fool! You will be dead in an instant."

Patrick's strength faded as the power of the evil eye drained him of life and the hands of the dead Coroticus tightened around his neck. But he stared at the demon defiantly, refusing to be frightened by it. As his sight faded, he saw a shadow cross over his face.

The hands suddenly released his neck and the corpse dropped to the ground in a heap. Patrick fell against a tree and gasped for air. He turned to find Ethrain standing at his side. Her dagger was plunged into Balor's evil eye and the wicked spirit had vanished. She hurried to Hadrian and examined his wound.

"I told you to run away," he said weakly.

She held him in her arms and realized that he was dying.

"No, Hadrian! Don't leave me!"

Patrick placed his hand on Hadrian's head.

"It is too late. We must get away from here!"

"Save her, Patrick," Hadrian whispered. "Save her for me."

The winds howled around them and the smoke of countless fires blinded them.

"I won't let you die!" Ethrain shouted.

"We will all die if we don't leave now!" Patrick insisted.

"So be it!" Ethrain cried out. "I will not live without him."

The ground trembled beneath them and fissures broke open all around.

"This island is going to erupt any moment!"

Patrick stood and looked toward the shore. The boat that had brought Coroticus rocked in the tumultuous waves. The fury on the island was stirring up the North Sea.

"We'll get him onto the boat!"

"No!" Hadrian whispered hoarsely. "Let me die here. Save yourselves."

"I can fight with demons," Patrick said as he kneeled next to his friend, " but I cannot overcome this woman. If she will not leave, we must die together."

He wrapped his arms around the two lovers as though protecting them from the hurling debris flying all around.

A light fell upon them. They looked up to see the archangel hovering over them. A radiant look of compassion and power emanated from the holy being. He made a gesture of blessing and suddenly the three were lifted into the air. The angel surrounded them with light and moved them quickly over the raging turmoil toward the island's shore.

They watched in silent amazement as they flew over the fiery landscape. They felt weightless and untouched by the drama below them as though they had been placed in the peaceful eye of the storm. They could see the rocks breaking open as a volcanic eruption prepared to shake the entire coastline.

They glided down upon the deck of the ship and landed gently on their feet. The angel remained in the air above them, smiling. The light being waved its hand and the boat's anchor broke off, causing the skiff to move out toward the open sea. A gust of wind quickly carried them far from the isle. They watched the angel hover over the shoreline, then swiftly disappear in the thick smoke rising into the sky.

The waves grew stronger as a rumble echoed across the horizon. Suddenly the entire island exploded in a jet of fire. The rocks of Mallor were hurled high into the heavens and rained back down upon the ocean, sinking in gigantic convulsions of steam to the bottom. When the smoke cleared, there was nothing left of Ethrain's home.

Patrick turned to his friends. Hadrian was terribly pale, but he seemed relieved of his pain. The monk examined his wound and saw that the bleeding had stopped.

"You have been healed once again, Roman. The Almighty must have a purpose for keeping you alive in spite of yourself."

Ethrain embraced her beloved with great joy.

chapter thirty

THEY SAILED back to Tara. Along the shores, the villagers gathered in vast numbers, drawn there by the explosions that had changed the color of the skies. Word spread that some mammoth event was taking place on the isle of Mallor, the well-known gateway to the spirit realm. It wasn't long before everyone knew that Coroticus and the High King's druid were dead and that unearthly sights were seen by fishermen across the bay.

Word finally came that the holy man, Patrick the Briton had been on the isle. The people knew then that extraordinary events were at hand. Hundreds watched in silence as the boat glided toward the rocks. Queen Ethne herself was on the coast, having learned of their return. She was eager to hear firsthand of this turning point in history.

In the fortress, King Laoghaire sat on his throne, grim and anxious. He knew that his men were dead along with his druid and that he had lost his battle with the monk. He would not be able to turn back the tide of admiration for this man's powers. The days of his reign were numbered as were those of the old ways. He would have to cooperate with the Briton in order to keep the peace. This was one adversary who could not be beaten by the brawn and metal that had won him his kingdom.

The boat entered the harbor. Queen Ethne stood at the head of the crowd, watching with great excitement. Patrick, Hadrian and Ethrain disembarked, wading through the shallow waters of the North Sea that had become strangely calm after the eerie turmoil of the past hours.

Hadrian moved slowly and limped, yet he felt himself a new man. He rejoiced at being able to live with his beloved and see their child born into the world. He knew there was no glory in death and that life was a blessed gift beyond all comprehension. The grim demeanor that had accompanied him for so long was now lifted from his brow like the cloak of night.

"Patrick!" the queen cried out. "Tell us what has happened."

"My Queen, it seems that the Almighty has chosen these isles as His throne. This will be a place of saints and loyal servants, free from the evil ways of the past."

"I have dreamt of such a time," the queen told him as she took his hands. "Is it truly possible?"

"We have seen with our own eyes," Ethrain said. "The forces of good have overpowered the underworld and the gods of the far north. The opportunity is here for a new day among our people."

"Is evil conquered then?" she asked with tears in her eyes.

"No, Queen Ethne," Patrick responded. "Evil will always be with us. Not only among us, but within us, seeking to claim dominion over our lives. The King himself will have to assist in making possible the entry of light upon these isles. There will have to be new laws and the banishment of sacrifices."

"I am sure that he will comply," the queen said confidently. "He is a soldier and he knows the difference between victory and defeat. There is no turning back now. Come, let us celebrate!"

Surrounded by her entourage, the three friends headed through the throng of people who stared at them in wonder.

"Is it true that Coroticus is dead?" someone asked.

"He is no more," Patrick answered.

"Then we can save the slaves on his island?" the queen inquired.

"Indeed! But that will require more warfare, my Queen," Hadrian stated. "The tyrant is dead, but his followers will not give up easily."

"We must free the prisoners!" Ethrain said to Hadrian. "Maybe it isn't too late for Maev after all."

"Who?" the queen asked.

"When I was imprisoned in the dungeon, I came upon a poor woman who had been locked away for three years and terribly abused by the beast. We must free her quickly! It would be such a tragedy for her to die when freedom was so near."

"I will arrange for the King to give you an army to take to the island and be rid of those wretched mercenaries forever," the queen announced.

"I am done with fighting, my Queen," Hadrian responded. "I want to be a man of peace now."

"A Roman centurion a man of peace? What strange transformation is this?"

"I've seen too much bloodshed, my Queen."

"Then I will have to send our commanders against them. I don't know if I can trust them to be victorious. What do you say, Patrick?"

"I am no man of war. Like my friend here I reject the ways of violence."

"But you are responsible for this!" the queen insisted.

"No, I am merely an instrument. A tool in the hands of Providence."

"They have used you to do battle against the forces of evil."

"I am a monk, not a warrior."

"Your mission is far from over, Patrick," the queen said anxiously. "If you want to claim these isles in the name of your god, they must be cleansed of the slave traders forever. My people will know no peace otherwise."

"What do you propose, Queen Ethne?" Patrick asked.

"I want you to lead our armies through the Firth of Clyde and conquer the kingdom of Dumbarton as the province of the High King. Perhaps the mercenaries will choose not to fight, knowing that you have defeated their leader. Otherwise, hundreds of men may be killed."

Patrick put his hand on the Roman's shoulder.

"Hadrian, will you join in this effort and advise me? I wouldn't know what to do with armed men at my disposal."

"Roman, I will give you land for you and your family as a reward," the queen proclaimed. "There is a glen in the plain of Breg watered by the river Boyne. It is the greenest meadow on this isle. It is yours if you complete this task for us."

"And then I will be left alone to plant my gardens and fish with my child?" he said as he took Ethrain in his arm.

"You have my word."

"Then I am with you, Patrick. It is the least I can offer for all that you have done for me."

"What about you, Ethrain?" Patrick asked. "Do I dare hope that you will wait at the King's castle for us?"

"You know my answer. I will not leave Hadrian's side."

"I thought as much. But you must stay away from all combat. You have a greater mission now. To bring your child into the world."

Ethrain looked at him in amazement. "How do you know this?"

Patrick smiled and a light seemed to twinkle in his eyes.

"It will be a boy and he has a special future. So take

good care of him even before he arrives among us."

The lovers looked at each other, thrilled at the monk's words.

"We will have a feast in your honor," the queen said joyfully. "To celebrate the birth of your child, and to wish you well on this last mission."

The crowd followed them at a distance as they headed for the castle on the hill of Slane.

THE FIRTH of Clyde in the kingdom of Dumbarton was a silent cemetery. The fortress of the King of the Rock rose like a monument to the dead. Nothing moved. The entire island seemed abandoned.

In the shadows of night, a ship dropped anchor near the shore. Hadrian stood on deck with Patrick. They studied the ramparts.

"Why don't we see any soldiers?" the Roman wondered.

"Do you think they've gotten word of the death of their leader?"

"I'm certain of it."

"Maybe they've all gone home."

"These mercenaries have no homes. This is their world and they will defend it to the end."

Ethrain approached them. "What do you make of it, Hadrian?"

"I don't understand why there are no guards on the towers."

"Why don't we send some soldiers in to scout the area?"

"If it's a trap, they'll massacre the men before they can make it back to the ship."

"What do you suggest? That we go in there and get massacred ourselves? Don't forget that Folchern is in command now. He's every bit as evil as Coroticus was."

"I do not have a good feeling about this," Hadrian muttered.

"They must be demoralized," Patrick suggested. "Without a leader, they have no more direction."

"They still know how to kill."

"How many prisoners would you say they are holding?" Patrick asked.

"Maybe a hundred," Ethrain surmised. "They took me through the slaves' quarters. I don't know how many have been shipped to foreign lands since then."

"How many soldiers?" Hadrian asked.

"Plenty. But if we can get to Folchern, then they'll be lost. These are not men with leadership ability. If they hadn't joined Coroticus, they would be thieves and murderers."

"But don't you think the eruption of Mallor would put fear into their bones?"

"Yes, but for now they have the advantage," Hadrian observed. "They're behind protective walls and we have to get to them."

"If we go around those cliffs," Ethrain suggested, "we can reach the dungeons. Maybe we can learn something from Maev."

"That's a good idea," Hadrian responded. "I'll send a dozen soldiers over there."

"No, I want to speak with her. She will trust me."

"Then I will go as well," Hadrian stated.

He called for several men to follow them and they left the boat. They quietly moved around the shoreline and approached the castle walls that rose at the edge of the sea.

"There is the opening!"

Ethrain pointed to a slit in the wall that served as window to the dungeon where she had stayed. They came to the side of the wall, trying to avoid the waves of the sea crashing at their feet. Hadrian ordered some of the soldiers to raise Ethrain to the window. She peered inside.

"Do you see anything?" Hadrian whispered.

"Nothing," Ethrain responded. "Maev! Can you hear me?"

No answer came.

"Is anyone in there? Answer me!"

One of the soldiers lit a torch and passed it to her. She slipped her arm through the narrow window and illumined the dungeon with the torch. The gruesome room was empty. Ethrain became worried over the fate of her friend and aimed the torch at different corners of the room. She saw the chains that had bound Maev piled in a heap in the corner.

"What have they done with you, Maev?" she wondered as sorrow filled her heart.

"No sign of her," she said as she pulled the torch out of the window. She handed to the soldiers who quickly put it out in order to avoid being seen.

"Perhaps she's died in these last days," Hadrian suggested. "Did you not tell me she was near death?"

"Yes, but she resisted its oncoming, out of spite for her captors."

They returned toward the boat and came upon a stream running alongside the fortress and into the sea.

"The water doesn't look right," Ethrain said anxiously. She kneeled and dipped her hand in the stream. She held it up to her face.

"It's red with blood! What have they done?"

They hurried to the ship and shared their findings with Patrick.

"You are the military commander," the monk said. "You tell us how to proceed."

"We must enter the fortress," Hadrian replied, tightening his sword around his waist.

"How do we do that?"

"We'll need to use the battering ram."

On the side of the boat was a huge tree trunk covered with the scars of many battles. Hadrian ordered the soldiers to lift it and carry it onto the shore. It took a dozen men to lift the huge tree. They climbed the cliff with difficulty and came to the door of the fortress.

Hadrian instructed them on how to use it most efficiently. Then he told them to standby.

"At my command," he said. "It should take no more than three assaults. Ready?"

The men nodded.

"Now!"

The soldiers rushed toward the door and smashed into it with the great trunk. It shook and rattled. A piece fell out of the wall.

"Again!" Hadrian called out.

The men rammed the door, this time cracking the wood on either side.

"One more time!" Hadrian said.

They took a deep breath and rushed the door again. This time it crashed backward into the fortress. The soldiers hurried in, drawing their swords. There was no one there. Hadrian signaled for the others to join them as they all hurried into the fortress. The Roman ordered several men to look in one direction, others to try the stairwells.

Followed by Ethrain and Patrick, Hadrian ran through the corridors, searching every room. The place seemed completely abandoned. They hurried up the stairs and came to the doors of the banquet hall.

"Wait!" Hadrian said as one of the soldiers was about to open the massive doors. "Listen first."

The soldier put his ear to the door. "Nothing."

Hadrian gestured for the men to open them. The great doors revealed a vast, empty room. The shadows were barely broken by moonlight entering through the windows.

The group entered carefully. They came to the center

of the room. Hadrian was about to order them to try another chamber when the doors suddenly shut with a terrible noise.

"What was that?" he asked.

"It must be the wind," a soldier said. "The doors have slammed shut."

Hadrian's warrior instincts took over. "Open them, quickly!"

The soldiers ran to the doors and pushed against them, but they wouldn't open. Several others joined in.

"They're locked!"

The rest of the group pushed on the great doors.

"There must be a bar on the other side keeping them shut."

Ethrain turned around and searched the darkness with her catlike sight.

"Over there!" she yelled.

Hadrian and Patrick turned around. She was pointing at the King of the Rock's throne. A form was in the chair.

"Welcome!" a voice said.

The soldiers prepared to fight.

"Don't bother!" the voice stated.

"Light a torch!" Hadrian called out. Several were lit and illuminated the room.

On the throne sat Folchern. The back wall was aligned with mercenaries armed to the teeth. Each one held a prisoner with a knife to their throat.

"I've been waiting for you," Folchern said. "I knew you would come."

"What do you plan to do?" Hadrian asked as he approached him.

"Don't come any closer. I've got something you want. You thought the battle was over, didn't you? But it isn't. Far from it!"

"Coroticus is dead!" Ethrain cried out.

"I know. The King is dead. Long live the King."

"And who would that be?" Hadrian asked.

"Who do you think, Roman? I've waited fifteen long years for this moment. If you hadn't killed him for me, I would have done it myself."

"You're surrounded by the High King's soldiers. You cannot win!"

"You don't understand, do you? This is not merely a human contest. I should think you knew that after what you witnessed on Mallor."

"The battle is over," Patrick said. "The evil forces have lost."

"This is the Day of Destruction, prophesied by the people of these isles for generations. Do you think one battle would do it?"

"Goodness has destroyed evil!" Patrick insisted.

"The decisive battle is won," Hadrian added angrily. "We're just here to clean up the vermin and free your captives."

"Well look closely, Roman!"

He raised his arm and his men prepared to slit fifty throats.

"Stop!" Hadrian cried out. "Don't do this, Folchern."

"We've been doing this all day. This is the last of them. One wrong move and you'll be responsible for the death of these people."

Ethrain scanned the faces of the terrified prisoners looking for her friend.

"Where's Maev?" she asked.

"Ah, Maev the witch. You came to know her, didn't you?"

"What have you done with her?"

Folchern stood and swaggered toward his men and their prisoners.

"She finally told us what we wanted to know."

"What do you mean?" Ethrain asked, her heart pounding.

"We learned of the sacred crystal."

"Why would she tell you now after all this time?"

"I promised her freedom. She saw the signs of Ragnarok on the horizon and knew that Coroticus would not be coming back."

"So where is she now?"

"Once she told me what I wanted to know, I had no more need of her."

"What did you do to her?" Ethrain shouted in horror.

"I crushed her skull with this!" he answered, brandishing the ax he wore at his side.

Ethrain lost control and attacked him. Before Hadrian could interfere, she reached him and cut him across the face with her dagger. He grabbed her arm but she kicked him and he released her. She plunged her weapon into his chest all the way to the hilt. Hadrian moved her away from him as his agitated men reacted in rage.

The king's soldiers faced the mercenaries and kept them at bay as Patrick leaned over Folchern.

"How could you think you could be victorious after what happened on Mallor?"

The dying man took hold of Patrick's tunic.

"Don't you understand? The powers that you invoked did not win!"

"That's impossible!"

Folchern snickered as blood ran from his mouth.

"They defeated the gods of the north, the warrior-spirits of Valhalla. But they have not overcome the underworld. We saw to that."

"How?"

"We killed men, women, and children by the dozen, right in the courtyard. The blood of the innocent has kept your powers from controlling our world. A worthy sacrifice!"

In shock, Patrick looked up at Hadrian.

"Evil is not defeated! The Almighty's angels can conquer the demons but not the souls of men. This creature's cruelty has interfered with the right order of things! As long as there are men like him, the dark forces will have entrance into our world."

He moved away from the dying man and whispered to Hadrian.

"You saw the power of the heavenly creatures, and yet there can be no victory without each person turning toward the good. These men have ruined this great opportunity to rid the world of dark influences."

"Another thing, monk," Folchern muttered with his last breath. "We have the crystal!"

"No! You cannot!" Ethrain yelled. "It vanished with the island."

Folchern shook his head and an evil grin distorted his features. "You can never defeat us."

"Where is it?" Ethrain shouted as she grabbed him by the hair.

Folchern convulsed and his eyes stared into emptiness. She shook him.

"Where is it? Where is it?"

Hadrian pulled her away from the corpse. He turned to the mercenaries.

"Men, your leaders are dead. I promise to treat you humanly as our prisoners if you will release these people. There is no need for more bloodshed."

"If we let them go, you will kill us!" one of the men shouted.

"You have my words as a Roman centurion. I will vouch for your safety."

"We can't believe you, Roman!"

"I tell you this. If you kill a single one of these people, we will slaughter you like beasts of the field."

He raised his arm and the king's soldiers prepared to attack.

"We'll fight to the death!" one of the mercenaries cried out.

"For what purpose?" Patrick asked.

"Because it is honorable!" the wretched man answered.

"There is no honor here. You hold children at knife point like cowards and you speak of honor. The only honor left is to do the right thing. Free them! Don't let the fate of your leaders be yours as well. They were not only killed, but their souls are in outer darkness for all eternity!"

"What do you mean, monk?" another mercenary asked, shaken by his words.

"There is punishment for evil deeds. The universe watches what you do. You cannot freely defy the laws of the Almighty and escape His justice. You may escape the High King's, but not your Maker's."

His words intensified the mercenaries' fear.

"Do not waste any more lives," Hadrian said.

"Then we will rot in the High King's dungeons until the rats eat us. I will not die that way."

The man raised his hand to strike the slave in front of him. Hadrian threw his sword through the air with all his strength. The weapon pierced him through and through and nailed him to the wooden beam holding up the wall. The soldiers moved forward. Red with rage, the Roman centurion cried out:

"This is your last chance! We will cut you down mercilessly if any one of you makes a move!"

"Wait!" Patrick said as Hadrian readied to order his men forward.

"Listen to me! You've all led wretched lives until now. You are given this opportunity to end your evil ways. If you put your weapons down, I will commit myself to visiting you regularly and sharing with you the mercy and forgiveness of the Almighty. I will lead you on a new path, and cleanse you of the darkness that has brought you to this moment."

As he spoke, some of the mercenaries began to weep.

Several of them dropped their weapons and let the prisoners go. Patrick radiated with compassion and unconditional love even for these miserable creatures. As he looked at each one of them deep into his soul, they seemed to melt before his gaze of goodness. Others among them wept like children as though the monk had placed a mirror before them and showed them what they truly were and the wrong they had done. He stood before them like the incarnation of their conscience and called forth their long-forgotten sense of right.

Ethrain held her breath before this phenomenon. She couldn't believe her eyes. The buried innocence of these bestial men surfaced from the depths of their depraved souls and broke onto the shores of their awareness like a tidal wave of emotion invoked by the power of the monk's simple goodness. The room echoed with the sound of dropping weapons as every man released his prisoner. The stunned slaves rushed away from them, exuberant.

Patrick approached the men and held out his arms. Several of them kneeled and kissed his hands. Others touched his robe as though seeking to be healed by his radiant spirit of compassion. All of them surrounded him, weeping and crying out for his help. Patrick serenely reached out to each one of them as though they were his own wayward children returning home to begin again.

Hadrian watched in utter amazement. Even the supernatural sights on Mallor could not match this miracle of metamorphosis among the mercenaries. He recognized in that moment the true power of the monk's religion. It was a power greater than any army. No conqueror could reach into the souls of men the way the humble monk was doing. He felt a tremor in his own spirit before the blessed presence of unconditional compassion.

One of the mercenaries rose and approached Ethrain. Hadrian was about to defend her but the man was as meek as a child, his face stained with tears.

"The witch Maev," he said. "She is not dead."

"What do you mean?" Ethrain cried out as she came up to him.

"She is alive. And she has the crystal."

"How can that be?" she asked as she took the man's hands.

"The few survivors brought it back. Folchern forced her to make use of it. That is how we knew you were coming. But as she did so, she told us that she would destroy all of us. She called upon the Fomorians to enter through her into our world. She helped them escape the higher powers on Mallor by giving them a channel through which to get away."

"Why would she do that?" Ethrain asked in horror.

"The bitterness in her heart," Hadrian said grimly. "She's been so hurt that she has taken the side of the very forces that oppressed her."

"We must find her to keep the crystal from becoming an entryway for the dark forces. They will be free to come and go through the power of the crystal."

She turned to the man standing before her. "Where did you see her last?"

"In the tower. That is where the crystal was taken. But she has used her magic to become invisible, along with the crystal."

Ethrain hurried out of the room, followed by Hadrian who ordered his soldiers to take the mercenaries aboard ship. They raced up the narrow winding stairs of the tower and came into a barren room perched over the ocean. The wind whistled through the narrow windows like a forlorn ghost.

"Maev!" Ethrain cried out. "I've come to help you."

The room seemed empty. Ethrain walked through the

chamber, looking for signs of the crystal's presence.

"Maev, if you're here, please make yourself known to us."

"Leave me!" a voice said from nowhere.

They looked around and saw nothing. "Where are you? We want to talk to you."

"Leave me," the voice said again. "You cannot help me now."

"Yes we can, Maev. I've come to free you." Ethrain said gently.

A shape formed in the far corner of the room. Maev partially appeared, translucent as a ghost. On her face was a look of sheer terror. Ethrain hurried to her.

"Don't come any closer!"

Ethrain studied her face. "What has happened to you?"

"I am a greater prisoner than ever! I've sold my spirit to the dark ones. I am their captive now. It's worse than the dungeon!"

"We can help you!" Ethrain said as she reached out to her.

"There is no help for me, Ethrain. I have made the final leap into the Otherworld."

"Why?"

"Revenge. I wanted the power to destroy life itself because of what it had done to me. The crystal gave me that. It allowed me to mingle with beings who have more power than Coroticus himself."

"What has this power given you?"

"I was able to escape Folchern who wanted to torture me one last time. But in escaping, I doomed myself to living in the in-between worlds. As you see, I cannot return fully into our own. I am caught."

Her form faded as she began slipping back into another dimension.

"Where is the crystal?"

"It is mine! I am its sole possessor now."

"What can you do with it?"

"Conjure the demons."

"Do they obey you?"

"No, they appear and then they use me for their purposes."

Patrick had entered the room a moment before and listened to the poor woman's sorrowful voice. He approached the half-formed figure.

"I will help you, my child."

"Who is this?" she asked.

"Patrick, the priest of the new religion. He has done amazing things. I've never seen powers like his before.

"Not even from Ubarra?"

"No, not even from him."

"I don't want to be seen like this!" she said, beginning to fade away.

"Wait!" Patrick said. "I will help you."

"You have no power here. This is not your world."

"It is the Almighty's world. There is no realm that escapes His dominion. And He can free you from this torment."

"I am a slave of the Fomorians now. Neither human nor spirit anymore."

"Child, behold the goodness of your Maker!"

Patrick reached out and grasped the shadowy appearance. Where is hand touched, the form became solid. He took her by the arm.

"In the name of the Holy One of God, be freed from this spell!"

He gently pulled her toward him and she slowly reconstituted into solid form. Ethrain gasped with awe as her body appeared into space. Maev was beautiful again. The scars and illnesses that had disfigured her were gone. She stood trembling before the monk, looking at her hands and seeing that the marks of her agony had vanished. Ethrain embraced her. They hugged with intense emotion.

Ethrain touched her face and her hair, laughing with joy.

"What magic is this?" Maev asked nearly hysterical, unable to believe what was happening to her.

"You're beautiful again, Maev! It's as though you never lived through the horrors of your confinement."

Maev felt her skin and hair. She laughed and cried at the same time.

"This can't be!" she said. "I had lost all hope."

Patrick smiled and took her hand.

"My child, there is always hope. Our Creator is good and wishes each of us to live in joy."

Maev sparkled with gratitude.

"I must know more about your religion, holy man."

"That is why I am here. Will you join me?"

She hugged Ethrain again. "I have no place to go now. What do I do?"

"I have a home that is open to you if you wish," Patrick said.

"I will never be able to thank you enough. Let me serve you."

"I seek no servant."

"Then let me be your helper in your mission."

"I can always use a companion for the great task."

Her face lit up with gratitude.

"What about the crystal?" Hadrian asked.

"It is lost in the in-between spaces. Neither part of this world, nor of the other one. It can do no harm now."

"Then our work is done," Hadrian announced. "Let us go home."

Ethrain took Maev by the hand.

"The Queen has given us land in the plain of Breg. We

will settle there and raise a family. I too want to learn more about what Patrick teaches. We will be neighbors."

They left the chamber and returned to the boat. On deck were all the freed slaves who greeted them with cries of joy and gratitude. The boat moved out into the waters of the North Sea, heading back to the hill of Slane where the High King and his queen awaited them. Hadrian placed his hand on Ethrain's stomach and they kissed. He knew that a good life awaited them and that the care of his wife and child would be the noblest mission ever awarded to a Roman centurion.

Patrick looked out across the ocean and quietly gave thanks to the forces of light that had manifested so strongly in the lives of his companions. He knew that much work lay ahead for him, but he was filled with confidence. He knew that the God in whom he trusted was ever present. He had felt the very goodness of Creation shine through his own heart. He knew he had nothing to fear even with the years of labor and hardship that lay ahead. They would be sweetened by the friendships he had made.

The fruits of his efforts were all around him. He rejoiced as he witnessed the sun break through the darkness of night and spread across the skies in a great song of colors celebrating the care of the Everlasting One for His earthly children.

epilogue

MAEV PROVED to be a deeply faithful disciple of the holy man. For the rest of her life, she would assist him in his work, always grateful for what had been done for her. She became a devout convert to his new religion and enlightened all her knowledge of the ancient ways with the wisdom of the new teaching. Alongside the humble monk, she cared for the sick and hungry.

Hadrian finally planted a little garden outside his cottage. He lived the long-deserved tranquility of a weary warrior. Ethrain would give birth in the spring. Their new life held the promise of daily joy warmed by a love that would never grow cold.

The High King oversaw the writing of the Sengus Mor, the great laws of the Irish isles, with the counsel of the Briton. Unlike his queen, he never became a follower of the new teaching yet he allowed the influence of the holy man to spread across the isles, forever changing the history of his people.

But evil continued to lurk in the shadows of human hearts. Balor of the Baleful Eye, though defeated, was not done with his nemesis. The Fomorians would rise again and seek dominion over human souls. They would meet a new adversary in Illadan, son of Hadrian and Ethrain, whose destiny was to shift the tides of history at great cost to himself and to his parents. Peace would always be elusive for the Roman centurion and the druid's daughter. But as long as Hadrian and Ethrain had each other, they could accept all that Fate required of them. For their strength came from a love that only grew stronger with each passing year and that sheltered them from all the trials which life would bring their way.

THE END

Future books in the

The Mystic Isle Legends

The Caves of Cruachan

The Phantom Queen

Beyond the Ninth Wave

The Stone of Destiny

The Cauldron of the Gods

About the Author

Theodore J. Nottingham has authored works in various genres including historical fiction, non-fiction works in spirituality, humor and metaphysical novels. He has published numerous articles and produced programs for national television. His writings are aimed at bringing together both entertainment and inspiration. He can be reached at Tnottingham@usa.net

Mr. Nottingham's other works include:

The Color of the Wind:
Fables for a New Age

The Final Prophet:
Book One of the Messiah Chronicles

The Tribulation
Book Two of the Messiah Chronicles

The Curse of Cain:
The Untold Story of John Wilkes Booth

Written in our Hearts:
The Practice of Spiritual Transformation

Further information is available at:
http://tedn.hypermart.net